Dear Friends,

For a very long time I reported on the television industry, and from that day to this I've been a self-confessed soap opera fan. *Temptation* was written with much love and respect for a genre of programming that networks have treated very shabbily in recent years.

More than that, though, it's a story of a woman coming to grips with the many unexpected changes in her life, building a new relationship with her estranged family and forging even stronger bonds with the people she loves.

I hope you'll enjoy this chance to catch up with a book that means a lot to me, and that Callie's story will make you laugh, shed a tear or two and sigh with satisfaction as she makes her way into an even brighter future.

All best,

Sherryl

Praise for #1 *New York Times* and *USA TODAY* bestselling author

SHERRYL WOODS

"Sherryl Woods returns with her usual wit and style in this latest tale of romance and suspense. Don't miss out on the newest winner by Ms. Woods."
—*RT Book Reviews*

"Woods is a master heartstring puller."
—*Publishers Weekly*

"Sherryl Woods writes emotionally satisfying novels about family, friendship and home. Truly feel-great reads!"
—#1 *New York Times* bestselling author Debbie Macomber

"Woods really knows what readers have come to expect from her stories, and she always gives them what they want."
—*RT Book Reviews*

"Love, marriage, family, and forgiveness all play an important part in Woods's latest richly nourishing, holiday-spiced novel."
—*Chicago Tribune* on *A Chesapeake Shores Christmas*

"Warm, complex, and satisfying."
—*Library Journal* on *Harbor Lights*

Also by **#1 New York Times** *and* **USA TODAY**
bestselling author Sherryl Woods

SEA GLASS ISLAND††
WIND CHIME POINT††
SAND CASTLE BAY††
WHERE AZALEAS BLOOM*
CATCHING FIREFLIES*
MIDNIGHT PROMISES*
THE SUMMER GARDEN***
AN O'BRIEN FAMILY CHRISTMAS***
BEACH LANE***
MOONLIGHT COVE***
DRIFTWOOD COTTAGE***
RETURN TO ROSE COTTAGE†
HOME AT ROSE COTTAGE†
A CHESAPEAKE SHORES CHRISTMAS***
HONEYSUCKLE SUMMER*
SWEET TEA AT SUNRISE*
HOME IN CAROLINA*
HARBOR LIGHTS***
FLOWERS ON MAIN***
THE INN AT EAGLE POINT***
WELCOME TO SERENITY*
SEAVIEW INN
MENDING FENCES
FEELS LIKE FAMILY*
A SLICE OF HEAVEN*
STEALING HOME*
WAKING UP IN CHARLESTON
FLIRTING WITH DISASTER
THE BACKUP PLAN
DESTINY UNLEASHED
FLAMINGO DINER
ALONG CAME TROUBLE**
ASK ANYONE**
ABOUT THAT MAN**
ANGEL MINE
AFTER TEX

*The Sweet Magnolias
**Trinity Harbor
***Chesapeake Shores
†The Rose Cottage Sisters
††Ocean Breeze

Look for Sherryl Woods's next novel
A SEASIDE CHRISTMAS
available soon from Harlequin MIRA

#1 *New York Times* Bestselling Author

SHERRYL WOODS

Temptation

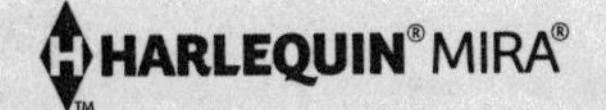

Recycling programs for this product may not exist in your area.

ISBN-13: 978-0-7783-1414-1

TEMPTATION

Harlequin MIRA September 2013

First Published by Zebra Books

For questions and comments about the quality of this book, please contact us at CustomerService@Harlequin.com.

Printed in U.S.A.

1

Jason Kane had finally seen a woman he wanted and no one in the whole incompetent world of television seemed to know who she was.

Okay, that was a slight exaggeration, he admitted as he replayed the brief scene. Surely some of those idiots on the set of *Within Our Reach,* his network's failing soap, knew her. She'd just sashayed across the screen in today's episode, wearing a formfitting uniform and displaying more shapely leg than any cop he'd ever seen on the streets of New York.

Unfortunately, they hadn't deigned to give her a credit. He'd run through the crawl listing the actors a half dozen times to no avail. He'd checked with the casting people, who seemed to have a vague recollection of the walk-on part but not the actress who'd gotten it. He'd had his secretary on the phone to the producers for the past hour. All she'd discovered was that the woman seemed to be a friend of someone connected to the show. That someone, whoever it was, had called in a favor to get her the tiny, nonspeaking role. Given the lack of a Social Security number on record, she apparently hadn't been paid a dime.

He played the video again, second-guessing himself, wondering if perhaps his initial reaction—okay, his first dozen reactions—had been aberrations. He homed in on her in the crowded scene, just as he had every other time. His body tightened with masculine appreciation, just as it had before. His pulse kicked in... again. His gut instinct, said to be the best in the entire television industry, went on red alert as he studied the close-up image enlarged to three times life-size on the giant screen before him. Her cute little tush and long, long legs might have aroused his most basic carnal instincts, but it was that image on the screen that had held his cooler, more professional fascination.

Her blond hair feathered softly around a delicate face so exquisite it would have had Marlene Dietrich in her prime weeping with envy. Her mouth was a lushly sculpted work of art. Her eyes, an impossible shade of vivid, summer-sky blue, were capable of such intense scrutiny he knew without a doubt that she could render a man weak with no more than a glance. In that bit part as a cop, every movement of her body, every expression that crossed her face, had hinted subtly of intriguing interrogation techniques.

So, he thought with yet another sigh of pure, heartfelt satisfaction, it hadn't been a fluke. She had a rare quality that eluded most women, no doubt about it. Even more important for television, the camera was able to capture it.

At thirty-five Jason Kane was a connoisseur of women, just as he was of fine wine and gourmet cuisine. He'd had to cultivate the latter, but his appreciation of women was pure instinct. He admired their beauty, reveled in their intelligence and enjoyed their sensuality, though not always in that order.

In his capacity as president of TGN—Trans-Global Network—he had been surrounded by some of the most gorgeous stars in the world. He'd worked with some of the brightest and most ambitious females ever to grace an executive suite.

And he had slept with… Well, the indiscreet truth of it was, he had slept with more than his share of the most incredible, most inventive, most incendiary ladies ever to don—or slide out of—a negligee.

But not a one held a candle to the charisma of that anonymous blonde whose perfect face was frozen on the giant screen in his office. Mysterious and a little sad, she fascinated him even more deeply than she affected his libido. His determination to have her doubled. He would pursue her as relentlessly as he had every other important acquisition he'd made in his life. There was no question in his mind that he would succeed.

"That," he snapped to the three junior executives who had been frantically scribbling notes all during the last-ditch strategy meeting to save the failing soap, "is what that show needs to drag it out of the ratings gutter."

When no one else had been able to devise a plan to rescue the show, Jason had taken it on himself. It was exactly the sort of challenge he loved. Hiring an unknown and making her a star would be the kind of bold, unexpected move he'd built his reputation on.

"Work with the producers," he instructed. "Get her under contract, long-term. Tell the writers I want her on-screen in a story line so hot it'll give the censors heartburn. Tell 'em to get her out of that uniform."

"But, boss, she plays a cop," Freddie Cramer had the temerity to point out.

Freddie Cramer was a recent graduate of UCLA. He couldn't seem to decide between Hollywood's casual chic of jeans, open-necked dress shirt and jacket and New York's more formal pinstriped suit. It was almost the only decision Freddie had trouble with. Today, probably in deference to the somber nature of the meeting, he'd gone with the pinstripes. Freddie was a big believer in ambience.

Freddie was also the only one in the whole bunch of junior executives who didn't cower when Jason spoke. To everyone else's astonishment and Jason's private amusement, Freddie's career at TGN was flourishing. He'd be a vice president before he turned thirty, maybe even before he hit twenty-five. If any of the others had had the guts to ask why, Jason would have explained that he didn't need to be surrounded by people who shared his opinion. Heads bobbing dutifully in agreement meant nothing to him.

He wanted people to argue with him, to keep him on his toes. He might be the person who was singlehandedly bringing this second-class network into ratings contention for the first time in its history, but he wasn't infallible. Not that he wanted too many people to figure that out just yet.

Freddie Cramer didn't question Jason's intelligence. He honed it. He didn't threaten Jason's power. He ensured it. Jason prayed daily for more men and women of Freddie's ilk to cross his path.

"No cop's on duty twenty-four hours a day," he shot right back. "If the writers can't figure out a way to make it happen, fire 'em and get me new writers. This show needs a dramatic overhaul, and this woman is going to be the linchpin for it. I want her in a front-burner story line within a month. Any questions?"

Naturally it was Freddie who dared one, even as the others dashed for the door, scrambling eagerly to do his bidding. "Who is she?" he asked, bringing his colleagues to a halt, their expressions suddenly uncertain.

Jason, his gaze once more glued to the screen and that incredible frozen image, said quietly, "That, gentlemen, seems to be the million-dollar question."

Whoever she was, Jason predicted with absolute certainty that not only her life but his own was about to be turned upside down.

The last time he'd felt the same surge of confidence and anticipation, he'd taken over an entire network. Surely one petite woman with an air of mystery about her would be a snap by comparison.

2

Callie Smith felt as if she'd been run over by a truck. Looked pretty much like it, too, she decided with brutal honesty as she gazed into the mirror above the sink in her minuscule bathroom.

Her eyes were red-rimmed and puffy from what felt like a solid two months of crying. Her skin was blotchy. Her hair had defied every weakhearted attempt she'd made to coax some curl into it.

Terence Walker peered over her shoulder and shook his head at her reflection. "Girl, you look sorrier than any cat Grandma ever dragged in."

"Thank you for that pick-me-up," she commented snidely to her neighbor and best friend. "Go away."

Unfortunately, Terry was not the sort of man easily dissuaded once he'd set his mind to something. Callie had learned that the hard way in the months since she'd been dumped by her Wall Street brokerage firm and her husband in a depressing burst of downsizing on all fronts of her life. Terry was harder to shake than a nagging midwinter cough and, especially on days like today, twice as irritating.

"This can't go on," he declared. "You've been a mess since that jerk you were married to walked out that door and flew to the Caribbean for a quickie divorce so he could marry the bimbo in spandex."

"That was six months ago. I'm over that," she said blithely. It wasn't entirely true, but she was convinced if she repeated it often enough, it would become true. Time, that reported healer, was crawling by at a snail's pace, it seemed.

"And losing your job two months ago? Are you over that, too?" Terry pressed.

Callie frowned. It probably said a lot about her priorities that that blow had been even harder to take. She'd never depended on a man, even her husband, for her sense of self-worth, but her self-esteem and her ambition were inextricably tied together. Still, she said determinedly, "I will be."

"Right," Terry said with a familiar disbelieving note in his voice. "The bottom line here is, you have to pull yourself together."

"For what?" she demanded, sniffling and patting ineffectually at her eyes with a damp cloth in an attempt to reduce the puffiness. She flatly refused to smooth on the hemorrhoid cream that Terry had assured her in a recent makeup tip session would work wonders. "I have no job. I have no love life. What's left?"

"Living, for one thing," Terry said. "Being forced to move back to Iowa and raise corn, for another. It could come to that, you know."

That dire reminder was almost enough to shake her out of her lethargy. Going home to the Iowa farm she'd always despised was a fate not to be endured.

Born Calliope Jane Gunderson almost thirty years ago, she had been named for a musical instrument in what must have been the last bit of whimsy in which her stern, rigid, Iowa-bred mother had ever indulged. Callie had always suspected she'd been conceived in the back of her father's pickup during the Iowa State Fair as a calliope played in the background. She'd never dared to ask either of her parents if some momentary lapse in judgment explained why two such wildly different and totally incompatible people had married.

Growing up in that strained household hadn't exactly been a picnic for her or her younger sister, Eunice. They had led a cold, harsh, sometimes desperate life, made more difficult by the lack of joy or affection between her parents. Eunice had married a dry, humorless man just like their father and was currently withering away on a farm of her own.

Callie had fled at the first opportunity. She had gravitated to New York the way a thirsty man might crawl toward an oasis in the middle of the desert. She loved the neon, the frenzied energy, the vibrant culture, the ethnic diversity, the quaint boutiques. She hadn't even minded the dirt and grime so much. After all, she had grown up on unrelenting acres of the stuff.

Now, it appeared, she was facing a return to more of the same unless she could haul herself out of this depression and pull her life together. If she hadn't known that already deep in her gut, Terry's constant reminders would have drilled it into her. She scowled at his reflection in the mirror.

"If this is your idea of cheering me up, it's a good thing you didn't choose comedy as a career," she said.

"I didn't choose comedy because I am a certifiable hunk," he retorted immodestly, grinning back at her and preening outrageously.

It was true. He had been blessed with the kind of interesting, rough-hewn features and muscular body that made women want to throw themselves at his feet and beg for just one of his endearing, crooked smiles. Ever since he'd become the leading actor on *Within Our Reach,* they had been doing just that with such regularity that Callie was embarrassed on behalf of the entire female half of the population.

Didn't they have lives? Didn't they realize that the character Terry played was make-believe? Apparently not, if the mail he periodically carted home was any indication. They really, really wanted his well-developed and carefully maintained thirty-three-year-old body.

"Stop bragging," she muttered, giving up on salvaging her face for the moment and turning away from the mirror. "One word to the soap opera magazines about your true sexual preferences and you'll be back trying to find work in some pitiful chorus line off Broadway."

"Discovering that I'm gay might force the writers to adjust the story line the teensiest little bit," he admitted without taking offense at the threat of blackmail. "But I could draw a whole new audience."

That was Terry, ever the optimist. No wonder he was wearing on her nerves. She wanted to sulk. In fact, she had been sulking off and on for most of the past six months. Just as Terry had diagnosed, it had begun with the departure of her husband and showed no signs of letting up. It was starting to put a strain on their friendship, if not her bank account, which was large enough to weather a few more months of self-pity if she stayed out of Bloomingdale's.

She scowled at him again. "Funny, I've never heard that the networks were battling for that particular demographic."

"I don't see why. We're young. We're upwardly mobile. We buy cars and clothes and beer."

Callie patted his sexily stubbled cheek. "Give it up. This is daytime TV we're talking about. The culture of Middle America. They'll never let you kiss on-screen again."

As she headed into the kitchen to see if there was anything in the refrigerator that could still be considered edible, Terry trailed after her.

"Speaking of kissing on-screen," he said, automatically leaning against the counter and striking a camera-ready pose that would have set most female hearts tripping. "Rumor has it that the network boss man himself has taken an interest in the show. He's out to spice up the ratings with some new femme fatale. When the word came down today, all the actresses on the set were in an absolute tizzy. I've never seen so many cell phones in use at one place at one time. Every agent in town must have been getting a blistering earful. I can't imagine why. At the rate soap time moves, it'll be months before the character does more than say hello."

Terry loved industry gossip. Since his long-time lover was bored to tears by what he considered to be the shallowness of television, Callie heard more than she'd ever wanted to know about Terry's coworkers.

She knew, for instance, that the sweet little ingenue

on the show had slept with almost every male in the cast and crew. She also had it on excellent authority that the man who played a pious, self-righteous physician with such dedication was addicted to cocaine. And the show's Emmy Award–winning villain was the softest touch on the set, to say nothing of being an Olympic-caliber ladies' man.

About the only thing she could say for being the beneficiary of all of this inside information was that it made the calls she received from Eunice almost bearable. Her sister was a die-hard viewer of *Within Our Reach.* Feeding her the show's latest gossip usually kept Callie from having to discuss anything at all about Iowa.

Lately, though, it was getting harder and harder to put off hearing about her mother's inability to cope with the farm now that her father was dead. Regina Gunderson was only in her fifties, but she had arthritis. She had a bad heart. In fact, she had so many ailments, Callie had given up trying to keep track of them all. No one had expected her to outlive her husband, but Jacob Gunderson had died of a stroke while harvesting last year's crop of corn.

Ever since the funeral, Eunice had been growing more and more determined to get the message across that, unless Callie had a very good reason for staying in New York, she ought to be at home bailing out that failing farm and taking care of Mama. The loss of her job and the failure of her marriage were a pretty good indication that she was washed up in the big city, according to Eunice.

Although she loved her mother and felt bad about her plight, she shuddered at the thought of going home, then dismissed it for now. She'd find work sooner or later. In the meantime, she was more interested in dinner.

She sighed heavily when her search of the refrigerator revealed nothing more than a spotty banana and a suspiciously green chunk of what must once have been cheese.

When she glanced up, she discovered Terry regarding her speculatively. "What?"

"I have just had a very bizarre thought."

"What else is new? Your thought process should be analyzed by some government grant," Callie observed. She eyed him hopefully. "Did you bring chicken soup, by any chance?"

"No, you're not sick. You're depressed."

"You used to bring chicken soup."

"I used to bring gin, too, but then I saw how maudlin it made you," he retorted. "If you mope around much longer, you can forget about little dabs of Preparation H. The best pancake makeup in the business won't hide those puffy circles under your eyes."

Callie frowned. "Is that supposed to upset me?"

"It would if you were thinking what I'm thinking."

"I'm thinking we ought to order in Chinese."

Terry shook his head. "Too much water retention. We'll go out for a nice, healthy salad as soon as Neil gets home," he suggested, referring to his live-in companion. "But that wasn't what I was thinking. I was thinking that you could very well be the woman who has all the actresses feeling so threatened."

Callie froze at the suggestion. She stopped rummaging around in her nearly bare cupboards to stare at him.

Surely she couldn't have heard him correctly. "Me?" she said eventually.

"Don't look so shocked. Word is that the woman Jason Kane is so hot to sign had a bit part on the show that aired a week ago. It just occurred to me. That fits you, dearie. I'm sure of it."

Callie had pretty much blocked the memory. The walk-on had been Terry's bright idea, another of his maddening attempts to get her out of her apartment and back into life. Stumbling from four decorator-designed rooms on the Upper West Side onto a soundstage filled with set-designed rooms in the fictional town of Glen River Falls hadn't struck her as a giant leap back into reality, but it had made Terry happy.

It had also killed ten hours that otherwise would have been spent bemoaning her fate and considering whether murder was too good for her ex-husband and her ex-boss.

The possibility that anyone had noticed her on-screen seemed completely ludicrous. Even Eunice claimed she'd blinked and missed it.

It hadn't exactly been a star-making role. Callie had walked from one corner of the dreary police headquarters set to the other. She had accomplished it without falling on her face or tripping over a cable. She had paused on cue and given one long, lingering look toward the camera, a look that supposedly conveyed all sorts of dire portent. Aside from shoving Terry out of the way of an unscripted falling file cabinet, that was it. The sum total of her acting experience, now and forever, amen. She had every intention of keeping it that way.

"You're delusional," she said just as the phone rang. "Work on getting back to reality while I grab this."

Five minutes later, head spinning, she hung up and stared at Terry.

"What is it, dollface? You're white as a sheet. Was it bad news? Did something happen on the farm?" He pushed her none too gently onto a chair. "Head down. Don't faint on me, please. As cute as some of those paramedics are, I really hate to cause a commotion by calling 9-1-1."

He hunkered down in front of her, hands on her thighs. "Callie, sweetie, are you okay? Talk to me."

"You..." Hysteria bubbled up in her throat. "You were right."

"Well, hallelujah! The girl finally sees what a genius I am!" He gave her a puzzled look. "Right about what?"

"It appears that *Within Our Reach* wants to hire me back."

"There now, see? I told you so," he exulted. "For another walk-on?"

Still dazed by the obscenely generous offer that had been rattled off, Callie could only shake her head.

"Recurring status?"

Apparently not even the ever-optimistic, ever-supportive Terry had bought that stuff about her being a femme fatale. Boy, was he in for a surprise.

"On contract," she said in a squeaky voice that would have made the producer who'd given her the news shudder. She gazed at Terry in total bewilderment. "It seems they want to make me a star."

3

"What do you mean she said no?" Jason Kane shouted at Freddie Cramer, who'd opted for a very sober navy suit to deliver his bad news. "What kind of actress says no to a chance to become a television star overnight?"

Freddie swallowed hard but didn't back up so much as an inch. "She's not an actress."

"Then what the devil was she doing in the middle of our soap?"

"It's a long story. At least, she says it's a long story," he added in a rush. "She wouldn't explain to the producer. She wouldn't explain to me. In fact, she hung up on me. Twice." He sounded stunned and a little hurt by her audacity.

Jason felt his blood begin to pump a little faster. The producers at *Within Our Reach,* despite their admirable award-winning track records, were wimps. He knew that firsthand. They'd been so busy bowing and scraping the last time he'd visited the set, it was a wonder they hadn't tripped over their own feet.

Freddie was made of tougher stuff, but he was at

heart a gentleman. If a lady slammed a phone down in his ear, he would take that as a final answer.

Jason was not so easily intimidated. He had learned long ago to fight fiercely for what he wanted. Nothing had ever come easily. He actually thrived on hard, demanding work. Resigned that this was going to be up to him, he held out his hand.

"Give me the address and the phone number for this—what did you say her name is?"

"Calliope Jane Gunderson Smith, according to the call sheet they finally found for that day's taping."

"My God!"

"She prefers Callie," Freddie said helpfully.

"I imagine she would." Jason tucked the address into his pocket and buzzed for his secretary. "Call this number and see if anyone answers. If they do, let me know and tell my driver to be down front in ten minutes."

"You're going to see her?" Freddie asked, looking a little awed that Jason intended to personally handle what was essentially a casting matter.

"I'm going to see her," Jason confirmed. Obviously no one else could be trusted to get the job done. And experience had taught him that the element of surprise was a distinct advantage.

Assured that Miss Calliope Jane Gunderson Smith was indeed at home, Jason set out to make her his.

Forty-five minutes later, after belatedly realizing it would have been faster to walk the twenty blocks than to deal with Manhattan's midmorning gridlock, he emerged from his limo. In front of him was an elegant old brownstone that had apparently been converted into apartments during the ongoing gentrification of the Upper West Side.

"Should I wait, sir?" Henry asked.

"Please," Jason said, then added with grim determination, "This won't take long."

He stood for a minute and assessed the building, its facade primped up by paint and a recent sandblasting. Living there had to cost a pretty penny. It increased his speculation about Miss Calliope Jane Gunderson Smith, who had dared to turn down the opportunity of a lifetime.

He glanced at the slip of paper in his hand. Naturally the irritating woman lived on the top floor. There was no elevator. He trotted up the four flights of stairs and leaned on the buzzer, already thinking of what a pleasure it was going to be to tame her.

Correction, to hire her, he reminded himself sternly.

"Who is it?" a muffled voice inquired.

That voice had a nasal quality that was worrisome, but an image of that incredible face, which he'd viewed again and again since first discovering it, stopped him from bolting.

"Jason Kane."

"Who?"

Clearly this woman wasn't going to do a lot for his ego. Fortunately, it was healthy enough without her adulation, or even her recognition, for that matter. He reminded himself once again that he was here to hire her, not to seduce her. Although in this business the two sometimes seemed a lot alike, he conceded.

"Jason Kane, president of TGN."

He thought he heard her sigh.

"Miss Smith?"

This time she did sigh. "Yes," she conceded with unmistakable reluctance.

"I'd like to talk, if you have a moment," he said, thinking of all the other women in the world who would have had the door open in a millisecond just at the sound of his voice or the mention of his name. The fact that he had to cajole this one into opening it so much as a crack increased his fascination with her. It had been a very long time since a professional or personal challenge had seemed so promising.

"I know why you're here. I really don't think there's anything left to say," she declared flatly, still from behind that firmly closed door. "I appreciate the offer, really I do, but it's not for me."

No was Jason's least favorite word. He might say it a lot, but he rarely heard it. Rejection wasn't even in his vocabulary. His determination mounted. "Perhaps I can change your mind," he suggested with more modesty than his well-tested powers of persuasion called for.

"I don't think so."

"I'd like to try."

"Really, there's nothing you can say that all those other people haven't said. That Freddie Cramer person was quite persistent."

Persistent but unsuccessful, Jason thought derisively. Winning was the only thing he credited with any respect. "Five minutes," he bargained.

"Will you go away, if I say no?" she inquired rather plaintively.

"Not likely."

She muttered something decidedly unladylike. "Do you have some ID?"

He chuckled at the display of temper, even as he admired the caution. "Business card or photo ID?"

"Both, if you don't mind."

He slid his driver's license and his embossed business card under the door. He sensed he was being studied through the tiny, round peephole. A minute later, he heard locks clicking and a chain being removed. His adrenaline kicked in as he waited for the door to open.

No stripper had ever been more adept at inspiring a man's anticipation. His breath snagged in his throat as the door handle turned. His heartbeat escalated more than it had when he'd climbed those four flights of stairs.

And then he saw her.

Sweet heaven, she was a mess, he thought, his spirits sinking. If he'd been anticipating heaven, this was definitely hell. With a cool, practiced eye, he ignored the bizarre leap of his pulse and examined her critically from head to toe to see if the disaster was fixable.

She was wearing a once-red T-shirt that had apparently had an unfortunate encounter with some bleach. Her jeans were practically threadbare, which aroused his masculine curiosity but did little to accentuate her beauty. Her hair had gone way past the tousled look. Seemingly untouched recently by brush or comb, it appeared to have been styled by nervous fingers, or by an electrical jolt.

She looked bone-deep weary, cranky and about as far from sophisticated as it was possible for any woman to get. Crying, which he deduced was responsible for her nasal voice and her red-rimmed eyes, definitely did not become her. It also terrified him. He truly hated coping with a bawling female.

Worse, though, he couldn't imagine a single, solitary viewer envying Calliope Jane Gunderson Smith.

Nor could he envision anyone wanting desperately for her to find true love in the arms of the soap's hottest hunk—that Terence Walker. Walker looked a little muscle-bound to him, but the ratings among women eighteen to forty-nine suggested he was alone in his opinion.

At any rate, based on the raw material in front of him, it seemed unlikely that this woebegone waif, barely five feet two and unlikely to be more than a hundred pounds soaking wet, could be transformed into a femme fatale. What on earth had he seen when he'd viewed that video? For the first time in a very long time, Jason was forced to question his instincts. He was thoroughly unaccustomed to self-doubt. He didn't like it.

Then he took a look into those cornflower-blue eyes. Even red-rimmed and puffy, they still sparkled, most likely with irritation. He lowered his glance to pursed lips so generous it was all he could do to tear his gaze away. Hope—and that something indefinable deep inside him—rebounded. He hadn't been mistaken, after all. Fixing her up would definitely be a challenge of monumental proportions, the very kind he loved.

It was a good thing, too. He really hated being wrong. He'd always figured the day that golden gut of his failed him would be the day he needed to get out of the television industry and into something safe, maybe reopen his father's plumbing business back in Virginia in memory of the man he'd loved and watched being destroyed by his mother. Given how he felt about the tedium of fixing leaks and installing copper pipes, he prayed daily that his instincts would last forever.

Before he could begin his persuasive sales pitch, Callie Smith crossed her arms over her meager chest and announced, "You're wasting your time. I'm not an actress."

"You were on *Within Our Reach,* though. Was that some sort of lark?" he asked, an unmistakable note of derision in his voice.

"Not exactly. Terry, that's Terence Walker," she added helpfully, as if he might be unfamiliar with his own show's star. "He lives downstairs."

Jason felt an odd surge of envy for the fortunate Terry. He couldn't help wondering just how close the two of them were. Women all over the country were clamoring for more of the sexy actor. Were they after something on which Callie Smith already had a claim?

"Anyway," she continued, "Terry thought it would give me something to focus on besides my unfortunate lack of employment and my divorce."

Jason seized on the revelations. They didn't answer his questions about her relationship with Terry Walker, but a woman with no income and no husband was a prime candidate for a contract with a couple of extra zeros tacked on to the offer. He promptly felt as if he were back on familiar turf. Negotiating a deal was right up there with good sex when it came to setting his adrenaline flowing.

"I've changed my mind," he announced, noting the sudden dull flush that climbed into her cheeks.

She hugged her arms a little more tightly around her middle. "I'm not surprised. As I'm sure you can see, I'm really not star material."

There was a note of defeat in her voice that made him feel like a heel for giving her a moment's doubt about the future he envisioned for her. She might claim not to want the career he was offering, but she unmistakably needed the hope he was holding out.

"Not about hiring you," he reassured her. "It's just that negotiations this delicate, this promising, should take place over lunch."

She drew herself up stiffly, pride radiating from every tiny pore. "I'm not starving, Mr. Kane. I can afford to buy food."

"You may not be starving, Miss Smith, but I am. Talking money always makes me work up a big appetite." He gestured toward the door. "Shall we?"

Her gaze went from his expensive, charcoal-gray suit to the white monogrammed cuffs just peeking out from the sleeves. She lingered on his Italian silk tie, then dropped her glance to the tips of his pricey leather loafers. The survey was so slow, so thorough, that Jason felt his blood heat, despite the fact that he knew its intent was more fashion assessment than seduction.

When she was done with her survey, she met his gaze. Her lips curved ever so slightly. "I really don't think I'm dressed for lunch, do you?"

He grinned at the massive understatement and decided at once it was meant as a challenge. "You'll do," he said briskly.

She shook her head. "I don't think so. People will think you took pity on some stray, homeless woman."

"It will be good for my image," he assured her. "Too many people think I'm coldhearted."

She considered that, then nodded. "I suppose we could go to the place on the corner. The pizza's not bad, though you don't look much like a pizza kind of person."

"Actually, I was thinking the Plaza," he countered on sheer impulse. "The Oak Room, perhaps."

"They'd throw me out on my ear," she said with certainty.

"Not if you're with me. Care to test it?"

For the first time since he'd walked into her apartment, he saw a little flare of defiance spark to life in her eyes. It transformed her. It also made him want to strangle the people responsible for dousing it in the first place. The husband who'd left and the boss who'd let her go were clearly fools.

"I'm game, if you are," she said. Her chin rose a notch at the dare. "Let me slip on some shoes and grab my jacket."

He wondered if she would also use the time to comb her hair and daub on some makeup. He was rather hoping she wouldn't, if only because it would mean she was enjoying holding his feet to the fire.

Sure enough, she returned in minutes wearing worn-out, red high-top sneakers and a too-large baseball jacket, but no makeup. He couldn't tell about her hair because she'd also added a baseball cap. He noticed the jacket and cap were for two highly competitive National League teams.

"Is that why your marriage ended?" he inquired, gesturing toward the team insignias.

An honest-to-God grin spread across her face. "It

should have been a hint, shouldn't it? Actually, the marriage ended over something far more serious...."

She allowed the thought to linger long enough for him to conjure up all sorts of dire scenarios of incompatibility before she added, "My use of his razor."

Oddly relieved by the flip explanation, Jason nodded. "Definitely a breach of marital etiquette, all right."

"He's lucky I didn't use it on his throat when I found out about the other woman," she murmured, slamming her door emphatically and twisting the various keys in the locks with visible anger.

"Touché," Jason said, thinking the man truly had been an idiot to walk away from a woman with such fire.

Downstairs, he ushered her across the street to his limo. His longtime driver swept open the door for her without so much as a blink. Jason resolved to give him a very large bonus at the end of the month.

"The Plaza, Henry."

That drew the tiniest hint of surprise, but nothing more. "Of course, sir."

As they rode toward the famed hotel on Central Park South, Jason studied the woman seated next to him. Despite her initial resistance to the idea of going out to lunch with him, she was now seated as regally as any queen. She didn't gaze around curiously, indicating this wasn't her first trip in such a luxurious car. She exited the limo in front of the Plaza with the same sort of aplomb, bestowing one of those rare, intoxicating smiles on the visibly bemused doorman. The man practically tripped over his own feet trying to open the door for her. He pretty much ignored Jason.

Jason was suddenly struck by the possibility that this was Callie's natural habitat, far more than any pizza joint on the corner in her neighborhood. He knew it when the maître d' in the Oak Room nodded politely at him, but beamed at Miss Calliope Jane Smith.

"Ms. Smith, it's been too long," he said, clasping her hand in his. "We've missed you."

She beamed at him. "Thank you, Charles. It's good to see you, too."

"I felt terrible when I heard what happened, just terrible."

Jason had no idea if the man was referring to the loss of her job or her divorce. Maybe the remark had been all-encompassing, which meant that Charles knew things about Callie Smith that Jason intended to find out before this lunch was over.

"Thank you," she said as Charles led them immediately to the best table in the room. "I appreciate your concern."

"You're getting along okay?" Charles inquired, sincere worry written all over his face. "If you need anything, anything at all, I'd be happy to help."

"I'm getting along," she reassured him.

When they'd been left alone, Jason regarded her with amusement. "You knew perfectly well you'd never be thrown out of here on your tush, didn't you?"

"It was always a possibility," she corrected, an impish grin in her eyes. "Charles can be temperamental."

Jason had seen the genuine warmth in the older man's gaze. Whatever temperamental outbursts he might be prone to, Jason doubted one would ever be directed toward the woman seated opposite him.

After they'd ordered—the sensible fish for him, an enviably thick, juicy burger for her—he leaned back and studied her.

The dark circles under her eyes and the weary slump to her shoulders hadn't vanished, but there was a bit more life in her expression.

"So, tell me how you and Charles came to be such pals," he suggested. "He usually radiates polite indifference to the customers."

"He mentioned to me once that he had a little nest egg put aside that wasn't growing fast enough to suit him. I offered a few suggestions. He tripled it. He's grateful," she said succinctly.

"You have a nose for investments?"

"I'm a broker," she said, then amended, "Or at least I was until a few months ago. Our firm downsized. I was one of the last ones hired, so I was one of the first fired. It didn't seem to matter that I was making a fortune for the company and for my clients."

Jason had to struggle to hide his astonishment. He tried to reconcile this bedraggled, ill-clad waif with the kind of barracudas who thrived on Wall Street in their expensive, stylish power suits. He couldn't.

Still, this latest discovery told him he'd seriously miscalculated the kind of negotiations that would lure her into the TGN fold. Cold hard cash and a simple appeal to her vanity were exactly the wrong things to offer. He had to make her see the long-term future she could have, the example she could become with her combination of brains and beauty, the good she could do for charity, perhaps.

First, though, he had to see if she had exhausted all

of the possibilities for another job on Wall Street. He didn't want her dallying with acting only until something in her field came along. This part on *Within Our Reach* was intended to be more than a quick fix. He needed a long-term commitment from her, a year at the very least. If things panned out as he expected, the soap could go on forever with Callie as its leading lady.

"Surely there are other jobs for someone with your qualifications," he suggested.

"Of course," she agreed. "If I'd been willing to move to some other city and start over. Even my own firm offered me that. So did half the other brokerages I contacted within hours after being canned. The rest were firing staff of their own."

"You didn't want to move because New York is where it's happening in the financial world," he concluded.

She lifted her gaze to his. "It was more than that. Going anyplace else would have been admitting defeat."

The response told him quite a bit about her determination and her priorities. He could understand that sort of drive, that sort of stubborn will. He'd needed it in spades for his own career climb.

"And, therefore," he surmised, "anything less than another position in the thick of the action was not to be tolerated."

"Exactly."

He leaned toward her. "Shall I tell you what I see for you in the future?"

She regarded him with a wry expression. "Is looking into crystal balls one of your hobbies?"

"No, making things happen is one of my skills," he declared flatly.

She shivered a little. Jason grinned. He enjoyed the effect such unbridled confidence had on people. "Gives you goose bumps just hearing such self-assurance, doesn't it?"

She leaned forward then. "Oh, I definitely think you're full of it, Mr. Kane."

"Jason," he corrected, deliberately ignoring the jibe, "since you and I are going to be very close."

"I doubt that, Mr. Kane."

He sat back and took a long, slow swallow of coffee, assessing his next step. "Are you a gambling woman, Callie?"

"I never gamble," she insisted.

"And yet you played the stock market with millions of dollars of other people's money."

"I took informed risks."

He grinned at the distinction. "Whatever. You spent your entire career researching companies, then placing bets on which ones would beat the odds, correct?"

"Something like that."

"Do you know anything about TGN?"

"The basics, of course."

"Know anything about the turnaround it's made in the past three years?"

For an instant she looked uneasy. "That you're credited with making it happen," she conceded. "The story made headlines as well as reassuring nervous stockholders. The price of shares has climbed as a result."

"What did that tell you about me?"

"That you're smart and relentless," she said at once.

"Exactly. Are you willing to gamble against a man like me getting my way?" he inquired lightly.

She sat up a little straighter at that, squaring her shoulders, lifting her chin. "You're forgetting who you're dealing with, Mr. Kane. I'm not an out-of-work actress. I'm no airhead. I'm not a pushover. And I'm not desperate."

He lifted her hand, as soft and light as a bird, and touched his lips to the delicate knuckles. A surprising shudder swept through both of them at the contact. "A challenge only makes things more interesting, wouldn't you say?"

She swallowed hard and practically yanked her hand from his. "You've guessed wrong this time, Mr. Kane. I am not an actress," she repeated stubbornly. "I don't want to be a star."

"So you've mentioned," he said without the slightest hint that he found the adamant rejection nearly as insulting as she'd clearly meant it to be. He'd trained himself to respond to subtleties, and her physical reaction to him told him far more than her deliberately dismissive attitude. She was susceptible to him and she didn't like it. He, to the contrary, found her responsiveness illuminating.

He directed a look straight into those baby-blue eyes of hers and dropped his voice to a seductive pitch. "I think changing your mind is going to be downright fascinating for both of us."

4

Callie was still regarding the huge, newly arrived arrangement of flowers from Jason Kane with dismay when the phone rang. She could barely find it—for all the flowers had been crammed on every available surface over the week since she'd had lunch with the arrogant, pushy network president. She couldn't imagine what good he thought this display of excess would accomplish. Maybe he hoped she had allergies that would eventually drive her out of her apartment and into his stupid show.

"Yes, hello," she said, then sneezed. Maybe she *was* allergic, dammit.

"Callie?"

Eunice, she thought with a sigh at the sound of her sister's whining voice. "Yes."

"You sound funny, like your nose is all stopped up or something. You haven't been crying again, have you?"

Ironically, Callie realized she hadn't shed a tear since her lunch with Jason Kane. It might be smart not to analyze that phenomenon too closely.

"No," she said, "but you sound as if you have been."

That was enough to encourage Eunice to launch into a familiar litany of her problems.

"It's Mother. She's driving me to distraction, Callie. She tried to run the tractor this morning, even though I told her over and over that Tom would come by as soon as he'd finished our fields and plow hers."

"Has it occurred to you that perhaps she'd prefer to be independent, rather than relying on you and your husband?" It was the one area in which Callie could totally sympathize with her mother. She could imagine the kind of price tag that came with Eunice and Tom's so-called help. Endless reminders of their generosity, no doubt.

"Of course she'd rather be independent," Eunice snapped. "That's not the point. She can't do the work. She'll wind up having a heart attack or something. And the other day in town she practically ran over Mr. Casey because she won't wear the glasses the doctor prescribed. She's fallen twice. Sooner or later, she's bound to break her hip. I'm scared to death she's going to burn the house down because she gets so distracted when she's cooking that she forgets all about whatever she's left on the stove."

She heaved a put-upon sigh. "I'm telling you, Callie, I can't take it anymore. You have to come home. She cannot be left in that big old house alone. And she certainly can't come here. Tom would have a fit."

Callie barely resisted the desire to scream, even though she suspected Eunice had plenty of cause to be anxious.

"It wouldn't work for the two of us to be under the same roof, either," she explained with careful patience.

"In case you've forgotten the cold wars waged before I left home—Mother and I have never gotten along. She blames me… Well, who knows what she blames me for? Her whole miserable life, I suppose." She couldn't help the rare note of confusion that crept into her voice with the admission.

"I swear to you, Callie, if you don't come back and take some responsibility for this, I'll…I'll…"

"What, Eunice? What will you do?" Callie prodded, tired of the guilt her sister had been heaping on her ever since the day she'd left Iowa.

It wasn't that she didn't love her mother. She did. But Regina Gunderson had not done anything to allow that love to flourish. Occasionally, in the darkest moments of the night, Callie regretted that their relationship wasn't stronger, but she'd tired of making efforts that were never returned. She'd long since stopped trying to figure out exactly what she was to blame for. She'd just accepted that the gulf between her and her mother was wider than any Iowa river at flood stage.

"I'll pack her bags and send her to New York, that's what I'll do," Eunice threatened.

Callie sucked in her breath, stunned by the possibility that Eunice might very well do as she'd said. "That's blackmail," she accused.

"You bet it is. I'm telling you I am at the end of my rope. It would be one thing if she were the least little bit grateful, but she's not. Tom's about had it, too, and you know what a saint he's been about helping out ever since Daddy died. I'm not ruining my marriage over this."

It was not the first time Eunice had declared her marriage on the brink of disaster. If it wasn't their mother's demanding, ungrateful attitude, then it was the failure of the corn crop or the lousy supper Eunice had fixed because she was too tired to stand in front of the stove for an hour.

Callie could have told her that Tom Foster was a selfish pig, who liked to throw his weight around just to keep his wife in a constant state of terror, but she kept silent. That was one realization her sister was going to have to come to all on her own. She wouldn't welcome Callie's observations or her advice.

"Give me a couple of days," she said. "I'll think of something to help Mother."

Jason Kane's job offer flashed through her mind. The money would offer a solution, a way to pay for a competent farmhand, she thought, then dismissed the idea as ridiculous. She was not an actress. It was absurd to think about wasting all of her education, all of her experience in business, to prance around playing a cop.

Maybe she was more Regina Gunderson's daughter than she'd ever realized. She could just imagine her mother's reaction to her choosing a frivolous career like acting, rather than something solid and dependable. In their family the sternest of work ethics had prevailed. A career in make-believe hardly qualified.

No, taking that job was out of the question. Resisting Jason Kane and all of his considerable powers of persuasion was essential, too. He was clearly a give-him-an-inch-he'd-take-a-mile kind of man. There had to be another way.

"Maybe we could sell most of the land," she began.

"Mother wouldn't hear of it," Eunice declared before she could finish the thought.

"She might have to," Callie said grimly. "Especially if it meant she could keep the house and hire someone to help out."

"But that land is our inheritance," Eunice protested.

That, of course, was the real source of her sister's objection, Callie knew. She and Tom wanted that land. Tom envisioned himself as some sort of land baron, the corn king of Iowa.

"Let me think about it," Callie repeated.

"I'm giving you until the end of the week, then, so help me, Mother will be on the first flight to New York." She slammed the phone down, apparently so Callie would get the message that she meant business.

"Well, that was pleasant," she muttered to herself.

A key turned in her door just as Terry called out, "Knock, knock, dollface. I know you're home because I can hear you talking to yourself."

"Unless you have a very large bottle of gin with you, go away."

Terry ignored the warning and came on in. "Uh-oh, Eunice must have called again," he said, regarding her sympathetically. "Why don't you change your number and not tell that witch?"

"Because that witch is my sister," she said, unwilling to admit how much appeal his suggestion held, especially after a conversation like the one they'd just had. Maybe she'd move while she was at it, so no one could find her at all.

Terry sat down beside her, shifted her bare feet into his lap and began to massage them. This, she reminded herself, was why she put up with Terry's tart tongue and his interference in her life. She sighed with pure pleasure, finally beginning to relax.

"I thought sisters were supposed to share some special bond," he said.

"So they say," she said wearily.

"On a scale of one to ten, how much guilt did she dump on you this time?"

"Seven," she said. "But that wasn't the worst of it." She summarized Eunice's threat to send Regina Gunderson to New York, if Callie didn't come home to take over her care.

"There's an obvious solution," he said with such nonchalance that every muscle in Callie's body tensed all over again.

"What?" she asked cautiously, though she knew perfectly well where he was headed. She'd taken a trip down that very road herself only moments before.

"You could become a star, darling."

She promptly removed her feet from his lap and drew her knees to her chest. "Forget it," she insisted. She might have been down that road, but she'd turned back.

He gestured toward Jason Kane's latest floral offering. "Am I wrong or is Mr. Kane still in hot pursuit?"

"So it seems."

"Would it be so terrible seeing your face on the cover of all the soap opera publications? Would it offend your sensibilities to be envied by several million women because you get something they all want—namely, me."

"I already have you."

He leered at her suggestively. "Who knows, a couple of love scenes with you, and I might go straight."

She scowled at him. "I know for a fact that sexier

women than I have tried and failed. Besides, you and Neil have a better relationship than most heterosexual couples I know. Why would I want to interfere with that?"

"The challenge, of course." He regarded her speculatively. "Unless you'd prefer the challenge of getting Jason Kane's pants off, something I hear is not all that difficult, by the way. Be careful with that one, dollface. He's wicked."

Callie prayed she wasn't blushing, since that very idea had crossed her mind a time or two over lunch. The reaction had stunned her. She'd been pretty much convinced that all men were lower than slime ever since her divorce. Not that she intended to admit that Jason Kane had stirred any sort of response at all, especially to a man who would use it against her every chance he got. Badgering and blabbing were two of Terry's less attractive traits.

"I am not interested in getting anybody's pants off," she said adamantly. "And aren't we getting a little far off the subject?"

"Which is?"

"What to do about my mother."

"I thought that was what we were talking about. If you become a rich, successful star, you'll be able to set your mother up with twenty-four-hour companions, if that's what she needs. You'll be able to hire some big burly guy to run the farm."

Terry seemed unduly fascinated by the latter. Callie shook her head. "You are such a fraud. I can't imagine how Neil puts up with you."

"That's personal, darling. Now, come on, say you'll

at least give serious consideration to Jason Kane's offer. If I have to do one more love scene with Penelope Frogface—"

"Her name is Frontier," Callie chided.

"Whatever. She wears too damned much Giorgio. One of these days I'm going to start sneezing and never stop. They'll have to close down the set and have it fumigated before I'll go back to work. It's up to you to save us all from that."

"It is not up to me to do any such thing."

"Besides that, a good friend would want to help out," he added slyly.

Callie eyed him warily. "With what?" she asked, certain that the subject had slipped away from excessive perfume.

"I seem to be getting these odd little notes," he confided with an air of mystery.

"Fan mail?"

His expression turned rueful. "Not exactly. My fans love me."

Something in his voice alerted her that this was more serious than he was pretending with all of these enigmatic hints. "Terry, exactly what's in these notes?"

He hesitated so long, Callie doubted it was just for dramatic effect. He seemed almost frightened to describe the notes aloud. "Terry?"

"I suppose someone totally paranoid might call them threats," he conceded eventually.

Callie stared at him. "Threats? What kind of threats? Dear heaven, have you told the police?"

"Darling, first of all, I am not that paranoid yet. Second, I couldn't possibly tell the police and risk the publicity."

Since Callie had never heard of an actor being averse to publicity, she guessed that these threats must have something to do with Terry's relationship with Neil. "Is someone threatening to reveal that you're gay?"

"It's nothing as overt as that," he admitted. "But it sure is pointing in that direction. I mean, what else could it be?"

"And you think someone on the show is behind them?"

"It has to be. The notes keep turning up in my dressing room with no postage, even though they're usually stuck in with the fan mail." He looked vaguely shaken by the implications.

Callie thought of the file cabinet that had inexplicably fallen during her one scene on the show. "Terry, is it possible when that file cabinet fell it was no accident?"

The question shook him visibly. The color drained from his face. "Of course not," he denied a little too heatedly. "I'm sure someone just tripped and knocked it over."

"Who?" Callie asked reasonably. "No one admitted to it."

"With the director carrying on the way he was, would you admit you'd caused an entire scene to be reshot?"

"No, I suppose not, but what if—"

"Forget it. The letters are probably nothing."

"Then why did you bring them up?"

"Why else? To get you to take the job," he said airily. His expression sobered. "Of course, just in case I'm wrong, you really would be doing me a huge favor if you came to work on the show and helped me figure out who's behind this."

It seemed everyone had new career plans for her. "I'm a stockbroker, not a private eye," she reminded him.

"But you'd be playing a cop," he said, as if that automatically would give her the requisite investigative skills. Terry had long since blurred the distinction between reality and fiction.

Callie groaned. She could tell he was dead serious about this. She wanted to help him, she really did.

"Terry, I'm having enough trouble with my own life without worrying about the little blips shaking up your serenity. If you think this is serious, you have to tell a real cop, not some pseudo-cop being played by a pseudo-actress."

"Sweetie, I know your problems are real, but at least you have a solution right in front of you." He plucked a business card out of his pocket and held it out. "The answer to your prayers is only a phone call away."

Callie eyed the card warily. "Unless that card belongs to a good psychiatrist, I don't want any part of it."

"Next best thing," he assured her. "A network president with the power to whisk away all your problems, answer all your prayers. Sort of a combination shrink and priest."

"How much did he pay you to do the commercial for him?" she inquired irritably just as the doorbell rang.

Terry jumped up before she could budge. "Not nearly as much as he paid me to see that he got in here to talk to you tonight," he admitted, flinging open the door to reveal a casually attired, devastatingly handsome Jason

Kane on the doorstep. "Bye-bye, sweetie." He turned and winked at her. "You, too, Callie."

"Quite an exit," Jason said, standing just inside the open doorway as if he actually meant to give her a choice about whether he stayed or went.

"Quite an entrance," she retorted. "I'm not sure which of you has better timing."

Hands shoved in his pockets, Jason rocked back on his heels and surveyed the room. "I see you got the flowers."

"Yes, thank you," she said politely. "I've been meaning to call."

"But you were afraid to risk another round with my powers of persuasion," he suggested.

"I was busy," she corrected defensively, knowing that he was exactly right. She hadn't wanted another encounter with the kind of temptation Jason Kane represented. It would be too easy to get swept up in the glamorous world he was offering her. Her inbred puritanical ethic required that success come through hard work, not some ridiculous fluke. She wasn't too crazy about testing his impact on her senses, either. She hadn't needed Terry's warning to know that Jason Kane was a dangerous man.

"New job keeping you busy?" he inquired.

"No." She had to fight to keep a defensive note from her voice.

"Volunteer work, perhaps?"

"No."

"A new relationship?"

There was a dark glint in his eyes with that last one.

Callie shuddered and reminded herself never to cross Jason Kane.

"I'm sure you have more important things to worry about than how I spend my days," she said.

"Not lately, as a matter of fact. Recently you've become my number-one priority."

"Why doesn't that reassure me?" she muttered under her breath. She glanced up to find amusement dancing in his gray eyes. He was clearly enjoying this cat-and-mouse game they were playing. She found that extremely irritating.

"Don't you have a home to get to?" she inquired testily, though she'd already gathered from Terry that Jason did not. Of course, that didn't mean that he hadn't once had a marriage that had fallen victim to the obsessive work habits she was beginning to suspect he had.

"Maybe some little kids who miss their daddy and are waiting to be tucked in?" she added hopefully.

He shook his head. "Nope. I'm free as a bird. I thought maybe we could take a little stroll over by Central Park. You look as if you could use a little fresh air, maybe some exercise."

"Do you moonlight as a personal trainer?"

"Only when I anticipate great rewards for my efforts."

"I don't do aerobics."

"You should. It relieves stress." He shrugged. "Of course, so does sex." He eyed her hopefully. "Would you prefer that?"

Callie met his gaze evenly. "I doubt you could keep up with me."

He chuckled. "Now, that, Miss Calliope Jane Smith, is a very dangerous dare."

He wasn't telling her anything she hadn't guessed the minute the words were out of her mouth. She couldn't imagine what had come over her. She did not engage in provocative repartee with men who were virtual strangers. She didn't engage in such banter with anyone, except perhaps for Terry, but he hardly counted. He was her buddy. They'd been taunting each other from the day he'd moved in downstairs. It had driven her homophobic husband batty. She couldn't classify Jason Kane in the same category as either Terry or the departed Chadwick Smith III. He clearly might take her up on her challenge. It was too late, though, to back down.

"I suppose that depends on which of us has the most at risk," she countered.

"An interesting way of looking at it," he said. "So, what about that walk? Maybe dinner. A little pleasant conversation."

"About?"

"You are a suspicious little thing, aren't you? Do you think I have an ulterior motive for showing up here?"

"Of course. You probably have those contracts you want me to sign tucked in your back pocket. You'll wait till I've had a few glasses of wine, then pluck them out, hand me a pen and, *bam,* I'll be yours."

He held his arms up in the air. "Care to frisk me?"

She chuckled to spite herself. "You'd love that, wouldn't you?"

"You bet." He grinned. "So would you."

Callie shook her head, feigning awe. "I didn't know

it was possible for an ego to get so huge without exploding from all the hot air."

"Perhaps you should make it your mission to cut me down to size," he said, reaching down to grab her hand and help her up from the sofa. "Come on, it'll be more fun than sitting here wallowing in self-pity all night."

"I do not wallow in self-pity," she grumbled, but she didn't resist nearly as hard as she should have. She was still muttering about his arrogance as they passed by Terry's open door two flights down.

"Behave outrageously, darlings," he called out. "I'll be waiting up to hear all about it when you come in."

Jason tucked her arm through his. "I guess we'll have to work really hard to make his wait worthwhile."

"You wish," Callie muttered.

She waited all evening for Jason to bring up the job on *Within Our Reach,* but he never once mentioned the show. Instead, he deliberately baited her about everything. There wasn't an opinion she held about which he didn't claim to believe the opposite. She was so riled up by the time they'd finished dinner, it was a wonder she didn't have serious heartburn.

"Do you really believe all that hogwash?" she demanded when they finally got back to her building.

"Which hogwash is that?"

"All of it, every word that has come out of your mouth since we walked out of here four hours ago."

Cool gray eyes attempted to feign innocence. "I can't imagine why you would think I'd lie."

"To make me mad," she guessed.

"Never." He grinned. "Perhaps to make you start living again." He dropped a kiss on her forehead. "Worked, too, didn't it?"

Before she could argue that point as well, he turned on his heel and walked away, whistling lightly. She stared after him in confusion.

"What was that all about?" she murmured, touching her forehead where the skin still burned from the all-too-brief brush of his lips. What kind of sneaky, low-down tactics was Jason Kane using on her now? If he thought he could seduce her into agreeing to join the soap opera cast, he was very much mistaken. If he thought he could seduce her at all, for that matter, he was out of his mind.

Brave words, she thought as she sank onto the top step and wrapped her arms around her knees. She was trembling from head to toe, which pretty much told the story. Jason Kane could have her any time he put his mind to it.

Her only hope was that he had a short attention span. Perhaps if she failed to give in on any front, he'd tire of the chase.

Then she recalled that dangerous gleam in his eyes earlier, when she'd dared him about his sexual prowess. The memory made her groan. There wasn't a male on the face of the earth who would ever walk away from a comment like that. She'd given him something to prove, something far more intriguing than the simple challenge of getting her to accept a job offer. No wonder he hadn't mentioned the show all evening. She'd changed not only the rules of their game but the prize.

And judging from his smug expression as he'd

walked away, he was ninety-eight percent certain that victory was within his grasp.

It was amazing how quickly life could take a totally unexpected twist and wind up with more complications than any soap opera script ever devised. Add in that earlier call from Eunice and her life was just about out of control.

5

Jason stared at the latest dismal ratings for *Within Our Reach* and muttered a string of expletives that had his junior executives turning pale. He scowled at Freddie.

"Is that new story line sketched out yet? The one for Ms. Smith?"

"Actually…"

He sensed he was about to hear a litany of excuses. "Is it or isn't it?" he demanded.

Freddie drew in a deep breath. "The writers are a little concerned that they might be wasting time since Ms. Smith hasn't even agreed to take the part yet." His brow knit worriedly. "She hasn't, has she?"

"Not yet," Jason conceded irritably. "But she will. It's only a matter of time."

He thought of the evening he had spent with her just the night before. She was definitely weakening. Her startled expression when he'd kissed her, then the fleeting glimpse of wistfulness he'd caught in her eyes, had told him quite a bit about her current state of mind.

Of course, her resistance to him wasn't exactly the issue. If he were being entirely truthful, he would have to admit that she was still pretty adamant about not taking the job. It occurred to him that she might be viewing it as some sort of windfall, perhaps even charity. Maybe he hadn't explained the stakes for the network clearly enough.

The sponsors were already getting restless. He doubted if he could hold them off with promises for much longer. Another week or two of ratings like the ones he had before him and they'd be yanking their ads in droves or demanding price cuts that wouldn't sustain the show's costs.

Maybe he hadn't fully expressed the bind he was in, the favor she would be doing him and her friend Terry, who stood to lose a job along with a lot of other people if Jason had to cancel the long-running series.

A smile slowly worked its way across his face as he considered this last. He'd seen for himself how tight Callie and Walker were. She was definitely the kind of compassionate, loyal woman who would do anything for a friend, maybe even take a job she claimed not to want.

"A few more days," he told Freddie, exuding more confidence than he had felt only moments earlier. "Tell those writers by the time they deliver that outline, I'll deliver Callie Smith."

"Can you be a little more specific?" Freddie pleaded. "I think a firm date would reassure them."

It was Thursday now. He glanced at his calendar and saw that he was tied up for the rest of the day, that evening and most of Friday. He didn't bother checking Saturday or Sunday. Anything he had scheduled for the weekend could be canceled.

"Monday morning," he said, his expression every

bit as grim as if he were setting a deadline for a major military maneuver, which, in a manner of speaking, he was. He was about to launch a full-scale assault on Callie, the likes of which she'd never seen before.

He hadn't looked forward to anything with more enthusiasm since he'd single-mindedly gone after the presidency of TGN. There were a lot of doubters at the network who'd said he couldn't get that, either. Some of the most vocal were now working for very small independent stations in cities it was very difficult to find on a map.

When no flowers arrived on her doorstep on Thursday, Callie considered it a reprieve. When none turned up on Friday, she had to acknowledge the tiniest hint of disappointment. Apparently Jason Kane's attention span was even shorter than she'd hoped. She indulged in half a bag of Hershey's Nuggets to console herself. To her deep regret, the chocolate didn't vastly improve her mood. All that sugar and caffeine just made her jittery.

What she really needed to boost her self-esteem was a job. Not a job as an actress but one in her chosen profession. It was time to aggressively go about getting one. She prayed that this wouldn't be one more futile attempt like all the others she had made with compulsive urgency in the first forty-eight hours after being fired. She had driven herself into an exhausted frenzy trying to find something new, only to be left feeling like even more of a failure. A month later she had tried, and failed, again. Maybe the third time would be the charm.

Filled with renewed determination, she flipped open her address book to the listings for brokerage firms and began making calls to various friends she'd made in the business.

As it turned out, two more had been fired. One had taken a transfer to Cleveland. And the others were all too nervous about their own shaky futures to be of much help to anyone who might ultimately be competing with them for the last remaining broker's job in the universe.

Callie finished the bag of candy, which did nothing for her mood and made her feel physically crummy to boot. At least her inability to find so much as a lead on a job took a backseat to her now-queasy stomach.

Then images of acre upon acre of corn flashed before her eyes as she envisioned the rest of her life. She really was a dismal failure, just as her parents had always predicted she would be. She had failed at marriage and failed at her career. Eunice had already seen it. Soon everyone in Iowa would know it, as well.

"Too many grandiose ideas," her mother had said with her lips pursed tightly as Callie had waited at the train station nearly ten years earlier. "They'll be your downfall, you mark my words."

"You'll be back with your tail tucked between your legs," her father had added.

They'd been no more supportive of her marriage. Maybe they had seen what she hadn't, that she could never fulfill the expectations of a man like Chad Smith, who'd grown up with wealth and power and class. Discovering that her replacement's credentials had more to do with her swimsuit size and her pedigree than her wit or intelligence had left her bitter and disillusioned, a reaction that admittedly was out of proportion to his actual worth, net or otherwise.

Maybe she was doomed to live out her days all alone on a farm in the middle of nowhere. Her skin would burn in the unrelenting summer sun, wrinkling up until she looked like a raisin. She'd be reduced to chopping off her own hair with a pair of kitchen shears or letting it grow until she could wind it into a tight little bun like the one her mother had worn as far back as she could remember. She was doomed to wind up her life right where she'd started it, in the middle of a cornfield.

It didn't take long for misery and defeat to spread through her like an eager virus. Tears trickled down her cheeks. The last remaining bit of spunk that had gotten her out of Iowa in the first place drained away in another soggy bout of uncharacteristic self-pity.

Naturally, that was when Jason Kane chose to make yet another of his unannounced entrances into her life. Callie stared at the door as he continued to pound on it and call out her name.

"Go away," she shouted back in a voice that was husky from crying.

To her shock and outrage, she heard a key turn in the lock. *Blast Terry to hell!* she thought. The lousy traitor had given the man his key.

"If you open that door, I am dialing 9-1-1," she threatened.

The door swung open. She picked up the phone. Jason smiled. It was a terrific smile, crooked, endearing. She forced herself to look away, focusing on the phone's keypad as she determinedly punched the nine.

"You don't want to do that," he said softly, plucking the phone from her hand.

"Yes, I do," she said stubbornly, trying to snatch it back. He lifted it beyond her reach.

"You won't when you see what I've brought for dinner," he promised.

"I'm not hungry," she said with absolute sincerity. The very thought of food on top of all that chocolate was enough to make her stomach flip over.

Or perhaps that was its indignant response to the sight of Jason strolling straight past her into the kitchen, two plastic bags of groceries in his hands. She noticed he'd tucked her portable phone into his back pocket as a safety precaution.

Thoroughly disgruntled, she followed him. "You really are an arrogant son of a gun, aren't you?" She didn't wait for a reply before adding, "Has it ever occurred to you that I might have plans on a Friday night? Didn't it cross your mind that you should call before dropping by with dinner?"

"No," he said. "Where are your pots and pans?"

"No what?"

"No, I don't think I'm arrogant. Just confident. No, it didn't occur to me you had plans. You haven't been out on a date since your divorce."

"Let me guess, Terry filled you in on the sorry state of my social life," she said irritably. She was going to strangle the blabbermouth. She really was.

"He's a very accommodating man," Jason said approvingly.

"Especially to the man who controls his paycheck."

"It didn't require blackmail, sweetie. He's worried about you. He thinks I'm the answer to your prayers."

"So he's said."

"In more ways than one," Jason added.

"Terry is a hopeless romantic," she acknowledged, then scowled. "I'm not."

"That's understandable," he soothed, "especially given your recent difficulties in the marriage department."

He made it sound as if she had an irritating malady that could be fixed right up with a couple of exposures to the right medicine—namely, him. Although she wouldn't have admitted it for anything, he might just possibly be right. She was feeling marginally better even though the aroma of the garlic he was sautéing was enough to cause her to seriously regret following him into the kitchen.

"What you need is a distraction," he added, as if he'd read her mind. "A little taste of success. Take me, for example. With a little effort, you could probably win my heart. I'll play hard to get, of course. I wouldn't want you to think I'm easy. The challenge and the ultimate victory will do wonders for your self-esteem."

Callie shook her head at the glib nonsense. "Maybe you'd better let me worry about my self-esteem. Your methods seem a little self-serving."

"Isn't that what you've been doing for the past few months? Sitting around here worrying about your self-esteem? Where has it gotten you?"

She had no ready response for that. Nor was she willing to tell him it had actually been six months, ever since she'd found out about the bimbo in spandex, as Terry had rather inaccurately dubbed her. Women like that wore cotton or very expensive silk. And dumb as they might be, they would almost never be described by anyone as bimbos, no matter how outrageously they behaved. Avoiding such a label was one of the privileges of class, she supposed.

"See, even you can't deny that I'm right about this," he said triumphantly when she remained silent. "I think you need an expert."

"And you're willing to sacrifice yourself on that particular altar?"

He deftly chopped up an onion and tossed it into the skillet. Only then did he glance her way. The heated, wicked gleam in his eyes could have melted steel, turned it right into a little puddle of molten metal.

"It would be my pleasure," he said softly.

Callie's already tremulous insides did yet another nervous little flip. Why in God's name did brash, bold men like Jason Kane turn her otherwise intelligent brain to mush?

"And what do you get out of this bargain?" she asked.

"Sweetheart, I should think that's obvious."

Her chin set stubbornly. She was determined to have him spell it out for her. "Not to me."

His gaze heated another ten degrees. "Satisfaction," he said in a slow, lazy way that gave the word more interpretations than Webster had ever dreamed of.

Callie sank onto the closest chair and tried to keep from reaching for a towel to fan her suddenly overheated skin. Her reaction to Jason Kane was disturbing. Very disturbing. She was actually tempted to go along with this bargain of his—her ingrained Middle American moral fiber be damned.

"Bad idea," she muttered under her breath.

Jason chuckled. "But you are thinking about it, aren't

you?" He tucked a finger under her chin and forced her to meet his gaze. "Tell the truth."

"No," she lied very firmly, looking straight into those challenging eyes. "Never in a million years."

He laughed. "Sweetheart, you are seriously overestimating your willpower or underestimating my powers of persuasion."

It was quite possible, Callie thought with a sigh of heartfelt regret, that he was right.

Dinner wasn't nearly the disaster it might have been, Callie decided as she sipped a glass of wine a couple of hours later. Jason definitely knew his way around a kitchen, even hers. He should have looked a little silly with one of her ruffled aprons tied around his middle, but he was far too masculine for that. The pink gingham had merely shrouded one of the more fascinating parts of his anatomy, a part Callie had no business looking at, anyway.

She jerked her gaze away only to encounter a pair of gray eyes dancing with amusement.

"See anything you like?" he inquired.

"I was just wondering whether that tomato sauce would come out in the wash," she retorted.

"Should I strip down so you can find out?"

"You wish. Besides, it's only on the apron."

"Oh, I'll bet if I looked hard enough I could find a splash or two on my shirt, maybe a little dab on my pants," he said with a wicked glint in his eyes. "I'm a messy cook."

He sounded proud of the fact. "Is that the technique

you always use to get out of your clothes right after dinner?" Callie asked.

"You have to admit it's more original than saying I'm going to slip into something more comfortable. Women have been saying that for eons."

"Maybe the women in your circle. When they're not at work, my friends are almost always wearing the most comfortable clothes they own."

He surveyed her denim cutoffs and oversize T-shirt. "So I've noticed. Is that the full extent of your wardrobe?"

"Actually, I was once one of Bloomingdale's best customers. I have an entire closet filled with outrageously expensive power suits. However, I almost never wear them when sitting around the house, especially when I am not expecting company," she added pointedly.

"Does that mean if I plan to take you to the theater tomorrow night, I should tell you now?"

"Unless you don't mind being totally embarrassed by your date's attire," she said without thinking. When the implication of his question sank in, she promptly tensed. "Are you asking me to go to the theater?"

He paused as if to give the matter some thought, then nodded. "Sounded that way to me."

"Why?"

"To see a play?" he suggested, as if he, too, were struggling to understand what had motivated the invitation.

Callie scowled at him. "I meant, why you and me?"

"Gee, that's a tough one," he taunted. "How about

because I have tickets, I don't have a date and you seem to be presentable enough."

Disappointed despite herself by the mundane response, she muttered irritably, "That sort of flattery will win a girl's heart every time."

He grinned unrepentantly. "I told you I was going to play hard to get."

Two could play at that game, Callie decided as a matter of self-preservation. Jason Kane clearly had ulterior motives up the wazoo, but there was no point in missing out on the theater because of them. She was confident she could hold her own in any battle of wits with him if she concentrated very hard on not falling prey to his charms.

"Comedy, drama or musical?" she demanded as if it truly mattered. The truth was, she loved it all. Broadway, off-Broadway, off-off-Broadway. She would have squandered half her income on tickets if she'd had the time to use them. She hadn't been inside a theater, though, since she'd lost her job.

He tilted his head consideringly. "You strike me as a musical kind of gal."

"Drama," she retorted, to be perverse.

He plucked two tickets from his shirt pocket and held them out. They were for the Tony Award–winning drama currently on Broadway.

"Why did you get tickets for a drama if you thought I was a musical kind of girl?"

"Maybe I didn't buy them for you," he suggested mildly. "Or maybe I just knew you'd be perverse, say drama to spite me and I'd be able to catch you in your own trap."

"Has anyone ever suggested to you that you have a devious mind?"

"Hourly," he said with a note of pride. "And in most media reports describing my talents."

"It's not something I'd brag about if I were you," she commented drily.

"So, do you want to have dinner before the theater or after?"

"Have I said I was going?"

"That's a given. We're talking about dinner."

"After," she said.

He grinned.

"Let me guess. You already have reservations for six."

"Wrong. Reservations at Tavern on the Green for ten-thirty."

Her expression brightened despite her attempts to control her reaction. "How did you know—"

"That it's your favorite?"

"Never mind. Terry, of course."

"In my business, it pays to do research," he retorted, neither confirming nor denying his source.

"I thought you dealt with Nielsen and Arbitron, not the FBI."

He chuckled. "Does the FBI have a file on your restaurant preferences?"

"If they've met Terry, they probably do," she grumbled as Jason stood and held out his hand.

"Come on. Walk me out. I'd better let you get your beauty sleep."

"Are you implying it will take eighteen hours or so of rest for me to look decent enough to be seen with you?"

"Actually, I was offering a polite excuse for my departure, even though I know you'd rather I stay here and ravage your body all night long."

Indignation promptly roared through her. "Why you egotistical—"

"Tsk-tsk, is that any way to talk about the man who's going to make you a star?"

"You're not going to make me anything," she shot right back in a determined effort to keep the game alive, even though she sensed it was all but over.

"We'll see," he murmured, leaving her still sputtering on the fourth-floor landing.

She leaned over the railing and shouted after him. "I'm a stockbroker, dammit!"

"You were a stockbroker," he called from right outside Terry's door, which immediately popped open.

"A lovers' tiff?" Terry inquired.

"The first of many, I'm sure," Jason agreed in a stage whisper designed to be heard in the rafters.

Callie wondered how much damage one of those many vases of flowers Jason had sent would do if she sent it crashing down on his head. Probably none. His head was clearly made of concrete.

It was a little late to change her mind and tell him not to bother showing up tomorrow night. Besides, why should she turn down a chance to see a play and to have an outrageously expensive meal at one of her favorite restaurants just to make a point? If he wanted to waste his money trying to bribe her into becoming an actress, so be it. It was probably all on his expense account, anyway. After the turnaround he'd accomplished at TGN, the network could afford it.

"Callie?"

At the sound of his voice, she peered over the railing once more. "What?"

"We're out the door at seven-fifteen. I really hate to be late when the seats are front row center."

"I am never late."

"No last-minute primping."

"I never primp."

He grinned at that. "Can't blame a man for hoping," he said.

She would have grabbed the vase after that, but it was too late. He was already gone.

"Whew!" Terry murmured, moving into full view in the hall and gazing up at her. "Darling, if he weren't so blatantly heterosexual, I might fall for him myself."

"Maybe you should be ready at seven-fifteen tomorrow night, instead of me."

Neil stuck his head out at that. "I don't think so," he said quietly. "If Terry spends any more time with people in television, his few remaining brain cells will rot. You go on your own date."

"It's not a date," Callie declared.

"It sounded like a date to me," Terry taunted. "Neil, what did it sound like to you?"

"Let's see, you're getting dressed up, going to the theater and then out to eat. Definitely a date," he confirmed.

"A date is social, this is business," Callie argued.

"Business is lunch at the Four Seasons," Terry corrected. "A date is an attractive man asking an attractive woman to spend Saturday night with him." He leered. "Al-l-l night long."

Callie trembled despite herself. What worried her was the fact that Terry's interpretation of Jason's wicked intentions didn't frighten her nearly as much as it should have. Somewhere deep inside she was apparently hoping that he was right.

6

There had been a time in Callie's life when she'd taken for granted an evening such as the one Jason had planned. Tonight, though, she felt as if she were back in college, about to go on a date—okay, Terry and Neil had convinced her that's what it was—with the most exciting, mysterious man on campus.

She retrieved a simple teal silk slip dress from the back of her closet, dug out her sexiest lace panties and matching garter belt, a pair of her sheerest iridescent hose and a strappy pair of high heels.

She spent a full hour soaking in a fragrant bubble bath, then fiddled with her makeup for another hour. Yes, she was primping, but it had nothing to do with Jason's wistful taunt. She had too much pride to go out tonight looking like a frump. The possibility of running into a former client, her ex-boss or her ex-husband and the bimbo dictated being dressed to the nines.

At seven-ten, Terry and Neil declared her efforts a success. At seven-fifteen, Jason looked as if he might faint dead away. All in all, she considered the reactions very rewarding. Bring on old Chad and her pedigreed replacement.

A half hour later she was wishing she'd said no to the entire evening. Nothing in her life had prepared her for an evening out with a man as eligible and recognizable as Jason. Before they'd even entered the theater, their picture had been snapped more times than hers *and* Eunice's had been for the family album back in Iowa.

"Who's the woman?" several photographers inquired as they snapped away.

They directed the question to Jason, as if she weren't perfectly capable of responding herself. She found that almost as irritating as the rude, intrusive nature of their behavior. Her natural instinct for privacy was deeply offended, which was one very good reason why she couldn't imagine taking a job on a daytime television show.

Within Our Reach might be failing, but it still had millions of fans and hundreds of promotional opportunities. She'd seen what had happened to Terry. Everyone wanted a piece of him for this event or that interview. Some might consider all that attention flattering. Just the thought of it made her shudder. She watched Jason closely to see how he intended to handle all of the probing questions about the new woman on his arm.

"You'll have to wait to find that out," he informed the photographers with the taunting skill of a true marketing genius. He slid his arm possessively around her waist, his hand resting an indecent inch or two below where it belonged. "I expect to have an announcement any day now."

She glared at him, but he was oblivious. He was too

busy answering another barrage of questions. She was smart enough to see that adjusting the placement of his hand would only draw attention to it. The next thing she knew her butt would be on the front page of some tabloid. She would get even, though. She really would.

"Can't you at least tell us her name?" one man pleaded.

Jason smiled down at her. "Oh, I think I'll keep that to myself a while longer, as well."

"A wise decision," she muttered under her breath.

Taking the very broad hint, he reluctantly broke away from the throng of photographers and ushered her into the theater.

"Sorry about that," he murmured as he led the way down the aisle to their seats.

"Are you really?"

"What's that supposed to mean?"

"It means I suspect you of making absolutely sure that those men were out there tonight. What did you do, call every tabloid in town?"

"Why would I do a thing like that?"

His innocence seemed genuine, which meant he was the one who ought to take up acting. "To give me a taste of the glamour that awaits me if I accept your offer," she suggested. "Maybe to give the *Within Our Reach* promotion machine a jump start."

She regarded him with a scathing look. "And to give you a chance to cop a feel when I couldn't protest without causing a scene."

"Interesting theories," he agreed. "But would I have dared that, given your tendency to dress down for most occasions? As for your being disinclined to cause a scene, I haven't noticed that your moods are exactly predictable."

She considered his response. It was true. She'd given him very little reason to expect that she would gussy up in her fanciest clothes tonight. As perverse as she'd been from the moment they'd met, she might very well have worn yet another pair of jeans and perhaps her red high-top sneakers. Would he have risked having photographers on the scene for that? She doubted it, although Jason had been turning her preconceived notions about him upside down from the moment they'd met. He wasn't nearly as stuffy and driven as she would have guessed him to be from the articles she'd read on the internet after he'd left the night before.

As for her accusation that he'd used the opportunity to cop a feel, they both knew he didn't have to be in public to accomplish that. He was sneaky enough to try it whenever he was of a mind to. To her deep regret, she hadn't exactly been resisting him.

"Okay, maybe I misjudged you about this," she conceded. "But did you have to make it sound as if you were about to make some big announcement about the two of us?"

That innocent expression came back. "Is that what I did?"

"Any journalist worth his salt in that crowd of vultures will have my name and the details of our association before tomorrow's editions," she predicted.

"I guess we'd better think of something to announce, then," he said, as if he'd unwittingly trapped himself and was resigned to his fate.

"Such as?"

"Our engagement?" he suggested a little too lightly for her to take him seriously.

"Very funny."

"It would fulfill their expectations," he pointed out.

Callie shook her head. "I don't think so. I refuse to fake an engagement just to get you out of a PR nightmare you created yourself."

"Hey, I'm past thirty. It's time to settle down. The engagement wouldn't have to be fake."

She regarded him grimly. "Oh, yes, it would."

He sighed, though she thought he didn't look quite as brokenhearted as she might have wished.

"Then I'll just have to sign you for a major role on *Within Our Reach,*" he said. He patted his pocket. "I have the contract right here."

"I love a man who's prepared for all eventualities. Is the engagement ring in the other pocket?" she inquired acidly.

He grinned. "Care to feel around for it?"

"You wish." She scowled at him. "As for that contract, it's ruining the lines of your jacket. I suggest you rip it to shreds and toss it in the nearest wastebasket during the first intermission."

He shrugged and plucked it from his pocket. "I'll do it now if it'll make you happy," he said, tearing it in half without missing a beat.

The gesture was a little too accommodating. Callie suspected the papers were perfectly blank, just meant to taunt her.

"Let me see those," she said, reaching for them just as the house lights went down.

"Too late," he said as darkness fell.

For the next hour the best drama on Broadway unfolded before her eyes, but Callie couldn't think of anything except those papers Jason had just destroyed.

No, she corrected. That wasn't entirely true. She was reasonably aware of the arm he'd stretched across the back of her seat. And she was shivery from the skimming touch of his fingers on her bare shoulder. All in all, Jason was doing a bang-up job of getting under her skin tonight.

In the lobby at intermission she demanded to see the papers, piecing the two sections together to study the front page. It was a contract, all right. A very lucrative contract. Her mouth gaped when she saw the outrageous sum he was willing to pay her to star in the daytime show. It was less than he was paying Terry, but Terry was a seasoned actor with proven credentials in attracting viewers. She was an unknown who belonged on Wall Street, not some West Side soundstage. It reinforced her belief that television was too far from reality to be taken seriously.

She gazed up into eyes that were watching her perfectly blandly. "You don't even know if I can act."

"You can," he said.

"How can you be so sure?"

"Because for the past week you've been pretending to dislike me. The act was amazingly believable," he assured her, then grinned. "At least to anyone who wasn't close enough to look into those blue eyes of yours."

"I wasn't acting," she swore.

"Want to bet?" he murmured, already leaning down to claim her lips before she could even form a protest.

Right there in the lobby of the theater, with tourists

from Michigan and Texas and Ohio looking on with fascination, with dressed-up New Yorkers totally oblivious, he kissed her, slowly and methodically and convincingly. Weak-kneed, Callie clung to his shoulders. Her resistance turned to ashes, burned to bits by the incendiary nature of that kiss.

Okay, she decided when she could form a coherent thought again, maybe she did like him just a little. But she really hated herself for the weakness.

Sunday morning, after a night during which her torrid dreams had starred the infuriating Jason, Callie had just about decided she ought to be sentenced back to Iowa. Clearly she was too easily manipulated by a sexy smile and a little persistence. At some point, she had actually considered taping that contract back together just to earn another one of Jason's devastating kisses.

The memory warmed her and made her want things she had no business wanting, especially with so many strings attached. Just as she yawned and stretched languorously, someone knocked. Since she wasn't quite sure which of the males in her life was in possession of her key at the moment, she hopped out of bed and dragged on her rattiest old robe. She refused to give Jason the idea that she cared what he thought of her attire.

"Who is it?" she called out as she crossed the living room.

"Me," Jason responded.

"And me," Terry added.

"And me," Neil chimed in.

Good grief, didn't anyone sleep in on Sunday morn-

ings anymore? She threw open the door and planted herself squarely in their path, as if that would bar them if they were intent on coming in.

"To what do I owe all this?" she asked.

"We were on our way out to brunch, when Jason came along and suggested we all go together," Terry explained, not quite meeting her eyes. "Get moving, dollface. We're starved."

Somehow Callie didn't believe for an instant that this could be explained away as innocently as Terry was suggesting. "You just happened to meet in the hall?" she asked skeptically.

"Cross my heart," Jason swore.

"Ditto," Terry said.

"Neil, you're awfully quiet," Callie observed. "Do you have a different version you'd like to share?"

Neil exchanged a highly suspect look with Terry's boss, then shook his head. "Nope."

"Satisfied?" Jason asked.

Callie supposed she was going to have to be. Based on prior experience, she knew a woman didn't have a chance of getting at the truth if men conspired to keep it from her. Her ex-husband had kept quite a lot of truths from her. It had tarnished her views on the male of the species for all time.

"Give me ten minutes," she said, turning away and leaving them to decide for themselves whether to wait inside or out.

When she emerged from her bedroom fifteen minutes later, she found them sprawled all over her living room furniture. Jason was settled in an easy chair, glancing through a magazine. Terry was stretched out on the sofa, eyes closed. Neil was perched awkwardly on a dainty chair meant for someone far smaller than his six feet two.

Callie gathered from the lack of clutter that Neil had spent most of the time tidying up as he did every time he walked into her apartment. Neil was compulsively neat, which probably explained why Terry retreated to her place so often. His own always looked as if it was about to be photographed for some interior-design magazine.

"Ready?" Jason inquired, glancing up. "Ah, I see we're back to casual wear."

Callie's cheeks burned at the implied criticism. It was true, she had deliberately tugged on a decrepit pair of jeans that had been ripped or worn through in several places. She'd topped the jeans with a badly wrinkled T-shirt in a fetching shade of faded blue.

"The peekaboo effect is really quite enticing," Terry observed. "Don't you think so, Jason?"

"That's certainly one word for it," he agreed.

Callie frowned. "I don't have to come along."

"Yes," Jason said. "You do."

"Says who?" she shot back.

"Play nice, children," Terry instructed. "We're all going."

He ushered them out the door with the skill of a parent dealing with a couple of squabbling toddlers. Callie was pretty sure she saw him glance at Neil and roll his eyes. She couldn't say she blamed him. There was some evidence that he was dealing with a couple of stubborn, spoiled brats. Callie resolved to behave for the rest of the morning. It wasn't Terry's or Neil's fault that she and Jason couldn't spend more than twenty minutes together before tempers flared.

She was about to fall into step with Terry, when Jason linked his arm through hers and pulled her alongside him.

"You know why you're so cranky, don't you?" he inquired with a lazy drawl, pitched for her ears only.

She had noticed before that he lapsed into something bordering on a Southern accent whenever it suited him. "Where are you from?" she asked, hoping to divert his attention. She'd guessed from his comment that whatever was on his mind was likely to set her teeth on edge.

"Virginia," he said. "Trying to change the subject?"

"You bet."

"I don't blame you. Acknowledging that you're sexually frustrated must be embarrassing."

Callie stopped in her tracks, causing Terry and Neil to come up short or run right over her. Hands on hips, she scowled up at Jason.

"How dare you!"

"Actually, I dare quite a lot," he said. "Come on. You're blocking traffic."

She dug in her heels. "I wouldn't go anywhere with you if you had the key to a buried treasure worth millions," she declared flatly.

Terry groaned. Neil sighed heavily.

"Well, I wouldn't," she insisted. "I'm going home."

Jason shook his head. "See what I mean? She's frustrated."

Terry regarded the pair of them worriedly. "Jason, could I give you just the teeniest bit of advice? Pointing out that Callie is sexually frustrated may not be the most diplomatic, gentlemanly thing to do."

"No, it's not," Callie concurred. "Especially since it's his fault."

The last slipped out before she realized the implication. "Oh, jeez," she murmured, covering her face with her hands as Terry murmured, "My, my, Mr. Kane. I gave you more credit than that."

It was Neil who took pity on her. He tucked an arm around her waist and urged her forward. "Pay no attention to the two of them. They're in television, you know. No class. No manners."

"You're telling me," she retorted, scowling at her two tormentors.

Neil continued to soothe her with his sympathetically derisive analysis of their companions. Before she realized it, he had guided her down the street and straight to a table at a sidewalk café near Lincoln Center. Terry and Jason, apparently content to let Neil smooth over the troubled waters they'd stirred up, slid up to the table as quietly as the pair of snakes they were.

When Jason hitched his chair a little too close to hers, Callie shot him a venomous look. He rested his arm across the back of her seat, then tugged her menu over so he could share it. There was a cozy sort of intimacy to his behavior that truly irked her under the circumstances.

"Do you have any idea how furious I am with you?" she inquired curiously.

"About?"

"That little remark you made back there."

"Just telling the truth."

"Don't you think the topic called for a little discretion?"

"What's wrong? We're among friends."

"My friends," she pointed out. "Why would you say something like that in front of anyone?"

He looked vaguely unsettled by her continued irritation. "Actually, it was a diversionary tactic."

She stared at him blankly. "Diversionary? I don't get it."

"You will," he said grimly.

"When?"

He glanced at the clusters of people seated around them, until he apparently found what he was seeking. "Now," he said. "Over there."

Callie followed the direction of his gaze and gasped as she saw a picture of the two of them kissing plastered across the front page of the Sunday edition of one of New York's tabloids. The headline trumpeted the question Has Network Romeo Found His Juliet?

"Oh, my God," she murmured, thunderstruck. That would certainly secure her a lot of respect the next time she went job hunting.

"It's a really good picture," Terry ventured.

Callie stared at him. "You've seen it?"

"I ran out and bought a copy as soon as Jason called this morning."

"So this was a setup," she said, glaring at the whole traitorous lot of them. She waved a finger under Jason's nose. "You didn't just bump into them into the hallway. You invited them along to protect you, didn't you?"

"Actually, I was thinking more in terms of moral support for you," he said.

"I'll bet."

"It's true," Terry said. "He thought it would be better for you to see it surrounded by your best friends, just in case you turned out not to be a publicity hound like most of the people in television."

"We're supposed to help you get over the shock," Neil said, shooting a condemning look at Jason that made it clear whose fault he thought it was that she was in shock at all.

"It's not so bad, really," Terry tried to reassure her. "It'll be forgotten by tomorrow. Remember that time the soap opera magazine reported I was having a steamy affair with my leading lady? No one even remembered her name a few weeks later."

"That's because you angled to have her fired for planting the rumor in the first place," Callie reminded him.

Terry shrugged unrepentantly. "She couldn't act worth beans, anyway."

"What am I supposed to do?" Callie asked. "Send a letter to all the TGN stockholders and enclose a copy of the front page of the paper and suggest Jason be voted out of office?"

"An intriguing form of retribution," Jason agreed, not looking the least bit panicked, probably because he owned a very large chunk of that stock himself. "Of course, I've long since convinced them that any time my name is mentioned, the network's call letters are, as well. It's good PR."

"Sounds a little self-serving to me," Callie contended. "It protects your butt since you seem like the kind of man who gets caught with his pants down relatively frequently." She paused, then added, "Pun absolutely intended."

"Maybe we should be thinking about a way to capitalize on this," Jason suggested with just the faintest hint of caution in his voice as he watched Callie closely.

"I don't think I like the sound of that," she said.

"There's bound to be a lot of fascination now that people have gotten a look at that picture," Jason insisted, trying to sound as if the idea had just occurred to him. "It's the perfect time to announce that you're the new star of *Within Our Reach.* People will think we were just sealing the deal with a kiss."

"Not that kiss," Terry commented drily. "You link the deal and that kiss and you'll be in court for sexual harassment."

Callie gritted her teeth. "Forget the kiss. I am not the new star of anything. Why can't you get that through your head?"

"Because I know what I'm doing," Jason responded. "You'll be spectacular." He glanced toward Terry for support.

"You do have the kind of face the camera loves," Terry concurred. He grabbed a paper someone had left behind on a neighboring chair. "Just look at this. You're beautiful, darling."

Despite herself, Callie found herself transfixed. It wasn't so much that she looked glamorous and sophisticated that stunned her. It was the luminous expression on her face as Jason's lips claimed hers. The photographer must have caught her before fascination had been transformed into irritation. She practically glowed. Jason appeared no less enchanted. No wonder the copywriters had jumped to all sorts of wild conclusions about their relationship.

"I don't know," she said, her certainty wavering for the first time. Would it be so terrible to take the job, especially considering what the amount of money mentioned in that contract would allow her to do to make her mother's life easier?

"Trust me, darling. Would I lie to you?" Terry asked.

"In a heartbeat," she asserted as her common sense reasserted itself. She could not allow herself to be manipulated into doing something that was totally alien to her talents and her personality. Not that closing huge stock deals didn't occasionally require a bit of acting, but the audience was very limited.

"His motives are especially suspect when you might be the only thing between him and the unemployment line," Neil contributed darkly.

Callie looked from Neil to Terry to Jason. "What does he mean? You aren't holding his job hostage to make sure I take this role, are you? Not even you would stoop that low."

"No, it's not like that," Jason said, though he didn't look particularly wounded by the charge, which meant she probably had some part of it right.

"The show is in serious trouble, though," he added. "The ratings are down."

"They're in the toilet," Terry confirmed.

"The sponsors are threatening to bail on us. No sponsors, no show. That's the nature of the business," Jason said. "But the minute I saw you on-screen, I knew we had a chance to turn things around."

"Could you dump a little more pressure on her?"

Neil asked with disgust. "Talk about a couple of manipulating bastards."

Callie reached over and patted his hand. "It's okay. They're not going to pressure me into doing anything," she assured him. Then she looked at Jason. "Is the show really in that much trouble? Are you seriously considering canceling it?"

"It may be the only option," Jason confirmed.

He said it so bluntly that she knew at once he wasn't playing mind games with her. Cancellation had been discussed at very high levels at the network.

"What about new writers? A hot new story line?" she suggested.

"That's where you come in," he explained.

"Wouldn't you be better off hiring some recognized actress who knows what the heck she's doing?"

"Too expensive," he insisted. "Besides, this will make a terrific sort of Cinderella story. The media will be all over it."

"Like vultures," Neil commented.

Callie sighed. She looked at Terry and thought of those vicious notes he'd wanted her to investigate, the mysterious falling cabinet. Then she considered the all-too-real threat of cancellation. Guilt weighed heavily on her.

Even so, she knew she was going to have to let him down. As silly as it seemed given her lack of alternatives, she couldn't walk away from the profession she'd chosen to play at acting.

She gazed at Terry with regret. "I'm sorry. I really am. I can't do it. I'm a stockbroker," she insisted one last time, "not an actress."

"That's okay, dollface," he reassured her. "If you can't, you can't. I'll survive."

Jason scowled at him. "Walker, you're not the only one whose career is at stake," he reminded him.

"Oh?" Neil said nastily. "Yours, too?"

"I was referring to the rest of the cast." He fixed his gaze on Callie. "Please, it's not as if I'm asking you to work the coal mines or to dig ditches. It's an acting job, a very lucrative acting job. You might have fun."

"And I might be publicly humiliated." She met his gaze evenly. "No. I'm sorry. I can't do it."

She looked around the table. Terry appeared resigned. Jason seemed to be gearing up for another battle. Only Neil shot her a look of understanding, even as he tried to cheer up Terry.

"I have to go," she said suddenly, tossing her napkin onto the table and taking off. To her relief, no one followed. She wasn't sure she could have said no a second time, knowing how much depended on her relenting.

Miserable over having to let Terry down twice when he'd asked for her help and furious with Jason for putting her in that position in the first place, she detoured to Central Park West and walked along the edge of the park to get a grip on her mixed emotions before finally venturing home again.

When she eventually trudged up the stairs, she fully expected Terry's door to be thrown open and at least two people to accost her for another round of badgering. When the door remained tightly shut, she sighed and continued to climb. She couldn't help wondering if her friendship with Terry would weather her letting him down.

Not until she turned on the third-floor landing and started up the last flight of steps did she realize that someone was waiting in the shadows.

"Jason?"

When no one replied, her steps became slower and more cautious. "Who's there?"

"Callie?" a frail, tentative voice called out.

Callie stopped in her tracks as the voice registered. "Mother? Is that you?"

"Yes."

She took the remaining steps two at a time to see for herself. Sure enough, sitting on the top step and huddled against the wall in a coat far too warm for the beautiful spring day was Regina Gunderson.

"Mother, what on earth? What are you doing here?"

"Eunice said she'd told you I was coming."

Callie thought back to the threat her sister had made a few days earlier. She'd forgotten all about it. Or maybe she'd just taken for granted that Eunice's temper would cool and the latest crisis would pass. Apparently it hadn't. The proof was right before her.

An hour ago she would have sworn that her life couldn't possibly get any more depressing, any more complicated. She sighed heavily. It appeared she'd been wrong about that, too.

7

Eunice had lied. Regina had figured that much out the minute she got a good look at Callie's face. Her daughter no more wanted her in New York than she wanted to be here.

The city hadn't improved in the thirty years since she'd last seen it. It was filthy and, if the TV news shows were anything to judge by, it was overrun by thugs and gangs. From the minute she'd gotten into a cab at LaGuardia Airport, she'd been overwhelmed by the changes…all for the worse, from what she could see. The enormity of what she'd done by leaving the safety of the farm had terrified her.

The changes weren't restricted to the city, either. Callie was showing signs of similar wear and tear. Her beautiful, full-of-life daughter appeared to have been beaten down by the twists her life had taken. First the divorce, then losing that job she'd been so crazy about. It was little wonder she appeared shell-shocked.

Regina regretted that more than she could ever say. She knew, though, that Callie would never believe her if she told her that she had envied her for breaking free of the farm, for fighting to go her own way. She had left such support unspoken for far too long, convinced that her loyalties lay with Jacob, who had violently opposed Callie's leaving home, especially to go to New York.

Still, feeling a little blue was no excuse for letting herself go to seed. If Callie had tried to wear those decrepit clothes she had on to go out in Iowa on a Sunday, Regina would have sent her back to her room to change. Her own circumstances were so uncertain, however, that she kept that opinion to herself and tried not to let her dismay show on her face.

"I suppose you're going to send me straight back," she said to her daughter.

Even she recognized the odd combination of resignation and hope in her voice. She'd viewed this trip as a mixed blessing from the beginning. If she'd had her way, she'd have stayed on the farm where she'd spent the past thirty years of her life, but Eunice had insisted that Callie wanted her to come. She had practically packed her bags for her. Relief had shone on her face when she and that sorry husband of hers had dropped Regina at the airport. They'd stood at the gate until the last possible minute, probably to be sure she didn't flee the plane before takeoff.

Regina would never understand her younger child's compulsive need to meddle in her life. She understood her son-in-law far more clearly. He was as transparent as an old piece of lace. Tom wanted the farm. Everything he did, every helpful gesture, was meant to ingratiate himself with her so that she would see that he and Eunice got all of it when she died, cutting Callie off completely.

It just proved they didn't know her at all. Even though she knew perfectly well that Callie wanted no part of the farm, her oldest was entitled to her share and Regina meant to see she had it. If Callie turned right around and sold it or gave it to her sister, that was her decision.

She risked another look at her daughter. "Do you want me to go?" she asked straight out. "Will I be in your way here?"

"Of course not," Callie declared with obviously forced enthusiasm.

Unlike Eunice, Callie was a lousy liar. The truth was plain as could be on her face. A deep sorrow spread through Regina when she thought of the wide gulf between herself and her firstborn child. She knew, too, where the blame for that could be placed, squarely on her own doorstep.

"I'm glad you're here," Callie insisted despite whatever reservations she was harboring. "I've been asking you to come ever since I moved to New York."

That was true, Regina conceded. But her husband had never wanted to set foot in a city he claimed was so filled with evil and she'd never been brave enough to cross him. Besides, she'd always feared that coming back to New York would remind her of all she had given up so many years ago. Her regrets ran deep enough as it was.

"I'm tired," she said because she couldn't bear to force more lies from Callie's lips. "I think I'd like to rest for a bit."

"Don't you even want to take a look around the apartment?" Callie asked.

"Maybe later," she said wearily, ignoring the vague

note of hurt in her daughter's voice. Maybe later she wouldn't feel this deep resentment at having been shuffled off like an unwanted piece of furniture.

Callie nodded, then led the way to the guest room. She had a sympathetic expression on her face, as if she could read her mother's mind.

Maybe she could, Regina thought as she slid between the cool, expensive sheets on the antique brass bed just like the one in Callie's room back home. She turned her face toward the wall to avoid meeting her daughter's eyes. After all, they'd both been trapped by Eunice and her selfish, controlling ways.

"How could you?" Callie demanded in a hushed, furious voice the minute she got through to her sister. "Why didn't you warn me she was coming? She was sitting out here in the hallway all alone like some poor, homeless woman. It was awful, to say nothing of dangerous. What if she'd gotten lost coming from the airport? Or hadn't had enough money for the cab? If she can't cope in Iowa, how did you think she'd manage here?"

"I told you I was putting her on a flight to New York unless you came up with a better solution," Eunice reminded her, her tone self-righteous. "I gave you until the weekend."

"You still could have let me know she was on the way."

"So you could have tried to buy more time with promises you never intended to keep?"

"So I could have met her at the airport or at least been here to welcome her."

"Yeah, right," Eunice said sarcastically. "Let's not kid ourselves. You're not mad because I didn't tell you. You're mad because she's there."

Callie clung to her patience by a thread. "Maybe so," she admitted honestly. "It's not the best time for me, but I wouldn't have let her see it. She's our mother, for goodness' sake, not a shipment of corn."

"I'm surprised you're aware of the distinction, for all the effort you've put into her care."

"God, Eunice, you are such a selfish pig," Callie muttered, and slammed the phone down before she really got angry. Maybe in her own way, she was just as selfish, she admitted to herself, but she wasn't cruel. That was the real difference between her and her sister.

As her mother slept—or hid out in her room, which is what Callie suspected she was doing—Callie considered her options. Her bank account, healthy enough when she'd first lost her job, was dwindling. There were no alimony payments. Pride had kept her from accepting one thin dime of Chad's guilt money. She wasn't in any immediate danger of starvation, even with another mouth to feed. But she could no longer be quite as cavalier about her joblessness.

Then she considered the size of the salary in that contract Jason had been waving under her nose. It was on a par with what she'd been earning on Wall Street and then some. Temptation whispered through her. If she accepted the offer, there would be enough money to send her mother back home and hire help for her, if that was what her mother wanted.

In addition, Terry's job would be safe, as well as the jobs of all those other cast and crew members Jason was threatening with unemployment. She wasn't entirely sure how seriously to take his remarks about canceling the soap, but it had been evident to her earlier that Terry was taking him seriously.

And then there were the threats Terry claimed he'd been receiving. For all of his pretended nonchalance, she knew he was worried. And the image of that falling file cabinet had been coming back to haunt her ever since he'd mentioned the mysterious notes he'd been getting. Maybe he could use another pair of eyes—albeit untrained eyes—to watch his backside in case the sender truly was dangerous.

She picked up Jason's business card, or the one closest to her. There must have been a dozen scattered around the living room. One had come with each flower arrangement. He'd dropped a few more each time he'd visited. He'd scrawled his home number across the back of each one. He obviously hadn't been taking any chances on her not being able to reach him when—not *if*—she changed her mind.

Could she do it? Could she actually get in front of a camera every day and pretend to be somebody else? Given the state of her own life, she thought ruefully, it might actually be a pleasure. At least she ought to explore the offer more thoughtfully than she had up until now.

Before she could change her mind, she grabbed the phone and dialed.

"Who is it?" Jason growled irritably when he picked up on the second ring.

Obviously his reserves of charm had worn thin. "Jason? It's Callie."

"Callie," he repeated, his voice softening to that sexy Southern drawl of his. "I didn't expect to hear from you."

"Yes, you did," she contradicted. "You probably just didn't expect it to be this soon."

He chuckled at that. "Maybe so. What's up? Still furious with me?"

"Yes, but that's not why I called. Actually, I was wondering something."

"What?"

She sucked in a deep breath, then blurted, "Exactly what role would I be playing if I should happen to decide to consider joining the cast of *Within Our Reach?*"

"The same one you played in your walk-on," he answered matter-of-factly.

The lack of triumph in his voice was to his credit, she decided. She tried to sound as cool as he had. "A cop's not especially glamorous."

"Depends on who's playing the role, wouldn't you say? Besides, I've told the writers to get you out of uniform."

"It'll get a little drafty running around without any clothes on, won't it?"

"Oh, you'll be dressed," he said, his voice suddenly tight. "Just not in dreary blue." He hesitated, then asked, "Are you going to do it?"

"I might consider it," she admitted. "But I'm not committing to anything without more information."

"Such as?"

"How long is the contract for?"

"A year, with options."

A year, she thought. That wasn't so long. If she truly

hated it, she would never have to set foot on a soundstage again. She could arrange for the character to be murdered in the line of duty, to go out in a blaze of glory, so to speak.

"Would I be working mostly with Terry?" That prospect implied a certain comfort level that was critical.

"That's the plan. He has the highest TVQ on the show. The viewers love him. Pairing you with him will guarantee awards as the hottest soap couple on the air."

How ironic, Callie thought wryly. She suspected even Jason must have guessed after meeting Neil that Terry was not quite the heterosexual hunk the public believed him to be. Just in case he was still clueless, though, she was careful not to spill the beans.

"What the heck is a TVQ?" she asked.

"Recognition factor."

"Ah."

"Are you weakening?" he asked hopefully.

"Shouldn't I have an agent or something?"

"The deal's virtually done already. You can have an entertainment lawyer look over the contract, fine-tune it. Once you're on the show, the best agents in the country will be beating down your door."

"I suppose I could ask Terry to recommend someone," she conceded, then thought of something else. "Terry belongs to the Screen Actors Guild. Isn't that some sort of requirement?"

"Trust me, I can take care of it." He laughed. "Any more roadblocks you'd care to trot out?"

She was sure Jason could handle each and every one. She doubted there was anyone who dared to cross him once he had his mind set on something. There was something almost irresistible about a man who exuded such confidence.

She thought it over. Other than the fact that her insides turned to Jell-O every time she pictured herself in front of a camera, she couldn't come up with anything Jason couldn't counter easily. If she dwelled too long on the potential for embarrassment and humiliation, she'd pack her bags and head back to Iowa, her mother in tow. As for the media frenzy Jason had planned, she supposed she could stand it for a little while.

"I can't think of any more roadblocks," she conceded.

"Well, then, are you going to do it?"

"Yes," she said quickly before she could come to her senses.

If he heard the doubts in her voice, he didn't acknowledge them. "Fantastic! You won't regret it," he promised.

"I already do," she said grimly.

Silence greeted the comment. "Callie, are you sure about this?" he asked eventually. "I know I've been pressuring you and I've had Terry heaping on guilt, too, but if you're really going to be miserable…"

She heard the reservation in his voice and was suddenly terrified that he was about to withdraw the offer. Then what would she do? She knew just how bleak her Wall Street options were. Given the volatile state of the market, they were likely to remain so for some time to come.

"I'll survive," she assured him hurriedly. "I'll make it work."

"What made you change your mind?"

"Let's just say it's an extremely extravagant Mother's Day present."

8

The contract negotiations in Jason's office were very brief. Every time he glanced at Callie's pale complexion and trembling hands, he panicked that she would bolt before her signature was on the papers. Even in her expensive, pinstriped, charcoal-gray skirt and jacket, she exuded more nervousness than the confidence such a power suit implied.

It took him a record-fast two hours to nail down the terms with the attorney Terry had recommended to her. He knew Walter Whittington very well, and he recognized the astonishment that the lawyer fought valiantly to hide every time Jason gave in readily to one of his increasingly outrageous demands.

Jason regarded Freddie Cramer with amusement. The junior executive had been invited to sit in on the discussions. He was clearly in a state of near apoplexy over the generous terms.

"Um, boss, could I speak to you for a minute in private?" Freddie pleaded right after Jason agreed that Callie would be allowed to keep any wardrobe she wore on the show.

"No," Jason said tersely. He intended to burn those frayed jeans and misshapen T-shirts in Callie's closet at the first opportunity, and he couldn't do that unless he was sure she had stylish alternatives. It was a matter of image. He intended to turn her into the most glamorous star on daytime television. A photo of her in her current casual wardrobe would destroy that in an instant, and there was no doubt that some paparazzi would succeed in capturing just that woebegone look.

"But, boss—"

"Later, Freddie." He regarded Whittington blandly. "Anything more?"

The attorney studied him intently, then glanced down at his yellow legal pad, which presumably held his standard list of demands. Jason had a feeling they'd gone well beyond the items on that list a half hour earlier. Whittington was no fool. He'd figured out at least an hour ago that he had the upper hand. Jason was doing very little to correct that impression.

"One last thing," Whittington said. "A car and driver." Somehow he managed to say it with a perfectly straight face.

A car? To travel, what, a mile or two from Callie's apartment on the Upper West Side to the soundstage on West Fifty-seventh? For an actress with a single bit part on her résumé? Jason held back the sharp retort that would have greeted the outlandish suggestion of such a perk under other circumstances. He knew the attorney was baiting him, trying to gauge exactly how eager he was to wrap up this deal. The request was clearly made less for Callie's sake than to satisfy Whittington's own curiosity.

The demand, however, played neatly into Jason's hands. He would grant the car and driver—his own, though Callie wouldn't know that until they showed up next Monday morning.

"You know the request is ridiculous," he pointed out to put up at least a token resistance. Half the fun of negotiating would be lost if he gave in too easily on every single point. Freddie looked vaguely relieved by the belated display of toughness.

"You claim you're going to make Ms. Smith into a very big star," Whittington countered, clearly improvising but doing it very adroitly. "She won't be able to walk down the street without being hounded by fans."

Jason saw the immediate alarm that spread across Callie's face at that suggestion and decided he'd played the game long enough. It was time to close the deal. "You win. She'll get the car and driver."

Freddie groaned. Callie looked relieved.

"Do we have a deal?" Jason inquired, praying Whittington wouldn't come up with any more outrageous perks to test his limits.

The lawyer exchanged a look with his client, who nodded, despite her shaken expression.

"We have a deal," Whittington agreed. "Damn, Jason, I wish all of our negotiations could go this smoothly."

Jason leveled his gaze on Callie. "I don't want everyone as badly as I want Ms. Smith," he said quietly, amused by the color that flooded her face as she interpreted the full meaning of the remark. "Freddie, have my secretary type up the contract. Let's get this over with now, so we can get to work making Ms. Smith a star."

Freddie looked as if he might rebel at the order, but after a sharp glance from Jason he reluctantly left the office. Twenty minutes later, thanks to hastily made alterations to the boilerplate contract kept in the computer, the papers were signed.

Jason wondered what Callie would think if she discovered how rare it was for anyone to sign a personal services contract with the network president rather than the network or a show's production company. He hoped Whittington was smart enough not to comment on it to her.

In fact, as soon as the signatures were dry, the lawyer practically ran out of the office with his client in tow. He seemed to be afraid that Jason was going to come to his senses and tear up that contract.

There was little chance of that, Jason thought as he watched Callie being ushered down the thickly carpeted hall toward the elevator, her tush swaying provocatively in that suit. Only after the doors had whooshed closed did he realize that the entire time she'd been in his office she had never said a single word.

And still she'd left him with desire slamming through him like a freight train. He'd foolishly expected that hunger to diminish once the deal was done. That was all he'd wanted, wasn't it? To lock her into a year on *Within Our Reach?*

"Boss?" Freddie's voice was tentative, but determined just the same.

Jason sighed. He could imagine the questions his junior executive must have. "What is it, Cramer?"

"Why?" he asked succinctly. "I mean, was it personal or something?"

Jason scowled at Freddie. "I never confuse business with pleasure," he assured him.

Though if he were brutally honest with himself, even he would have to admit the waters were suddenly incredibly muddy.

"You're going to do what?" Regina Gunderson looked as if Callie had just announced plans to become a stripper. Her eyes, a faded shade of Callie's own blue, were wide with shock and her face was pinched with disapproval.

"I'm going to be on television," she repeated, still so astounded herself that she couldn't entirely blame her mother for her stunned reaction.

"On that soap opera, the one your sister is glued to every afternoon?" Regina asked, clearly struggling with the full import of Callie's news.

"That's right. *Within Our Reach.*"

"I don't understand. What happened to being a stockbroker? I thought you loved working on Wall Street."

"I did. That's what I am, but right now there's no work. I've been looking, but it's too competitive. Too many people, not enough jobs, unless I want to move to some branch in the boondocks."

"Iowa, perhaps?" her mother asked in a surprisingly dry tone.

Callie ignored the comment. "I can't go on sitting around in here, staring at the walls. You and Dad ingrained too rigid a work ethic in me. This is temporary, just until a job in my field opens up."

In fact, reminding herself of the temporary nature of the job was the only thing that had enabled her to sign the contract in Jason's office. She'd been able to tell herself she wasn't selling out, not for all eternity, anyway. One year of her life. One year. It wasn't as if it was a forever-after bargain with the devil.

"So you decided to become an actress," her mother said with a note of derision. "That's certainly a stable alternative. Have you ever acted a day in your life? Weren't you the one who got sick at the first rehearsal of your class play? Didn't you quit that very night?"

Callie vividly recalled the humiliation of that moment. Up until just this instant, she had successfully blocked it from recall. It was not a reminder she needed right now. "This will be different," she said, as much to reassure herself as her mother. "I won't be able to see the audience."

"There wasn't an audience then, either," her mother pointed out grimly. "Just some kids you'd known all your life and your teacher." She shook her head. "Callie, I can't imagine what you were thinking taking on something like this."

She was beginning to wonder that very thing herself. It was all Jason's doing. He'd sweet-talked her into believing that it would be a snap, that she was gorgeous and sexy and capable.

After six months of feeling as if she didn't measure up as a woman and two of feeling like a failure in her profession, she had needed that reassurance. Even though she suspected that half of the things he'd said to her had been designed to manipulate her into agreeing to take the job, hearing them had bolstered her flagging self-esteem and reminded her of the kind of confidence that had once been second nature.

Now, after just five minutes with her mother, as always, her self-esteem was in the toilet. Doubts rampaged through her.

"I took this for you," she said tightly.

Regina looked genuinely shocked at that. "I can't imagine why you'd think I'd want you prancing all over television for all the neighbors to see."

"Not so you'd be proud of me, that's for sure," Callie shot back bitterly, almost as furious with herself as she was with her mother for the rapid disintegration of the conversation. How many times had she come home bursting with excitement and pride, only to have either or both of her parents promptly cut her back down to size. A B-plus should have been an A. An award wouldn't put food on the table. A compliment from a boy shouldn't be trusted. The litany of negativity had gone on and on.

"I figured I'd be earning enough to hire some help for you back on the farm, if that's where you want to be," she explained, wearied by having tried and failed yet again to please.

A flicker of something that might have been guilt registered in her mother's eyes, but it didn't last.

"No need for you to be doing something just for my sake," she said stiffly. "Despite what Eunice thinks, I can manage."

Callie finally realized once again that she couldn't win. She grabbed her jacket before they both said things they would regret. "I'm going for a walk."

She was almost out the door, when her mother called her name hesitantly. She turned back. She couldn't read her mother's expression. "Yes?"

"Maybe…I mean, would you mind…"

Callie's patience was too frayed for this verbal tap dancing. "What?"

"I could come along," her mother offered. "If you wouldn't mind."

The whole point of going out had been to escape her mother's oppressive censure, but Callie thought she detected a certain wistfulness in her mother that she'd never seen before. She couldn't bring herself to say no. Besides, it was an overture, the first she could ever recall her mother making.

"Of course," she said, if not enthusiastically, at least without any hint of her mixed feelings.

"It won't take me a second to be ready. I'll just grab my coat."

"It's too warm for that heavy winter coat," Callie said. "I'll lend you one of my jackets."

"No, no," her mother protested automatically. "The coat will be fine."

"Come on, Mother," Callie coaxed, pulling a hot-pink Windbreaker from the closet in the foyer. "This color will look great on you."

Despite her expressed objections, her mother reached for the jacket eagerly. Suddenly, seeing that light in her mother's eyes, Callie recalled a time, years and years before, when she had seen her mother wearing bright colors. When had her mother begun settling for bland grays and beiges? When had her wardrobe turned dark and dreary and depressing, right along with her mood?

In that instant, Callie resolved to find some way to restore the once-happy, bright-eyed Regina Gunderson who lurked in the dim recesses of her memory.

* * *

Jason waited impatiently in front of Callie's apartment at six-thirty on Monday morning. She was due at the studio for her first day of script consultations and rehearsals at seven.

He had deliberately avoided calling her during the week since the contract had been signed. He'd wanted to prove to himself that he could withstand temptation for at least that long. It had been the most difficult battle of his life. He was not a man used to depriving himself of anything he wanted as badly as he now admitted he wanted Callie, not just for the show, but in his bed.

He realized as he kept his gaze fixed on the front door of her building that the only thing the delay had accomplished was to increase the hunger just for the sight of her. It was pitiful, that's what it was. Even Henry had smirked when he'd described the arrangement he'd made.

He watched as his driver went inside and rang the buzzer, waited and then emerged with Callie trailing along behind with the expression of a scared schoolgirl on her first day of classes. He thought she looked magnificent just the same.

When Henry opened the car door, she started to step inside, caught sight of Jason and hesitated.

"What are you doing here?" she demanded.

"You wanted a car and driver. You got a car and driver. Come on in."

Still, she hesitated. "Actually, Mr. Whittington wanted that. I thought it was absurd. I can walk to the studio." She frowned slightly. "I wouldn't want to take you out of your way."

She sounded miffed. That was good. Very good. It was about time she got her spirit back. He grinned and avoided looking at Henry, whose amusement was growing by the minute.

"You wouldn't want me to violate the terms of your contract on your very first day, would you? Whittington would be in my office by noon."

"I don't recall you being part of any bargain we made," she said.

"I'm just a bonus. I come with the car and driver."

She regarded him uneasily. "Every day?"

"Morning and night," he replied cheerfully.

She stepped back into the street. "I really do think I'd rather walk."

Jason didn't waste his breath arguing. He slid out and joined her. "Then I'll come along with you. Of course, you'll probably be late," he pointed out. "And it is your first day. You know how important first impressions are."

"Which is precisely why I don't think showing up in the network president's limo is too smart," she countered. "No one will take me seriously."

"Oh, they'll take you seriously," he assured her. He had seen to that in a series of extremely volatile meetings that had almost cost a couple of highly paid producers and writers their jobs. He'd made sure they understood that if they held that little private discussion against Callie, he would find out about it and make good on his threat.

"Stop worrying," he instructed. "No one will ever see me. You'll slip out of the car and I'll shrink back in the shadows like a wallflower."

Apparently the image amused her because the tight expression around her mouth eased. He could think of another good way to relax her, but kissing her on a five-minute ride was a very good way to assure he'd never get another thing done the rest of the day. He'd spend every minute between her exit from his car and picking her up again that night thinking about the way she melted in his arms. Down that path lay the ruination of his career, which Freddie Cramer seemed to think was doomed, anyway. He needed to keep his wits about him, he decided, studying her mouth with some regret.

Callie finally got into the car and sank back against the leather seat. To his amusement, when he took his place beside her, she moved a few inches, carefully keeping what she apparently assumed was a safe distance between them. He could have told her that it was only the strength of his willpower, not that invisible line she'd drawn, that was keeping them apart.

They made the too-short drive in silence. Only when the limo had pulled to a stop in front of the studio did she turn to face him.

"Morning and night, huh?" she inquired.

"That's right."

A smile suddenly tilted the corners of her mouth. "Maybe I could get used to this, after all."

Jason grinned. "I can assure you it's habit-forming," he said, his gaze fixed on her mouth again.

She blushed furiously and rushed from the car the instant Henry opened the door.

"Break a leg," Jason called after her.

She turned back and regarded him soberly. "If you

knew what a klutz I am onstage, you'd never in a million years say something like that."

"It's a theater expression," he reassured her. "It's for luck. You're not supposed to take it literally."

"I'll try to remember that when I start tripping over a cable."

Jason started to slide toward her, but she held up her hand in a warning gesture.

"In the shadows," she reminded him.

"I just wanted to tell you that you're going to be fantastic."

"Is that a promise?"

"A guarantee."

She grinned. "I don't believe you, but thanks."

Only after she'd walked away did Jason allow himself to murmur a little prayer for both their sakes that this wouldn't be the one time that renowned golden gut of his had failed him.

9

This was such a mistake, Callie thought desperately as she prepared to tape her first real scene for *Within Our Reach.* Every time she glanced across the soundstage and saw the little red light on the camera blink on, her throat clogged up as if it had been stuffed with cotton. Her palms were so slippery she couldn't have grasped anything smoother than industrial-grade sandpaper.

She hated Jason for his so-called discovery of "tomorrow's greatest daytime star," as he'd been describing her to the media for the past fourteen days. She hated Terry for heaping guilt on her and waving the existence of threatening little notes under her nose. But most of all she despised Eunice for pushing her over the edge by delivering her mother to her doorstep.

It wasn't that the visit was going all that badly. Callie had been so caught up in preparing for her soap opera debut that she'd spent very little time at home. Her mother seemed content enough to be left alone. She hadn't even wanted to come to the set today for the taping.

Callie had no idea how her mother spent her time.

They were almost like roommates with very little in common and very separate lives. When she had time to think about it, that struck her as awfully sad. She became irritated with Eunice all over again, because it was easier than trying to bridge the huge gulf between herself and her mother. That one afternoon they'd spent together had apparently been only an interlude, not the genuine new beginning she'd hoped for.

As if the tension between Callie and her sister hadn't been thick enough, Eunice was now in a snit because Callie had landed what her sister considered the dream job of a lifetime. At this precise instant, Callie would gladly have turned over the role of Kelly Piper to her sister. Maybe Eunice would have been able to remember the lines. She was certainly able to recall in vivid detail every slight by Callie, going all the way back to kindergarten, it seemed.

"Quiet on the set!" shouted Paul Locklear, a veteran soap director who'd been hired specifically to coach Callie through her first nerve-racking scenes. Tall, with thinning hair and a slight paunch, he was the most unprepossessing man Callie had ever met, yet he could command the most difficult actor with a mild suggestion. He was so calm and unflappable that a tank could roll through the set and he'd never bat an eye. Given the odd little accidents that had been occurring on the set the past few days, his focus had been critical. Everyone's nerves were on edge.

"Callie, are you ready?" he asked quietly.

She swallowed hard and nodded.

Terry leaned down and whispered, "You're going to knock 'em dead, dollface."

It was an interesting turn of phrase given the fact that they were standing over a body, the corpse of Terry's most recent leading lady. Cop Kelly had been called in to solve the murder and—if subsequent, hastily revised scripts were to be believed—console the grieving fiancé.

Callie wouldn't be surprised if somewhere down the line he also turned out to be the prime suspect—probably right after he made her pregnant. Terry's character had developed a dangerous edge the writers seemed all too eager to explore.

Try as she might to take the taping in stride, Callie felt as if she were in the middle of some otherworldly experience. If she looked anywhere except in the direction of the cameras, she was surrounded by luxury.

Lauren Fox's penthouse apartment, where the body had been discovered, was filled with incredible artwork, on loan from a Madison Avenue gallery. She had been the show's resident fashion queen, with a wardrobe more elegant than two or three designer showrooms combined and a lifestyle to match. A good many of those clothes had been tossed from one end of the set to another in a ransacking apparently meant to make the murder appear to be a robbery.

That wardrobe was probably one reason why she'd been killed, Callie decided cynically. The show's tightening budget hadn't been able to afford another selection of outrageously expensive clothes.

To top it off, the character had already had more weddings than Zsa Zsa Gabor or Elizabeth Taylor. Terry had been her latest conquest and he'd been only days away from walking down the aisle, which would have meant another lavish wedding episode, followed by a blissful honeymoon on location. That bullet wound in Lauren's temple had been far cheaper than a new gown, a trousseau, buckets of flowers and a trip to some Caribbean island for the location shoot.

"Let's do it," Paul said, snapping Callie back to the present. "In five, four, three, two, one… Action!" He indicated which camera was on in case Callie couldn't find the red light through the haze of terror clouding her vision.

She stared down at the body at her feet, trying to keep her expression as bland and professional as a cop's might be.

"She's dead?" she said in a squeaky voice that rose and fell in a rhythm that made it sound more like a question than a confident statement of fact by the seasoned detective she was supposed to be.

"Cut." Paul strolled over. "A little more authority, okay?" He smiled at her. "It's all right, sweetheart. Don't panic. You'll get it."

"And even if you don't, nobody will be listening," Terry whispered. "They'll be too stunned by your beauty and the sparks already flying between the two of us."

Her gaze shot to his. "Sparks? Already? What kind of coldhearted cad are you?"

"If you'd been watching, you'd know," he said.

She had been watching, disc after disc of back episodes, in fact, but the flickering images hadn't really registered. As she'd stared at the screen, she'd tried valiantly to memorize the various characters and their convoluted relationships.

But in the end, all she'd been able to think about was how ill-prepared she was to join such a cast of consummate professionals—one of whom was apparently out to get Terry, she kept reminding herself. At any rate, watching them work, seeing the number of lines they were required to memorize practically overnight, witnessing flawless performances with little rehearsal time, she'd been in awe. She wasn't even remotely in their league. Recognition of that fact had her knees practically knocking together.

She backed up a step, making sure she was off her mark to indicate she wasn't ready for the camera to roll. "Where the hell is Jason?" she muttered under her breath. "You'd think he'd want to be here for the debacle."

"Maybe he thought he'd make you nervous," Terry suggested, rubbing her frozen hands in an attempt to get the circulation going again.

"Maybe he realized he was the one whose body ought to be lying down there in a pool of blood," she shot right back. "Maybe he saw the network stockholders circling for the kill."

"And maybe you ought to get back on your mark," Jason's disembodied voice called out cheerfully.

Callie peered into the darkness. "Where are you, you coward?" She didn't care that the question would arouse the cast's curiosity about her relationship with the network president. It was too late for that kind of worry, anyway. Rumors had been circulating since her first day. Discretion didn't seem to matter a hoot.

"In the control booth," he responded.

Of course he was. *Control* was the man's middle

name. Unbelievably, though, the tight knot in Callie's stomach eased. She realized that on some level she'd been terrified that Jason had realized what a terrible mistake he'd made and stayed away precisely so he wouldn't have to witness her disastrous debut. His absolute confidence in her abilities was the only thing that had gotten her onto the soundstage day after day. If it had been shaken, she would never have set foot in front of the camera. She needed him here for moral support.

Reassured that he was still solidly behind her, she drew in a deep breath, glanced at Paul and announced she was ready.

"Way to go, Jason," Terry murmured, shooting her one of his trademark, irrepressible grins. "If I'd known the effect that man's mere presence would have, I wouldn't have offered you those Valiums. I'd have made a phone call to him instead."

"If you two are finished chatting, maybe we could get on with the show," the actress who was playing the now-dead Lauren Fox snapped. "This floor is cold as ice."

Callie winced. For a moment there, she'd actually forgotten that the woman wasn't really dead. She'd also forgotten that she was the one responsible for Lauren Fox's rushed demise and actress Penelope Frontier's untimely unemployment.

"God, I'm sorry," she apologized. That otherworldly sensation came back as she stared at the gaping hole that makeup had created on the side of the woman's head and the fake blood that had trickled into her hair.

"I'm sure," Penelope said nastily, then rearranged her

clothes just so before collapsing into a glamorous pose that gave audiences one last view of her exquisite body.

This time Callie ran through the brief scene without a single mistake. It might not have been the greatest performance ever recorded, but the line delivery was flawless. At the moment, she was satisfied with that.

There were two more scenes, including a preliminary interrogation of the man initially suspected of killing Lauren Fox. With his sharp features and chilling eyes, Jonathan Baines was so adept at portraying a villain that just being on the set with him gave Callie goose bumps. She forgot completely that Terry had told her time and again what a soft touch the man was in real life.

When she removed her gun from its holster, set it on the desk between them and kept her hand on top of it as she interrogated him, the gesture was pure instinct. She wanted protection.

"Cut! That's a wrap," Paul called out, then came over to Callie and draped an arm around her shoulders. "What was that bit with the gun? We hadn't rehearsed that."

"I know. I'm sorry," she said contritely. She'd accepted from the first that the director was the final authority and no one made changes without his approval. Her first day on the job and she'd already violated that unwritten rule. "Victor is just so creepy that I needed the gun in plain sight."

"Stop apologizing," Paul said at once. "It was wonderful. That's exactly the kind of subtle reaction that was needed to bring it home to the audience that he's a dangerous man. I wish I'd thought of it."

Callie stared at him, astonished by the approval. "You mean that?"

"Of course. Once you get over those jitters and lose yourself in the part, you're fantastic."

"I told you so," Jason chimed in, joining them on the seat.

He cupped her face in his hands and kissed her. Unfortunately, it was merely the sort of celebratory kiss a boss might share with a protégé. Callie could have used a passionate, bone-melting, male-female sort of kiss about now. She regretted that need more than she could say, especially since Jason had been disgustingly discreet and impersonal in recent days.

Fortunately, several of the other cast members circled around to offer their congratulations. Despite their otherwise superb acting talent, few of them sounded particularly sincere. In fact, she suspected that without Jason's presence and Terry's very visible welcome earlier, her first day of taping the show would have gone unnoted by most of them. She'd sensed a lot of resentment seething just under the surface since she'd arrived on the set what seemed like a lifetime ago. There was no question that a lot of people would be happier if she failed. She was determined that wouldn't happen. She intended to be the best prepared actress on the set, if not the most experienced or talented.

"Where's that champagne I ordered to toast Ms. Smith's first day?" Jason demanded.

"Coming right up," someone called out from behind the sets.

"And the hors d'oeuvres," Terry shouted. "I paid a fortune for little wieners wrapped in blankets because

I know how much Penelope loves them and there won't be any at her farewell party tomorrow night."

"Walker, you have so much pizzazz," observed the actor who played the villainous Victor. Jonathan Baines smiled benevolently at Callie. The smile transformed him.

"Darling, that bit with the gun scared the daylights out of me," he said. "It always makes me nervous when I see a woman with a weapon."

"Perhaps that should tell you something about the way you live your life," Paul Locklear chimed, then added for Callie's benefit, "Jonathan has what might best be referred to as a love-'em-and-leave-'em philosophy. Some of his conquests don't take too kindly to being abandoned, which is why he has to work so hard to make all those generous alimony payments."

Even after spending a whirlwind two weeks on the set, working with the writers and rehearsing informally with her costars, Callie was still a little bemused by the cavalier barbs they exchanged. Often, there was an underlying affection to the remarks, but just as frequently they were made with acidic sincerity.

She supposed it wasn't all that surprising, then, that one of them had gone a step further and started leaving nasty little notes in Terry's dressing room. So far, though, she didn't have a clue who might be behind the handful of subtly threatening notes or whether they were linked in any way to the recent spurt of minor accidents that had disrupted scenes.

No new notes had arrived since she'd started to work, perhaps because she'd been in the way, spending most of her time in Terry's dressing room, running lines with him. Until her arrival, Terry had apparently been a gadabout. He'd left his dressing room unlocked and accessible to anyone who wanted to slip a warning in amid the stacks of fan mail.

The small celebration was barely under way when Jason pulled Callie aside and complained, "Except for driving you to and from the studio, I've hardly seen you since you started work."

She grinned at his disgruntled tone. "This was your idea," she pointed out.

"I guess I figured I could pull rank and get a few minutes alone with you every now and then. Then the producers explained a few hard facts of life about the taping schedule and the script changes needed to work in your story line."

"So I fell victim to the bottom line. You are such a sentimental soul, Mr. Kane."

"A pragmatic soul," he corrected. "What would be the point of hiring you to save the show, then sabotaging it for my own prurient interests?"

"Prurient interests, huh? Sounds fascinating."

His expression suddenly turned serious. "Want to sneak away with me?"

"To?"

"Someplace private, where I can explain my prurient thoughts in more detail."

"Why do I suspect it would be more show than tell?" she inquired lightly. She checked her watch, then patted his cheek. "Sorry, no can do. I have an interview in ten minutes."

"How long can that take? I'll wait."

"Then I have to go shopping with the woman from

wardrobe, so we can make some decisions about what Cop Kelly would wear once she sheds that depressing uniform."

"Now there's where I come in," Jason said eagerly. "I have very clear ideas about that. I'll come, too."

"We're supposed to have a magazine photographer along to do a layout. I don't think it would be so good for your image to be seen hanging out in women's boutiques, instead of running the network."

"Of course it will. It's after-hours. It'll show what a dedicated, hands-on president I am."

"Hands-on, huh? Maybe we can work this out. It'll be very convenient to have the man with the checkbook along, in case my tastes run to excess."

"I've seen your taste," he countered. "I'm not worried."

"You've only seen my I'm-depressed-and-sulking wardrobe," she corrected. "One reason I came to New York was because I refused to buy one more cheap outfit in a discount warehouse. I really love expensive little dress shops. Remember Julia Roberts in *Pretty Woman* once Richard Gere gave her the run of Rodeo Drive? That's me."

He grinned. "You're not going to scare me off. Besides, your wardrobe budget is set. You're a financial whiz. You can imagine the consequences of going overbudget. I'd probably have to insist on another actor being written out. Do you want the responsibility for that on your head?"

Unfortunately, Callie guessed that his threats weren't entirely idle. There was an undercurrent of hard practicality required for a man to achieve what Jason had accomplished by the age of thirty-five. She had certainly been subjected to his relentless determination. She would hate to be the one to trigger any decision to start making cast cuts. Whatever resentments were already seething on the set would only deepen.

"Actually, I was thinking you could pick up the tab personally since this was all your idea," she challenged.

He took a step closer, backing her against the wooden framework of the set for the police station. She found it was surprisingly sturdy and unyielding.

"Why, Callie Smith, I had no idea you were that kind of woman," he taunted.

Her eyes widened. "What kind of woman?" she asked weakly.

"The kind who could be bought for a few pretty frocks."

If he hadn't been right smack in her face, his warm breath fanning over her cheek, she might have laughed. Frocks, indeed! But he was too delightfully close to inspire laughter. Instead, her breath snagged in her throat. Her gaze locked with eyes that gleamed silver in the shadowy light. Once again, she was reminded of danger, but in an odd way she found the thought exhilarating.

She dared a step forward, closing the already infinitesimal distance between them. Her breasts brushed against his chest. Her hips and thighs were close enough to feel the heat radiating from his body.

With a sense of inevitability she turned her face up just as he slowly lowered his. Their lips brushed lightly, then clung in a kiss that was by turns fierce and gentle, desperate and relieved. The aroma of his aftershave was late-in-the-day subtle and very provocative, like a lover's scent lingering on a pillowcase.

Somewhere deep inside, Callie recognized that just as walking in front of that camera for the first time a few hours earlier had been a turning point in her professional life, walking into Jason's arms was a pivotal moment for her emotions. The jury was still out on whether, in both instances, she was heading for disaster.

10

The fictional town of Glen River Falls had a population of about forty, most of whom were incestuously interconnected, as far as Callie could determine. There had been a minor baby boom a few seasons before, but those children were apparently locked away in the attic because they never appeared on-screen. No doubt they'd return as teenagers in time for steamy summer episodes filled with adolescent lovers.

At any rate, ever since Callie had been cast, the previously quiet town had been plunged into the middle of a crime wave of metropolitan proportions to keep her character on-screen as much as possible. By soap opera standards, her romance with Terry's character was racing faster than a runaway train.

By the end of her second week, fan mail was already pouring in. Only a handful of the letters expressed much regret over the departure of her predecessor, Penelope Frontier. Apparently a lot of women thought a relationship between Terry and the promiscuous character of Lauren Fox was a bad idea.

Surprised by how all of the praise was affecting her,

Callie plucked a handful of the best letters from the growing pile and tucked them into her purse to share with Jason and her mother. She'd never dreamed how much fun it would be to get all this admiring mail. It beat the occasional grudging memo from her supervisor at the brokerage firm all to heck.

Total strangers actually liked her. Well, they liked her character, but that was close enough to suit her. To her chagrin, she was beginning to understand why Terry was so addicted to his fan mail, even though it was directed toward his fictional persona. The whole experience was very seductive.

As if she'd conjured him up, she glanced up to find Terry's amused reflection staring back at her in her dressing table mirror.

"It's a kick, isn't it?" he asked.

"It is, indeed," she confessed. "What do I do with all these?"

"That depends."

"On?"

"Whether you want the public to love you or to think you're an ungrateful snob." He grinned wickedly. "Since we both know you're an approval junkie, you might as well get a zillion copies of your best publicity shot made, autograph them and start popping them in the return mail. If someone sounds particularly intelligent, you could always make them president of your fan club and turn the job over to them."

Callie stared from the pile of envelopes on the dressing table to the half-full mailbag on the floor. "I'm supposed to answer all these myself? I never even wrote home." She couldn't recall ever seeing Terry carting a load of mail to the post office. "Do you answer every letter?"

"Every one."

She regarded him suspiciously. "Personally? Or do you have a fan club that handles it?"

"Actually, I just hired a personal assistant to take care of it."

Given the speed with which the mail was accumulating, Terry's solution held tremendous appeal. "Maybe that's what I should do. Is it expensive?"

"Minimum wage by the hour."

"Do you think this person could take me on, too?"

"You'd have to ask, but I don't see why not."

Something in his expression struck her as awfully smug. "Okay, why that look? Do I already know this person?"

"Sure. Your mom."

Callie's mouth dropped open. "You hired my mother to answer your fan mail?"

"Actually, Neil hired her. He said she was looking for something to do to keep occupied. He was getting tired of my mail cluttering up our apartment until I got around to hiring some kid in the neighborhood to answer it for me. Presto, the deal was struck."

"Since when are Neil and my mom so tight?" she inquired, an unmistakable edge in her voice.

"Whoa," Terry warned, promptly beginning to massage away the tension in her neck. "Don't go getting your drawers in a knot, sweetheart. It's only been since you and I have been taping late every night. They've shared a few dinners, a little conversation. Besides, what difference does it make?"

None, she supposed, except it was yet another indication of just how wide that gap was between herself and her mother. They were living under the same roof and she still didn't know how her mother was spending her time, much less what was going on in her head. What kind of a daughter did that make her?

"I should have known, that's all," she said wearily.

"Uh-oh, here goes the bad-daughter routine again," Terry replied.

"Well, what else would you call me when I didn't even know she'd taken a job?"

"It's not a job. It's something to occupy her time," Terry corrected. "You didn't expect her to sit around all day watching soaps, did you? Except for ours, of course."

Callie sighed. "I don't know what I expected," she admitted. But, she thought resolutely, it was about time she figured it out.

Regina glanced up guiltily when she heard Callie's key turning in the lock. If there'd been time, she would have swept the huge stack of mail into the tote bag Neil had delivered earlier, but something told her it was just as well that she was about to be caught. It was a silly secret to be keeping in the first place. She and Callie had little enough to say to each other as it was. She still didn't understand how a mother and daughter who'd once shared everything could have drifted so far apart.

As she waited for Callie to discover her at the kitchen table surrounded by Terry's fan mail, she tightened her grip on the fancy fountain pen Neil had insisted she use.

"Mom?"

"In here."

Callie appeared in the doorway and surveyed the neat piles of envelopes that were already prepared for the morning mail. Regina watched her closely for some hint of surprise or disapproval. Instead, the expression on her daughter's face was unreadable. When had she become so adept at hiding her feelings? Regina wondered.

"Terry's mail?" Callie asked.

Regina nodded. "He told you, I suppose."

"He mentioned that you and Neil had worked out an arrangement."

Regina still couldn't gauge her mood. "Are you upset about it?"

Callie shrugged, feigning indifference as she always had when she'd felt slighted. Regina recognized the gesture at once.

"Why on earth would I be upset?" Callie asked, her tone neutral. "If you were looking for something to do, though, you should have told me."

"I didn't want you to think I was complaining."

Callie sighed and pulled out a chair opposite her. "Mother, as long as you're here, I want you to be happy. Get out, see things, meet people, whatever you want to do."

That said, Callie studied her so intently that Regina found herself squirming.

"Are you just doing this for the money?" Callie asked worriedly. "Because if that's it, I can certainly give you more spending money. I don't want you shut up in here because you don't think you can afford to do things."

"The money has nothing to do with it," Regina denied vehemently. "I wanted to make myself useful. It doesn't take a minute to keep this apartment straightened up. You're almost never home for meals, so there's no point in cooking. I'm used to going from sunrise to sunset. Idleness doesn't suit me."

"You should have told me," Callie repeated.

"And what would you have suggested?" Regina retorted, anticipating exactly the sort of guilty expression she got. "There, I knew it. You would have gotten that precise look on your face while you tried desperately to figure out what to do with me. It didn't take Neil but a minute to think up this idea."

Not until the words were out of her mouth and she saw Callie's hurt reaction did she realize that she'd compared her daughter to a near-stranger and implied that Callie had come up wanting. "I'm sorry," she said at once. "I didn't mean that the way it sounded."

"Sure you did," Callie said. "And it's okay. I deserve it." She looked Regina straight in the eye. "Maybe I've just thought of you for so long as my mother, I've never stopped to think about you being a person. Of course, Neil would see you in a different light."

Regina did something then that she hadn't done in years. She reached across the table and clasped her daughter's hand. Such a small gesture but one so rare she couldn't even recall the last time she'd made it, the last time Callie had allowed it, for that matter.

"Why wouldn't you think of me as your mother?" she chided gently. "That's who I am."

"But you're more than that, and I should have seen it."

"Then maybe it's a good thing I'm here, after all.

Maybe we can both spend this time discovering who we've become."

To Regina's surprise, Callie's eyes shimmered with unshed tears. "I'd like that, Mother. I really would."

"Me, too." She released Callie's hand, stood up and put a kettle on to boil water. "Why don't we toast that with a cup of hot chocolate."

"With marshmallows?" Callie asked. "The way we used to celebrate special occasions?"

Regina grinned at this sophisticated young woman who suddenly sounded so much like the child with whom she had once taken such joy in sharing things. "Is there any other way?"

"When did you buy hot chocolate and marshmallows?" Callie asked as she retrieved a pair of mugs and set them on the table.

"The minute I saw you didn't have any in the cupboard." She winked at Callie. "Seemed to me you must have just run out."

"Nine or ten years ago, more likely. Chad wasn't exactly a hot-chocolate kind of man."

"Forget about that terrible man and what he liked and didn't like," she said. Then she added more gently, "Not everything from the past has to be sacrificed when you make a new future, you know." She put the steaming cup of hot chocolate in front of her daughter, then fixed her own and sat back down. "Tell me about your day."

With startling eagerness, Callie did just that. As her daughter described this strange make-believe world she worked in, Regina sat back and let the words flow over her. Five words, she thought with a sense of amazement. That was all it had taken—"tell me about your day"—

and she and Callie were communicating, really communicating, for the first time in years.

"So, anyway, there I was with all this mail piled up around me, trying to figure out what on earth I was going to do with it, when Terry came along and told me about this deal Neil had made with you."

Regina found herself laughing at Callie's put-upon expression. She'd always displayed the same hint of jealousy whenever Eunice had gotten some sliver of parental attention that Callie had craved for herself but been too proud to ask for. She wouldn't ask this time, either, Regina guessed.

"I suppose now you want me to do your mail, too," Regina grumbled lightly.

Callie grinned. "Well, you are my mother."

"I'm not cheap."

"Terry said he was paying minimum wage."

"But I am your *mother,*" Regina countered.

"Extortionist," Callie accused.

"Good business. I suddenly sense a demand I never knew existed."

"Don't tell me I got all those business genes from you," Callie said.

"And where else would you have gotten them? Not from your father certainly. Why do you think he agreed to let me take the corn to market?"

"I always figured it was because he was trying to work you into an early grave," Callie said so bitterly that Regina winced.

"Oh, baby, that's not true."

"Never mind. I don't want to talk about it." To prove

it, she reached for a handful of Terry's mail. "So what are the ladies writing about our favorite hunk?"

"Callie?" Regina said softly.

Blue eyes clashed with hers. "Another time, Mother," Callie insisted, her tone forbidding.

Regina accepted defeat for the moment. So much bitterness, though. Too much for a child to harbor into adulthood. It was so obvious to her now. How had she missed it for so long?

Holding back a sigh of regret, she glanced across the table and saw that the color had washed out of Callie's face.

"Darling, what on earth? What's wrong? You're white as a sheet." She reached for the piece of stationery Callie was clutching, assuming that it must have something to do with her obvious distress. Callie refused to give it to her.

"Let me see it," Regina insisted, gently trying to pry it loose.

"No," Callie said sharply. "Don't touch it."

"Why not?"

"Fingerprints."

Regina stared at her. "Fingerprints," she echoed blankly. "I don't understand."

Callie met her gaze then, her expression so serious and shaken that Regina felt the dull thud of her heart begin to pick up speed.

"It's a threat, Mother. Against Terry."

Surely not, Regina wanted to say. She had read a hundred letters or more tonight alone, all of them gushing with praise for the nice young man who lived downstairs. Why would one person want to threaten him?

She knew, of course, that there were a lot of crazy people in the world. Even in Iowa, old Mr. Kinsale had periodically waved his shotgun around, complaining about the government and scaring the entire town to death. He hadn't shot anyone yet, though, and Regina doubted he ever would. She could see from Callie's expression that this letter couldn't be dismissed so lightly.

"You think it's serious?"

"I do. Do we have any little plastic bags in the kitchen?" she asked, already heading in that direction.

"In the drawer beside the refrigerator," Regina responded distractedly, her entire focus on the threat.

"What do you know about all of this?" she asked when Callie came back with the note sealed inside a clear bag.

"It's not the first," Callie said. "He told me about the others, but this is the first one I've seen."

Regina's heart skipped a beat. She didn't like the idea of her daughter and danger being so closely linked. "You knew about these and you still took a job on that show? Callie, what were you thinking?"

Callie leveled a look straight at her, a look devoid of fear and filled with such determination that Regina saw no point in arguing even before Callie declared, "I was thinking that a friend needed my help."

Regina knew she should have felt pride in that courageous answer, but she didn't. She felt an unfamiliar sense of terror chilling her all the way through.

11

"It's crap," Jason declared, referring to the situation-comedy pilot that had been on the screen in his office for less than five minutes. "Next."

"But, boss—" Freddie protested. As usual he was the only one of the three junior executives in the room to have the temerity to speak up.

Jason cut him off. "I don't need to see any more. What else have we got?"

"Nothing that will impress you given your current mood," Freddie responded, hugging the DVDs protectively. "I'll bring these back tomorrow."

Jason's astonished gaze clashed with Freddie's determined one. It had been a long day. They had started practically at dawn. Everyone was clearly exhausted, but Freddie was very close to crossing over the line. Jason sighed. So, what else was new? That's why he regarded the young man as his most promising junior executive.

"Okay, everybody out," Jason ordered. When all three men rose, he added, "Not you, Cramer. We need to talk."

While the others made a hasty exit, Jason swiveled his chair to stare out at the Manhattan skyline. Shrouded in low-lying clouds and dripping wet from two days of constant rain, it was as gray and gloomy as his disposition. Not that the weather was responsible. He could lay his mood directly at the feet of one Callie Smith.

He'd made a cold-blooded decision two weeks ago that there was no longer any reason for him to see her. She was safely locked into a year-long contract. He'd personally overseen her wardrobe selection and knew she was going to be the fashion envy of women everywhere. The latest soap episodes he'd screened were dynamite. The media coverage had been nothing short of fabulous. The ratings were already showing the first faint signs of improvement. His job to save *Within Our Reach* was done. He had an entire television schedule to worry about. He'd already spent more time than he should have on curing the ills of one daytime drama.

The litany of excuses went on and on, but the truth was that the woman, or rather, the way she made him feel, scared the spit out of him.

His limo continued to pick her up morning and night, but he was no longer in it. He walked to work, hoping the exercise would dull the unexpected longing he felt. He deliberately didn't bother with explanations or excuses for his driver to deliver. He ignored Henry's disapproving scowls and shoved aside thoughts of Callie's likely confusion over his sudden absence. A clean break was for the best. He had a lifetime of experience at getting them right.

To his shock, however, he hadn't been able to simply dismiss Callie from his mind. Images popped up when he least expected them. His body ached with the kind of turned-on longing he hadn't experienced since his teens. Clearly, at some point, she had gone from being the solution to a business problem to something more, something personal. That was a first and he didn't like it. He didn't like it one bit. He should have seen it coming and cut her out of his life sooner, the minute the ink was dry on that contract, for example.

Now, as Freddie had dared to suggest, her absence was turning him into a foul-tempered beast, one of those capricious network executives who dismissed months of hard work with a snap of his fingers. He really hated having his flaws pointed out to him as Freddie just had.

Fighting to bring his temper under control, he slowly turned back to confront his audacious junior executive.

"I'm not apologizing," Freddie said defiantly before Jason could open his mouth.

"Have you done something that calls for an apology?"

Freddie regarded him warily, clearly uncertain what to make of Jason's quiet, tempered response.

"That depends on your point of view, I suppose," Freddie admitted. "You are the boss around here."

Jason nodded, keeping his expression bland. "So they tell me."

"You were also wrong about that show."

"Wrong?" Jason repeated, his tone deadly.

Freddie didn't even flinch. "Wrong," he repeated with renewed defiance, jamming the DVD back into the player as he spoke. "Watch this."

Impressed by Freddie's conviction, if not by his insubordination, Jason watched, resisting the urge this time to stop it before the first scene was over.

The sitcom did improve. The stars were charming and fresh. The premise was unremarkable but had potential. By the end of the half hour the writing and the performances sparkled. There were some genuinely funny moments. He was forced to admit that he could see what had caught Freddie's attention.

Unfortunately, most viewers would have switched channels long before the end, just as he in essence had. In the competitive world of prime-time television, shows rarely got a second chance to hook viewers.

"It's weak," he said.

"But promising," Freddie insisted.

"I'll give you that," Jason conceded, "but we can't go with it the way it is. It'll be dead after the first fifteen minutes. Any suggestions?"

Freddie didn't hesitate. "Order another script. Everything was coming together at the end in this one. One more script ought to prove whether or not there's something here. If it works, we shoot another pilot."

"You're throwing a lot of money around on something that's far from a sure thing."

"My gut tells me it will work," Freddie countered. He regarded Jason slyly. "You've spent a lot more going with your gut. Need I remind you of—"

"No, you needn't," Jason was quick to reply before Freddie could mention Callie's name. Hearing it set off responses he had no idea how to deal with. A man with less practice at remaining unscathed by emotions might describe what he was feeling as vulnerability. Jason refused to concede that possibility. It was just a matter of shoring up his willpower as he always had.

"She was just a game to you, wasn't she?" Freddie asked, an unexpected note of derision in his voice.

Jason scowled at him. There was no need to ask to whom the young man was referring. He deeply resented the implication that Callie had been no more than a business challenge, but could he deny it? Not truthfully, he confessed silently.

At least that was how it had started, as a pragmatic, coldhearted decision to use her to bolster his soap's flagging ratings. He'd pursued dozens of big-name actors and actresses for precisely the same reason. That was the name of the game—wheeling and dealing for talent, gambling megabucks on instinct. The adrenaline rush it gave him was unequaled, or it had been until recently.

"Since you're not answering, I must be right," Freddie concluded. "Did she know that?"

Ah, Jason thought with a sick sensation in the pit of his stomach, *that was the rub.* Callie Smith hadn't played in the network big leagues before. She didn't know the rules. Which made him a son of a bitch.

"You know, Freddie, your network career could be shortened considerably if you persist in trying to be my conscience," he said, reaching for his jacket as he headed for the door.

Freddie grinned unrepentantly. "I'll take my chances. Does that mean I can give the go-ahead for another script?"

"That means you can tell my secretary to send the biggest bouquet of flowers in the shop to Callie first thing in the morning," Jason retorted. "*Then* you can give the writers another script order."

He was on his cell phone, calling for the limo before he hit the lobby thirty-five floors down. He felt better than he had in days.

Callie had been surprised the first time she'd dashed into Jason's limo and discovered it empty. She hadn't had the nerve to ask Henry where Jason was, though she had the distinct impression the driver might have had quite a bit to say on the subject. He'd been even more solicitous than usual, as if he felt he had to make up for someone else's crummy treatment.

As the days passed, her pride had kicked in until she would have chewed nails before asking about the man to whom the limo belonged.

She had also managed to evade most of Terry's direct questions about her relationship with "the big shot," but she could tell his curiosity wasn't going to be put off much longer. He was getting that worried, protective gleam in his eyes more and more frequently.

Which made two of them. She still hadn't gotten over that nasty threat that had been tucked in with Terry's fan mail: "Tell all or I will…soon!"

Simple but very clear. Callie shivered every time she thought about it.

She'd sworn her mother to secrecy and put the plastic Baggie containing the letter into a manila envelope for safekeeping until she could figure out the best thing to do. From the beginning Terry had been so adamant about keeping the police out of it that she knew it wasn't an option. Not yet, at least. There might come a time when she would be forced to overrule his objections and insist that they talk to a real policeman.

For now, all she could do was keep her eyes open around the studio. If she couldn't catch someone leaving a note in Terry's office, perhaps she would catch a glimpse of the perpetrator of the rash of pranks that so far hadn't resulted in serious injury to anyone.

She had decided to pick a different cast member each day to observe intently, studying the interaction with Terry, the movements, any hints of hostility. It wasn't much, but it was better than asking too many questions and drawing attention to what some might view as an excessive interest in her new coworkers.

"Okay, detective, you're off-duty," Terry declared.

The comment interrupted her surreptitious survey of perky ingenue Lisa Calvert, who was currently trying to seduce the town's leading citizen. She was practicing her wiles on-screen and off. Callie's dressing table mirror offered an amazing view of the even more astonishing activities backstage.

"Did you know that much about seduction when you were her age?" Callie inquired, unable to take her eyes off the scene currently being played just out of camera range. Lisa had her tongue down Randall Trent's throat. Her hands were very active, as well.

Callie tore her gaze away from the absorbed couple and turned to look at Terry. "Well, did you?"

"No comment."

"Did she ever come on to you?"

Terry shrugged. "She's come on to every male on the set at one time or another."

"What did you do?"

"Jealous, dollface?"

"Oh, for heaven's sake, be serious," Callie retorted. "Tell me what happened. Could you have offended her when you rejected her? Could she have guessed that your lack of interest was gender-related rather than personal?"

"I'm sure her ego is plenty big enough to survive without adding me to her list of conquests, if that's what you mean. Lisa didn't send those notes. I'm sure of it."

"I'm not," Callie said succinctly. "Scorned women can turn vicious."

"Only if they had something invested in the relationship in the first place."

"You'll excuse me if I don't take your word on this," she countered, her attention returning to Lisa's activities, which had progressed several heated degrees toward indecency. Her eyes widened. "My, oh, my. No doubt about it, she stays on my list."

Terry grinned. "Don't look now, but your envy is showing. Why not ask the big shot to demonstrate what you've been missing?"

"My suspicions have nothing to do with…" Callie scowled at him. "Oh, never mind." She picked up her purse and headed for the door. Terry stayed right on her heels, his expression puzzled.

"Hey, what did I say?"

"Nothing. Forget it."

"Callie?"

"Look, I'm tired. I'm heading home. Do you want a lift?"

"In the limo? Won't the big shot object?"

"To what? There's room enough in there for an army."

"I've always heard three's a crowd."

"And two's company," she retorted, giving the phrase an unexpectedly bitter significance. "I could use the company."

"Uh-oh, trouble in paradise, dollface?" he asked, scrambling into his jacket as he followed her out of the studio.

"What paradise?" she inquired as she looked up and down Fifty-seventh for some sign of the limo. Henry was late. Henry was never late. He was the most reliable man she knew—far more reliable than his boss, whom she hadn't seen since the night he'd accompanied her and the wardrobe mistress on a shopping excursion from one end of Manhattan to the other.

Terry's hands locked on her shoulders, stilling her impatient pacing. "Okay, dollface, what's up? Did you and the big shot have a spat?"

"No," she said honestly. In fact, he'd left her that night with a blistering kiss that had stolen her breath. Terry didn't need to know about that. It was too humiliating to admit that she'd been rejected just when she thought things were really heating up.

"Come on. Let's get to the bottom of this. Tell me exactly what happened the last time you saw him," he persisted.

She debated answering, then decided that perhaps Terry would see something in Jason's behavior that she'd missed. "We went shopping," she admitted finally.

Terry made a dramatic display of dismay. "Well, no wonder. There's not a man alive who can tolerate more than five minutes of shopping with a woman, not even me and you know what a fashion hound I am."

She surveyed his khaki shorts, T-shirt and well-worn leather jacket. "I'm not sure the ever-elegant Neil would agree. Anyway, Jason wanted to go. In fact, he insisted on it. We were picking out the wardrobe for my character. He had a certain image in mind."

"I'll bet."

"Watch it!"

"Okay, okay. So, it was strictly a business excursion, then?"

For most of the evening it had been, Callie recalled. Jason had displayed an astonishing sense of what would look good on her. He'd examined and discarded clothes so fast it had made her head spin. The wardrobe mistress, who'd been at her job for thirty years, had been equally awed by his skill. She'd gone back to the studio laden down with their purchases.

All except one very slinky midnight-blue dress that Jason had insisted Callie wear to dinner. That dress seemed to have had quite an impact on him. He'd finished three quick glasses of water before the wine steward even showed up at the table.

"Mostly," she hedged.

"Mostly. What does that mean, mostly?"

"Just what you think it means." She scowled at him. "I don't want to deal with this."

Terry glanced over her shoulder. "Don't look now, but you're going to have to," he said.

"It's none of your business."

"How about his?" Terry inquired quietly.

Callie turned just as Jason emerged from his limo.

His gaze locked with hers and fireworks erupted in the pit of her stomach. She swore to herself that they'd been set off by fury and nothing else.

Terry brushed a kiss across her cheek and squeezed her hand. "See you."

Her startled gaze flew to his. "Where are you going?"

"I've just remembered an important engagement across town."

"Liar," she muttered as she warily watched Jason's approach.

"Traitor," she added for good measure as he waved cheerfully at Jason.

"Not very nice names to be tossing around about your friend," Jason chided.

"You should hear the ones I have saved up for you," she shot back, then clamped her mouth shut.

"I take it you missed me."

"Oh? Have you been somewhere?" The jaunty tone was valiant, but even she knew it was too late. His smug expression was proof enough of that.

"Just working. We're getting down to the final decisions on the fall season schedule. If you'll have dinner with me, I'll tell you all about it."

"Sorry, I have plans." His expression was so skeptical, she quickly improvised. "I promised my mother I'd take her out tonight."

"Terrific. She can come along."

Callie stared at him. He seemed totally sincere. He seemed anxious to make amends. Okay, maybe she had overreacted to his absence. Maybe she'd just gotten addicted to his attention far more rapidly than she'd had any right to. The past few days had been a warning not to take him too seriously. But that didn't mean she shouldn't enjoy his company occasionally.

"You're sure you wouldn't mind having my mother along?" she asked, trying not to show her disappointment that he wasn't as eager to be alone with her as she was to be with him.

"No, indeed. I can pick her brain to see what viewers in the Midwest really want to see."

"Farm reports," Callie said drily. "Weather predictions."

"Surely there must be more."

"Not in my household. Television was considered a frivolous waste of time unless it was providing crop-related information. You can just imagine how overjoyed my mother is that I am now working in that very medium. The two of you should get along famously, assuming you don't mind being told that you fry brains for a living."

Jason's startled and suddenly wary expression provided her with the most amusement she'd had in days. The evening promised to be a revelation of the depths of his tolerance. Given his abandonment over the past two weeks, she figured it was no more than he deserved.

12

Callie's excuse to avoid being alone with Jason wasn't home. Callie called out to her mother as they walked in the front door, then went from room to room for good measure, but there was no sign of Regina Gunderson.

"I guess your mother forgot about those plans the two of you had," Jason observed drily.

"It's not like her," Callie said, more worried about her mother's absence than she was embarrassed over being caught in a blatant lie.

"It's not like her to forget something?"

"No, to leave the apartment. She's been here every day when I got home."

"Obviously she likes to be here to welcome you."

"No, she hasn't been going out, unless it was with me or Terry or Neil. I could swear it. She's intimidated by the city. She's never been very adventurous. She never even left Iowa, as far as I know."

She stood at the window and peered anxiously down at the street below, hoping to catch a glimpse of her mother heading home. "What if something's happened to her? She doesn't know her way around. She could have gotten lost or mugged."

Jason came closer and cupped her face in his hands. "Whoa, you're getting carried away. I'm sure there's a simple explanation. She probably just ran out to the store for a minute."

Callie could feel panic—rational or not—churning inside. Jason didn't know her mother. He couldn't possibly understand how ill-equipped she was to deal with a city like New York. She'd always resisted trips into Iowa City, for heaven's sake, claiming she preferred to stick close to home.

"I'm telling you, I don't think she even knows where the store is."

"Maybe she's with Terry."

"No, you saw him. He left the studio when we did. He couldn't have beat us by much, assuming he even came directly home."

"Neil, then," Jason said, persisting with his maddening attempts to offer a rational explanation for something Callie knew was anything but rational. "Perhaps she's downstairs visiting with him."

It was a possibility, Callie thought, grabbing the phone and pressing the number she'd set to automatically dial the apartment downstairs. No one answered. She hung up when the answering machine picked up.

"Nothing," she said.

"Okay, then, sit down and let's think about this," Jason said calmly. He nudged her onto the sofa, sat beside her and took her hands in his. The firm grip was reassuring, but Callie's imagination went spinning out of control, anyway.

"What if—"

"Stop it. There's no point in wild speculation," he said, accurately guessing the gruesome direction her thoughts were taking.

Callie bounced back up. "Maybe I should call the police."

"They won't do a thing until she's been missing twenty-four hours," he reminded her. "Now let's think about the chores she might have decided to run—grocery store, cleaners…what else?"

"I didn't have her doing my errands," Callie snapped.

Jason's eyes remained level with hers. "Maybe she had errands of her own."

Another tide of hysteria washed through her. "I'm telling you—" she began just as she heard a key turning in the lock. She flew off the sofa and flung the door open. Relief warred with anger at the sight of her mother clutching a plastic bag filled with groceries.

"Where have you been?" she demanded, knowing the question was totally irrational given the evidence right before her eyes.

Her mother looked taken aback by the attack. "Callie, what on earth?"

Callie drew in a deep breath and tried to calm down. "I'm sorry. I got here and you were gone. I panicked. I had no idea how long you'd been out or where you might have gone."

She caught the amused look Jason exchanged with her mother and wanted to strangle them both. "Okay, I overreacted. I'm an idiot."

"Sweetie, you're not an idiot," her mother said. "But I am capable of buying a few things at the store. How do you think the cupboards have been getting stocked the past few weeks?"

Callie sighed. "I guess I hadn't even noticed that they were."

"Because you've been working far too hard." Her mother glanced pointedly at Jason. "And you're the young man who's responsible for that, aren't you?"

Jason stood. "I suppose I am," he said apologetically, even as Callie scrambled to figure out how her mother could possibly have known. "It's the nature of the television business, I'm afraid."

"Well, I don't know a thing about that, but I do know hard work and long hours take their toll. Just look at her," her mother said, regarding Jason accusingly. "She's pale as a ghost."

Jason grinned. "Now, I think you're the one to blame for that, Mrs. Smith."

"It's Gunderson," Callie corrected automatically. "Regina Gunderson. Mother, this is Jason Kane."

"I recognize him from his picture in the paper."

Callie shot a puzzled look at her. "What picture?"

"The one of the two of you kissing in plain view of God and all the world," she said. "Neil showed me a copy of it."

Callie was startled less by the reference to that picture than by the sparkle in her mother's eyes when she brought it up. She actually seemed amused, rather than appalled, by it. Callie, to the contrary, had no desire to discuss that particular photo ever again.

"Give me the groceries, Mother. As soon as I put them away, we can go to dinner. Jason's invited both of us to join him."

Her mother's cheeks turned pink at that. "Oh, my, I couldn't possibly go along on your date."

"Of course you can," Jason insisted. "Callie told me the two of you had plans to eat out tonight. Since I'm intruding on those, it's only fair I take you both out."

Callie caught the startled look her mother sent her way, but Regina turned out to be surprisingly quick on her feet. "Well, when you put it that way, young man, how could I possibly say no? Just let me change. I won't take but a minute."

"Absolutely not. You look lovely just as you are," Jason said.

At the sight of yet more color blooming in her mother's cheeks, Callie was forced to give Jason high marks. There was no way she'd shatter her mother's pleasure by suggesting that she was actually being brought along so the man could conduct a little market research on her.

By pinpointing Jason's ulterior motives so clearly and so readily and comparing them to her ex-husband's shoddy behavior patterns, Callie realized a sad truth. If her lousy track record in choosing men kept up much longer, she could very well wind up one heck of a cynic about love.

Based on his first glimpse of Regina Gunderson, combined with Callie's overwrought reaction to her mother's absence from the apartment on their arrival, Jason would have predicted a very strained and essentially dull evening. He'd known a lot of women like Callie's mother back in Virginia—women who were essentially gray in appearance and in personality, women who were mere shadows of the men in their lives.

His own mother had been the exact opposite. She had been like an exotic bird of paradise amid all the traditional, pale Southern flowers. Ambitious, colorful, outspoken, she had been his father's downfall. Too much woman for a man like Wendall Kane, a man content to run his plumbing business and bask in the reflected glory of his wife's achievements. He'd realized too late that she would cut him loose when she'd surpassed him in accomplishments. He'd never been the same after she'd left.

And neither had Jason.

Seeing his mother ride roughshod over his father and the way his father's spirit had slowly seeped out of him after she'd gone had convinced Jason that success was all that mattered. He'd chosen the most competitive career he could think of, one that would command all of his attention, one that would give him power over any woman who happened to cross his path.

And that's exactly the way it had been with Callie. Something about her threatened to undermine all his hard work to stay unattached and uninvolved.

A few short weeks ago he would never have left his office with so many programming decisions still to be made. He would have stayed as late as it took to view every one of those videos. He would have eaten stale sandwiches and drunk gallons of rank coffee until every magnetic strip on his giant program scheduling board was exactly where he wanted it. He would have thrived on every exhausting minute of it.

Tonight he had seized on Freddie's chiding comments as the excuse he'd been waiting for to break his vow to stay away from Callie. His eager bolt from his office had been downright pitiful. The flare of excitement he'd felt when he'd seen her after fourteen days of total abstinence told him he was in deep trouble with this woman. She lured him like a siren, straight onto treacherous emotional shoals he'd always vowed to avoid at any cost.

He couldn't for the life of him figure out why. She was beautiful, no doubt about that. It was what had drawn him to her image on the screen in the first place. But something beyond beauty had captured his attention and kept it, something indefinable and dangerous.

Studying her now, he viewed such thoughts as ludicrous. With professional detachment, he tried to figure out the allure. Her hair was tousled in no particular style. Her makeup had been scrubbed off before she'd left the studio and not replaced with anything more than a sheer dash of pale pink lipstick. For the first time he noticed the lightest dusting of freckles across her nose, testament to long-ago summer days in the sun. She looked every bit the innocent farm girl she had once been and nothing like the kind of woman who typically attracted him.

"Tell me about your farm," he suggested impulsively midway through dinner. He addressed the question to Mrs. Gunderson, but kept his gaze fixed on Callie. He saw the unmistakable shadow that darkened her eyes, the instantaneous blandness in her expression that told him more than any overt protest would have that she found the subject distasteful.

Callie stayed perfectly silent as her mother described the acres of corn that had surrounded their home, perfectly still at the description of the harsh winters and blisteringly hot summers.

When he finally focused his attention on Mrs. Gunderson again, he guessed from her even, unemotional tone that she was no more enamored by the life they'd led than Callie had been. He wondered if Callie heard the same vague distancing from the past that he did. He wondered if she realized that there was an adventurous spirit in her mother just waiting to be freed. Judging from her earlier comments, she did not.

He glanced at Callie again. "What is your favorite memory of living on the farm?"

"Leaving," she said succinctly.

Her mother looked as if she'd been slapped. Callie saw it the same instant he did.

"Mother, I'm sorry, but you know it's true."

Regina Gunderson managed a sad smile. "You were always so eager to go. I never understood how someone who'd never known anything but farm life could long so for places they'd never been. Eunice was like your daddy, content to live her whole life in one place. You running off like you did broke your daddy's heart."

"I didn't 'run off,' as you put it," Callie retorted defensively. "I went away to college."

"And never came back, not even on school vacations."

"I had to work to pay for school. You know that."

Jason sensed it was an old and bitterly fought argument. He regretted now pursuing the subject at all, but it did tell him quite a lot about Callie. He realized now why she had battled so fiercely not to admit failure as a stockbroker and why, ultimately, she had succumbed to his pressure. It was the only option she'd felt she had left to avoid going back to that farm she so clearly hated, to avoid admitting that she'd been defeated by the big city.

There were more undercurrents between the two women; Jason had no doubt about that. He feared any topic he broached might pull them all into deep and perilous waters. He could understand that, too. His own rare meetings with his mother were strained. Conversations skimmed over polite, indifferent topics because neither of them dared to stray onto more personal turf.

Maybe, as he'd promised earlier, what they all needed right now was a stimulating, intellectual battle over television. He figured he could easily hold his own against any derisive comments Mrs. Gunderson might direct his way.

"So, Mrs. Gunderson, tell me what you watch on TV," he suggested, ignoring the gentle, warning kick Callie directed his way under the table.

"Farm reports and the weather," she said flatly. "The rest's a bunch of nonsense."

"Told you so," Callie murmured.

Jason persisted, anyway. "You haven't even sneaked a peak at *Within Our Reach* since your daughter's been on?" Her immediate blush told him he'd hit a nerve. "She's terrific on the show, isn't she?"

"I'm no judge of whether she is or she isn't," Mrs. Gunderson replied, carefully evading Callie's transparently hopeful gaze.

The terse comment confirmed his guess without offering her daughter so much as a smidgen of praise. Jason grew more determined to drag a compliment out of her. If ever he'd seen a woman in need of parental approval, Callie was it. She was blinking furiously in a near-futile attempt to hide her tears.

"You know, we're really counting on her at the network," he said. "I think Callie has the talent to become a superstar, if that's what she wants."

Mrs. Gunderson regarded him skeptically. "Callie, a star?"

"If that's what she wants," he repeated firmly.

"What I want is to change the subject," Callie stated. "There's no point in trying to talk television with Mother. She's never approved of it."

He directed a look straight into Mrs. Gunderson's blue eyes. "Why is that?"

"Like my husband always said, it's a waste of time."

"That's what he thought," Jason persisted. "What about you?"

"I just said," she retorted irritably.

"No, you echoed his opinion. Do you share it?"

"For goodness' sake, young man, I said I did, didn't I?"

Callie touched his hand with another light, warning gesture. Jason pretended he hadn't gotten the message.

"You could really do me a huge favor," he said.

Mrs. Gunderson regarded him warily. "What would that be?"

"Take a look at *Within Our Reach* over the next few days," he requested blandly. "Tell me what you think. I'd really like to hear your opinion."

"Why mine?"

Because he wanted her to watch Callie. He wanted her to appreciate the talent, the emotional depth her daughter was displaying on the show. And he wanted her to admit it aloud, not so much to him, but to Callie. Clearly, though, he couldn't say that.

"Because you obviously represent the segment of the audience we haven't been reaching," he said instead. "I'd like to know if there's something we could do that would capture your attention, maybe a certain kind of character or story line that you'd like to see."

"I may not like it at all," she warned him. "And I won't be shy about telling you so."

Jason grinned. "I can take it."

"I just hope I can," Callie muttered.

"No need to worry, sweetheart," he said. "You've already won over the only audience that counts."

"Oh?"

"Sure. That would be me."

The comment finally coaxed a half smile from her. "That'll last how long?" she inquired drily. "Until the ratings start to slide again?"

"I'm not that fickle," he denied. Besides, he had a sinking feeling that she was going to be twisting him around her finger for a lot longer than the run of any show he had on the air.

13

Jason's faith in her talent kept Callie going, even when she began to hear the renewed gossip making the rounds on the set. The rumor had it that she was on the show only because the network president had insisted on it. She couldn't very well argue with that. It was the truth. But behind the whispered remarks were all sorts of unspoken innuendos about exactly where her skills lay. And the comments were getting nastier all the time, fueled by jealousy and fear, according to Terry.

If someone had questioned her abilities as a stockbroker, her ego had been strong enough to withstand any sort of speculation. As an actress, she had only Jason's conviction, bolstered by Terry's support, to rely on. Most of the time that was sufficient. Some days—and today was one of them—it wasn't nearly enough. She felt as if she were drowning in a sea of uncertainty. The first few days of shooting, which had run smoothly enough, had convinced her that she had a lock on acting. More recent disasters had told her otherwise.

"Don't mind them, dollface," Terry whispered just as they were about to shoot a scene for the third time because of her inability to respond to a flubbed line by another actress quickly enough.

Reacting to the scowls of derision being sent her way, she moaned, “But it’s my fault.”

“Hardly,” Terry snapped, returning the scowls of their costars with a quelling look of his own. “They’re blowing lines deliberately to rattle you.”

“Well, it’s working,” she said. “If we have to do this again, I won’t even be able to remember my name, much less save the scene by covering for them.”

“It’s not just you. Everyone’s nerves are shot today,” he consoled her. “One of the sponsors has been making noises again about pulling out.”

“Even though the ratings are up?”

Terry shrugged. “Ratings fluctuate all the time. They dipped again at the end of last week. The sponsor has been looking for an excuse to cancel for months. Now he has it.”

The butterflies in Callie’s stomach danced a rumba. No wonder the other actors were taking it out on her. She was supposed to save the show. That had been the very public explanation for bringing in an unknown. Now the show appeared to be sinking, even with her on board.

Suddenly the pressure overwhelmed her. How had she gotten herself into this position in the first place? She had no business being on television. She couldn’t even get a simple scene right. And every time the camera stopped rolling because she’d fouled up, costs escalated. The producers had coldly made her aware of that basic fact very early on.

“I must have been out of my mind when I agreed to

this," she muttered to Terry as she awaited a cue from Paul Locklear to begin the scene again. Even the habitually complacent director was impatient today.

"You have no control over other people not knowing their lines," Terry retorted just loudly enough to be overheard by the two other actresses in the scene. "It is not your job to ad lib them out of the mess they created."

"A professional would be able to," Lindsay Gentry shot back. "Instead, we get this amateur who's sleeping with the network president."

The unexpectedly crude and vicious attack left Callie breathless for the space of a heartbeat. Just as Terry was about to leap to her defense, her own temper kicked in and she found her voice. She had finally had all she could take. At least the resentment was finally out in the open, where she could deal with it head-on, instead of simmering behind the scenes.

"I'll deal with this, Terry. It's my battle," she said as she crossed to stand toe-to-toe with the other woman, who played a saintly character whose vocabulary was considerably less vulgar than the actress's.

"How dare you imply that I got this job by sleeping with anyone," she said in a tight, barely controlled voice. "Until the day he asked me to join the cast to save this sinking ship, I'd never even met Jason Kane. Obviously he didn't think you were capable of turning the ratings around. Frankly, I don't know why he thought I could, either, but I'm here and I'm trying my best to do just that. Now isn't it about time for you to stop whining and start acting like the so-called professional you claim to be?"

"Whoa, honey," Terry murmured, stepping closer as

if he were preparing to intervene in an inevitable fist-fight. "That's telling her like it is."

Callie's temper was so hot, she didn't even acknowledge the interruption. "I'm the first to admit that I have a lot to learn. Since I'm apparently here to stay, at least for the next eleven months, it would be nice if you could see your way clear to helping me, instead of trying to sabotage me at every turn. Otherwise, I won't be the one responsible for the ship going down."

"Bravo," Jonathan Baines called from the shadows, where he'd apparently overheard every word. He applauded slowly and emphatically to underscore his praise.

As one of the show's three leading men, even though his character was currently mired in villainy, Jonathan was widely respected by other members of the cast, including the suddenly red-faced Lindsay. His quick jump to Callie's defense apparently signaled the others that it was time to start behaving like adults, rather than jealous, sniping kids. A guilty silence fell over the set. Lindsay sullenly retreated to her mark without responding.

"Now that that's settled, could we try this scene again?" director Paul Locklear inquired in his usual calm, matter-of-fact tone. Apparently the explosion had had the effect of soothing everyone's frayed tempers.

Once again, by remaining coolly professional, Paul got them back on track.

But only seconds later, just as the scene was finally progressing flawlessly, a light overhead exploded, sending a shower of glass raining down on everyone. Callie took the worst of it as a jagged piece nicked her head. Blood spurted everywhere, ruining her clothes and the sofa on which she'd been seated. The terrifying and potentially deadly incident shut down the set for the rest of the afternoon as the producers tried to figure out what had caused the explosion.

More frightened than she wanted to acknowledge, Callie retreated to her dressing room. The lighting accident, the flash of tempers and the subsequent tension had left her thoroughly drained. Head resting on her arms, she cursed Jason and the circumstances that had forced her onto such unfamiliar turf and possibly into the path of some deadly mischief maker.

She had to find some way to garner some respect from her costars or this was going to be the longest year of her life, longer even than a year on the family farm. Standing up to Lindsay Gentry had been a start, but she knew better than to think today's incident would be the end of it. She would be tested time and again, and more than anyone else on the show, she couldn't ever be found wanting. Worse, she had probably made an enemy of the woman.

She wondered how long it would be before there were leaks in the media about dissension on the set of *Within Our Reach,* all blamed on the newest addition to the cast.

Befriending Lindsay Gentry or any of the others was probably less important, though, than turning in a decent performance time after time. Maybe she should hire an acting coach or take classes at one of the prestigious acting academies in the city. It seemed like a lot of trouble to go to for what in essence was a temporary job.

No one, least of all she, expected Jason's predictions of superstardom to come true. A year from now she'd be making the rounds of brokerage houses on Wall Street again. A fat lot of good it would do her then to be able to play a scene skillfully. Of course, it would be nice to get through a job interview without conveying any hint of the desperation she would likely be feeling.

At any rate, she was in no mood to cooperate when the show's publicity person tapped on her door a few minutes later and told her she'd been scheduled to appear at three shopping mall events and one charity bowl-a-thon over the next few weekends.

Callie stared at Jenny Harding as if she'd just announced that Callie was booked on a trip to the moon. During her initial round of media interviews she had grown used to Jenny's perky good humor, but not to her enthusiasm for activities that seemed to Callie an awful lot like torture. Jenny was young and energetic and determined to make a mark for herself in publicity and promotion. Callie was her dream assignment.

"You're kidding, right?" Callie said as she scanned the demanding schedule Jenny had prepared for her. Counting travel time, it appeared she wouldn't have a day to herself for weeks.

"Oh, no, this is wonderful," Jenny insisted enthusiastically. "Requests are pouring in. People can't wait to see you in person. Mr. Kane said to book you for as many events as possible to keep the momentum going. He called it the Big Mo. He said some guy who ran for president a long time ago called it that."

Callie was not about to educate Jenny on American politics. She had far more pressing concerns.

"A bowl-a-thon?" she repeated incredulously, her gaze locking on the first event listed. "I don't bowl."

A minor inconvenience, according to Jenny. "People don't care if you win. You just have to be a good sport."

"I'm not feeling like a good sport at the moment," Callie said direly.

"Oh, you'll do just fine," Jenny said, apparently unaware of the events that had preceded her arrival.

She handed over the itinerary and the necessary airline tickets for all of the distant events, one of which Callie noted with an impending sense of doom was in Iowa City, far too close to home and Eunice.

"Everybody just loves doing these things once they're there," Jenny assured her. "People are so sweet. You might want to talk to the writers before you go because fans always have lots and lots of questions about what's going to happen next on the show."

She literally bounced toward the dressing room door, then turned back. "Oh, and they want to know all about you and Terry."

The sparkle in Jenny's eyes was a bit worrisome. "Such as?" Callie asked.

"If you all are lovers mostly."

"On-screen, you mean."

"Off, too," Jenny said, then waved a cheery little bye-bye as she exited.

Callie stared after her. She was going to kill Jason for getting her into this. She really was.

"You want me to go where with you?" Jason inquired, convinced he couldn't possibly have heard Callie directly. It was the first time she had ever invited him to spend time with her, but the implication of that was diluted considerably by the destination.

"It's a bowl-a-thon in Newark," she repeated.

With her low, breathy tone, she made it sound like a cross between an IRS audit and heaven. Jason wouldn't have been even remotely tempted to say yes, if it hadn't been for that seductive promise in her voice. A dozen excuses were on the tip of his tongue, but she didn't seem inclined to take no for an answer.

"If I have to go, I think you should, too," she concluded rather emphatically. "For me, I believe it's referred to as paying my dues. You can think of it as marketing research, perhaps."

"I don't bowl," he countered, wondering if he could convince her to exchange this outing for a more romantic evening of dinner, dancing and gambling in Atlantic City after the charity bowling event.

"Neither do I," she shot back. "But no one seems to care about that."

"Do I detect some kind of retaliatory mood behind this invitation?" he asked, surmising that she wasn't likely to be coaxed into anything, much less the intimate compromise he had in mind.

"You've got it, buster. Saturday at noon. Be here."

Jason chuckled as the phone slammed in his ear. Apparently she hadn't quite grasped what an honor it was to be in such high demand. Maybe he could explain it to her on the drive to Newark.

If she didn't strangle him en route.

When Jason arrived promptly at noon on Saturday, Callie surveyed him with astonishment. His fancy suits had been traded for well-worn blue jeans. His expensive Italian loafers had been exchanged for sneakers that appeared to be about five years past their prime. He was wearing a *Within Our Reach* T-shirt exactly like her own, along with a baseball cap and sunglasses. He looked sexy as hell.

"Traveling incognito?" she inquired as she slid into the limo. She winked at Henry, who quickly hid a smile.

"Just one of the fans," Jason agreed. "I'll blend right in with the crowd."

Callie doubted it. She anticipated a bowling alley crammed with women. Jason would stand out like Kevin Costner in his field of dreams.

"I just hope you're bowling on my team," she muttered. "Somebody has to get our score up."

"Not me, sweetheart. I'll be right there on the sidelines cheering for you, though."

"Witnessing my humiliation," she corrected. She scowled at him. "And don't tell me all anybody cares about is my being a good sport. I am not a good sport."

Jason grinned. "You really do hate to lose at anything, don't you?"

"No more than you do, *sweetheart*."

"Maybe we should talk about what today is all about," he ventured. "Charity, Callie. It's about soap stars coming out to raise money for a good cause. It is not about bowling."

"Then why hold the stupid event in a bowling alley?"

"Because it's fun."

She rolled her eyes at that.

"You'll see," he promised.

Next thing she knew, he'd be telling her the world was flat. The man would lie through his teeth if it meant upping the ratings by half a point. She knew that better than anyone.

So, why was she even remotely considering getting involved with him? Why had she invited him along today? Retaliation, as he'd suggested? Or was it far more complex, a pitiful excuse to spend the day with him without having to admit that she craved a few hours in his company? When no answers came, she sighed.

He clasped her hand in his. "Not to worry. I'll cheer for you, even if you roll nothing but gutter balls."

Callie met his gaze. "What's a gutter ball?"

Jason sighed at that. "It really is going to be a long afternoon, isn't it?"

"Haven't I been trying to tell you that from the beginning?" she grumbled.

Her spirits perked up marginally when the limo pulled into the huge bowling alley parking lot and she saw the welcoming masses of balloons and banners. Fans, cordoned off behind velvet ropes more suitable for the Emmy Awards than a bowl-a-thon, screamed her name as she exited the car ahead of Jason. She stopped so suddenly at the sound of it echoing across the parking lot that Jason stumbled into her heels.

She turned to him, eyes shining. She clutched his hand as the most incredible feeling of warmth spread through her. She'd never experienced anything like it before. These people liked her. They admired her.

Later she would be able to analyze the moment and accept that the outpouring of emotion was meant for the character she played, that not one of these people really knew her, Callie Smith, at all. But right now she felt as special as anyone on earth had ever felt. She recognized it as an emotion that she'd been waiting for all her life.

Glancing up into Jason's face, she caught a glimpse of smug satisfaction. He'd anticipated this. He'd made it happen.

"I could get used to this," she admitted.

"In a few brief weeks, you've already touched thousands more just like them," he told her. "Did anything you ever did on Wall Street compare to that?"

Callie was sure there had been predictions that had paid off big for her clients. She knew there had been wheeling and dealing that had seemed incredibly rewarding at the time.

But right now, with her name being shouted by hundreds of fans, with requests for autographs coming from every direction, she couldn't think of any single day or even a week as a stockbroker that was this moment's equal.

That heady sense of excitement should have terrified her, but it didn't.

And neither did the possibility that she might be falling in love with the man responsible for giving it to her.

14

Thanks to the mob scene outside the bowling alley and the equally enthusiastic crowd inside, Jason noticed that Callie quickly got into the spirit of the event. Every pin she struck down was a triumph. Every gutter ball was laughed off.

Her teammates from his other network soaps welcomed her as an old friend. There was none of the animosity Terry had described her experiencing on her own set every day. To his relief, these actors and actresses reserved their competitiveness for the teams from the ABC, CBS and NBC soaps, not for one of their own. Some members of the *Within Our Reach* cast could take a lesson from them. He would have pointed that out to Callie's costars, but Terry had made him swear to stay out of it.

As he'd vowed to do today, he blended into the background, watching from a red plastic-covered bar stool, an icy mug of beer in hand. He'd picked the location in an attempt to remain out of the limelight, which belonged to his network's stars. He found it served another purpose, as well. It allowed him to observe Callie for hours on end without being caught at it.

More and more, he liked what he saw. Not just the cute little tush that sashayed halfway down the alley before she plunked down her bowling ball. Not just that high-voltage smile that had her teammates and fans alike falling under her spell. He saw more and it went far deeper than the lust that slammed through him every time she was near.

He saw the grit of which she was made, the core of pride that made her try harder, the streak of determination that had her rolling spares by the last frames.

He also saw her graciousness in defeat and wondered at the reserves of strength that helped her to rise above the humiliation she had feared. All this just from watching her bowl. Who knew what he could discover if he allowed himself to go on seeing her, if he risked the kind of emotional entanglement she threatened to stir in him.

More than once, her gaze sought out his in the shadows and clung, a smile of such sweet pleasure on her lips that it made his heart ache. He had never guessed how desperately she needed the kind of acclamation she was receiving today. After meeting her mother, after sensing the stinginess with which praise had been doled out all of Callie's life, he should have known.

For one brief instant, her reaction troubled him. He knew all too well how easily manipulated such adulation was with the right marketing and how quickly it could fade. Soap audiences were among the most loyal in the world, but even they could prove fickle. He reassured himself that Callie might thrill to this outpouring of love for now but that later she would put it neatly into its proper perspective. Gut-deep instinct told him she was too levelheaded not to. And that, too, was something to be admired in her.

The TGN team came in third, but all of the celebrities were treated as winners. For two solid hours after the bowling ended, they signed autographs and chatted with fans.

Not until they were back in the limo did Jason glimpse the exhaustion shadowing Callie's eyes.

"They like me," she told him, her astonishment evident. "They really like me."

Like a child for whom excitement had finally taken its toll, she leaned her head trustingly on Jason's shoulder and fell sound asleep. His arms settled gently around her as he watched the slow rise and fall of her chest and felt the warm whisper of her breath against his cheek. It was the sweetest torture he'd ever known.

"Will Miss Callie be going directly home?" Henry inquired as they crossed into Manhattan.

Jason stared down at the woman responsible for making both his heart and his body ache with longing and wondered if he had her strength. If he did, he would deliver her to her doorstep and leave all of these risky feelings unexplored. On some level he knew that making love to her would be no casual proposition. It would be the start of something. He didn't allow himself to consider exactly where it might lead. If he had, he would have had to admit it was a path he'd sworn never to take, a path experience had taught him led only to complications and tragedy.

Callie sighed just then and shifted position, bringing

her breasts in contact with his chest. He sucked in his breath and saw himself for the weak fool he was. His willpower, which had withstood all sorts of feminine temptations, was no match for this woman. For once it didn't seem to matter so much.

"No, Henry. We'll be dining at my apartment."

"Very well, sir. And will you be needing me later?"

"No," Jason said, overriding all of the doubts ripping through him. "We'll be fine for the rest of the evening."

He glanced up then, just in time to catch Henry's satisfied smile in the rearview mirror.

"Henry?"

"Yes, sir."

"You can be replaced."

The smile only broadened. "Doubtful, sir."

With that, the darkened glass between the two compartments slid silently and deliberately closed. It was no doubt Henry's subtle way of encouraging him to take advantage of the privacy in any way he liked.

For a man who'd always treasured the illusion of independence, Jason couldn't help thinking that his life was suddenly becoming filled with indispensable people—Freddie at the network, Henry who'd been with him for years now, not just as a driver but as a stoic guardian angel, and Callie. He trusted the two men implicitly. It remained to be seen if he could trust Callie with the same degree of certainty.

His arms tightened around her instinctively. He hoped he wouldn't live to regret his involvement with her as his father had regretted his life with Jason's mother.

* * *

"Where are we?" Callie inquired sleepily as the limo slowed to a stop in front of an unfamiliar tower rising high into the New York skyline.

"My place," Jason said.

He sounded oddly tentative. Callie looked into his eyes and saw a surprising hint of vulnerability there. Was he expecting rejection? Surely he knew by now that there was very little she could deny him.

"Taking me up to see your etchings?" she inquired.

"Oils," he corrected. "Impressionists, mostly."

He sounded vaguely defensive, as if awaiting some comment on the incongruity of a tough-as-nails network president owning such romanticized, softened views of the world. Callie resisted the temptation to do just that.

"I can't wait," she said, thinking unexpectedly of long-ago days when her mother had showed her a dog-eared book filled with pictures of great paintings and told her about the artists. She had fallen in love with the splashy sunflowers of van Gogh and the pastel world of Monet. It was something they had once shared and lost. It had been years since Callie had set eyes on that book. She wondered if it had been stored away in the attic or simply left forgotten in some drawer. She'd always sensed it was something of which her father didn't approve, that in showing it to her, her mother had been sharing something vaguely wicked.

"Any van Goghs in the lot?" she asked Jason without any real hope that there would be. Van Goghs were priceless museum pieces, not wall decorations for mere mortals.

"One," he said with a characteristic air of understatement. "A very, very small one."

Stunned by his reply and his nonchalance, she grinned. "If you own a Monet, I'll be yours forever."

The partition between front and back slid down just then and she heard what might have been a choked-back laugh from the front seat. Jason cast a forbidding look in that direction.

"Henry seems amused," she noted.

"Based on your comment, Henry is apparently already making plans to see that we get to the church on time," Jason said wryly.

"In other words, you have a Monet."

"Or two," Jason corrected.

Actually, there were four, Callie discovered to her amazement when they arrived in Jason's penthouse. All were small, all were lit with exquisite care unequaled by any gallery she'd ever visited. The sight of them, so close she could touch them, brought tears to her eyes.

"Are you crying?" Jason asked as he turned her around gently. He scanned her face with obvious bemusement. "You are. Why?"

"They're just so magnificent."

She noticed then that Jason's expression as he gazed at the paintings wasn't one of awe or even real appreciation. Vaguely disappointed by what she thought she'd discovered, she asked, "They're just possessions to you, aren't they?"

He shrugged. "I suppose."

"Proof that you've succeeded," she guessed. "Or do they represent some sort of competitive victory at an auction?"

Eyes suddenly shuttered, Jason turned away without answering. "Would you like a cabernet with dinner? Or maybe champagne?"

"I'd like an answer," she insisted.

"Why?" He tossed the question over his shoulder as he opened the door to an impressive wine cellar.

"Because I want to understand you."

He stood slowly, the wine temporarily forgotten. His gaze remained averted. He seemed to be staring out at the Manhattan skyline. His reflection showed a face that was distant and moody. Callie almost regretted pressing him, but she knew this was too important to let it pass.

"And the reason I bought those paintings will help you to do that?" he asked.

The stiff set of his shoulders told her the response to that was yes. She gazed around at the rest of the exquisitely decorated but impersonal apartment and knew there were no real answers to be found in anything except those paintings. They had some deep meaning to him, meaning that had nothing to do with their actual worth in the art world or their beauty.

"I think so, yes," she said quietly, silently commanding him to look at her, to tell the truth. The soft classical music Jason had flipped on when they'd entered the apartment built to a crescendo, emphasizing the air of expectancy as she waited.

He turned then and looked directly into her eyes. "Maybe someday I'll tell you," he said, dangling it like a carrot for their future.

"But not tonight," she concluded.

"Not tonight."

"Then I think I ought to be going."

To her regret, he seemed amused, rather than dismayed, by her mild touch of defiance. “Because I won’t answer all your personal questions?”

“Because you don’t trust me.”

His bold gaze clashed with hers, defiant and dark with unexpected passion. Callie trembled, but she couldn’t look away. He took a step toward her, then another.

“But I want you,” he said with such stark hunger that Callie was taken aback. “Isn’t that enough?”

He reached for her before she could answer and crushed her lips beneath his own in a kiss as urgent and demanding as anything Callie had ever known. He plunged his tongue deep into her mouth, tasting her, possessing her as surely as he had claimed those Monets.

For one brief, determined moment, Callie fought him, struggling to keep her senses from spinning out of control. Then the fire of his need swept through her, heating her blood as it clearly had his. The paintings, her unanswered questions, the wine, everything was forgotten except the sensations stirred by his touch.

The demanding hunger, the hint of yearning, should have come as a surprise, but it didn’t. Not really. It had been simmering just below the surface for weeks now, practically from the moment they’d met.

Callie knew she was lost. Desire, uncontrolled and desperate, blinded her to everything except the slow slide of his fingers under her shirt, the rough caress of his thumb over her already sensitive nipple. Her body hummed. Instinctively, she fit herself to him, molding soft curves to hard contours.

As if he sensed that she was his, his mouth on hers gentled, coaxed, tasted, even as his caresses teased, inflamed.

She wanted him. Too much.

He wanted her. There was no mistake about that.

Callie wanted more. To her amazement, she realized that she wanted his heart. But for now, if this desperate need and the promise of magnificent fulfillment were all he had to give, she would content herself with that.

15

Regina woke on the living room couch Sunday morning, her arthritic bones stiff and aching. She was aware instantly that Callie hadn't come home. She would have awakened if her daughter had come in.

She was embarrassed to admit she'd been waiting up for her as she had when Callie was just a girl. She promised herself it would be the last time. Callie would probably call it being overprotective. Just as important, she was too old to be sleeping all cramped up on a couch.

She thought about the implications of Callie's absence. It appeared she had stayed overnight with that nice young man. Regina tried to work up the sort of moral outrage that her husband would have, the fly-off-the-handle temper that would have caused heated words to be exchanged and doors to slam shut. Even after all those years of marriage, she couldn't manage it.

The truth was, she liked Jason Kane, even if he was in television. He was strong-willed and sure of himself, a man who'd already achieved what most men never even dreamed of accomplishing. Callie needed someone like that in her life, whether she knew it or not.

She'd also seen the way he looked at Callie, the way his gaze followed her every move. He had stars in his eyes, all right, whether he knew it or not.

Regina smiled to herself. It seemed so long ago that she had felt that way about anyone.

But she had once. She had felt her pulse race and her skin heat just the way she suspected Callie's did now at the sight of her young man. The memories of those sensations might dim for a woman, but they never went away. They lingered, taunting, sparking an occasional regret, an even rarer sigh of remembered pleasure.

Sitting on the sofa, flexing her fingers and knees to work out the stiffness, she considered what to do with the day that stretched out ahead of her. She had quickly grown used to having Callie around on Sundays, puttering around the apartment, doing laundry, reading the *New York Times,* doing the crossword puzzle. It had been comforting to share the day with someone again, even though they had precious little to say to each other. The farm was home, but it had been lonely despite Eunice's duty calls. Sad to say she'd never been entirely sure if Eunice was hoping to find her alive or dead.

At any rate, she couldn't let a spectacular spring day like this go to waste. The sun glistening on the window hinted of balmy temperatures. It had been a long time since she'd awakened to a day like this without having to worry about plowing fields or planting crops.

She decided on a walk. Maybe she'd even stop at the café a few blocks away that Callie loved so much and have breakfast there, one of those sinful croissants with strawberry jam. And a cappuccino. Usually she liked her coffee strong and black, but she'd developed a certain fondness for the frothy steamed milk that made a cup of coffee seem like an extravagant treat. It was hard to believe she could afford such little luxuries, but the money Terry had been paying her to answer his fan mail had been adding up.

She felt like a teenager playing hooky as she dressed hurriedly and stole out of the apartment. She slipped quietly past Terry and Neil's. They were lovely young men and they were dears for being so kind to her, but it was about time she started doing things on her own. It was time to rediscover the city she had once called home so many, many years ago. Memories, kept secret from everyone except her husband, called to her.

Once outside, the soft, cool breeze invigorated her. She strolled over to Broadway, then headed south toward Lincoln Center. She wasn't sure whether it was the air or the promise of adventure, but she felt emboldened, rejuvenated for the first time in decades.

She felt almost as giddy as she had when she'd first stolen away to New York to study art, something neither of her daughters knew about. She wondered what they would think if they found out that she hadn't always been tied to a farm in Iowa, that their father hadn't been her first love.

She lingered over her breakfast, watching the people who passed by, especially the young ones, who were so full of life, so energetic. One girl, dressed in those tight bicycle shorts and a practically indecent top, skated to a halt right beside her table, clinging to the outdoor café's railing for support. She grinned at Regina.

"Looks like fun," Regina commented, indicating the in-line skates.

"It's a blast," the girl said. "You ought to try it."

Regina laughed at the ridiculousness of the idea. "Not me. I'd break my neck, my hip and probably a lot of things in between."

The girl surveyed her with the brazenness of youth. "I don't know, you look pretty fit to me."

"Which just shows that looks can be deceiving."

"My mom does it. You're not much older than her." She grinned. "Think about it." Joined by her boyfriend then, she skated off with a wave.

Regina stared after her, trying to adjust to the idea that she didn't look any older than that girl's mother. When had she grown used to thinking of herself as frail and tired and over the hill? The possibility that she might not be gave her something to consider for the rest of the day as she wandered farther afield than she had before.

When she found herself on Madison Avenue, far across town from Callie's, she realized that instinct had pointed her in that direction. There were art galleries tucked amid the boutiques on block after block. She stared in the windows, one after another, fascinated by the displays of paintings and sculptures by artists she'd never heard of.

Deep inside, a part of her ached for a long-forgotten dream. Then, thinking of the young woman on her skates, she wondered if perhaps it was not too late for dreams to come true, after all.

Not until she was in a cab going back to Callie's did she glance at her watch and realize that she had wasted the whole day with her nonsense. She couldn't go back in time, even if she wanted to, she told herself sternly. Her daughters would have her committed if she suddenly went out and bought an easel and acrylics and took up painting. Who did she think she was—Grandma Moses?

Suddenly exhausted and feeling ridiculous over her absurd daydreams, she trudged up the stairs to Callie's apartment. She was barely at the landing, when the door flew open and Callie ran out.

"Mother! Are you all right? Where on earth have you been? You've been gone for hours."

Regina might have laughed at the turnabout in their roles if she hadn't been so tired. As it was, the flurry of questions only irritated her.

"Did I ask where you were when you didn't come home all night long?" she retorted, striking the first blow for her own independence. It was something Callie certainly ought to understand. She'd left Iowa quick enough when she was of a mind to and expected everyone left behind to understand. Only Regina had, and ironically, she hadn't been able to tell her.

Apparently her daughter had forgotten her own tough stance for independence. Callie's mouth dropped open, her expression of astonishment almost comical.

"Well, no, but—"

"No buts. We're both grown women. If I want to go out for a bit, I will."

Callie blinked, then glanced at Jason, who was watching the two of them from across the room. Regina thought she detected amusement in his eyes.

"Well, of course, but..." Callie's voice trailed off in apparent confusion.

Impulsively, Regina patted her daughter's cheek.

"It's okay, dear. As you can see, I'm perfectly fine, as are you. Now, if you'll excuse me, I think I'll go to my room and rest a bit. All that walking has worn me out."

As she sank onto her bed, slid her swollen feet out of her shoes and rested her head against the pillows, Regina couldn't help feeling exhilarated by the day and the mild argument that had concluded it. She wondered, though, which of them would recover from the shock of that exchange first.

Callie stood in the middle of the living room and stared after her mother. Something akin to shock kept her speechless for several minutes after her mother had gone.

"Now, what do you suppose that was about?" she asked Jason when she could finally gather her thoughts.

"Sounded to me like a woman standing up for herself."

Callie turned and regarded him with a puzzled expression. "I know. It sounded that way to me, too. It didn't sound like my mother at all."

He grinned at her. "Look on the bright side. At least she didn't read you the riot act for staying out all night with me. That was what you were expecting, wasn't it?"

She shuddered as she thought of the way her stern father had always stood in judgment of her every move. Her mother had always supported him, if only by her stoic silence. "I was expecting to catch holy hell, actually."

Jason looped his arms around her waist from behind and nuzzled the back of her neck, reminding her instantly of the long, wildly passionate night they'd just shared.

"Wasn't this better?" he asked. "We now seem to have her tacit approval."

Callie twisted around until she was facing him. He seemed extraordinarily pleased by the turn of events. "You were even more nervous than I was, weren't you?"

"Hey, I've seen all those documentaries about the viciousness of mothers protecting their young from danger."

"I think those were probably mother bears or lions or something."

"Same principle. I've also heard a whole bunch about shotgun weddings. Your mother does know how to fire a shotgun, doesn't she?"

Callie nodded, unable to hide the grin spreading across her face as she contemplated the image of her mother nudging Jason down a church aisle with a shotgun. "I doubt she brought one with her to New York, though."

"Maybe you should sneak into her room some night and check, just to be sure."

"Coward," she accused.

"No way," he protested. "You're far more dangerous than your mother, even if she happens to be armed. You don't see me running from you."

Callie sighed. *Yet,* she thought. She'd seen enough of Jason in recent weeks to figure out that he was a man who had a serious case of commitment phobia. It hadn't particularly bothered her before because she had a fairly severe case herself.

Now, though, she was beginning to wonder if she would ever get enough of him.

"I don't suppose you could be talked into going to a major shopping-mall event in Iowa?" she inquired wistfully, thinking of the next assignment on Jenny's dreaded list.

"Would that be the test of my devotion, by any chance?"

"Actually, I was thinking of it more as a rescue mission. I really, really don't want to be alone when I see my sister again."

"You could always take your mother along. She could visit with friends while you charm the socks off all those shoppers. You'd make her very proud."

Callie shook her head. "I doubt it. She'd probably be humiliated by having to explain to all those rigid acquaintances of hers that I am practically buck naked on TV, in bed with a man I hardly know—according to the story line, that is—and trying very, very hard to get pregnant so I can trap him into marrying me."

Jason chuckled. "My, my, you have been busy since the last time I tuned in."

Callie's gaze narrowed. "I thought you watched every day."

"I do. You're taping two weeks ahead, remember?"

"Oh."

"So, you and the nation's favorite hunk are getting it on?"

He sounded awfully testy about it. Actually, Callie had had a great deal of difficulty not giggling the first time she and Terry had stripped down strategically and climbed into bed in front of the cameras. Only Terry's dire warning of evil consequences if she laughed had kept her serious enough to deliver her lines.

"Jealous?" she inquired.

Jason's brows rose slightly. "Of Terry?" he asked a bit incredulously.

So, she thought, he knew that Terry was gay. And apparently it made no difference to him. Bless the man.

"You are a wonder," she whispered as she lifted her mouth to his.

The front door clicked open before she could lose herself thoroughly in the kiss.

"My, my," Terry observed. "There is definitely progress being made. Neil, would you look at these two?"

When Callie would have shrugged free of Jason's embrace, he tightened it.

"Are you two into voyeurism?" Jason inquired. "Go away. I was just about to get lucky."

"You wish," Callie retorted, shoving him away with a little more force. "My mother's here, remember?"

"But she likes me," Jason reminded her. "She's all but given us her blessing."

"Not to carry on while she's in the room next door," Callie assured him. She turned her attention to Terry. "What have you guys been up to?"

"Reading my fan mail," Terry said. "It gets me all psyched up to go back to work on Monday."

"The man is shameless," Neil commented as he dropped a Saks Fifth Avenue bag filled with mail beside the sofa, presumably for Callie's mother to answer. "He reads them all aloud. Every Sunday. Week after week. All those entranced women. It's enough to make a person gag."

Callie regarded both men closely for any hint that there had been another threat tucked among this latest batch of gushing compliments. Apparently not, judging from their perfectly bland expressions. Either that or they were both exhibiting their acting skills for Jason's benefit. Since Terry rarely wasted his talent on an audience this small, she doubted that was the case.

"I have an idea," Jason said. "Since we're all here, why don't we have Chinese food for dinner?"

Callie and Terry exchanged glances. "Too much water retention," they chimed in unison.

Neil rolled his eyes. "I may never forgive you for putting Callie on the air," he said to Jason. "One actor around was bad enough. Now there are two of them primping and worrying about what they eat all the time. I haven't had a decent *moo shu pork* with plum sauce in months."

"Tonight you will," Jason assured him. "I will fix it myself and if anyone gains so much as an ounce from retained fluid, I will personally provide access to a private steam room first thing in the morning."

His gaze was locked on Callie when he made the promise. She had the feeling he wouldn't mind at all starting the day stripped down and sweaty with her. She grinned at him. The prospect held a certain appeal for her, too.

"In that case, be my guest," she said, pointing the way to the kitchen.

"I've seen your cupboards," Jason protested. "Even with your mother here, your supplies are pathetic. So first, we have to shop for ingredients." He glanced at Terry and Neil. "Do you two want to come along?"

"Callie and I will get things ready here. You and Neil go," Terry said at once. "He gets absolutely rapturous over fresh produce."

Jason seemed a little disconcerted by that particular prospect, but he shrugged gamely. "Let's go, then."

As he and Neil reached the door, Terry frowned at Neil with mock ferocity. "Now you be nice to the man. Don't tell him the business he's in sucks."

Jason groaned. "Not another one. Between you and Callie's mother, I may be forced to change careers."

Neil grinned at him. "We can talk about it," he said. "Did I mention I was a management headhunter?"

Callie laughed at Jason's slightly frantic expression as the door closed behind them. She glanced at Terry. "Do you suppose by the time they get back, Jason will be CEO of some other corporation?"

"Entirely possible," Terry confirmed as he grabbed silverware and plates from the kitchen and began setting the table as if he were in his own home. "Neil is very good at what he does."

"I don't know about that," Callie retorted. "You're still an actor, aren't you? And he's been working to change you for years now."

"All talk," Terry declared, folding the napkins into a fancy shape Callie would never have attempted. "I think he watches our show every day."

"What makes you think that?"

"He's gotten very nervous since you and I started having love scenes." He winked at her. "Frankly, so have I."

"I'm sure," Callie retorted drily. "Be serious for a minute." She gestured toward the new sack of mail.

"Any problems in there? Is that why you wanted to see me alone?"

"What makes you think I wanted to see you alone?"

"The fact that you sent Neil off grocery shopping with Jason, instead of letting him stay here and rewash all my dishes so they shine to his satisfaction." She noticed that he didn't even try to contradict her guesswork. "What's in the bag?"

Terry's expression finally sobered. "Nothing."

"Maybe that's the end of it, then. It's been, what, a week now since the last one?"

"Not quite," he said.

He said it while looking everywhere but at her. It didn't take a genius to figure out he was hiding something. "Terry, what are you keeping from me?"

"It was nothing," he said defensively.

"What was nothing?"

"It was just a phone call."

"Just a phone call!" She regarded him incredulously. "Are you crazy? Why didn't you tell me the minute it happened?"

"Because it was nothing," he repeated, continuing to downplay it. Clearly, though, it had upset him enough for him to bring it up now, even with such a show of reluctance.

"Just a hang-up?" she persisted.

"No, the same message that's been in the notes."

Callie had done a lot of interrogations on the soap in the past few weeks. The technique had almost become second nature. "Was the caller a man or woman?"

"I couldn't tell. The voice was muffled."

"What time was it?"

"Ten-fifty-seven."

"Were you on the set or in your dressing room?"

"Actually, I was in bed. It was 10:57 at night. Last night, as a matter of fact."

Callie's heart skipped a beat. Terry's home number was unlisted and known to only a few close friends and even fewer people connected with the soap. He was obsessive about maintaining his privacy, determined to protect his secret for Neil's sake and his own. Now he'd been called at home on a Saturday night by someone who, at the very least, wanted to embarrass him publicly if that's what that "tell all" instruction was all about.

Was the caller hoping to ruin him? Was he or she counting on the public turning on Terry once his homosexuality had been revealed? Who would stand to gain from that? Another actor on the show? Or was it someone who was gay himself and resented that Terry was trying to pass as straight? Whatever the motivations, it appeared the stakes had just risen. The warnings were hitting too close to home to be ignored any longer.

"That's it," she declared. "We're talking to the police first thing tomorrow."

"We are not," Terry retorted just as emphatically. "You'll just step up your investigation a bit."

"What investigation? I've been keeping my eye on people on the set to see if anyone's been behaving suspiciously, but I'd hardly call that an investigation. I'm more and more convinced that those little accidents on the set weren't accidents at all. This is serious, Terry. It's not some story line with a predictable ending."

Before she could say more, she heard the key Terry

had given Jason turn in the lock. Terry latched on to her hand with a tight grip.

"Not a word," he demanded. "Promise me. Neil will freak if he hears about this. He'll insist I quit the show and go into hiding in some isolated house in Vermont, for God's sake."

"What does he think now? How did you explain the call?"

"I told him it was just a wrong number."

Callie wrenched her hand away. "I won't tell Neil if you'll agree to let me talk to one of the cops I've been consulting for my work on the show. You've met Hank. He's terrific."

Terry looked dubious. "You'll talk to him off the record? No names?"

She sighed. "For now," she agreed.

She just prayed she wasn't misjudging the seriousness or the immediacy of the danger.

16

Detective Hank Parker of the NYPD had a crumpled face that looked as if it had been through one too many boxing matches, which it had. He'd told Callie that by twenty his nose had been practically flattened. By twenty-two his left cheek had an oddly irregular shape, the result of inexpert plastic surgery following his final bout. His right eyebrow was split in two by a thin, jagged white line, a scar from an early round in the same fight.

Despite all of those flaws, at the age of twenty-nine he had a certain gruff charisma that made women flock to him. Ever since he'd made his first appearance on the set as a consultant to Callie, the actresses had hovered around him, drawn by his unmistakable aura of raw masculinity.

He also had very impressive biceps and triceps and abs. Callie knew about the latter firsthand because he'd invited her to punch him in the abdomen during one of their training sessions. She'd bruised all her knuckles. He hadn't even winced. In fact, he'd smirked with satisfaction.

He visited the set only rarely now, usually because he was called by one of the writers to check out some twist or other in the script. On Monday he came in response to Callie's call and just in time to share the leftover Chinese food she'd promised him.

"This is fantastic," he said, wolfing down his second plateful of the *moo shu pork* Jason had prepared the night before. Either his appetite was naturally huge or he hadn't eaten in days. "Where'd you order from?"

"Actually, it's homemade."

His eyes widened, which sent that jagged scar skyward. "Oh, baby, marry me."

"Actually, I'm not the one you want if you're after more *moo shu pork.*"

"Who, then?" he asked eagerly. "Is she married? Is she as beautiful as you?"

"Actually, the cook is a man."

He sighed with such genuine disappointment that Callie couldn't help grinning at him.

"Hank Parker, you are by no means desperate for companionship," she chided.

"For companionship, no," he agreed cheerfully. "But I'd kill for a woman who could cook like this. Now that I'm fed, tell me why I'm here. You gotta take out a bad guy today? You want some advice on aiming for the heart?"

"I'm worried about you, detective. You seem a little too eager to put a gun in my hand."

"Turns me on to see a woman handle a weapon."

"Anything in a skirt turns you on," she corrected.

He grinned unrepentantly. "True. In fact, if you could

set me up with that Lisa Calvert, I'd name our first six children after you."

Callie considered the sexy ingenue. "Six children? Lisa? I don't see it."

"Okay, five, but that's my bottom line. I was an only child. I want a big family."

"I'll see if she's interested," Callie promised. "In the meantime, could you answer a question for me?"

"That's what I get paid for."

"Actually, this question is personal. I need a favor. Actually, what I need is your professional opinion on something."

His expression sobered at once. "You in trouble?"

"Not me. A friend."

He regarded her skeptically but nodded for her to continue.

"There have been some threatening notes—at least, I guess you could say they were threatening. Maybe it was more like blackmail, except there was no demand for money or anything."

A grin slid across Hank's face as she inexpertly tried to explain without revealing anything.

"Maybe you could just tell me what the notes said and let me decide," he suggested.

Callie debated a way to phrase it without giving away anything that might link the notes to Terry. "Just that this person should tell all."

"Tell all?" he repeated. "What the devil is that supposed to mean?"

"It means this person has a secret and the writer of the notes knows about it and wants this person to go public."

"Like in the tabloids or something?"

"Maybe with a banner across Broadway," Callie snapped, suddenly losing patience with Hank and the whole incredible set of circumstances that had put her smack in the middle of some devious plot. She was equally put out with Terry for tying her hands this way. It would be a lot simpler if she could just tell Hank the whole story.

She glanced over and caught Hank's hurt expression. "Sorry, but how would I know what would satisfy the writer? The important thing here is whether the recipient should take the threats seriously."

"I suppose it depends on how badly this person wants the secret kept. How damaging would it be to go public?"

"Damaging enough," Callie assessed, thinking of the hue and cry that would arise if all those female fans discovered the object of their affections was gay.

Hank studied her intently. "You have a kid no one knows about?"

"It's not me. It's a friend."

He held up his hands. "Okay, okay. It's just that this 'friend' ploy gets worked a lot. Nobody ever believes it."

"Well, believe it. This isn't my problem beyond the fact that I'm worried about my friend. Does something like this ever turn dangerous?"

"Ever? That's a long time and a lot of possibilities. Sure, it could turn dangerous, but it could also be benign, nothing more than a power play. I'd have to have a lot more to go on before I could determine that." He looked straight into her eyes then. "Any chance you could tell me what we're actually talking about?"

"Not now," she said with an air of resignation. "I promised."

"I suppose you also promised you'd stick your nose into it and try to find out who's behind the threats."

Callie shrugged. "Just a question here and there."

"Don't do it," he advised. "On the off chance that you are dealing with a real loony toon here, talk your friend into letting you fill me in on the whole story. Then maybe I could give you some advice that makes sense."

"I've tried."

"Keep trying. And whatever you do, don't go getting the idea that the fake badge in your pocket and that unloaded gun you strap on before you go in front of the cameras gives you any actual police skills. Got it?"

Since it was more or less exactly what she'd told Terry weeks ago, she nodded dutifully. "Got it."

He stood up and tucked a beefy hand under her chin. "I mean it, sugar. I'd hate to get a call one day and find you dead in an alley."

"How pleasantly graphic of you to say so."

"Remember the image," he advised. "And call me before you go and do something stupid."

She thought of her plans to have dinner with Lisa that night and to pry for information on the rest of the cast. Hank would probably think that qualified as stupid. She couldn't risk telling him about it and having him invite himself along, either to protect her or for his own nefarious, libidinous purposes.

Maybe if she spent part of the evening convincing Lisa to go on a date with the detective, he wouldn't be too furious with her. He'd probably be too besotted to even care if Callie managed to get herself killed for poking her nose in where it didn't belong.

"This is really fun," Lisa said, settling gingerly into the booth opposite Callie and reaching for the menu. "I don't have all that many women friends. I think they're afraid I'll steal their boyfriends or something."

Given Lisa's reputation and her skintight wardrobe, it was not an idle consideration, Callie thought, but kept the unkind thought to herself. If she wanted this woman to open up to her, she couldn't start out by insulting her.

"Oh, I'm sure that's not true," Callie said instead. "I'm sure it's just because your social life is too busy to fit in many evenings out with the girls."

Lisa gave her a provocative little smile that would no doubt have been more effective on the males she was used to dealing with. "Actually, I had to rearrange my evening to fit you in."

Before Callie could offer the thanks that Lisa clearly expected, the actress waved her off. "Oh, I was glad to do it. My date will wait," she said confidently. "Besides, I've been dying to get the real scoop on you and Jason Kane."

Oh, goody, Callie thought. *Lisa wanted to exchange confidences.*

"There's really not much to say. He saw me on the show when I did that walk-on, decided I had some quality that would benefit the show and he hired me."

"Oh, please, nobody believes that PR crap," Lisa said. "Are you sleeping with him?"

"Are you?" Callie retorted pleasantly.

Lisa blinked hard, looking vaguely uncertain. Apparently she wasn't nearly as used to being on the receiving end of blunt talk as she was to dishing it out. Callie plastered her most fascinated expression on her face, took a slow sip of her iced tea and repeated, "Well, are you?"

Lisa finally settled on giggling. "Me? Never. Not that I would mind if he looked at me twice, but he hasn't."

"Glad to hear it," Callie muttered under her breath.

Lisa leaned forward. "What?"

Callie beamed at her. "Nothing. As a matter of fact, I do know of a certain man who's crazy to go out with you, if you're interested."

Lisa immediately looked fascinated. Callie supposed a woman could never have too many men panting after her.

"Who? It's not Paul Locklear, is it? He's a sweetie, but he's way too old for me."

Paul was all of forty-five, but it was nice to know that Lisa had some limits. "No," Callie said. "Actually, it's Hank Parker."

Lisa looked blank for a second before recognition of the name dawned. "That cop who consults on the show?"

"That's the one."

Lisa seemed to consider the proposition thoughtfully. Or maybe she was just calling up an image of Hank's physique.

"I never thought about going out with a cop before," she said eventually. "I mean, I've only dated guys in the business."

Probably because of what she thought they could do for her, Callie imagined. She kept the thought to herself. A whole evening of this and her head was likely to burst from all the unspoken thoughts crammed into it.

"Maybe it would be fun to date someone who lives in the real world," she suggested instead.

Her expression still uncertain, Lisa eventually nodded. "Sure, why not? Tell him to give me a call sometime."

"He'll be ecstatic," Callie told her with absolute sincerity. She wondered to herself how long it would last, though. Lisa's relationships didn't seem to have a lot of staying power. Still, that wasn't her problem.

Her promised matchmaking out of the way, she propped her chin on her hands and said, "Why don't you fill me in on everybody. It's funny how you can work with people all day long and not be able to get a fix on them. Maybe it's because we're all pretending to be somebody else most of the time."

"I know exactly what you mean," Lisa gushed. "I mean, who would have guessed that sweet Dr. Thornton would turn out to be hotter than a Texas barbecue at high noon."

Lisa waved her napkin in front of her face to emphasize exactly how steamy Randall Trent, the actor who played the good doctor, was. That came as no news to Callie since she'd seen the two of them engaged in their intimate quest for each other's tonsils.

"Don't you worry about getting so involved with someone on the show?" Callie asked if this were Lisa's first costar fling, even though she knew perfectly well that it was just her most recent. "What if things go sour? Won't it be a little awkward? How's Randall going to feel about you going out with Hank?" Left unasked was who would be left to date by the time she turned thirty.

Lisa shrugged. "Why should working together be a problem? We're all professionals. Besides, it's not as if we're really serious, you know. It's just something to make the day go by a little faster."

Callie's head was spinning at the logic. "You don't actually date, then?"

"Oh, heavens, no. Randall's way too old for me, almost as old as Paul."

Callie decided then and there that she had lived far too sheltered a life.

"Then jealousy's not a problem?" she asked.

"Not usually. I mean, we all know the rules."

"And what rules are those?" Callie asked.

"That our private lives are just that, private. At the end of the day, we go home to whomever."

Callie nodded. "I see. Whom does Randall go home to?"

"His wife, of course."

Of course, Callie thought drily. "And you?"

"No one special, if that's what you mean. I share an apartment with a couple of other actresses. We've been so busy trying to make it, we haven't had a lot of time for serious relationship stuff."

"So you just get your physical kicks on the set," Callie said, trying to be sure she'd grasped the concept.

"In the dressing rooms, actually, but that's the idea," Lisa confirmed, wolfing down her pasta as if it were the only meal she'd had in weeks.

Dear heaven, what had she gotten Hank into? Callie wondered, feeling almost sorry for the amorous cop. Still, he was a big boy. She wondered if there were others who hadn't known the rules.

"Doesn't it get complicated?" she asked again, trying once more to get a handle on whether jealousy was ever a problem. Surely these men were no less competitive or possessive than others in the universe.

"Just once," Lisa confessed. "There was one guy who thought he owned me just because we'd gotten it on a couple of times. He was almost, you know, like stalking me."

"What happened?"

"I set him straight. He ended up leaving the show. I felt bad about that, too. He was a real good actor. He's over on CBS now." Her expression suddenly turned nostalgic. "We had some really hot scenes together. It took a long time for them to find someone to replace him. My story line went to hell in the meantime. I had my agent on the phone to the producers twice a day, sometimes more, threatening to pull me if they didn't beef up my part again."

She beamed, the man and the troubles apparently forgotten. "It worked, too. They turned me into a real homewrecker. You should see the hate mail I get. It's fantastic."

To each his own, Callie thought. "Speaking of hate mail, does any of it ever scare you?"

"You mean, like, do I take it seriously?"

Callie nodded.

"Don't be silly. It just shows I'm doing my job."

"Then you don't get actual threats."

"Sure I do. All the time. But, come on, these people aren't going to act on it. They know this stuff is make-believe."

Callie wasn't nearly as convinced of that as Lisa appeared to be, but it did put another slant on those notes Terry was getting. Maybe someone was threatening his character, not him. Of course, if the sender was a nut, that could be just as dangerous. Despite Lisa's conviction to the contrary, this person might not know the difference between reality and make-believe.

But even as she considered the possibility of a misguided fan, Callie dismissed it. These notes weren't coming through the mail as a deranged viewer's would. Logic indicated that they were being hand-delivered by someone with much closer ties to the show.

"How about anyone else on the show? Has anyone ever gotten mail they thought was over the edge, maybe a little too scary to dismiss?"

Lisa's eyes widened as she considered that. "Oh, wow, you mean like threats on their lives or something?"

"Maybe," Callie confirmed. "Or not even something that direct, just weird."

Lisa tilted her head and studied Callie intently. "You know, you sound just like a cop. You're not a plant or something, are you?"

"What do you mean?"

"You know, like, working undercover because somebody on the show really is being stalked."

Callie felt her cheeks turning pink. "No. I'm just curious. This is all so new to me. It's like a whole other world. I was just wondering if people ever get spooked by their mail."

"I suppose it's happened once or twice," Lisa said, looking bored with the topic.

Callie persisted. "Who would they tell about it? Would they go to the police?"

"I wouldn't. I'd tell the producers and let them handle it."

"Good idea." Callie resolved to talk to the producers first thing in the morning and see if there had been other threats reported. In the meantime, she had one more avenue to explore with Lisa. Getting into it, though, was going to be tricky.

"You know," she began casually, "I've been wondering about Terry."

"Oh, gosh," Lisa said at once, her wide eyes sparkling. "Haven't we all? He's a hunk, all right. There was a time when I thought he and I—well, you know what I mean."

"It didn't work out?"

"No, he made it real clear he wasn't interested. He was sweet about it, though. It wasn't like some big, embarrassing rejection or something. He just told me he was, like, really involved and not into messing around. You have to respect a guy for being honest, you know." She sighed wistfully. "I hope someday I meet a guy like that, one who won't fool around on me."

She seemed thoroughly sincere, and if she'd guessed the real reason for Terry's rejection, she certainly wasn't letting on. She didn't seem to be harboring any hidden resentments toward him, either. Callie dismissed her as being the one behind the notes.

Nor did it seem likely that Terry's rebuff of Lisa could have fueled speculation about his sexual preference. She doubted Lisa would have made a big thing of it and spoiled her reputation as the show's resident sexpot.

It wouldn't hurt to find out what others thought of Terry, though. "He's a sweetheart to work with," she ventured. "He seems to get along with everybody."

"Oh, everybody adores him," Lisa confirmed. "He's not, like, on some star trip or something. He doesn't steal scenes or insist on extra lines, the way some of the big shots on the show do. He's real sweet to the crew, too. Not everybody is, you know. I mean, just because they're not on camera, what difference does it make? They're people. We couldn't very well do the show without them, but you wouldn't know that from the way some people treat them, like they're slaves or something. Not Terry, though. He's nice to everybody. I know Paul thinks he's the best actor on the show, too. He says he's a dream to direct. I'll bet if we had a popularity contest, Terry would win hands down."

High praise, Callie supposed. Unfortunately, it wasn't quite true. Somebody was writing those notes. And whoever it was clearly wasn't one of Terry's biggest fans.

17

Callie arranged to have lunch with the producers of *Within Our Reach* the next day. She set it up under the guise of determining the direction her character was intended to take over the next few months.

Marty Malloy and Katrina Devon had been coproducing the series since its inception. They had been part of the original creative process and its evolution. They had weathered ratings slides and writing upheavals. Somewhere along the way they had formed a romantic liaison, as well. Even so, they clung to their singlehood with all the fervor of two successful people terrified of losing the identities they'd worked so hard to achieve.

Whatever resentment they felt about having Callie forced on them was well hidden.

Skinny, balding and bespectacled, Marty was the more passionate and voluble of the two, talking so fast at times that he kept the crew in an uproar trying to follow his orders. He was Woody Allen on speed.

As plump as Marty was thin, Katrina was the sweet voice of reason, a soothing counterpoint to Marty's hyper behavior. Her more diplomatic style couldn't disguise the fact that she was tough as nails in her own right. The term *steel magnolia* had been created to describe Katrina's style of demeanor, though she carried it off without a honeyed Southern accent.

They both intimidated Callie. Lunch promised to be an adventure. Only for a friend as dear as Terry would she have willingly subjected herself to it.

The shooting schedule prevented long, leisurely, getting-to-know-you meals. That meant that the three of them were closeted in Marty's cramped office with takeout from the deli down the block. The aroma of Marty's pastrami permeated the room. Callie and Katrina dutifully sipped from steaming, low-cal cups of chicken broth. Callie noticed that Katrina kept her gaze enviously pinned on Marty's sandwich as if waiting for an opportunity to snatch up any leftovers. He hunched over his food as if he knew it was in danger from his constantly dieting significant other.

"Okay, so what's on your mind, Callie?" he asked between gargantuan bites.

"My role," she said, her gaze locked on his mouth as he chewed…and chewed. She worried he'd strangle before their meeting ended.

"You're already complaining it isn't big enough?" Marty asked.

There was an edge to his voice that gave away his irritation that she had any part at all. It was the first time the facade of welcome had slipped since she'd joined the cast. Callie guessed that Jason had been responsible for any facade being there in the first place. He'd probably issued some sort of be-sweet-or-else order.

"Of course not," she said at once, hoping to correct

any impression he had that she was ungrateful for the opportunity she'd been given or that she was going to become unduly demanding. She'd learned a lot about walking on eggshells the past few weeks.

"I don't know a lot about writing for soaps, but I'm sure it was difficult to fit in a new character so quickly," she said smoothly. "The writers have been incredible."

"Glad you know that," he grumbled, sounding somewhat mollified.

Katrina jumped in. "What Marty means is—"

"I can say what I mean," he snapped. "You don't have to go making nice on my behalf."

"I do if we're all going to get along," she corrected without any hint of rancor. She grinned at Callie. "Marty went to Harvard. He's afraid it polished away all his rough edges, so he likes to play tough."

Callie surprised herself by warming to Katrina's unexpected openness. She smiled back. "He's very good at it."

"Hey, you two, I am in the room," he reminded them.

"We know," Katrina soothed. "I get goose bumps when I know you're close."

Marty scowled at her for several seconds, then grinned, ruining the tough-guy effect once and for all. "Damn, woman, you're going to turn my head one of these days."

"That's the general idea," Katrina confirmed. She glanced at Callie. "He thinks I've been trying to get him to marry me for ten years," she said, her tone suggesting that was the most ridiculous idea she'd ever heard. "He's still holding out."

"For what?" Callie asked, playing what she gathered was a familiar game.

"Someone who's not so sassy," he replied. "Okay, enough of this chitchat. Lunch is almost over and we still don't know what Callie wants."

Callie decided to tap dance through an explanation and see which part of her response struck a chord. "Just some idea of where you see this character heading," she began. "Part of this is my own curiosity, but there's a practical side to the question, as well. I'm about to go to a bunch of public appearances where I'm told people will want to know if Terry and I really will get married eventually. Personally, I'm wondering why I can't see through the fact that he's such a cad."

"Maybe you can, but Cop Kelly can't," Katrina said. "All she sees are his muscles and that endearing grin. She is definitely hot for his body."

"In other words, he's fooled her the same way he's fooled millions of fans," Callie said, deliberately phrasing the statement so it could be interpreted in two ways. If they knew Terry was gay, now was the perfect moment for them to reveal it.

They didn't.

"Exactly," they both said blandly.

"Surely there must be some women in the world who see through all that charm and get furious with him, maybe even send warnings about his lousy track record to his female conquests."

"You should know the answer to that better than we do," Katrina reminded her. "Have they?"

"Nope," she admitted. "As a matter of fact, they all envy me."

"See," Marty said. "They want to believe that underneath those roguish ways, he's really a man worth taming. It's our job to make them believe you're just the woman to do it."

"In other words, a femme fatale," she said.

"Just like Jason Kane wanted," Marty confirmed, that edge back in his voice, though perhaps a shade less resentful than it had been earlier.

Maybe she'd won him over, maybe she hadn't, but Callie decided she'd pressed as hard as she could for the moment. She stood up to leave, then turned to Katrina. "One last question, do any of the actors ever get serious hate mail?"

Before Katrina could answer, Marty jumped in, looking vaguely alarmed. "Have you gotten some?"

"No, but I've read about that kind of thing. People get angry at a character and come up and smack 'em on the street or send nasty letters. I just wondered what I should do about it, if it ever happens."

"Turn any mail like that over to us," Marty said grimly. "We'll deal with it."

"Does it happen a lot?"

"Only once since the show started," Katrina said. "That was scary enough."

"What happened?"

"We hired a bodyguard for the actress for a while."

"Did you ever catch the person responsible?"

"No. Nothing ever came of it. The letters stopped. We finally decided it had to be a crank. Most of them are. Even so, we don't like to take chances until we know that for sure." She exchanged a glance with her coproducer. "The last thing this show needs is a dead star."

Callie was already cynical enough about television to wonder if the publicity department would agree.

"So, how come you've been locked away with our illustrious producers for the past half hour?" Terry demanded when Callie walked into his dressing room to run through her lines for the scene they were shooting together that afternoon. He sounded miffed.

"Don't act like there's been a party and you didn't get invited," she retorted. "I was doing research for you."

He eyed her skeptically. "What kind of research?"

"I was trying to discover whether anyone else in the cast has ever been threatened."

"Oh," he said with surprising indifference. He picked up his script. "Ready to tackle this scene?"

Callie didn't get the nonchalance. Terry was too much of a worrier to dismiss anything which might shed light on the mail he'd been getting. "Terry?" she prodded.

"What?"

"Don't you want to know what I found out?"

"Not especially."

"Why not?"

"Because I think it's a waste of time trying to figure out who's sending these notes. They probably don't mean a thing."

Callie couldn't believe she'd heard him correctly. "Wait a minute. That's not what you were saying just a few days ago. That phone call Saturday night really spooked you. Admit it."

He shrugged. "I've had time to think about that, too. I'm sure that was the end of it. It was probably just a practical joke."

"Is anybody laughing? Have you seen any smirks around the set?" It wasn't entirely an idle question.

"You know what I mean," Terry said defensively.

"No, I do not know what you mean," she snapped impatiently. "Are you or are you not concerned about these threats?"

"Not." He avoided looking directly at her when he said it.

Callie moved into his line of vision so there could be no evasions. "Okay, what's the deal?"

"I just think maybe I got rattled over nothing," he insisted, his jaw set stubbornly.

Callie might have believed him, if he hadn't been gazing somewhere over her left shoulder when he'd said it. For a good actor, he was a lousy liar. She had two choices: she could call him on it or she could allow the lie to stand and forget all about her so-called investigation. Something told her that getting to the bottom of the threats was suddenly more important than ever.

"You're lying," she accused. "Now tell me what's happened or I swear I will tell the world about these threats and call the cops myself."

He leaped up and slammed his dressing room door. "Jesus, Callie, watch what you say around here."

"Worried that your letter writer will overhear me?"

"As a matter of fact, yes. You're already stirring things up just by asking questions. I'm more convinced than ever that that crashing light the other day was meant as a warning."

"What makes you think that?" When he didn't answer, she grabbed his brawny shoulders and shook him. It was a relatively ineffective gesture given the difference in their sizes, but she had to do something. "Dammit, Terry, talk to me. How do you know I'm stirring things up?"

He closed his eyes and sighed. As he did, he reached into his pocket and pulled out an envelope. It had been folded into thirds. "This was sitting on top of my fan mail today. I just opened it."

Callie took the envelope from him and lifted the flap. She removed the letter carefully by one corner and shook it to open the single, typewritten page.

"Keep the woman out of it!"

The message was succinct and not especially dire, but it gave Callie goose bumps just the same. Clearly someone knew she'd been asking questions, which meant that someone was watching not only Terry but her. That someone had to be on the set. There was no way an outsider could know what she was up to. And it had to be someone who'd seen her with Hank, knew about her dinner with Lisa, or maybe even her just-concluded lunch with Marty and Katrina.

"Exactly when did you first see this?" she asked.

"When I got back from lunch, about ten minutes before you walked in here."

"The mail wasn't there before you left?"

"No."

So the writer could have seen her in the producer's office, Callie thought with a sinking sensation in the pit of her stomach. He or she could have slipped into Terry's dressing room just minutes before he got back from lunch. Trying to compose herself for Terry's sake, since the note had clearly rattled him enough to make him try to call off her investigation, she glanced over the single page again.

"Well, that's not so bad, really," she said, attempting a smile of pure bravado.

"Not so bad," Terry echoed incredulously. "It means I've drawn you into the middle of this."

"Whatever *this* is," Callie said. "Let's think a minute. It seems to me there are a couple of things we need to figure out."

"Figuring out one would suit me just fine—namely, who's doing this."

"Somebody with an ax to grind."

"Well, duh," Terry said sarcastically. "I guess so."

"Don't get smart with me, mister. I'm the cop, remember?"

He grinned at that. "Sweet heaven, I've created a monster."

"You don't want me on the case, there's always Hank Parker. He's hot to start digging."

Terry looked alarmed. "Exactly how much did you tell him?"

"Just enough to get some advice."

"Which was?"

"To tell him the rest of it."

"You know I can't do that."

"I don't know any such thing. You can, but you won't. Terry, he'll keep it confidential."

"And exactly how do you envision him investigating it—from his beat in midtown?" He paced from one side of the cramped office to the other, pausing only to say, "I'll tell you how. He'll be lurking around the set, poking and prodding until he has everyone in a complete tizzy. How long do you figure it will take before our mysterious fan guesses why he's really here? Five minutes? Ten? Don't you imagine his little visit with you yesterday was behind this latest note?"

"It could have been that," Callie conceded, then added with some reluctance, "Or it could have been my dinner last night with Lisa."

"Lisa?" he repeated with a groan. "I suppose you asked her all sorts of innocent little questions, too."

Callie glared at him. "You're the one who wanted me to investigate. Don't start criticizing the way I decided to go about it."

"But Lisa, of all people. She's the biggest gossip on the set."

"Exactly, which means she knows the most about what goes on."

"Did Little Miss Mouth give you any hot leads?"

Callie was growing increasingly tired of his mocking attitude. "Terry, I don't have to do this. I don't even want to do this. I want you to turn it over to a professional. Maybe he'll know how to investigate without getting caught at it. That is why they call them undercover cops, you know."

Terry ran his fingers through his hair, which had already been sexily tousled for that afternoon's taping. The hairstylist was going to have a conniption.

"Look, I'm sorry," he apologized with enough sincerity to cool her temper. "I know you're doing the best you can. It's my fault for dragging you into the middle of it. Maybe it's time to stop, though."

"Do you honestly think if you leave it alone, it's going to go away?"

"It might."

"If all the person wanted was to rattle your chains, maybe so, but I think it's more than that. There's an agenda here that we're just not getting, and frankly, it's beginning to scare me."

Terry sank back down into his chair, his shoulders sagging. "You and me both, dollface. You and me both."

18

The litter of coffee cups in Jason's office was testament to the long hours he and his programming team had put in finalizing the fall season schedule. Not that it was ever final. When the other networks made their announcements, he and his staff would be scrambling to fine-tune and counter-program what the competition had planned.

As always, Freddie Cramer was the last to leave. He poked his head into the office. "Anything I can do for you before I go, boss?"

Jason barely resisted the urge to grin. Freddie looked as if he'd been through combat. His normally pristine silk-blend shirt had coffee and ketchup stains on the front. His tie had been unknotted hours ago and was now draped unevenly around his neck. One sleeve was rolled up. The other was missing a cuff link but still hung to his wrist. His shirttail had pulled free. He looked a lot like the kid in the *Peanuts* comic strip who walked around in a haze of dirt.

"No, go home and get some sleep," Jason advised. "You did a great job today."

Freddie appeared too exhausted to be affected much by the praise. He murmured a vague thanks just as Jason's phone rang. "Want me to get that?" he asked.

"No, I'll grab it. You get out of here."

When Freddie had gone, Jason stared at the phone and debated answering. Who would be calling his office at ten-thirty at night? Some media hound trying to scoop his competitors on the fall schedule probably.

Or maybe Callie? His pulse picked up speed just thinking about her. The overeager thump of his heart convinced him to take the call, even though he'd been resisting seeing her again lately just to prove that his willpower was still intact.

Unfortunately, although the voice he heard was feminine, it was definitely not Callie.

"Hello, Mother," he said wearily. "What can I do for you?"

"Whatever happened to 'How are you?' Or 'Mother, I'm so glad to hear from you'?" When Jason remained stonily silent, she sighed. "Oh, never mind. I suppose it was too much to hope that you'd be pleasant for once."

"Mother, I am very tired. If there's a point to this, I wish you'd get to it."

"Actually, I was hoping we could have dinner one night this week."

"Sorry, I'm booked up," he said without bothering to take so much as a glance at his calendar. When it came to spending an evening with his mother, his calendar was always full. He thought she'd taken the hint and given up on masterminding some tender reunion long ago. Apparently he'd been wrong.

"You're all tied up with that new young woman, I

suppose, the one I've seen you with on the cover of all the tabloids lately," she said.

Jason was beginning to get the picture. His mother was concerned that he might be about to disgrace her. Nothing less would have stirred her up enough to track him down at this late hour.

"Her name is Callie Smith," he pointed out. "I'm sure that's not too difficult for someone with your social skills to recall."

"Why does every conversation we have disintegrate so quickly?" she asked as if the answer actually mattered yet totally eluded her.

"Maybe it's because I find your motive in calling suspect."

"I was only hoping that we could get together for dinner so that I could meet the new woman in your life. Is that so unusual?"

"For you, yes. Your motherly concern is about twenty years too late. Or are you simply interested in checking her pedigree? I can save you the time. I doubt you'd approve, and frankly, I don't care whether you do or not."

Harriet Walters Kane Pennington sighed heavily at that. "You've never understood me, have you, son?"

"Oh, I think I've understood you only too well. I suggest we don't rehash my opinions at this late date. As always, Mother, it's been a pleasure. Do check in the next time you have a spare minute in your busy life." He hung up before the conversation could slide any farther downhill.

Every now and then, he tried to recall the last time they had had a civil chat. He was pretty sure it was on the day she'd tried to explain that she was leaving his father because he was holding her back. Although she'd been very earnest, as if she'd wanted his approval for her actions, Jason hadn't really understood what she meant at the time.

Only when he'd witnessed his father's slow decline into sorrow and depression and his mother's quick grab onto the social coattails of New York investment banker Franklin D. Pennington had he fully understood her desertion. She'd had social and political ambitions far beyond being a plumber's wife or even mayor of their small Virginia town. The indulgent Pennington had been able to give her everything she'd ever dreamed of, including a sufficient campaign war chest to run for any office she chose. She was currently a representative to the New York General Assembly.

Since his father's death, Jason hadn't actively fueled his distaste for his mother's ambitions. His sole blatant screw-you message had been delivered the day he'd outbid her for those Monets she'd wanted so badly. It had been a sweet victory, but he still didn't feel they were even for all the pain and suffering she'd caused both him and his father.

As for her sudden fascination with his social life, hell would freeze over before he would ever introduce her to Callie. Not that Callie couldn't hold her own against a barracuda like his mother, but why should she have to, especially when his mother's opinion mattered so little to him?

He sighed as he considered what a pair they were. Callie's relationship with her own mother might be vaguely dysfunctional, but his with the Honorable Mrs. Pennington was the stuff that made psychoanalysts rich.

* * *

The lines on the pages of the script were blurring. Callie had been memorizing her scenes for the next day for what seemed like an eternity, but she couldn't seem to get them. Maybe it was because she had too many other things on her mind.

Terry's latest threat, for one thing. Her own upcoming trip to Iowa City, for another. She still hadn't mentioned the latter to her mother. She glanced over and found Regina thoroughly absorbed in answering yet another stack of Terry's fan mail.

"Any more surprises in there?" she asked, gesturing toward the letters.

Her mother glanced up. "You mean like that odd note you found the other day?"

"Exactly."

"I really don't understand how a thing like that could happen to a boy as nice as Terry. The world's a crazy place these days."

"You're telling me," Callie agreed. "If you do find another threat, you'll tell me right away, won't you?"

Regina regarded her worriedly. "You're not getting mixed up in this, are you? Callie, you're not a policewoman. Stay out of it. Let a real policeman handle it."

"Terry refuses to tell a real policeman."

"Why would he do that?"

"He's afraid."

"Of what?"

Callie realized too late that she'd walked right into a trap. Clearly her mother hadn't guessed about Terry and Neil's relationship, or if she had, she hadn't realized it might be a secret they wouldn't want revealed.

Callie settled for explaining that it could mean bad publicity for the show, which was an understatement if ever there was one.

"Nonsense," Regina said. "What's more important? A TV show or protecting a nice young man?"

"I think Terry might pick the show." To say nothing of his own career, she added to herself.

"Well, he'd be wrong. I doubt even your friend Jason would agree with that. Does he know about this?"

"No."

"Well, why on earth not?" her mother demanded with indignation. "It's his network. Seems to me he's responsible for what goes on around there."

Jason would probably see it that way, too, but Callie had been sworn to secrecy. She would honor Terry's request as long as the danger didn't go beyond receiving a few obliquely threatening letters and an occasional hang-up phone call. The pranks on the set were nerve-racking, but nothing more, so far. She had only suspicions but no proof that they were connected to the notes.

"Just let me know if you find any more letters, okay?"

"Of course."

Callie hesitated a minute, then decided there was no time like the present to get into a subject she'd been deliberately avoiding. "Mother, I've been wondering about something. Would you like to make a trip home with me next weekend?"

"You mean to visit the farm?"

Callie was startled by the odd mix of hopefulness and fear in her mother's expression. "Not exactly," she explained. "I have to do a publicity appearance in Iowa City. I was thinking you might want to go along and see some of your friends, maybe spend a little time with Eunice and Tom."

"Just for the weekend, then?"

"Yes."

Regina shook her head firmly. "No, you go on along. I'll be just fine right here."

Callie didn't know what to make of the hasty refusal. Her gaze narrowed as she tried to read her mother's mood. "Are you sure? Don't worry about the expense."

"It's not that. I just don't feel much like bouncing halfway across the country and back again for a day's visit with people I just left behind."

"You're not homesick, then?"

"I miss the farm sometimes," she admitted. "Not much else."

Callie regarded her with astonishment. "Really?"

Regina's smile came and went in a heartbeat. "Don't look so shocked, girl. You're not the only one capable of seeing that life for what it was."

Even as Callie tried to absorb the meaning of that, her mother gathered up the mail she'd finished, set it on a table by the front door for Callie to take out in the morning and put the rest away.

"I think I'll be going to bed now." She leaned down and kissed Callie's forehead. "Don't stay up too late."

Callie had the feeling, though, that the shock at her mother's totally unexpected, soft-spoken revelation about the way she viewed the farm would keep her awake for hours.

A little over a week later, Callie was all alone in Iowa City. Not only had her mother continued to refuse to go, but Jason had balked at making the trip, as well.

He'd said it would be bad PR for him to be seen trailing around the country after her.

"People will begin to think I'm exerting some sort of Pygmalion-like control over you, that I'm afraid to let you loose in public on your own," he'd told her.

"If that's not the most ridiculous, self-serving remark I've ever heard," Callie shot back. "If you don't want to go to Iowa, just say so."

"I thought I had."

"Only if I read between the lines," she countered.

"Which you have," he reminded her.

She couldn't believe he was bailing out on her now. "If you leave me to deal with my sister on my own, I will never forgive you."

"I'll risk it," he'd said smoothly. "Have a good trip."

"Have a good trip," she mimicked as she prepared to walk out to the makeshift stage in the middle of the mall and confront what looked to be three hundred or so fans being worked into a frenzy by some local DJ. If Eunice and Tom were out there, Callie hadn't spotted them yet. With a little luck, their car had stalled en route.

This was the last of the scheduled mall appearances. The first two had gone every bit as smoothly as the bowl-a-thon, so the only thing that could possibly account for the butterflies in her stomach was the prospect of seeing her sister.

She dreaded it, no doubt about it. But if she allowed herself to get too worked up over spending time with Eunice, she'd head for the closest exit. She settled for running through a familiar litany of curses aimed at Jason instead.

She really didn't intend to forgive him for abandoning her. All that Pygmalion garbage was just that, so much hastily improvised nonsense to explain the fact that he was distancing himself from her again.

Even in the few weeks they'd known each other, she'd begun to detect a certain pattern. Every time it appeared that their relationship was actually developing into something serious, he took not just one step back but a dozen or more. Now he'd managed to put several hundred miles between them.

He must be feeling very safe back in his sterile, lonely New York penthouse about now. At least, he'd better be lonely, she thought with a sudden, unexpected flash of pure possessiveness. She realized that until just that instant she had never considered the possibility that a man as desirable as Jason might have other women in his life. How naive! Women probably threw themselves at him hourly. It was hardly sensible to assume that he never caught a single one of them. He was probably cheating on her at this very instant with some glamorous actress or some brainy executive. Could a man even cheat on a woman to whom he'd made love but no promises?

A nudge from the PR assistant assigned to her for the mall event snapped her out of her wild imaginings barely an instant before she would have snatched up the nearest phone and made a call she would wind up regretting.

"You're on," he pointed out, gesturing toward the steps leading up to the stage.

Callie plastered a smile on her face and made her entrance to thunderous applause. She spotted half a dozen familiar faces in the crowd, women she'd gone to school with mostly, along with their husbands, some of whom had been in the same class. Once she wouldn't have envied them at all. In fact, she would have mocked them for choosing such a safe, dull path for their lives. But as she spotted one couple with an infant, another with a baby in a stroller and one or two with toddlers, an odd sensation spread through her. It felt an awful lot like longing.

What was happening to her? Was she losing her edge? Was it living in this peculiar make-believe world that was changing her? Or was it Jason? Funny, but he had struck her as being just as independent as she was, an unlikely candidate for marriage or parenthood. And yet she suddenly couldn't shake the thought of making a baby with him.

"Tell us about that gorgeous Terence Walker," someone demanded. It was a woman who looked to be in her fifties, but the very mention of Terry had her giggling like a schoolgirl.

Thankfully, the question broke Callie's train of thought. She grinned. "Want to know just how sexy he is?" she asked in a seductive whisper, playing the game.

"Oooh, yes," several women shouted back.

Callie dropped her voice to an even lower, even huskier pitch. "He is every bit as handsome, every bit as dangerous and every bit as desirable as he appears onscreen."

"When are you two finally going to be married?" one girl, barely out of her teens, asked, proving that Terry's appeal crossed generational lines.

"They haven't told me that yet."

"Do you see each other off-screen, too?"

"All the time," Callie said honestly.

"Oh, my God," one woman moaned. "It's true, then. You two are having an affair in real life?"

This was tricky turf. The publicity people had warned her to let people cling to their illusions, within reason. Claiming to be involved with Terry off-screen seemed to be a little extreme.

"No," she said, as if she wished it were otherwise. "We're just friends."

One of her old schoolmates, class brain Wanda Harris, waved her hand. "I heard you were living together. Is that wrong?"

Wanda glanced pointedly toward the edge of the crowd when she said it. Callie followed her gaze and spotted Eunice, who blushed furiously and avoided looking directly at her. Dear heaven, what had Eunice been telling the neighbors?

"Actually, we live in the same building," Callie responded. "I knew Terry before I joined the cast. He got me the bit part that led to my being hired."

"Will you and Terry end up together on the show, I mean, forever?" another woman called out. Either she'd missed the earlier question about marriage or she didn't want to believe that Callie didn't really know the answer to that.

"This is daytime TV," Callie reminded her, drawing laughs. "Nothing is forever."

"Just like real life," some male cynic in the crowd muttered loudly enough to be overheard.

It went on like that for another fifteen minutes before Callie called a halt and offered to sign autographs. The line snaked past for over an hour, allowing little time to catch up with the women she'd once gone to school with. At the end, Eunice was waiting—alone, Callie noted with relief—her expression stiff and unhappy.

"You had to put me down, didn't you?" she said by way of a hello.

Callie stared at her. "Excuse me?"

"You had to make me look like I'd lied about you and Terry living together."

"If that's what you told people, then you were lying," Callie reminded her.

"Just stretching the truth a little," she said defensively. "What was the big deal? Would it have hurt you to play along?"

"It was a big deal to me, and it would be an even bigger deal to Terry. We're both seeing other people. I'm sorry if you thought I was telling the truth to deliberately hurt your credibility."

Eunice remained stonily silent. Callie drew in a deep breath and tried to make peace. She looked around to see if there was any sign of her brother-in-law.

"Isn't Tom with you?"

"No, he was too busy to leave the farm."

"That's too bad," Callie said without much sincerity. "Look, I have an hour before I have to go back to the airport. Don't you want to go somewhere and have a nice lunch?"

Her sister shrugged indifferently. "If you're sure you can spare the time."

Callie bit back a sharp retort. It was one hour of her life. Surely she could force herself to be pleasant for that long. There had been a time when her sister had been the closest thing she'd had to a best friend. It was way past time they tried to recapture that closeness.

When they were settled into the mall's only non-fast-food restaurant, she studied her sister. Eunice's thick brown hair, which she had once envied, had been scooped into an unbecoming ponytail. She'd applied too much blush to her cheeks and done nothing to accent her lovely dark eyes. Callie's fingers itched to take her makeup case from her purse and do the job right. Eunice would only have resented her for it, though.

"You look good," she said instead.

Eunice's lips almost curved into a smile at that. "Now who's lying," she said. "I look like the devil. I meant to take more time getting myself together, but Tom needed help in the fields this morning. I almost didn't get here at all."

Callie thought about what it must be like being chained to a man and a lifestyle that demanded so much unrewarded attention. Compassion stole through her. Eunice might have chosen this life for herself, but she didn't deserve to be so miserable.

"I'm glad you made it," she said.

Eunice looked as if she didn't quite believe her, but she did begin to visibly relax at last.

"How's Mother?" she asked eventually.

"Doing surprisingly well. She's doing some work for Terry and me, answering our fan mail. I asked her if she wanted to come on this trip with me, but she said she'd be fine in New York."

"Of course. Why would she want to see me?" Eunice said with startling bitterness. "Why would she want to see the daughter who stayed behind and took care of her?"

"She misses you," Callie said. "I know she does."

"Oh, really? She hardly ever calls."

"She probably worries about it being too expensive," Callie improvised in an attempt to soothe Eunice's ruffled feathers. "You should see the way she grumbles over the price of groceries. She pinches pennies like an old miser."

Eunice didn't seem inclined to buy the excuse, but she let it drop. "Do you think she'll come back here?"

"She hasn't mentioned it lately. I don't intend to rush her, either. It's been good for us to be together. I think we're slowly but surely mending fences. She's said some surprising things lately. I guess maybe I never really understood before what she might be feeling." She smiled ruefully. "Not that she's exactly pouring out her soul, but we are communicating better than we used to."

Eunice sighed and picked disconsolately at her salad. "You're so lucky, Callie. Things just fall into place for you."

"Not everything," Callie reminded her. "I lost my husband this year and my job."

"But you landed on your feet with something better than ever."

With so little time before her flight, Callie debated asking the obvious, but Eunice seemed to need someone to talk to. "Are you so very unhappy?"

Eunice gave her a mocking half smile. "What's not to like? My husband is faithful. Our farm provides us with an adequate living." She sounded as if she were saying it by rote.

"I asked about you. Does that make you happy?"

"It should," her sister said in a voice so low Callie could barely hear her.

"But does it?"

Eunice slowly shook her head. A single tear leaked out of her tightly closed eyes and slid down her cheek. Callie thought her heart would break at the sight.

Impulsively, she reached over and hugged her sister. "Oh, sweetie, I'm sorry. What can I do?"

"Nothing," Eunice murmured. "As mother would say, I've made my bed, now I just have to lie in it."

"You don't," Callie retorted. "Not if you're miserable. Decide what it is you really want, and if it's within my power, I will help you get it."

"What can I do? I married Tom right out of high school, even though everyone, including you, told me it was a mistake not to go to college. Knowing me, I probably did it just to prove you all wrong. Isn't that ironic?" She swiped at another tear. "Getting a divorce and working at McDonald's for the rest of my life hardly seems like a solution."

"What does, then? Do you want to see a marriage counselor?"

"Tom would never hear of it."

"Then go alone. I'll pay for it."

"I can't ask you to do that."

"You're not asking, I'm offering."

"First I shove the responsibility for Mother off on you and now I'm asking you to solve my problems. That's not fair."

"I can't solve your problems," Callie corrected. "But maybe I can make it easier for you to solve them. Think about it. Decide what you really want and I'll do whatever I can to help you get it." She glanced at her watch. "Damn, I'm really sorry, sweetie, but I have to go or I'll miss my plane."

Eunice nodded. "Go. I'll be fine. I think I'll sit here for a bit and have another cup of coffee. I never get any time to myself anymore."

Callie pulled a hundred dollar bill from her purse and pressed it into her sister's hand. "Lunch is my treat. Use the rest to buy yourself something special, okay?"

"I don't need your charity," Eunice said with stiff pride.

"Please, let me do something nice for my only sister, okay?"

Eunice struggled with herself for a minute before finally nodding. "Thank you."

"You'll call me?" Callie prodded. "Promise?"

"I promise."

Callie bent down and gave her sister another hug. On the long flight back to New York, all she could think about was how all of the Gunderson women—as different as each of them were—had reached such critical turning points in their lives at the same time.

19

When Callie stepped off the plane in New York, she found Henry patiently waiting for her by the gate. He unfolded his lanky body from a chair and tucked a dog-eared book into his pocket before she could get a good look at the cover. Horror, she thought. It didn't seem to suit his placid personality.

A welcoming grin spread across his rugged face as she neared. At least Henry seemed to have missed her, Callie thought with a trace of bitterness directed toward his boss.

"There you are, Miss Callie." He reached for her bag. "Let me take that for you."

Although it was easy enough to handle the small makeup bag, she handed it over without argument. He would have been offended if she hadn't.

"I didn't expect to see you here," she said as she hurried to keep up with his long strides. "How did you know when my flight was getting in?"

At his wry look, she nodded. "Mr. Kane, I suppose."

"He does keep track of such details," Henry agreed blandly.

"Too bad he couldn't be here himself," she muttered under her breath as she followed the driver from the terminal to the limo waiting at the curb.

Before Henry could reach for the handle, the door was opened from the inside and Jason himself stepped out. Callie frowned at Henry. "You could have told me."

"Much better to let you be surprised," he informed her with a wink.

Callie regarded Jason speculatively and tried to ignore the rush of pure pleasure that raced through her at the mere sight of him. She was falling for him, all right. The prospect struck her as far more dangerous than anything that had happened to Terry so far.

"Was this in my contract or something?" she asked tartly.

His gaze locked with hers, and his expression turned very serious and sincere. "No, my sweet, this is strictly personal."

She allowed herself a faint smile as her irritation faded far too readily. "Oh, in that case…"

Unable to resist, she stepped straight into Jason's arms and lifted her face for his kiss. His lips met hers with a coaxing, consuming hunger that stunned her. Apparently he had missed her, after all. The distancing maneuvers seemed to be over for the moment. She intended to take full advantage of the reprieve.

"Maybe I'll make threats about never forgiving you and go away more often," she said when she could catch her breath. "It seems to have the most amazing results."

"So, am I forgiven for not going along?" he inquired when they were settled in the car and heading for Manhattan.

After that kiss, he didn't seem especially worried about her reply, so Callie tilted her head consideringly and said, "I'll let you know. Maybe I should make you beg for it a little longer."

"Sweetheart, I never beg."

"Then kiss me senseless," she suggested instead. "It seems to work pretty effectively."

He tucked a finger under her chin and tilted her face up. His gaze lingered on her lips until they tingled with anticipation. Then slowly, so slowly that her heart began to race, he lowered his head until his mouth hovered just over hers.

"Jason, please," she murmured, suddenly starving for another kiss.

"Now who's begging?" he whispered back.

Her indignant protest was lost as his lips finally met hers. She savored the mint-sweet taste of his breath, the soft-as-satin caress of his mouth against hers, before shoving him away with all her might.

"You are a dirty, rotten, sneaky jerk," she informed him, withdrawing to the far corner of the luxuriously wide seat.

He grinned. "I've been called worse."

"By anyone who matters?"

"Not really. I thought you knew by now that there are very few opinions I really care about."

"And mine obviously isn't one of them."

"Oh, I don't know. I was at the airport, wasn't I?"

There was an odd undercurrent to the comment that made Callie study him more intently. Clearly he considered meeting her plane to be an overture of some importance.

"Jason, when was the last time you admitted you missed somebody?"

The question clearly made him uncomfortable. He looked as if he desperately wanted to reach into his briefcase and find a batch of papers to hide behind. There was even a hint of a blush tinting his cheeks.

"Never," he finally bit out.

"But you did miss me?" she persisted.

He scowled at her. "What is it about women that requires a bunch of words to state the obvious? I thought my actions were clear enough. Maybe I should have let you take a damned cab home."

"Jason?" she prodded relentlessly.

His frown deepened, before he finally sighed. "All right, yes. I missed you, okay? Are you satisfied?"

She beamed at him and slid back across the seat until she was tucked against his side. "Okay," she said softly, ridiculously pleased by the tiny victory.

When he took her hand and placed it intimately on his thigh, her heart thundered wildly. A sweet and gentle kiss, a daring touch, that was all it took for Jason to drive her senses to distraction. She glanced toward the front seat.

"Exactly how well tinted is that window and how long would it take you to close it?" she inquired lightly, sliding her hand ever so slightly higher. She wasn't sure who was more surprised by her daring gesture, her or Jason.

"It is there for total privacy," he assured her. He touched the intercom and added in an ominous tone, "And once it's closed, if Henry touches the button to lower that window between here and home, I will personally exile him to Siberia for the rest of his days."

"Ah, gee, boss, and here I was hoping to hear all about Miss Callie's trip," Henry retorted, his amused expression reflected in the rearview mirror.

"Impertinent son of a bitch," Jason commented as he personally closed the window between the two compartments and shut off the intercom.

Callie grinned as she reached for the zipper of his pants. "So much for any interruptions."

Straightening their clothes when they reached the city took an almost comical effort of coordination, to say nothing of an untangling of limbs. If Jason had his way, he would have ordered Henry to park the limo somewhere and leave them be for another day or two. It was amazing how inventive two people could be in such a confined space.

As the car slid to a stop in front of Callie's apartment, Jason was still breathless from her unexpectedly wicked seduction. The woman was clearly filled with more surprises than he'd ever imagined. Her actions certainly confirmed the notion that being honest had its rewards. He wondered what she would do if he ever admitted he thought he might be falling just a little in love with her. Not that he'd ever admit such a thing, he reminded himself grimly. He didn't believe in love.

He tried to beg off going inside with her, sure that their activities would be plain to Mrs. Gunderson, but Callie insisted she wasn't going to face her mother alone and try to explain her disheveled appearance.

They'd made it up only two flights of stairs when

Terry's door popped open. The man had to have radar where Callie was concerned. It was an irksome trait. Still, Jason took one look at Terry's face and saw that something was seriously wrong.

"What's up?" he asked, keeping his own tone light when Terry's expression was anything but.

"Come on in," Terry suggested, avoiding Callie's gaze.

Apparently oblivious to her friend's anxiety, Callie shook her head. "I really need to go up and let Mother know I'm back."

"Actually, she's here," Terry said. He opened the door wider so they could see Mrs. Gunderson seated stiffly on the sofa, her hands clasped tightly in her lap.

Callie finally picked up on the undertones that Jason had spotted at once. "Mother, are you okay?" she demanded, looking from her to Terry and back again.

Mrs. Gunderson looked up with a shaky but determined smile that Jason couldn't help admiring. Clearly she'd passed along that same level of gumption to her daughter.

"Don't go getting in a tizzy," she said. "I just had a little scare, that's all."

"What kind of scare?" Callie asked worriedly, sitting down beside her and clasping her hands.

Jason stood behind them and willed Terry to look at him, but the other man was clearly every bit as upset as Callie's mother. Neil walked into the room just then with a tea tray. He took one look at Jason, plunked the tray down unceremoniously in front of the women and headed for the door, beckoning for Jason to follow.

Outside, with the door to the apartment firmly closed, Jason demanded, "What on earth is going on?"

"Come with me," Neil said, his jaw set furiously as he led the way up to Callie's apartment. He took out a key and unlocked the door. "See for yourself."

Jason stepped inside and halted, dismay spreading through him. The place had been tossed, not professionally, it appeared, but by vandals. Furniture was upside down, upholstery was shredded, plants had been upended on top of everything.

And on one wall, in bright red paint, it said: Stay Out of It!

"Stay out of what?" Jason asked, half to himself. He looked at Neil, whose expression was more grim than ever. "Do you have any idea what this is about?"

"I wish I did. Those two downstairs are as silent as a pair of clams. I'd like to strangle them."

"Where was Callie's mother when this happened?"

"We'd all gone out for lunch. She's not sure if she locked the door or not, but she thinks she did."

"Did you call the police?"

"Of course. They've been through the place. They didn't see any evidence of forced entry, which is odd given the number of locks. Surely she'd left at least one of them locked, even if it was just the flimsy lock in the doorknob. I'd lay odds she turned a dead bolt or two, as well, which means somebody got their hands on keys."

Jason shoved his fingers through his hair. "Who would do something like this? And what is that message supposed to mean?"

"It beats me," Neil said. "But I'll tell you one thing, Terry and Regina both know more than they're saying.

I always know when Terry's lying through his teeth. As for Regina, she just gets this pinched expression around her mouth and swears she has no idea how such a thing could have happened. She and Terry are so busy avoiding looking at each other that it's clear to me there's something they don't want the rest of us to know."

"And if the two of them know, then Callie more than likely does, too," Jason said grimly.

He glanced around just then and caught sight of Callie in the hallway, frozen in place. Her complexion was so pale he wanted to gather her up and take her away to some sun-kissed beach where all of this would be far from her mind.

"How bad is it?" she asked, her voice uncharacteristically hesitant.

"Bad enough," Jason replied.

"I would have started cleaning up," Neil said. "Terry and your mother thought you ought to be here to decide what you want done."

"That's a very good idea," Jason decided, blocking Callie's entry into the apartment. "But it's something we can do tomorrow."

Callie scowled at him. "I might as well get it over with. It won't be any better tomorrow."

"But you'll have had a good night's sleep then. It's late now and you're bound to be tired from your trip. Things always look better in the morning."

"If you tell me every cloud has a silver lining, I'll hit you," she threatened.

He grinned. "Okay, it won't look that much better in the morning, but you'll be rested."

She regarded him stubbornly. "Jason, get out of my way."

He shrugged and reluctantly stepped aside. She inched her way into the apartment, stopping just inside the door with a gasp. "Dear God," she murmured. "I had no idea… Terry didn't explain…"

"Because he's a coward," Neil said succinctly.

Callie's startled gaze flew to his, as if she weren't quite certain what or how much Neil actually knew. The reaction was very telling, as far as Jason was concerned. It confirmed Neil's guess that everyone but he and Jason knew a whole lot more about what was going on.

"Maybe you'd better tell me what this is all about," Jason said. "Starting at the beginning."

"I…I don't know what you mean."

He and Neil exchanged looks.

"I think you do," Jason said.

"So do I," Neil added.

She regarded them both with huffy indignation. "What are you two, the Hardy Boys?"

"Or Castle and Beckett. We're whatever gets us answers," Jason said.

"What makes you think I know anything about this?"

"Because you're a crummy liar," Jason suggested. "You haven't looked either one of us in the eye since we started asking for answers."

Neil nodded agreement. "Worse than Terry or your mother. And don't try that see no evil, hear no evil, speak no evil crap, because I'm not buying it. Something weird is going on here, and it's about time you let the rest of us in on it."

"Amen," Jason chimed in.

"Oh, give it a rest," Callie retorted. "Isn't it bad enough that my apartment has been trashed without my having to go through an inquisition on top of it?"

"If this were some random act, I'd say yes," Jason replied. He gestured toward the wall. "That message changes things."

"'Stay out of it,'" Callie quoted in a monotone. "What does that mean? It could mean anything."

"But it doesn't mean just anything," Jason said, forcing her chin up until she met his gaze. "Does it?"

A shudder washed through her, and she shook her head, her expression bleak.

"What's it all about?" Jason persisted.

"Let's go downstairs," she said. "I'll explain there."

"Why not explain right here?" Neil asked.

Callie gave him a rueful look. "What is this? Some sort of divide and conquer strategy?"

"Whatever works," Neil said.

"Downstairs," she insisted, and headed for the door.

"What about the mess?" Neil asked, clearly appalled by the clutter.

"I'll hire someone to clean it up," she said. "I know how compulsive you are about neatness, but just leave it for now."

Back downstairs, they found Terry and Regina huddled together on the sofa like a couple of misbehaving kids awaiting punishment. Terry's gaze instantly shot toward Callie, and he rose to meet her.

"Did you tell them?" he asked.

She shook her head.

He looked relieved. "Thank you."

"Don't thank me. It's up to you to tell them."

Terry looked as if he'd rather be floating down the Amazon on a leaky raft. Jason would cheerfully have beat the truth out of him, but it appeared Neil was inclined to do it for him. The two men were standing toe-to-toe, the silence between them charged with electricity.

"Talk or so help me I'll throw you out into the street," Neil threatened eventually in a low, lethal tone that clearly shook Terry as not even the vandalism upstairs had.

Jason realized then that his suspicions about the relationship between the two of them were accurate. The prospect of a publicity nightmare flashed through his mind, then vanished. Whatever was happening right here and now was far more pressing than any damage Terry's sexual preference might have on *Within Our Reach.* He spent a fortune on the best spin doctors in the business. Maybe they could finally earn their keep with a challenge of this magnitude.

Terry shoved his hands in his pockets and turned away from them. It was several minutes before he finally spoke, describing a series of notes tucked in with his fan mail. The mild threats had been enough to shake him but not enough to scare him into going to the police. He'd gone to Callie instead.

"Dear God," Jason muttered, his fists clenching. "You deliberately dragged her into this?"

"You hired her. I just took advantage of the fact that she's playing a cop," Terry retorted.

"No wonder you were so eager for her to take the job," Neil said. "You wanted her to save your ass."

"Yours, too," Terry shot back. "You don't want the

truth about our relationship spread all over the tabloids any more than I do."

At that, both Callie and Jason looked at her mother, clearly wondering what Regina's reaction was going to be.

"Why is everyone staring at me?" she demanded. "I'm not blind. I've known all about Terry and Neil from the first day I met them. It's none of my business how they live their lives, as long as they're happy."

Neil leaned down and kissed her cheek. "Thank you."

Regina patted his hand. "There's nothing to thank me for."

"Oh, yes, there is," Neil said. "There are a whole lot of people who wouldn't be so understanding."

"Well, we know of one, for sure," Jason said direly. "Let's concentrate on figuring out who that might be."

"I've racked my brain," Terry said.

"And I've asked questions," Callie offered. "Everyone connected to the show seems to adore Terry. I've dropped hints about his sexual preference, but no one has so much as blinked. If someone knows about him and Neil, I sure can't figure out who it could be or why they would want him to go public."

Jason considered what they'd all said. "You seem certain this has something to do with Terry and Neil. Why? Were the notes more specific than you mentioned?"

Terry stared at him. "No, but that has to be what they're talking about when they insist I tell all."

"Is this the only secret you have?"

"It's the only one that matters," Terry insisted.

"Maybe to you, but what about to someone else?"

Jason persisted. "Is there anything in your life, anything at all, that somebody in the cast might think you'd want kept quiet?"

Callie shook her head. "Jason, I think you're way off base here. It's obvious that somebody wants Terry to come out of the closet and admit he's gay. You know perfectly well that there are whole groups dedicated to making sure that public figures who are gay are exposed."

Jason kept his gaze pinned on Terry. Although Callie was expressing what Terry himself had said only moments before, he didn't look quite as certain as he had when the conversation had begun.

But it was Neil who finally spoke out. "Tell them, Terry. Tell them about your child."

20

"Damn," Terry muttered over and over, his face buried in his hands. He cast a betrayed look toward Neil. "How could you?"

Neil clasped his shoulder. "To save your neck," he said simply. "And Callie's."

Callie stared at her friend, openmouthed with astonishment. "Terry, is that true? Do you have a child?"

He nodded without meeting her gaze. When he finally lifted his head and faced them all, his expression was bleaker than she'd ever seen it. All traces of his usual exuberance and optimism were absent.

"It was a long time ago," he began, his gaze fixed on Neil as if for moral support from the one person in the room who obviously already knew the whole story and hadn't judged him.

"I was married my sophomore year of college," he explained, his tone flat. "I was just nineteen and trying to prove I was straight, I guess. It lasted all of six weeks before I realized the relationship was all wrong. I was cheating both of us, not just because of the sex stuff but because we were both ruining our chances of pursuing the careers we wanted.

"Hannah..." He paused and drew in a deep breath. "Hannah was upset, as I'm sure you can imagine. She ended up leaving Northwestern. I never saw her again. But not quite a year later I got a note telling me I was a father, nothing else. No request for child support. Nothing. I have no idea where they are. I don't even know if the baby was a boy or a girl. I suppose she thought it would be the ultimate revenge, telling me I had a baby but nothing more."

"How old would the child be now?" Jason asked.

Terry considered the question before answering. "Thirteen, I guess. Maybe fourteen. I don't even know the exact birth date, but it would be right around now."

"Old enough to be asking a lot of questions about his or her father," Callie's mother said, *tsk-tsking* in sympathy. "Poor child."

Callie was astounded at how well her mother was taking all of this. For someone who'd always seemed so rigid and unyielding in her beliefs, she was coping with everything with amazing open-mindedness. For the first time she wondered just how much of her mother's seemingly judgmental attitude could be attributed directly to her father's influence. Freed from that pressure, her innate compassion seemed to be flourishing.

"Is there any way someone connected to the show could have found out about all of this?" Jason asked.

"Not unless they know my ex," Terry said with absolute certainty. "I never discuss it. For obvious reasons, it's not exactly written up in my bio. I only told Neil so he would be prepared in case something exactly like this ever happened."

"Any ideas at all about where your ex-wife might be living now?" Callie asked.

"No. Like I said, we didn't exactly keep in touch. Her family was from just outside Chicago, but I don't think she went back there after the divorce. For some reason she blamed herself for not being woman enough for me. Nothing I said could make her see that my choice wasn't about her at all. It was about who I was."

"Where was she when she sent the note?" Callie asked.

"I don't remember," Terry said.

"You didn't save the note?" she asked.

"For what? To torment myself?"

"Maybe so you could track down your child," Callie retorted more sharply than she intended. "Didn't you care about that baby at all?"

Terry looked hurt that she'd even asked such a question. "I cared enough to stay away," he said softly. "That was all I had to offer."

"But you're a wonderful man," Callie protested. "Any child would be lucky to have you for a father."

"Very few people would have thought that thirteen or fourteen years ago," Neil reminded her.

"Look, it's too late to change the past, but think, man," Jason ordered. "Surely you at least glanced at the envelope. You must have wondered where they were. Try to picture that envelope."

Terry looked doubtful, but he dutifully closed his eyes as if trying to dredge up the image or maybe just some long-forgotten memory. Suddenly his expression brightened. "Wait, I do remember. It was Wisconsin. I remember thinking that at least they were close enough to visit her family, so they wouldn't be so terribly alone."

Jason still wasn't satisfied. "Milwaukee? Madison? Green Bay? Racine?"

"Madison," Terry said readily. "It had to be."

"Why?" Callie asked.

"Because my ex planned to teach college history. The University of Wisconsin is in Madison. She was too ambitious to pick anyplace smaller than another Big Ten School."

Callie stood up and hugged him. "There, you see. We have a lead. First thing tomorrow we'll start trying to track her down."

"No," Terry said sharply, his tone startling them all. "I won't let you do it."

"But, Terry, that could be the answer to everything," Callie said. "We have to check it out."

"I won't disrupt their lives."

"But they could be disrupting yours," Jason reminded him. "And maybe Callie's, as well. It's gone beyond a few innocuous little notes now. That mess upstairs is serious."

"I'll hire someone to watch out for Callie," Terry said stubbornly. "I'm not worried about myself."

"Well, I am," Neil shot back. He looked at Jason. "Do whatever you think is best to get to the bottom of this," he said, overruling Terry's objections.

Jason nodded. He turned a grim look on Callie that instantly started warning flags waving.

"As of this moment," he said, "you are out of the off-screen investigating business, is that clear?"

She glowered right back at him. "I beg your pardon? Who put you in charge of my life?"

His lips curved into a wry smile she knew all too well. It was his power-trip smile. Something told her she wasn't going to like his answer one bit.

"You did," he reminded her. "Read your contract."

She tried very hard not to let him see how shaken she was by the reply. "I'll call my lawyer. Contracts were made to be broken," she said with far more confidence than she was feeling.

"Not this one, sweetheart," he said just as confidently. "I am very good at what I do, and I made very sure that you and I would be joined at the hip for one solid year with options."

She deliberately surveyed him from head to toe, lingering pointedly on the area below his waist. "So that explains it," she said sarcastically as she headed for the door. "And here I thought our relationship was based on mutual desire."

She fled quickly, but Jason caught her halfway up the stairs. He spun her around to face him. She had never seen him quite so angry. That made them pretty much even. She was livid.

"You know that wasn't what I meant," he bit out furiously, his hands locked on her shoulders.

She smacked his hands away. "And how do I know that? For all I know there's some clause indicating that you're just one of the perks in my deal. Just a little sex to keep the starlet contented and in line. Tell me, Mr. Kane, do you provide the same service for all your actresses?"

"Dammit, you know better," he repeated.

"No, I don't," she said softly but emphatically. After giving him one last regretful look, she turned away and started up the steps.

Only when she was inside her trashed apartment, huddled against the remains of her upturned sofa did she allow herself to cry. Her emotions by then were in such a tangle, she couldn't even have sworn with absolute accuracy what her tears were for.

That was how her mother found her a few minutes later, sobbing as though her heart were broken, which perhaps it was.

"Oh, baby, don't cry," Regina whispered, taking Callie into her arms. "We'll have this place back in order in no time."

"And my life?" Callie inquired with a sniff.

"You listen to what that nice young man has to say. He'll take care of you."

Another conquest for Jason, Callie thought bitterly. "I don't want anybody to take care of me," she snapped instinctively. "I can take care of myself."

"Never hurts to have a strong man like that on your side, though, does it? He's only worried that something might happen to you. You can't blame him for that. He cares about you."

"But he's just taken over, as if I didn't have a brain in my head."

"Maybe it's not your brain he's worried about. It's your soft heart. Trying to protect Terry could land you in more trouble than you know how to cope with, that's all Jason is saying."

"Funny, I thought I heard him saying I was incompetent to make rational decisions," Callie said.

Her mother grinned at her. "You always were quick to jump to wrong conclusions when your pride was at stake."

She brushed the tears from Callie's cheeks as she hadn't since Callie was a child. The gesture was oddly comforting.

"You know what I see when I look at Jason Kane?" she asked.

Curiosity won out over the desire to make some smart remark. "What?" Callie asked.

"A man with stars in his eyes."

Despite herself, Callie grinned. "I could have sworn those were macho sparks of anger."

Her mother shrugged. "With some men it's pretty much the same thing." She scanned Callie's face. "You love him, don't you?"

"I don't know what I feel," Callie claimed, reluctant to admit what seemed obvious to her mother.

"Well, you don't have to figure everything out tonight. Come on, now."

"Where?"

"Back downstairs. Terry and Neil insist we stay in their guest room tonight. Jason had other ideas, but he gave in eventually."

Callie found the concept of Jason relenting under pressure fascinating. "He gave in?"

"He did. Actually, though, I believe we can expect to find him sleeping on the sofa. He doesn't seem inclined to let you too far out of his sight."

An image of the contortions necessary to fit Jason's

body on one of Neil and Terry's dainty matching love seats cheered Callie considerably. There was something to be said for his protectiveness, as well. When she wasn't so busy being huffy, she could actually admit that she found it rather sweet.

She glanced at her mother closely. "How come you came up here to talk to me instead of Jason?"

"He seemed worried that you would break the few remaining dishes by throwing them at him."

Callie chuckled. "I never much liked that fancy pattern, anyway. It was Chad's idea."

Back downstairs, Jason wasn't even pretending to be asleep when they returned. He looked from Regina to Callie and back again.

"Everything okay?"

"Just peachy," Callie assured him. She gestured toward the cramped love seat. "Sleep well."

"You have a vengeful streak that worries me," he muttered, but that familiar sparkle was back in his eyes when he said it.

Callie viewed that twinkle with new insight, given her mother's analysis of Jason's state of mind. She paused long enough to caress his cheek as she passed.

"Thank you."

He regarded her suspiciously. "For?"

"Caring."

He promptly looked as if he wanted to deny it, but Callie didn't give him a chance. She sashayed on past and headed for the guest room, making sure he'd have an image that would keep him awake the rest of the night.

Maybe he was right about that vindictive streak, she

decided with a slight smile as she closed the bedroom door firmly behind her. There really was nothing quite like sweet revenge.

Callie was awake at daybreak. Judging from the whisper of sound she heard coming from the living room so was Jason.

She pulled on her wrinkled clothes from the day before and went out to join him, leaving her mother sound asleep in the room's other twin bed.

She found Jason pacing the room, each long stride revealing his impatience and his anxiety. He was barking orders into his cell phone. A steaming mug of coffee sat untouched on the coffee table. Since no one else appeared to be up, Jason had clearly had a busy morning.

Callie found the freshly brewed pot of coffee in the kitchen and poured herself a cup. Judging from its pitch-black color, it was strong enough to wake the dead. She added a hefty splash of cream to weaken the effect on her already jangled nerves.

When she crossed Jason's path again, he snagged her hand and tugged her close without so much as a hesitation in his conversation.

"You'll get on it right away, then?" he said. "I need answers and I need them in a hurry. I'll double your fee if you get 'em for me by the end of the day."

He chuckled at something said on the other end of the line. "Okay, I'll triple it for the impossible and double it if you come up with something by tomorrow morning. Thanks. I owe you. Again."

He clicked off the phone and turned his full attention to Callie. Using the arm he'd pinned around her waist, he curled her into his body. His gaze searched her face intently.

"Did you get any sleep at all?" he muttered, stroking a thumb across the delicate skin beneath her eyes.

Callie trembled despite her determination to make him pay for the control he'd tried to exert over her life. "Did you?" she inquired sweetly.

"Yes," he said, clearly enjoying her disappointment. "But no thanks to you."

She accepted the concession as the most she was likely to get. "Who was that on the phone?"

"A friend of mine."

"He must be a very good friend for you to be calling him at this hour. It's barely 6:00 a.m."

"Five in Chicago," he pointed out. "And it wasn't a he, it was a she. Dana Miller, the best private investigator in the Midwest. She'll be on her way to Madison in a half hour, as soon as she's gone through the Chicago area phone books to see if there's a listing for Terry's ex's family."

"How do you happen to know the best P.I. in the Midwest?" Callie asked with what she hoped sounded more like innocent curiosity than jealousy.

"You'd be amazed at the friends I have," he retorted. "Jealous?"

"I'm not sure," she admitted. "Is she gorgeous?"

"Yes."

"Did you ever have an affair with her?"

"No comment."

A decidedly jealous flutter began in the pit of her stomach. "Are you still seeing her?"

"On occasion."

"Oh."

"I'm godfather to her oldest son."

Callie felt better at once. "I probably shouldn't be relieved to think of you guiding the moral values of a child, but I am."

Jason chuckled. "His father's a better influence in that area than I am. He's a minister. I take care of supplying the computer games. The kid's a genius."

He said it with such genuine pride that Callie could see more clearly than ever what a wonderful father Jason was going to make someday. She felt that odd little tug in the region of her heart once more. The last of her irritation with him from the night before vanished for the time being.

"I called Henry earlier," he told her then. "His wife and her sister will be here at eight to help with the cleanup."

Callie was startled. "Henry has a wife?"

"Sure he does. It's the only thing that keeps him from meddling in my life."

"How much did you have to do with getting him married off?" she asked suspiciously.

"It was self-defense," he insisted, looking embarrassed. "Not matchmaking."

"No wonder the man seems inclined to return the favor."

He silenced her with a quick brush of his lips across hers. "Do you really want to waste this time we have to ourselves talking about Henry?" he asked.

Callie pretended to give the matter some thought, then shook her head. "No, I can think of far more interesting things to do."

He gave a nod of smug satisfaction, but before he could claim her mouth with another kiss, Callie backed away. "Let's go over the cast list for *Within Our Reach.*"

He stared at her. "Why would we want to do that?"

"Because you may know more about these people than I do. I still don't think these notes have anything to do with Terry's kid. I'm more convinced than ever that someone on the show is responsible."

"You've already said everyone seems to like Terry."

"Maybe someone likes him too much," she suggested.

"Meaning?"

"Maybe we have someone else in the cast who's gay." At Jason's snort of disbelief, Callie said, "No, I mean it. I was assuming maybe one of the women resented him for rejecting them, but maybe that's not it at all. Maybe it's one of the guys who's after his body."

"Don't you think threatening him would be an odd way of courting by anybody's standards?"

"True enough. Okay, maybe they just resent his success as a hunk and figure he ought to pay for passing as a straight guy."

"That sounds slightly more plausible, but I think Dana is going to find our answers in Madison."

"Would it kill you to go over this cast list in the meantime?"

"Do you have a copy here?"

"In my makeup bag," she said, grabbing it from the chair where she'd tossed it the night before. "I go over it before my mall appearances so I can remember people by their real names and their soap personas."

Jason eyed the sheet with resignation. "Let's do it,

but I think we're wasting time. I can't think of a male on the show whose sexual preference has ever been questioned."

"Terry's hasn't been, either," she reminded him. "In fact, America thinks he's as macho as they come."

"Touché."

Callie read off the names one by one, as much to trigger her own instinctive impressions of the men as to get Jason's insights. There were fourteen contract men and a handful more with recurring status. A review of all of them didn't turn up a single clue, not so much as a whiff of suspicion. The two Callie knew most about—Jonathan Baines and Randall Trent—were clearly heterosexual. Baines had the alimony payments to prove it and Trent had a wife and Lisa.

"Don't be discouraged," Jason consoled her. "There's also the crew to think about. They have access to his dressing room and fan mail, too."

Despite Jason's attempt to comfort her, Callie felt as if she'd failed Terry. Worse, it appeared that the stakes were getting higher by the minute.

21

The cleanup of Callie's apartment took all day Sunday, despite the help of those nice women Jason had hired. Regina was exhausted and emotionally drained not only by the hard work but from thinking about those intruders going through all of Callie's lovely things and destroying them. She'd like to get her hands on them for a few minutes and teach them a few lessons about respect for other people's possessions. Obviously their parents had failed at the task.

Although everything was pretty much back in order by Monday morning, Regina found she was too jittery to sit around the apartment all by herself and worry over whether there was likely to be a return visit.

At least that was the excuse she came up with when she found herself in a taxi heading toward Soho. She swore she was only going for a little outing to distract herself. She'd spend a few minutes looking in gallery windows, maybe stop for a cup of fancy cappuccino. She intended to be back home in no time.

But even as she made that vow to herself, she found herself turning in a once-familiar direction the minute she set foot outside the taxi. A lot had changed in the area, but she couldn't help the vague stirring of excitement in the pit of her stomach as she checked the addresses closely. It ought to be right along in here, she thought, walking a little faster. An oddly familiar flutter of anticipation began to build inside her.

Suddenly she came to a stop, her heart pounding so loud she was sure the passersby must be able to hear it. It hadn't changed at all, she thought with a sense of astonishment. The seven in the address was still a little crooked on the faded blue door. The zero had fallen away years ago. At the time the paint on the door had been darker beneath where the number had been, but the years had washed away the difference in color. Only the eight was firmly tacked into place.

Mikel Rolanski's School of Art had been elegantly lettered above the number. It, too, looked sadly neglected. Why an artist as gifted as Mikel hadn't spruced up the front of his building was beyond her, but that had always been his way. He'd cared nothing for appearances, nor much more about making money. His art had been everything. His and his students'.

Regina sighed. She had once been considered one of his best.

Suddenly she wasn't so sure that what she was about to do was a good idea. What if she'd changed so much that he didn't even recognize her? What if he was disappointed in her when he discovered that she hadn't even held a paintbrush in all these years? At one time Mikel's approval had meant everything to her. In some tiny, almost forgotten part of her heart, it obviously still did.

She glanced at her reflection in a narrow window

beside the door and saw the toll the years had taken, the lines on her face, the tiredness beneath her eyes. Perhaps, though, time had been no kinder to Mikel, she consoled herself. Few escaped its ravages forever.

But even acknowledging that, she couldn't bring herself to take the last few steps that would carry her back into his life. Some things could never be recaptured. To try would only lead to disappointment.

Filled with uncertainty, she stood frozen to the spot until, suddenly, the decision was taken out of her hands. The door flew open and Mikel was there, his disbelieving gaze locked on hers.

"Gina?" he whispered, scanning her face intently. "My God, it is you, isn't it? I saw from inside and couldn't believe my eyes."

Her heart thundered at the sound of his deep, almost raspy voice. Her senses spun as giddily as they had as a girl.

"Yes, Mikel. It is I."

He reached out his hand as if he still couldn't quite believe her presence was real. When his fingers brushed the curve of her cheek so, so gently, she trembled…just as she once had at caresses far more intimate. Memories came flooding back—sweet, sweet memories, long buried, where they could not torment her for the choices she had made.

His sensual lips curved into a wistful smile then, as if responding to his own memories. "You are here to take a lesson, perhaps?" he asked, as if she'd only been gone since yesterday or the day before.

"I…I don't know," she said honestly.

"You are here because you must be," he said more

briskly, planting his big hand squarely in the middle of her back and pushing her toward the door, taking charge as always.

Just inside he hesitated, looking down into her eyes. "I always knew one day you would return, my Gina. I *knew*."

If only she had always been so certain, she thought as he swept her inside with such eagerness, such confidence, perhaps then her life would have been more bearable.

Upstairs in the huge loft with its perfect artist's lighting cascading through the high northern windows, a dozen sensations assailed Regina all at once, carrying her back so many years—the smell of the paints, the vibrant splashes of color, the soft Hungarian music that always played in the background, the dust motes swirling in sunlight.

"It hasn't changed," she said in wonder, drawing one of Mikel's once-familiar and very dear smiles.

"And I?" he asked. "Have I changed?"

His thick black hair shone with threads of silver now. His craggy, self-described peasant's face was a bit more lined. His massive shoulders were slightly stooped. But his eyes, those wonderfully soulful black-as-midnight eyes, sparkled with the light and eagerness of a much younger man.

"You are the same," she vowed. "Just as I remembered."

He grabbed a palette and dabbed it with an array of colors, then pushed her toward an easel on which a blank white canvas waited. He pressed a brush into her hand and ordered, "Paint for me. Paint what you see when you look at me."

From anyone else, it might have been an egotistical request, but Regina understood exactly what he wanted from her, what he needed.

But too much time had passed. She feared she could not give it to him, could not express on canvas the passion and the excitement she had once felt in his arms. The colors and images had flowed back then. Now her arthritic fingers ached just trying to clasp the brush that had once felt like a natural extension of her soul.

Tears filled her eyes as she looked at him. "I can't. It's been too long."

Shock spread across his face. "You have not painted in all these years?"

She shook her head, filled with regret.

"But it was your life."

Her art and him, she thought with silent dismay. She had given them both up to marry a man her family thought solid and dependable, Callie's father. Jacob had dismissed her art as nonsense and thrown her paints away. She had come as close to leaving him then as she ever had, but in the end she had stayed. For her daughters.

Mikel tenderly brushed the dampness from her cheeks. "Then we will begin again, you and I. From the beginning."

A sigh shuddered through her at his words. Could it possibly be so simple? "From the beginning," she echoed, suddenly filled with hope for the first time in a very long time.

* * *

Jason was so distracted, they could have stolen the entire network out from under him and he would have barely noticed. He'd waited all day Sunday and most of Monday for some word from Dana. His private line and his cell phone had remained ominously silent.

It required every bit of restraint he possessed to keep from racing over to the studio where he could personally keep an eye on Callie, but he knew Terry would protect her with his life. Hopefully such a dramatic gesture would never be called for.

He didn't know what to make of these threats and the break-in at Callie's. Dana, who had far more experience with such things, hadn't seemed overly alarmed, but she had agreed they couldn't just wait to see what developed. She'd felt the need was urgent enough that she'd disrupted her precious time with her family to go charging off to Wisconsin.

He'd exaggerated only slightly when he'd told Callie that Dana was the best P.I. in the Midwest. She'd actually been out of the business for a few years now, content to be the wife of a parish minister and mother of three brilliant sons, of whom his six-year-old godson was the oldest.

He sat scowling at his phone, willing it to ring. When it didn't, he snatched it up and punched in Dana's home number. Ken Miller answered on the first ring. He didn't sound overjoyed to hear Jason on the other end of the line.

"Couldn't you have just asked Dana for a referral?" he grumbled, then shouted something to a squalling child in the background.

"You're just mad because you got stuck with baby-sitting," Jason charged, amused despite himself at the image of this gentle, distracted man coping with the chaos of the children.

"And you don't think I'm justified? You fly out here and try it for a few days," Ken said wearily. "Running the Eighty-second Airborne would be less stressful."

Jason chuckled. "Just think how much more you'll appreciate your wife when she returns."

"If she returns," he said disconsolately. "Now that she has a taste of the hunt again, I'm afraid her retirement may be over. If it is, I will personally strangle you."

"Now is that any kind of threat for a minister to make," Jason chided.

"Would it be more suitable if I damned your soul to eternal hell?"

"Don't go throwing your professional weight around, padre. Have you heard from your wife, by any chance?"

"Not since last night, when she gave me my orders for the day. Do you know how much carpooling is required for three children, even at this age?"

"You'll get no sympathy from me," Jason taunted. "You stole the best woman in the world right out of my grasp, remember?"

"I did, didn't I?" Ken said, sounding vastly pleased with himself. "I suppose I can afford to be more generous toward you, then. Dana said if you called to give you her cell phone number. She said she'd forgotten to give it to you yesterday."

He rattled off the numbers, then asked, "You haven't got her involved in something dangerous, have you?"

Jason heard the genuine worry in his voice. "No, I promise," he reassured him. "She's just tracing a missing person for me."

The answer was sketchy but true enough. The danger, if there was any, was in New York.

Callie was jumping at shadows. Given the fact that Terry was not more than a step or two away at any given instant, there were a lot of shadows. He was making a nuisance of himself, probably at Jason's behest.

"Will you go away?" she pleaded eventually.

"No can do," he said. "I promised."

"I don't think Jason meant for you to follow me into the ladies' room," she said, standing outside the door.

Terry looked up as if he hadn't realized where she was heading. He shrugged at the sign on the door. "Sorry. I'll wait right here."

Callie shook her head. "Whatever," she muttered as she went inside.

"Oh, Callie, I'm so glad I ran into you," the ever-perky Jenny said when she spotted her. "I need to talk to you about another publicity event. These others have gone so well that everyone's clamoring for more. Marty and Katrina said we should go for it."

Callie resigned herself to hearing the entire pitch right in the middle of the restroom. "What now?"

"A charity softball game in Central Park," Jenny said. "Isn't that cool?"

"Cool," Callie agreed without enthusiasm. "I don't suppose it matters that I do not play softball."

"You didn't bowl, either, and look how well that went," Jenny reminded her. "So I can go ahead and make the arrangements? You'll put a team from the show together? It's really short notice, actually. The game was already scheduled when I approached them with the idea of us having a team."

"How short is short?"

"Two weeks from Saturday."

Callie stared at her, uncomprehending. "I'm supposed to put together a team from *Within Our Reach* and I'm supposed to do it in two weeks?"

"I know it won't be a problem. Everyone loves to do this stuff. Be sure to get Terry, though. The fans want to see the two of you together. You're hot. I'm predicting a *Soap Opera Digest* award for hottest couple, I swear it."

Apparently that was something Jenny and Jason agreed on. They both mentioned it often enough. "I can't wait," Callie retorted drily. She was also willing to bet that if the truth about Terry came out, that award nomination would vanish like a puff of smoke. She wondered what this mysterious "everyone" would think then.

"He will do it, won't he?" Jenny persisted.

The girl was indefatigable when it came to selling the show and its stars. "Ask him yourself," Callie suggested. "He's right outside."

"But you're in charge of the team."

"I think he'll respond more favorably if the suggestion comes from you," Callie told her. Hopefully the flattery would get the perky media flack out of the restroom before Callie's bladder burst.

Sure enough, Jenny scurried out, intent on signing Terry up for the event.

When Callie finally emerged, Terry had a scowl on his face. "What did you tell that little whirlwind?"

"That you'd be susceptible to her charms," Callie said blithely. "Did you agree to play?"

"I had to," he said without enthusiasm. "To paraphrase a friend of yours, you and I are joined at the hip until this whole mess is straightened out."

"Why did that sound a whole lot more promising when Jason said it?" she asked.

"Because you two are in mutual lust. Though, as I recall, at the time he said it, you didn't take it so well. In fact, you got downright irritable."

Callie linked her arm through his. "Never mind Jason. The public thinks you and I have the hots for each other. Let's go get undressed."

He grinned at her. "For a shy little girl from Iowa, you sure have adapted well to playing these seminude scenes of ours. Does your mama know she raised an exhibitionist?"

Callie shuddered. "God, I hope not. She keeps surprising me with her fairly liberated reactions, but my exhibitionism might be a little too much for her to take. I'm still a little rattled by it myself."

"And sister dearest?"

Callie hadn't spoken to Eunice since their visit in Iowa City. "I think she has more important things on her mind these days than whether I'm keeping my clothes on."

Her expression suddenly turned serious. "Terry, have you ever gotten weird vibes from any of the men on the set when we've been doing our scenes?"

"Such as?"

"That one of them was overly fascinated by you showing a little skin?"

He stared at her blankly. "You mean do I think one of them is gay?"

"Exactly."

"Sorry. My radar's not that finely tuned."

"Maybe it should be."

He scowled. "Terrific. Could you make me any more self-conscious. Isn't it bad enough that I'm supposed to be making love on-screen to my best friend, who doesn't stir so much as a twinge of excitement in me?"

"Not even a twinge?" Callie teased.

"Callie!" he protested. "Does every male in the universe have to swoon at your feet for you to be happy?"

"We can blame Chad and the bimbo for that," she said. "So how about it? Maybe a little twinge?"

He shook his head. "Okay, maybe once," he conceded for her ego's sake, "but let's get serious here. I really do not want to think that someone on the set is lusting for me when we shoot those scenes, any more than you do."

"We already know the women are hot for your body and jealous as sin of me. That doesn't seem to bother you."

"I can't explain why your suggestion makes me crazy. It just does."

"Well, forget all about your squeamishness and pay attention because I think that's what's going on here." She paused thoughtfully. "Have any of those magazines ever outed anybody from the show?"

"How would I know?"

"You don't read them?"

"Have you ever seen one around my apartment? I

read the *New York Times,* the trades and *Architectural Digest.* When my face is on the cover, I read the soap magazines. That's it. Neil reads business magazines, stacks of them."

"Okay, okay, you don't have to get huffy. I'm just trying to help."

"I thought the big shot had ordered you off the case."

She frowned at him. "Do you see him anywhere around here right now?"

"In other words, what he doesn't know won't hurt him?"

"Something like that."

"If your snooping gets you killed, I think he'll figure out what you've been up to. He won't be happy."

Callie shuddered, despite herself. "Neither will I."

22

There was something different about her mother. Callie spotted it the minute she walked into the apartment. It was more than the faint flush in her cheeks, more even than the very visible sparkle in her eyes. It was as if some terrible weight had been removed from her shoulders. She looked happy, Callie realized with a sense of shock. Happy and more self-confident.

"What did you do today?" she asked, hoping to discover what was behind her mother's intriguing transformation.

"Nothing much," Regina said, avoiding Callie's fascinated gaze. "And you? How did your day go? Did anything happen on the set?"

The quick change of subject left Callie feeling thoroughly frustrated. She knew from past experience that trying to turn the conversation back toward her mother would be next to fruitless. Maybe it was some self-effacing, maternal thing, but Regina Gunderson had always preferred to talk more about her daughters' lives than her own. That probably explained why Callie had never realized before the other night's inadvertent comment that her mother hadn't been especially happy on the farm.

Still, this one time Callie was determined she wouldn't be put off by the deliberate shift in topic. She wanted to discover what was behind this new outlook on life her mother seemed to have developed overnight.

"You didn't spend the whole day shut up inside, did you?" she asked.

"No, I got out for a bit. Wasn't it a lovely day?"

"From the few minutes I had outdoors, it seemed to be," Callie said, thinking of the way Jason had shuttled her into the limo that morning, into the studio and back into the limo that night as if he were certain some sharpshooter was hovering on a nearby rooftop. Henry had stood guard in a similarly alert manner. For the first time, she'd been almost certain that there was a gun beneath his jacket. She'd shivered at the realization that Henry's duties went beyond just driving the limo.

"Where did you go?" she asked, forcing herself to forget that moment of awareness and concentrate on her mother.

"Here and there," Regina said evasively, her cheeks pinker than ever. "Why don't we go for a walk now? The fresh air will do you good. You look a little peaked."

Callie sighed. Her mother was clearly determined not to reveal any more than she already had. "I would like nothing more than going for a walk with you, but Jason will be back any minute with dinner. The great outdoors seems to make him nervous at the moment."

Regina's expression grew troubled. "I hadn't thought of that."

"And you don't need to," Callie reassured her. "Jason is overreacting."

At a knock on the door, she flung it open, only to find herself facing a scowling Jason.

"You didn't even ask who it was," he accused, juggling several bags of groceries as he deliberately turned every single one of her locks to assure they were safe within the fortress.

"No one knocks as imperiously as you do," she explained. "Besides, I looked through the peephole."

He glanced toward her mother, clearly for confirmation. Regina, bless her loyal heart, nodded dutifully.

"She did."

"Well, I should hope so. This isn't a game, you know."

"Actually, I don't know that," Callie informed him, following him into the kitchen, where he began unloading supplies for some complicated Thai dish he claimed he'd been wanting to fix for ages. She wondered idly when he'd had time to learn all of these culinary masterpieces, how often he prepared them and for whom.

"And you don't know any more about whether this is a game than I do," she pointed out.

"What's it going to take to convince you, a knife in your back?"

"How delightfully reassuring of you to mention the possibility," she retorted, glad that her mother hadn't followed them into the kitchen. Jason's remark would have set off panic.

He carefully placed some exotic-looking ingredient on the table and reached for Callie's shoulders, dragging her to stand within inches of him. "I...am...not...

trying…to…be…reassuring," he explained very slowly and patiently. "I am trying to keep you alive."

Callie shuddered despite her best attempt to maintain an air of bravado. "Oh, please," she said, pulling away. "Stop exaggerating. Nobody is going to get killed."

"When did you become an expert on the psychotic mind?"

"About the same time I became an actress," she retorted. "*Within Our Reach* had a character who was one very sick puppy for months last year. I watched all the episodes."

"Well, as much faith as I have that the writers did their homework, I'd prefer it if you thought of yourself as an amateur and played it safe."

"Why? Has the network made too big an investment in my continued well-being?"

He seemed to be gritting his teeth at that. "If you don't know better than that," he said eventually, "then you're not nearly as bright as I credited you with being."

She stared into his blazing eyes and saw the turbulent emotions he was fighting to keep in check. "Oh," she said softly.

He grinned. "Yes, 'oh' sums it up very nicely." He turned his attention back to dinner. "By the way, what has your mother looking so chipper tonight?"

"I wish I knew."

"Don't tell me she's keeping secrets, too."

"Afraid so."

"Well, with any luck at all, at least hers won't be potentially lethal."

For the first time in her life, when it came to her mother, Callie realized that she was totally at a loss.

The rigid, predictable woman she'd known back in Iowa seemed to have metamorphosed into someone else entirely.

"Who knows?" she said a little wistfully. "I'm beginning to think I never really knew her at all."

Dana called while they were eating dinner. Judging from Callie's expression when she answered the phone, Jason decided it might be best if the two women never met. One look at the gorgeous P.I. and all of Callie's insecurities would come bubbling to the surface no matter what he did to reassure her. That ex-husband of hers had left her self-confidence in a shambles. If a million new fans couldn't combat that, how was he supposed to do it alone?

When he took the phone from her, he deliberately kept her hand clasped in his. "Hey, Dana, what's up?"

"Nothing, that's what," she said, sounding disgusted. "Your ex-Mrs. Walker has vanished into thin air."

"She isn't teaching at the University of Wisconsin?"

"Not for the past ten years," she told him. "The chairman of the history department has been around for a couple of decades, though. He remembers her. He says she just quit at the end of the school term one year and left town. He has no idea why she quit or where she went. He doesn't believe she ever asked for references."

"It's a dead end, then," he said.

"Maybe not. He gave me the names of a couple of her friends from back then. I'm trying to track them down to see if they stayed in touch with her. Unfortunately, one's on sabbatical at Oxford and the other's in the hospital recovering from surgery. I've got a phone number for the one in England, but with the time difference it's too late to call. The other woman should be feeling well enough to see me tomorrow, according to her son."

"I don't suppose the son remembers anything about Terry's ex."

"He says he vaguely remembers her coming by the house, but he was a teenager then and pretty self-absorbed. He doesn't recall anything about a kid."

Jason sighed. "I'll hear from you tomorrow, then."

"Unless I catch a break tonight tracking down her brother."

"Her brother? Terry didn't say anything about a brother."

"I figured you would have mentioned it if he had. I found out about him when I spoke to people in the family's old neighborhood outside of Chicago. I stopped there on the way to Madison. Her parents are both dead, but the neighbors say she has a brother in L.A. None of them had heard anything about Hannah in years."

"Any luck in locating this brother?"

"I've checked directory assistance and there are half a dozen listings that could be right," Dana told him. "I may be able to start reaching some of them about now. People should be getting home after the rush-hour, freeway demolition derby out there."

"If you have any luck, call me. I don't care what time it is. If I'm not at this number, try me at home or on my cell. Thanks, Dana. You're an angel."

She chuckled. "I'm married to a minister. What else could I be?"

"I remember a time—"

She cut him off. "Don't remind me. Those days are long gone. I'll talk to you soon."

He slowly replaced the receiver in its cradle. The silence in the room was almost palpable.

"Jason," Callie prodded eventually. "Any news?"

"Nothing solid," he admitted. "But we do have some leads." He glanced at Callie. "Terry didn't mention anything about having a brother-in-law, did he?"

She shook her head. "Not the other night. Why?"

"You'll see." He picked the phone back up and glanced at Callie. "Is his number on speed dial?"

"Yes. It's six."

He punched it in and waited. It was Neil who answered. Jason explained what Dana had discovered about Terry's ex-in-laws.

"Is he there? I want to ask him about this brother-in-law who's supposedly in L.A."

"I'll get him," Neil said.

Jason heard Neil explaining the latest news to Terry. When Terry picked up, he said at once, "I haven't even thought about Bryan in years. He was just a kid when Hannah and I were married."

"I don't suppose he ever expressed an interest in show business."

"Why would you ask that?"

"Just a hunch. It is one of the main reasons people go to Los Angeles."

"Sorry," Terry said. "I don't remember. After the wedding I doubt if I saw Bryan more than once or twice for some holiday meal or other we couldn't avoid. Hannah saw him more often than that."

"When you did see him, he didn't plague you with questions about getting into show business?"

"No, not that I recall, but I was just doing some dinner theater stuff then, mostly amateur. I doubt he would have been impressed. You know, though..." He hesitated.

"What?" Jason asked.

"I seem to remember him asking me one time if I'd do an interview for his school paper. Everyone thought his asking was so cute and grown-up. I think I told him I would, but it never came up again."

"So he might have been interested in journalism," Jason said thoughtfully, suddenly wondering if he might be a reporter after a scoop on a major TV celebrity. That would be motive enough for someone to encourage Terry to tell all. And who better to tell than an ex-brother-in-law, who might paint him in a more sympathetic light.

"Maybe," Terry said, sounding doubtful. "But again, he was just a kid, no more than twelve, I'd say. He could have changed his mind a dozen times before he grew up. Why is he so important, anyway? I thought we were looking for Hannah."

"We are, but you never know what might turn up along the way. He might be easier to catch up with and he might know where Hannah is."

"I suppose so," Terry said. "They were pretty tight once."

Knowing that, Jason felt slightly better about the flimsy lead. "Thanks, Terry. I'll keep you posted if we learn anything."

By the time Jason got off the phone, Callie and her

mother had cleared the table and done the dishes. Regina had retreated to her room.

"We're all alone?" he inquired, sinking onto the sofa and pulling Callie down into his lap.

"Pretty much," she agreed.

"How shall we spend the time?"

She grinned at him. "Not the way you clearly have in mind. I have lines to learn between now and tomorrow."

"A love scene by any chance?"

"As a matter of fact, yes."

"How many lines can there be?" he asked drily, thinking of the significant close-ups that usually took the place of dialogue in such scenes. "Get your script. I'll help you rehearse."

He regarded her intently. "Of course, if Terry puts his hands anyplace near where I intend to put mine, I'll have to cut them off at the wrist."

"It's called acting," Callie reminded him. "And we're talking about Terry. He doesn't put his hands on me anyplace the director doesn't tell him to."

"How reassuring."

She wriggled deliberately, setting his senses aflame. "It wouldn't be if you knew how seductive Paul Locklear wanted these scenes to be," she said.

"If you're trying to provoke me, it's working. Maybe I'd better have a chat with the director tomorrow, too."

"Not if you want those ratings to soar," Callie reminded him a little too cheerfully. "Besides, you don't have a thing to worry about. When Terry's making mad, passionate love to me, I promise to pretend it's you."

"Is that supposed to thrill me?" he grumbled.

"No, it's supposed to console you. A very famous

network president once told me that this business is all about thrilling the viewers."

"The man must be a fool," he murmured, sliding his hands under her blouse until he found satin-soft, warm flesh. "The real thrills are real life."

"Aren't they ever," Callie agreed with a sigh.

23

The next morning Callie found Hank Parker sitting in her dressing room contentedly sipping coffee, munching on a powdered doughnut and looking like the proverbial cat that swallowed the canary. Or in his case, like a man who'd very recently had fireworks-caliber sex.

She paused beside him to wipe a smudge of powdered sugar from his upper lip. She didn't bother trying to erase the streak of lipstick from his cheek. She didn't want to get her hand smacked. He probably considered it a souvenir.

"Let me guess," she said. "You and Lisa got together."

"All thanks to you," he said, looking disgustingly besotted.

She wasn't at all sure gratitude was in order. To make that point as gently as possible, she said, "Good luck."

His gaze narrowed. "What's that supposed to mean?"

"It means, my sweet, that holding on to her is not nearly the snap that getting her into bed might be."

"That's a pretty rotten thing to say," he said, puffing up with indignation on Lisa's behalf. A true gentleman.

"Sometimes the truth sucks," she agreed. "I just don't want you to get hurt. Why are you here, by the way, to gloat?"

"No, as a matter of fact, I am here to look after your sorry behind. The producers called me in and hired me full-time for a while."

Callie tried to think of something in the script that required Hank's professional coaching, especially on a daily basis. Unless his experience with Lisa had taught him a few new bedroom tricks, she couldn't think of any. That meant the phrase "protecting her sorry behind" had nothing to do with the show.

"Exactly what are you consulting on?" she asked, hoping she was wrong.

"I'm not consulting. I'm here to play bodyguard."

The confirmation set her teeth on edge. "Excuse me?" She wanted details before she started strangling people.

"They seem to think that there's trouble on the horizon for their fledgling superstar—off-screen, that is."

"And why would they think that?" she asked, her voice tight with barely suppressed and rapidly growing fury.

"Because a little birdie told them," he guessed.

Callie knew exactly which little birdie she had to thank for this. The one perched in the network president's penthouse office. "Okay, out of here. You're fired."

Hank didn't seem to be taking his firing seriously. He shrugged and remained firmly planted right where he was. "Sorry, sweet pea, no can do. You're not the one paying the bill."

But she certainly knew who was. She snatched up the phone on her dresser and punched in the number for the limo. With any luck it was caught in morning gridlock.

"Henry? Is your boss still in the back or have you already delivered him to his ivory tower?"

"He's still here, Miss Callie. Traffic's a bitch this morning. You want to talk to him?"

"Absolutely not," she said. "But would you please make a U-turn and haul his butt back over here?"

"Uh-oh, what'd he do now?"

"He hired a babysitter for me, one with a gun," she said, not even trying to hide her outrage.

Henry didn't have any more luck trying to stifle a chuckle, assuming he tried at all. He seemed to find their more volatile exchanges amusing. "We'll be right there, Miss Callie," he promised with the eagerness of a man looking forward to a barroom brawl. "Ten minutes, tops."

She was pretty sure she heard Jason asking what the hell was going on right before she hung up and headed for the street, Hank hard on her heels.

She whirled around and poked a finger in his very solid chest. "Stay," she ordered.

He grinned. "Personally, I would be happy to oblige you, but like I said, I have my instructions. You go nowhere without me."

She couldn't blame Hank for all of this and the last thing she wanted to do was get him into trouble with the producers or, knowing Jason, with the police commissioner himself. Some very high-level negotiations had probably gone on to free up Hank's time.

"Okay, but you wait at the door," she instructed. "You do not follow me to the limo."

He looked doubtful but finally conceded, "As long as you're in plain sight, I suppose that would work."

"Make it work," she muttered as she crossed the sidewalk to wait at the curb. As the limo cruised to a stop, she yanked open the back door and glared at Jason.

"Fire him," she demanded, pointing over her shoulder toward Hank, who was leaning against the studio wall, enjoying the scene a little too much. Between him and Henry, who'd rolled down his window to listen more attentively, she was definitely playing to an appreciative audience.

Jason followed the direction of her gesture and asked with a look of pure innocence, "Who's he?"

"He is the policeman who was consulting on the show. He is now the policeman who has been assigned to protect me."

Jason gave a nod of satisfaction. "Good."

"Good?" she repeated incredulously. "It is not good. It is lousy. If our perp—do you like that word? It's cop lingo. Hank over there taught it to me. If our perp discovers that I'm under guard, don't you think he's going to guess that I am very involved in this—whatever the hell this is—and decide I'm more of a danger than ever? You're turning me into the damned target instead of Terry."

"And just maybe the sight of a guard will scare him off," Jason countered. "I like my version better."

"Are you willing to take a chance that you're right and I'm not?"

Jason surveyed Hank from his well-developed shoulders to the tips of his boots. He seemed especially fond of the gun handle, barely visible inside Hank's denim jacket. "He looks as if he's ready for that possibility."

Callie groaned. Saints protect her from macho men! "Let's just hope his attention's on me and not on the little starlet he finds so fascinating," she snapped.

"It will be," Jason said grimly, exchanging a look with Hank that spoke volumes.

Clearly the two of them were communicating on some level that a mere woman couldn't possibly hope to comprehend or contradict. Callie gave up. She stepped back and spoke to Henry, who'd been blatantly eavesdropping, a grin on his face.

"Why don't you take Mr. Kane and drive him straight into the East River," she suggested pleasantly.

"I'll give it some thought," he promised. "Long as I can figure a way to do it that won't ruin the finish on the car."

"We'll discuss this later," Jason said to her. He was disgustingly unruffled by her indignation.

"Not with me, you won't," Callie said. "I'm going back inside to investigate my brains out, now that I have all this backup."

With that, she whirled and went into the studio, leaving three men staring after her. Hank caught up with her before she'd gone two feet down the corridor.

"Maybe you'd better fill me in on this investigation business," he said.

"Sorry, no can do," she said, mimicking his earlier comment. "You're just going to have to sit this one out. Maybe Lisa will keep you company."

As it turned out, though, Hank and Lisa stuck to her

like glue. The only person Callie got to speak to without the pair of them hovering over her was Terry, during their scenes in front of the camera.

"Why is that cop hanging around?" Terry whispered as they finished taping their first scene.

"Three guesses," Callie muttered, scowling in Hank's direction.

Terry's eyes widened with dismay. "He knows?"

Callie shook her head. "Of course not. Heaven forbid anyone would actually give him any useful information. He was just hired to protect me from evil forces."

"And who's going to protect him?" Terry wondered.

His gaze traveled to Lisa, who was nibbling on Hank's ear, causing the cop's complexion to turn beet-red when he realized they were being observed.

"He's been warned," Callie replied.

"A two-by-four between the eyes wouldn't be enough warning for a man under Lisa's spell," Terry predicted.

"Look, could you take your eyes off Hank and Lisa long enough to help me figure out who I ought to be questioning next? Who on the set knows the most gossip? Besides Lisa, I mean."

"That would be me, darling," Lindsay Gentry announced.

She had slipped up beside them so quietly, Callie hadn't heard a thing. Clearly that was a skill that aided in eavesdropping on the good stuff. Lindsay tucked her arm possessively through Terry's and regarded Callie smugly.

"What I don't know, I make up," she informed them. "It keeps the day from getting too, too boring."

Ever since the day Terry had openly chastised her for

trying to sabotage Callie's scenes, Lindsay had behaved with cool professionalism in Callie's presence. Callie doubted they would ever become bosom buddies, but at least the off-camera sniping and deliberate flubbing of lines on camera had stopped.

"I should have guessed you'd pride yourself on being well-informed," Callie told her, giving a charitable spin to the other woman's claim to knowing all the latest dirt on her costars. Lindsay looked as if she weren't too sure whether Callie had meant it as a compliment. Callie doubted she was astute enough to figure out it wasn't.

"People just love to tell me their little secrets," Lindsay confided. "Maybe it's because I play a psychologist so convincingly."

Or because she made it her business to snoop, Callie thought to herself. She cast a quick glance at Terry for some hint as to whether he had ever revealed any of his secrets to the soap's resident shrink. An "oh, please" expression indicated he had not.

Callie gave Lindsay her most congenial smile, the one she'd practiced on potential Wall Street clients she was trying to lure away from other brokerages. She called up the same flattering hogwash she'd used on Lisa.

"I wish I had your insights into the cast," she confided. "It would really help me to fit in faster around here. Do you know there are still people on the show I've never met in person because of the shooting schedule? I don't suppose you'd like to bring me up to speed."

Lindsay looked vaguely intrigued by the idea of becoming Callie's mentor. The concept clearly played to her ego, so much so that she never seemed to wonder why Terry hadn't already spilled the beans on his costars. Unlike Lisa, though, Lindsay was far too circumspect to start blurting out secrets in the middle of the set.

With a dismissive little wave at Terry, she latched on to Callie's arm and led her toward the dressing rooms. "Come with me, dear. You and I definitely have a lot to talk about."

Terry shot Callie a warning look. She guessed he wanted her to beware giving away more secrets than she gleaned. He had no idea how skilled she was at pumping people for information. That's why she'd been such a success on Wall Street. She'd known which questions to ask which people to stay one step ahead of the crowd without tumbling into some insider information scandal.

They were almost to the large dressing room Lindsay shared with two other actresses when a shot rang out. The sound sent Callie diving to the floor. Someone landed squarely on top of her, pinning her down. Judging from the weight, it was probably Hank. She'd forgotten how closely he was shadowing her.

When Callie finally realized that she was uninjured, except for any broken bones Hank might have caused when he tackled her, she opened her eyes to peek at the scene around them. The first thing she saw was Lindsay Gentry's stunned face staring down at her.

"What on earth?" the actress murmured. Her gaze went rather quickly from Callie to the hulking man on top of her. "My, my, my, who have we here?"

"Could we save the introductions?" Callie grumbled. "Hank, get up. You're squishing me. Don't you think you ought to try to figure out who fired that shot?"

"That would be Jonathan," Lindsay said matter-of-factly. "Why?"

Hank finally scrambled up and held out his hand to help Callie to her feet. "How would you know that, ma'am?"

Lindsay was still regarding him in a way that suggested she found all that brawn to be extremely provocative. "What?" she murmured distractedly, her gaze pinned to his chest, rather than the gun in his hand. It was a definite indication of her priorities.

"What makes you think this Jonathan person fired that shot?" Hank asked patiently.

"Because he's trying to kill the one witness who can connect him to Terry's late fiancée's death."

Callie groaned as she realized that the shot had been part of that day's script. Hank simply looked bemused by all this matter-of-fact talk about killing.

"On the show," Callie explained to him.

"Oh," he said, and shook his head. "Jeez, this Glen River Falls place is a blasted crime capital."

"So says a member of New York's finest," Callie retorted.

"You're a policeman?" Lindsay asked, looking as if she found the idea absolutely fascinating. "Do tell me more." Apparently she'd forgotten all about her intention to tell Callie all the latest gossip about the cast.

Fortunately, Lisa detected competition and came over to practically twine herself around Hank in a manner that left no doubt about whose man he was. To Callie's dismay, he didn't seem to mind in the least. Even some of the brightest men didn't always think with their brains. Not that this was news. Just look at Chad and the bimbo, a couple even more horrifying than Hank and Lisa, not that Callie was particularly biased on the subject.

At any rate, for the moment, Hank's fascination with Lisa permitted Callie to remind Lindsay Gentry that they'd been about to share a little girl talk. The actress cast one last look of regret in Hank's direction as she allowed Callie to propel her toward their original destination.

Seated before her dressing room mirror, Lindsay began removing her makeup while Callie sat raptly to her right observing the deft ritual.

"Tell me about some of the men in the cast," Callie suggested when she thought Lindsay was just distracted enough not to ascribe any ulterior motive to the question.

"Oh, darling, you don't want to get involved with an actor. They're so tedious. Everything is always about *me, me, me.*"

"I'm not looking for a date," Callie reassured her. "I just want to get to know them a little better."

"Then take them to lunch. One at a time, of course. Most of them can barely stand one another. Your treat, naturally, since they're all so tight they squeak." She lifted her gaze until her eyes met Callie's in the mirror. "Of course, you already know Terry quite well."

Callie could think of no reason to deny it. "He's been my neighbor for years now. He's gotten me through some rough patches in my life."

"He does seem to have an uncommon decent streak," Lindsay conceded. "Of course, that could get him into trouble. One of these days someone who's not so ethical is likely to blindside him."

Callie's breath came a little faster. This was exactly what she'd been hoping for. "Anyone in particular?"

"Darling, in this business just about everyone is capable of stabbing you in the back."

"You're very cynical."

"I'm very realistic," Lindsay corrected. "I've been around the block a few times. Nothing surprises me anymore."

"Why do you stay in the business if it makes you so unhappy?"

The actress smiled. "Who said I was unhappy? The important thing is to know your enemies. Once your backside is protected, you can relax and enjoy yourself. The adulation from all those people out in TV land is a real rush. You must have felt it at all those appearances you've been making."

Callie nodded. "But it's not real. It's not for me. It's for the character I play."

"That's close enough to satisfy me," Lindsay said. "I'll take applause wherever it comes. I've done some real stinkers off-Broadway just to hear people clap. Of course, there you get the boos and hisses firsthand, too."

Callie thought of the charity event for which she needed to rally a team. She hadn't done much about it. If Lindsay loved adulation so, perhaps she could be convinced to play. "I don't suppose you'd like to play softball in Central Park in a couple of weeks."

Lindsay stared at her as if Callie had just invited her to romp naked through the tulips. "Softball?"

There was a world of meaning in the way she said

that single word. Callie could relate to the incredulity and the disdain.

"I don't think so," Lindsay added.

"My reaction exactly," Callie told the other actress. "Unfortunately, they want a team from this show for a charity event. I have to pull it together. There will be scads of publicity, I'm told. Jenny Harding practically salivates when she talks about it."

Lindsay appeared to be weighing her ego against the thought of all that dust and physical activity. Her ego won. "When and where?" she said with a resigned sigh.

Callie filled her in. "Anyone else who'd be good?"

"Forget good. Go for the ones who'll actually show up. Who do you have so far?"

"You, me and Terry."

"My God, you are in a jam, aren't you?" Lindsay said. "Okay, then, ask Lisa and Jonathan, for sure. Randall Trent, I suppose. He hates to be left out, and it will do him good to see that Lisa has moved on to greener pastures, so to speak."

She suggested several others, including Paul Locklear, the show's frequent director. "He'll make a great captain, darling. You do know how he loves to order people around."

Callie considered the quiet, unflappable, low-key man with his balding head and slight paunch. He looked more suited to a slow-paced game of chess than anything requiring physical exertion.

"He doesn't exactly strike me as the baseball type," she said.

"Maybe not, but he'll come if you tell him Terry's playing. I can promise you that."

Callie swallowed hard and tried not to seem too eager when she asked, "Why is that?"

"Oh, darling, everyone in town knows Paul is gay. Haven't you seen how the camera hugs Terry's cute butt whenever Paul's directing?"

Callie hadn't noticed that. She'd been all too self-conscious thinking it was focused on her own butt. What was it someone had once said? Essentially that people wouldn't worry so much about people talking about them if they realized how seldom they did. Apparently the same general thing applied to camerawork.

24

"No, no, no, Gina. Like this," Mikel ordered. His large hand enveloped hers and directed her brush across the canvas in bold, sure strokes.

"No, not like that," Regina said, surprising herself as much as Mikel when she resisted. Her confidence must be coming back if she was willing to pit her own artistic instincts against Mikel's genius.

Or perhaps she just enjoyed seeing the flare of temper such defiance put into his dark eyes. They smoldered with suppressed passion, reminding her of days long ago when all too often paints and canvas and artistic differences had been forgotten in the heat of lovemaking. It had been a scandalous, incredible time in her life, one for which no amount of penance in Iowa could atone.

He grinned at her now, the deep creases in his face curving into laugh lines. "You plague me deliberately, do you not?"

"Perhaps," she admitted. "Just a little."

"Why is that, my Gina?"

"Because it is so easy," she said, smiling.

For too many years she had had to stifle such wicked impulses. There had been little teasing between her and the somber man she had married. Perhaps the fault had not been solely Jacob's. He had known from the beginning that she had agreed to marry him only to give her daughter her father's name.

Their affair had come in the aftermath of her fleeing New York and Mikel's apparent disinterest in marrying her. She had turned to Jacob, a man she had known all of her life, for comfort. Her parents had encouraged the relationship. It had been easy for comfort to become physical as well as emotional after a time. They had been careless, and the result was Callie and a marriage that should never have been, not when her heart belonged to someone else.

One small mistake. A mistake that had had so many tragic consequences for all of them, she thought sadly. Wasted years of her life. Heartache even for the daughters she had borne Jacob Gunderson. She could never regret her children, never, but the lost time with Mikel? Only now, aware of the vast difference between being alive and merely surviving, did she realize what a waste those years had been.

Everything in Iowa had been hard, from the weather to farming to surviving Jacob's constant criticism. By contrast, being with Mikel was astonishingly simple. It felt so right that it scared her to think she might never have found it again had it not been for Eunice's selfishness. More terrifying was the possibility that she could lose it all again.

"What is it?" Mikel asked gently, apparently reading her disturbing thoughts in her expression.

"I was just wondering how I ever survived staying away all these years," she admitted with surprising candor.

He smiled sadly at that. "I, too, have wondered how I survived losing you. Not a day has passed that I haven't regretted letting you go. I was a stubborn fool for not following and bringing you back. I was so sure I was right, but I found that being right is cold comfort on a lonely night."

He turned her to face him and plucked the brush from her hands. Then he touched her cheeks with his fingertips with astonishing tenderness.

"You will not go again," he said fiercely. "This time you will stay and marry me as it was meant to be."

Regina stared at him. "Marry you?" she whispered.

"Yes."

Her incredulous gaze swept his face. "You never asked before."

He sighed deeply. "Is that why you went running off to Iowa? Did you not know that marriage was our destiny?"

"How was I supposed to know that?" she asked irritably. "Was I supposed to read your mind?"

"I could read yours," he said.

It sounded like an accusation. Regina wanted to explain that she'd been able to read his heart but never his mind. Instead, she merely said, "You should have said what you were thinking."

"I understand that now," he said with wry humor. "Which is why I asked you to marry me not more than a minute ago. I still have no answer."

The thought of marrying this man who'd owned her

heart for most of her life both thrilled and terrified her. Could she do it at her age? Could she reach out and claim the happiness that had been stolen from her so long ago when she'd foolishly fled from an uncertain future?

Just thinking about Callie and Eunice's likely reactions was enough to make her cringe inside. Perhaps Callie was caught up enough in her own romance that she would see the wonder of what was happening to her mother, but Eunice? Eunice would probably try to have her locked away in some psychiatric ward.

She broke free of Mikel's embrace. "I will have to think about this," she said, meeting his hopeful gaze with regret.

Hurt darkened his eyes, but he nodded. "Do not wait too long, my love. We have lost far too much time already."

Regina set out on foot from Mikel's loft. It was a brilliant spring day with a soft, gentle breeze to catch the occasional fragrance of the gardens she passed. She needed the time to think, just as she had promised.

Oddly, something Jason had said to her the first night they met came back to her now. When she had dutifully recited Jacob's opinions about television, he had prodded, "What about you? What do you think?"

Perhaps all this worry over what Callie and Eunice might think was just as wrong. What she should be deciding was what she wanted after all this time.

And there was no mistake about that, she concluded. She wanted a life with Mikel for whatever time either of them had left. Her spirit soared just contemplating it. Her pulse raced as it hadn't in years. He was her destiny. He always had been. She had known it the instant she set eyes on him as a girl and felt her heart thunder wildly. Nothing had changed that, not even more than thirty years of separation.

She paused in front of a fancy department store window and studied her reflection, awestruck by the fact that a man like Mikel had proclaimed his love for her, had apparently found no replacement for her in all this time. She was no longer the young girl with the thick brown hair and unlined complexion he had taken under his wing when she first came to New York determined to discover if she had any talent as an artist.

She touched her fingers to the fine lines feathering out from the corners of her eyes. Hands trembling, she tugged a few wisps of graying hair free from the severe knot atop her head. The effect softened her face, but she still looked old, older than her years.

Suddenly she thought of the money Callie had been tucking into her purse like clockwork every week since she'd been in New York, payment for helping with the fan mail and more besides. And there was Terry's money, too. Other than what she'd spent on groceries and a few meals in neighborhood restaurants, she'd saved most of it. What if she took the rest and splurged on a complete makeover in some elegant salon? Did she dare? Was she crazy for thinking she could recapture her youth with a little hair dye and a facial?

And where would she go? She knew nothing of such things. Perhaps Neil would know. And he was discreet enough to keep her secret from Callie just a little longer. It was funny how fond she had become of him and Terry. It felt as if she'd known the two of them forever, and there were times when she thought she knew and understood them better than her own daughter.

Yes, she decided, if Neil would help her, she would do it. Anxious to make an appointment now that the decision had been made, she hailed a taxi. Back on the West Side, she practically raced up the stairs to Neil's apartment, praying that he had come home from work early for once.

She rapped on his door and waited. She was almost certain she heard voices coming from inside, so when he didn't answer at once, she knocked again.

"That's odd," she murmured, positive now that she heard someone speaking in the apartment. She decided that perhaps they had left the radio or TV on in the morning. Terry especially was always in a rush. Suddenly, though, the voices faded.

Images of the chaotic ruins intruders had made of Callie's apartment came back in a flood. "Oh, sweet heaven," she murmured, and hurried toward the stairs. The police. She had to call the police at once.

Heart racing, she had climbed half a flight when she finally heard the door to Neil and Terry's apartment open. Filled with dread, she peeked over the railing. Sure enough, the man she saw slipping out was a stranger. But there had been voices. More than one. She was sure of it.

She crept up the remaining steps to Callie's and slid the keys in the locks one by nerve-racking one. Inside, with the door securely bolted behind her, she grabbed the phone and dialed 9-1-1. She was too frantic to search for the names of the polite young policemen who'd come to investigate Callie's break-in. They'd left a card behind, but right now anyone would do.

But before the call had connected, a knock on her own door nearly had her jumping out of her skin.

"Regina! Are you in there? It's Neil."

Regina glanced at the phone in her hand, then quickly placed it back in the cradle. She rushed over to unlock the door.

"Neil, my goodness, you were home. I thought I heard someone, but when you didn't answer the door, I panicked. I was just about to call the police."

"I'm sorry. I came home from work with a migraine and went to bed, so it took me a few minutes to wake up when you knocked."

He sounded nervous. Regina thought of the man she'd seen slipping away and knew at once that he was lying. She thought of poor Terry, who probably had no idea he was being betrayed, and looked Neil straight in the eye until finally he sighed heavily.

"Okay, I didn't have a migraine," he admitted. "I had a friend over."

"Does Terry know about this friend?" she demanded protectively.

Neil winced at the condemning tone. "It's nothing like that, I swear it. But I knew what it would look like. That's why I didn't answer the door."

Regina continued to regard him skeptically. She might not be so worldly, but she knew there was more to the story than Neil was letting on.

"Why don't we sit down and have a cup of tea?" she suggested.

He looked as if he wanted desperately to refuse, but

he was too polite to do it. He followed her into the kitchen and paced while she put the kettle on and took out the fancy selection of herbal teas that Callie kept on hand.

"Why were you looking for me?" he asked eventually.

Regina had almost forgotten all about her plan to have a makeover. "There was something I was hoping you could help me with," she said. Maybe the change of subject would make Neil relax enough to finally open up and tell her what was so clearly troubling him.

"What?" he asked, looking relieved.

Regina blushed just thinking about it. "I was considering getting my hair done," she admitted. "Not just trimmed, you know, but a whole new look. Maybe even some color to get rid of the gray."

Neil grinned. "What a fantastic idea! You're a beautiful woman, you know. I always wondered why you'd let yourself look older than you need to."

"It never seemed important before now."

"Before now," he repeated, clearly speculating on the implications.

"Don't go making anything out of that, young man. It's just that being around Callie and the rest of you, you always look so nice, I thought maybe it was time I was more in style. Do you know someplace I could go, someplace that wouldn't go overboard? I don't want to look like an old lady pretending to be twenty again."

Neil surveyed her intently. "I know just the place. One of their top stylists is a friend. I'd be happy to make an appointment. I'll even take you myself."

"Oh, would you? I'm so afraid I'd make a complete fool of myself."

"Not a chance." He regarded her worriedly. "But why aren't you asking Callie about this? I'm sure she would love to help you."

Regina wasn't sure she had an adequate answer to that. Maybe she was afraid Callie would ask too many questions. She wasn't sure she was ready to explain about Mikel yet. She didn't want her daughters making judgments and ruining the happiness she'd found before she'd even had time to enjoy it.

"I wanted it to be a surprise," she said, praying Neil would accept the answer at face value. "I've saved up some of the money she's been giving me for groceries plus what Terry's been paying me, and I suddenly had this impulse to indulge myself."

Neil nodded, his expression understanding. "Well, I'm sure Callie would approve. I'll set it up for the first available opening. Frank might even be able to squeeze you in tomorrow. Is that okay? Are you free?"

"Absolutely," she said, already edgy with anticipation. The sooner, the better.

She studied Neil and decided he looked like a man who'd just dodged a bullet. As grateful as she was to him for his willingness to help her, she couldn't forget what she'd seen earlier.

"Neil, do you want to tell me what's going on?"

Startled, he stared at her. "Going on?"

"With you and that man I saw leaving your apartment."

He shook his head slowly. "I can't. I'm sorry."

She put her hand over his and squeezed gently. "If I can help, you know I want to."

"Thanks," he said. "But no one can help with this. It's too late."

Too late for what? she wondered, dismayed by his dire tone. "As long as there's breath left in a body, it is never too late," she told him firmly, thinking of both Callie and Mikel when she said it. "I'm living proof of that."

Jason was barely listening to what Callie had to say as they made the trip from the studio to her apartment. He couldn't get his mind off what Dana had told him when she'd called earlier. She had traced Terry's ex-brother-in-law to New York. He was apparently working for some sleazy tabloid.

Jason kept thinking of the message in those notes Terry had received: *Tell all.* More and more he was convinced that might be the hope of someone interested in grabbing a celebrity exposé to launch his own career.

But why hadn't Bryan contacted Terry directly? Or simply written the story? Clearly he had firsthand knowledge of many of the facts, including the breakup of Terry's marriage and the reason for it. Whether he actually knew about Neil was another question.

"Jason, have you heard a word I said?" Callie demanded.

"Sorry."

"I was trying to tell you that I may have discovered a break in the case."

He blinked at that. "You have?"

"Paul Locklear is gay."

He stared at her blankly, trying to picture the man he knew only by his award-winning reputation. "The director?"

"That's right. And the person who told me is convinced he has the hots for Terry."

"Then why would he threaten him?"

Callie's excitement visibly faded. "I don't know. He's such a sweet man, I can't imagine him wanting to force Terry to come out of the closet publicly. What purpose would that serve? It might even force him out of the show and then where would Paul be? He wouldn't be seeing him on a regular basis at all."

"Unless he has the twisted idea that Terry would be driven into his arms for comfort."

Callie waved off the suggestion. "He has Neil for that."

"When it comes to love, though, hope springs eternal. He could think that the publicity would ruin the relationship."

"I suppose." She gazed at Jason with wide, worried eyes. "Has your sexy P.I. discovered anything?"

"As a matter of fact, she does have a lead." He described what Dana had learned about Bryan. "Has this guy ever approached you for a story?"

Callie shook her head. "The name's not familiar at all, but Jenny doesn't usually come to us with requests from the tabloids. She knows most of us will turn them down."

"I'll do some checking on him tomorrow with the corporate publicity people. They know everyone in town, no matter how sleazy." He glanced down into her upturned face. "In the meantime, I can think of far better things to be doing with these few minutes we have alone before we get to your place."

Fire flared in Callie's eyes. "Have you forgotten that I am mad at you? Hiring Hank behind my back was a sneaky, underhanded thing to do."

Jason chuckled at the prompt renewal of indignation. "No, I haven't forgotten, but I was hoping that you had."

"Not a chance. I hold a grudge."

"For how long?"

"Maybe forever."

"How about days?" he countered, rubbing his thumb over the sensual curve of her lips.

"Not days. Weeks, at least," she said, but she sounded a little breathless and less than certain.

"Minutes," he proposed, brushing a kiss across her forehead. "You've made your point."

"Have I really?" she said doubtfully.

"Definitely."

She edged away and shook her head. "I don't know. You look like a man capable of lying to get his way."

"There's no need to lie," he protested. "All I really have to do is kiss you."

He proceeded to demonstrate before she could gather her wits to argue with him. He would probably pay for the sensual assault eventually, but right now her irritation over the hiring of Hank Parker was definitely fading.

And, even more important, this mess with Terry was clearly the last thing on her mind.

25

First thing the next morning, when Callie asked Paul Locklear if he'd join the *Within Our Reach* softball team, she watched his expression very closely as she listed the others who'd already committed to playing. She was hoping he'd reveal just how deep his fascination with Terry was. Instead of eagerly jumping at the chance to spend a Saturday in Central Park with the object of his affections, however, Paul shook his head at once.

"Softball's a little out of my league," he said. "No pun intended."

"You don't have to be good," Callie insisted, then added in total honesty, "At this point, I just need warm bodies to show up. We'll put you way out in one of those field positions, where nobody hits the ball. At least, I hope nobody hits that hard. If I get enough people, you won't even have to do that—you can direct. I mean, coach. Jeez, how did I get myself into this?"

"You sound desperate."

"I am way past desperate," she assured him.

He regarded her with amusement. "Okay, then, but don't say I didn't warn you."

"Thanks, Paul. You're an angel."

"Remember that the next time you want to strangle me because you don't like the way I'm directing a scene."

"I will," she promised.

Heading back to her dressing room, she tried to make sense of his reluctance to get involved. Had Lindsay been wrong about his interest in Terry? Or was he simply worried about making a fool of himself in public, the way the rest of them were? Directors were rarely called on to make personal appearances, except to pick up awards. Maybe Paul was simply shy, especially out of his professional milieu.

Before she could reach any conclusions about that, one of the show's gofers ran up to tell her she had a phone call.

"It's some Mrs. Pennington," the girl said. "She was quite adamant about speaking to you right now, even though I told her I thought you were in a meeting with the director. Sounds like she thinks she's the Queen Mother, if you ask me. Do you know her?"

"No, but thanks, Cindy. I'll take it."

She picked up the extension closest to her dressing room. "Mrs. Pennington? This is Callie Smith. May I help you?"

"Ah, there you are. I was afraid that insolent young woman wasn't going to give you the message, even though I told her it was extremely important."

"Our staff is really very reliable," Callie countered,

already concluding that Mrs. Pennington, whoever she was, was a first-class bitch. "What can I do for you?"

"You can agree to have lunch with me, today if possible."

It sounded more like an order than an invitation. "I'm sorry. Our shooting schedule doesn't permit enough time for me to go out for lunch very often." For once, she was grateful for the tight timetable.

"I insist."

The woman was really beginning to get on Callie's nerves. "Could you tell me what this is about? If you're a reporter, you should be arranging this through our publicity person. I can transfer you."

"I am definitely not a reporter," she said with obvious distaste.

That left Callie at a loss. "Do I know you?"

"No, but I believe you know my son."

"Your son?"

"Jason Kane."

Jason had a mother? No, Callie corrected. What was unbelievable was that he had a mother like this. Then again, they did share a certain touch of arrogance. "I'm sorry, Mrs. Pennington. Jason hasn't mentioned you."

"I'm not surprised," she said drily. "He'd very much like to forget I exist."

Callie had absolutely no difficulty at all understanding why. "I really am very sorry, Mrs. Pennington, but I can't go out to lunch."

"Cocktails, then," she said, sounding very put-upon at having her plans upset. "The Oak Room at the Plaza. I will see you there promptly at six."

She hung up before Callie could counter that that

wasn't convenient, either—that no time in this century would be convenient unless Jason himself deemed it so.

She promptly dialed Jason's office and was put through immediately. It was Freddie Cramer, not Jason, who picked up.

"He's meeting with some sponsors right now, Ms. Smith. Can he call you back?"

She heard a muttered exchange, then Jason's voice. "Sorry. Freddie hates having my meetings disrupted."

"And you? How do you feel about it?"

"The more often, the better, especially if it's by you."

"You may not feel that way when you hear why I've called."

"Oh?"

"I just had a call from a woman who claims to be your mother. She has scheduled a command performance for me at the Plaza at six o'clock. Mrs. Harriet Pennington," she said cheerfully. "Does the name ring a bell?"

"Damn."

"I gather it does."

"Don't worry about it. I'll call her. She won't bother you again."

Callie impulsively changed her mind. Jason's reaction roused her curiosity. "Actually, I'm thinking of going."

"Why in God's name would you do that?"

He sounded genuinely horrified, which made the prospect of meeting Mrs. Pennington more intriguing than Callie would have guessed a few short minutes ago. "Maybe she'll have your baby pictures with her," she told him.

"I doubt she owns any," Jason said with surprising bitterness. "Unless, perhaps, they're on some campaign poster."

"Campaign poster?" Before Jason could explain, Callie made the connection. "Oh, my God, she's *that* Mrs. Pennington?"

"The one and only."

"Jason, I don't get it. Why don't you ever talk about her?"

"Why should I? She doesn't talk about me."

Undercurrents swirled, leaving Callie a bit dazed by it all. "Okay, there is clearly a lot more going on here than I know about. Care to clue me in?"

"No, just forget all about going to that little tête-à-tête. It'll be a waste of your time."

Callie was less convinced of that than she had been. "Uh-huh," she murmured evasively. "Okay, gotta run."

"Callie!"

"Bye."

At five as she borrowed one of the more sedate suits the show had purchased for Cop Kelly's professional wardrobe and dressed carefully. At five-fifteen, she convinced herself that going to meet Jason's mother, especially over his rather adamant objections, would be a big mistake. At five-thirty, curiosity won out over logic and fear of displeasing Jason. This was her chance to gain more insight into the complex man she was falling for. She didn't intend to miss it.

When she walked into the Oak Room promptly at six, she was greeted exuberantly by Charles, who insisted on hearing all about her soap opera experiences. He seemed even more impressed by her now than he had been when she'd multiplied his savings through savvy investments.

"Charles, I promise to fill you in on all the details some other time. Right now, I'm supposed to be meeting someone."

"I know," he said with a subtle lift of his eyebrows that suggested he was well acquainted with the woman in question and didn't approve.

"They're right over there by the window," he added.

"They?"

"Mr. Kane and his mother."

Uh-oh, Callie thought. A very dry martini suddenly sounded extremely appealing. By the time she caught a glimpse of Jason's grim expression and his mother's equally hostile one, she decided to order a double. In fact, if she were smart, she'd duck out right now. Unfortunately, it was too late. Jason had spotted her.

As Charles led her to the table, Jason stood, scowling ferociously—at either her, his mother or women in general. Callie couldn't be sure which. Only Charles seemed to escape his wrath. Of course, he scooted out of sight rather quickly as if he sensed the tension in the air.

"Mother, this is Callie Smith," Jason said with clearly forced politeness.

Mrs. Pennington was too much a product of the campaign trail not to force a smile of her own and hold out her hand. "I'm very happy to meet you," she said.

Callie beamed at Jason. She might as well lie with the rest of them. "I had no idea you'd be joining us."

"Neither did I," his mother grumbled with an accusing look at Callie.

"I couldn't let you two get together without me," he

declared, as if they were the leaders of warring factions and he were the peace negotiator. He regarded his mother impassively. "Callie thought perhaps you'd have some of my baby pictures with you."

There was an obvious barb in the comment, but Mrs. Pennington didn't even flinch. "As a matter of fact, I do," she said, reaching into her purse.

To Jason's obvious astonishment, she flipped open not a campaign flyer, as he'd predicted, but her wallet. There were two fading photos facing each other. One was a studio shot of a smiling, bald, chubby-cheeked baby. The other was a snapshot of a gap-toothed boy of eight or so, holding a baseball bat in grubby hands, his elbows and knees skinned. Evidently facing the sun, he was squinting at the camera. Both were dog-eared from frequent handling, a fact Callie found a little poignant.

Although she would have loved to examine the photos more closely, Callie couldn't help focusing most of her attention on Jason, who appeared torn between embarrassment and being unwillingly touched that his mother still carried those old photos with her. Clearly he was bemused by it.

"I had no idea you were so sentimental, Mother," he said stiffly. "Or is it just that you haven't replaced that wallet in years?"

"The wallet is brand-new," his mother responded tartly. "A gift from a grateful constituent. As for these pictures, I've always treasured them. I took very few when I left your father."

"How noble, when you robbed him of everything else that really mattered."

Not even the very polished Mrs. Pennington could

hide her shock at the deliberately cruel comment. Callie was stunned by the depth of his scorn. Clearly she was way out of her depths in these particular waters. She felt as if she'd wandered into some dark Ibsen drama and didn't know her lines. It probably didn't matter since her companions had clearly been rehearsing theirs for years.

Mrs. Pennington, her cheeks flushed pink, looked at Callie. "I'm terribly sorry you got caught in the crossfire. This is an old disagreement between Jason and myself. Sometimes my son doesn't understand that family squabbles shouldn't be played out in front of strangers."

"Callie is hardly a stranger," Jason snapped.

"She is to me, which is why I invited her to cocktails. If you can't be civil, then you may leave," she suggested with an imperious wave of her bejeweled hand. She was wearing a diamond-and-ruby ring big enough to knock out anyone she happened to strike with it.

"I'm too old to be ordered off to my room," Jason countered. "If Callie stays, then I stay."

Callie looked from one scowling countenance to the other and decided it was time to cut and run before there was bloodshed. "Maybe this was a bad idea. We can do it another time."

"It won't be any better another time," Mrs. Pennington assured her with a wry smile. "You see my son doesn't approve of me."

"Which makes your determination to meddle in my life all the more perplexing," Jason said. He stood and glanced down at Callie. "Are you ready?"

"Yes." She shot a regretful look at Mrs. Pennington, who suddenly looked incredibly sad. "Thank you for inviting me."

She had to practically run to catch up with Jason, who was striding toward the exit as if a whole squadron of outraged viewers were after him.

Outside, Henry appeared as if he'd known precisely how to time the arrival. Apparently Jason's get-togethers with his mother rarely lasted long.

Only when they were in the back of the waiting limo did Jason speak. "Satisfied?" he inquired, his tone chilly.

Callie glared right back at him. "As a matter of fact, no. You have a lot of explaining to do."

The look he turned on her was lethal. "Oh?"

"Starting with why you never even mentioned you had a mother living right here in New York, much less that particular mother."

He shrugged. "You may have noticed, we don't get along."

"I noticed that you don't. She seems to be trying."

"Do I tell you how to deal with your mother?"

"All the time."

"Well, from now on you can ignore me, just the way I'm going to ignore you. The subject of mothers is hereby declared off-limits."

"I don't think so."

They were still arguing about it when they got to Callie's apartment. All further discussion was tabled the minute Callie caught a glimpse of her own mother, who looked as if she were ready to model for some magazine cover. Even Jason seemed dumbfounded by the change.

"Mother, what on earth?" Callie murmured, circling her mother as if she were an intriguing stranger.

Her mother's cheeks, now more clearly defined by

subtle makeup, turned bright pink. "Do you like it?" she asked hesitantly, patting the soft brown curls that skimmed her chin.

"You look absolutely…" Words failed her.

"Ravishing," Jason chimed in.

"Don't overdo," her mother chided Jason.

"I'm not," he swore. "You look twenty years younger."

"Maybe five," her mother said shyly.

"No, Jason's right," Callie said. "Mother, you are gorgeous. But why? How?"

"I got this idea in my head yesterday and Neil helped me. He made an appointment at a salon and took me there himself."

Callie thought she had never seen her mother look quite so happy. Something told her, though, that makeup couldn't account for all the color in her mother's cheeks. She had the distinct impression that there was more behind this makeover than her mother had admitted to and that whatever it was was likely to be far more disconcerting than a new haircut.

26

Callie was exhausted. She'd been trying to disguise the circles under her eyes for the past ten minutes, but none of the tricks Terry had taught her were working. She gathered up her makeup sponges and various tubes of foundation and cover-up and headed for his dressing room. Since the circles were his fault, he could repair the damage.

Once he'd shown up the night before to admire her mother's new look, they'd all sat around her apartment until the wee hours of the morning dissecting what they knew—and didn't know—about the threats. There was so little new information to go on that they'd all finally given up in defeat but not before they'd nitpicked the subject to death.

"I think the crisis is past," Terry had said, hopefully, at the end. "No mail, no phone calls, no visits, no pranks."

Jason had been adamant about not letting their guard down. He'd scowled at Callie. "You stay in Hank's sight while you're at the studio, okay? I think it's safe to say those little accidents were meant as warnings. I want

Hank to examine every single prop you're supposed to use."

Callie stared at him. "How did you find out about…" She glanced over and caught Terry's guilty expression. "Never mind."

Jason wasn't through yet. "And make sure Hank is going to be at that softball game."

"There will be a zillion people around that day," Callie protested. "No one would dare to try anything."

"Having a zillion people around means that we won't know most of them," Jason pointed out. "It's the perfect time for someone to act. Tell Hank I want him there. If he needs help, he's authorized to hire it, okay?"

Callie had finally agreed just so that everyone would leave and she could get at least a couple of hours of sleep before dawn. Today she was definitely paying the price. Her brain felt like mush and her face didn't look much better. This glamorous image was harder to maintain than she'd imagined. In fact, her whole impression that acting was a frivolous career had been turned on its ear. It was hard work.

She walked into Terry's dressing room and flopped down in the big easy chair in front of his mirror. He glanced up from his script.

"Hey, dollface, what's up?"

"I look like I've got two small carry-ons under my eyes. Fix it."

He grinned. "I'm talented, but I'm no plastic surgeon. Go see Suzy," he said, referring to their makeup genius.

"If Suzy sees these, she'll quit the business rather than have her reputation compromised."

Terry came over, grabbed her elbow and hauled her

up. "You don't need makeup. You need food, something to revive you."

"I don't have time for food."

"We'll make time. We're not shooting until one. It's still early for the lunch crowd. We can run across the street, eat our soup and be back here in fifteen minutes with plenty of time to get dolled up for the camera."

"Fifteen minutes to get served at the deli? Since when?"

"You'll be with me, remember?"

"Oh, of course. I'd forgotten how the waitresses fall all over themselves trying to catch your attention," she said snidely. "The rest of us could die of starvation."

"Yes, well, fame does have its privileges," he remarked drily.

"Forget fame," Callie retorted. "It's that sexy dimple that gets them. It would work if you were a bus driver."

"Whatever," he mumbled, clearly embarrassed. "Are you coming or not?"

"I'm coming," she said, patting his cheek affectionately. "Cutie."

Terry groaned but otherwise let the taunt slide.

Slipping out of the studio in the middle of the day made Callie feel as if she were playing hooky. She usually relied on Terry to bring her back a cup of soup or a salad. He made the trek to the nearby deli just before noon every day like clockwork.

Because she usually holed up in her own dressing room for a final rehearsal of her lines, Hank wasn't expecting her to head for the exit. She caught a glimpse of him engaged in one of his increasingly heated exchanges with Lisa. This one, at least, was verbal. At the last instant, she thought of Jason's warning.

"Maybe I should tell Hank we're going," she said, hesitating at the door.

"We'll be back before he even notices we're gone," Terry reassured her. "I'll protect you."

"Who's going to protect you?"

"No need," he promised, doing an elaborate scan of the sidewalk. "The coast is clear."

Callie rolled her eyes and followed him to the curb. Terry took her hand and led her between two parked cars, glancing up the one-way street to be sure there was no traffic in sight. Callie followed the direction of his gaze and assured herself that the nearest car was waiting for the red light to change on the other side of Eighth Avenue, a hundred or more yards away.

They had taken no more than two steps into the street when Callie heard an engine accelerating as if it were coming out of a turn at the Indy 500. It squealed around the corner on two wheels and took aim straight at them.

In the blink of an eye, the car was on top of them. Terry reacted with lightning-quick reflexes, shoving Callie backward so hard that she landed on her tailbone with a painful thud. He dove after her but not in time to avoid the car, which grazed his side and sent him sprawling.

The driver never even touched the brakes. Callie closed her eyes and prayed harder than she'd ever prayed in her life as she painfully scrambled toward Terry's inert form.

Within seconds, it seemed, Hank came racing out of the studio, apparently alerted to the near-miss by one of the other cast members, who'd been exiting behind them and had seen everything. He knelt beside Callie. "You okay?"

"Just shaken up a little. Check on Terry. I think the car hit him."

"I'm okay," Terry insisted, barely stifling a groan as he straightened up. "Just a little dust on my pants."

"You're damned lucky you don't have tire treads over your middle," Jonathan Baines said, joining them. "It happened so fast, I didn't even have time to scream a warning."

"Did you see the car?" Hank asked, going instantly into his professional cop mode. "Make, model, color? What about the driver?"

Callie couldn't dredge up anything but that instant of terror. Terry was no more helpful.

However, Jonathan, whose photographic memory was much envied by others in the cast, closed his eyes and withdrew into some sort of trancelike state. Then he, too, shook his head.

"It happened too quickly for me to get much of a look at the driver," he said with regret.

"What about the car?" Hank asked.

"Older, maybe an '85 or '86," Jonathan guessed. "Some kind of Chevy, I think. Dull blue or gray. Pretty nondescript, actually."

"The perfect car for a planned hit-and-run," Hank said.

The actor's eyes widened. "You think it was intentional?"

Hank fixed his gaze on Callie and Terry. "Don't you?"

Terry sighed heavily. “If so, then it had to be me they were after. I cross here every day about this time. Callie never does.”

“Which means it’s not over, after all,” Callie whispered, trembling so hard she felt as if she’d been caught in a blizzard without her coat. Even her teeth were chattering.

Terry wrapped an arm around her. “Sorry, dollface. Looks like I’ve done it again.”

“Not you, this crazy person,” Callie said adamantly.

“It’s because of me, though, that you’re at risk,” Terry repeated.

Jonathan regarded them all with curiosity. “What the devil is going on?”

“Nothing you need to concern yourself about,” Hank assured him. He looked as if he’d be happier if Jonathan disappeared so that he could fuss over Callie and Terry.

Jonathan drew himself up to stare regally at the rest of them. His gaze lingered affectionately on Terry. “If my friends here are in danger, then I would like to do what I can to help.”

“Just try to remember anything more you can about that car or the person driving it,” Hank suggested. “We could use a good solid lead.”

Callie saw the genuine concern in Jonathan’s expression and said, “Hank, maybe we should fill him in. Another pair of eyes wouldn’t hurt, especially with the softball game coming up.”

Hank looked as reluctant as would any cop asked to confide in a civilian. His gaze clashed with Callie’s, but when she didn’t back down, he relented. “Okay, I suppose it can't hurt. Let's go on over to the deli since I assume that's where you all were headed."

Jonathan *tsk-tsked* as he heard the whole story about everything that had gone on since before Callie had joined the show. They skipped over any hint of what the person might be holding over Terry's head.

When the explanation concluded, Jonathan looked at Callie. "Let me get this straight. Are you an actress or some kind of an investigator?"

"Actually, I'm really a Wall Street broker pretending to be an actress until something better comes along," she said. The response was automatic, and not until it was out of her mouth did Callie realize that she no longer felt that way about the job. She'd actually begun to enjoy herself in this world of make-believe into which Jason had drawn her. She wasn't too sure what to make of the discovery and now was hardly the moment to be reassessing her career goals.

"What?" Terry said, his gaze fixed on her.

"I'm actually beginning to feel more like an actress than a broker."

He grinned. "I hear the ham factor is very similar."

"Could we get away from the subject of acting for a moment and concentrate on coming up with a plan for that ball game?" Hank suggested. "Is there any way to withdraw the team?"

"Not a chance," Callie said. "Jenny would have heart failure."

Hank looked resigned…and worried. "Then we have to set up some sort of security perimeter."

"Short of surrounding the ball field with cops on

horseback, I don't see what we can do," Terry protested. "There's not much control at an event like this."

"You're probably right," Hank conceded with a sigh. "Maybe I can get some of my buddies to go undercover and help me keep an eye on things. I don't want you two left alone for a minute." He glanced at Jonathan. "You can't say a word to the rest of the cast about this. There are some suspects there we'd rather not alert."

The older man's gaze widened. "You suspect people in the cast? My God, who?"

"It's better if you don't know that for now," Hank told him. "This person has a nasty habit of going after anyone who gets involved. I don't need to be worrying about another potential victim. Just stay alert to anything peculiar going on."

Terry glanced at his watch. "We'd better get back."

Callie's muscles had stiffened up from her fall in the few minutes they had been sitting in the restaurant. She stood up gingerly. Terry watched her with obvious alarm.

"Are you okay? Maybe we should have you checked out at the hospital."

"I'm fine," she assured him. "I'm just not used to being bounced around on asphalt like that. The kinks will work out in no time. We're just lucky we're not shooting some torrid love scene today. I have a feeling there's a nasty bruise on my tush that all the makeup in Suzy's kit wouldn't hide."

Jonathan chuckled. "You two are amazing. A close brush with death and here you are making jokes."

Callie shivered at the reminder that the accident was meant to be far more serious than it had turned out.

Only Terry's hand, wrapped firmly around her own, kept her from bolting to the safe haven of her own apartment—though, come to think of it, that wasn't so safe anymore, either.

Jenny Harding greeted them as they returned to the studio. "My God, are you all right?" she demanded, some sort of weird, breathless excitement in her voice. "I just heard about the accident."

Hank stared hard at her. "From?"

"It's all over," she assured him. "Everyone's heard by now."

Hank muttered an expletive and kicked a metal chair into the wall. Jenny watched him, wide-eyed with dismay. Callie decided she'd better get Hank into her dressing room before he scared the poor PR girl to death.

"It's okay," she assured Jenny. "We were just hoping word wouldn't leak out."

Jenny's head bobbed. "Oh, it won't. Not to the media. I promise." She looked vaguely disappointed. "Of course, the sympathy factor would be terrific for ratings."

"Forget it," Terry said tersely, brushing past her. He glanced back at her. "One word of this hits the papers and I will personally see to it that your career as a PR flack for this network goes up in flames. Got it?"

Tears welled up in Jenny's eyes at the unexpected attack. She turned and ran.

"Did you have to be so hard on her?" Callie asked.

"Can you think of any other way to get through to someone who thinks only about what will increase ratings?"

"I suppose not."

"I know not," he assured her. "Which means we probably shouldn't fill Jason in, either." He gazed at Callie. "Should we?"

Callie had her own reasons for not wanting Jason to hear about this near-miss, and they had little to do with a debate over the merits of publicizing it. "No," she said with a pointed look at Hank. "I vote he stays in the dark about this one. Hank?"

"I suppose," he conceded with obvious reluctance. "For now, anyway."

It was probably only concern over his own job security that made him agree, Callie thought cynically.

Terry glanced at Hank, who still looked angry enough to spit nails over having been caught with his attention misdirected. "Maybe I should send Lisa in to soothe your temper."

"Not now," Hank said tersely, following Callie down the hall.

Callie guessed what was on his mind. "Hank, this was not your fault."

"I'm being paid to watch you," he argued. "It wouldn't have happened if I had been."

"You can't help it if I slipped out while you weren't looking."

"If I hadn't been all caught up with my hormones, you'd never have slipped out," he insisted. "Sometimes I wonder…"

He hesitated, looking about as miserable as anyone Callie had ever seen. "If Lisa is deliberately— No, that can't be it," he said with more wistfulness than conviction. "At any rate, it won't happen again."

Callie thought she could guess what he'd been about

to say. He was worried that Lisa might be part of the plot. Lisa's innocence was one of the few things Callie was certain about, but reassurance from her wouldn't convince Hank. She didn't even try.

"Look, detective, stop beating yourself up over this. I'm a big girl. I should have known better."

He scowled at her. "Yeah, you should have. Whose idea was it to go over there, anyway?"

"Terry's. He thought some soup would perk me up."

"From now on you don't go anywhere with Terry unless either Mr. Kane or I are along."

Callie started to form a protest, but something in Hank's expression told her his patience was at the breaking point. "I promise," she said dutifully. She stood up and headed for the door.

"Where are you going?"

"To makeup. I have a call in fifteen minutes."

Hank stood up. "Let's go, then."

"Do you really think you need to watch them put my makeup on?"

"From now on I need to watch if you decide to catch fifty winks all by your lonesome."

"This is really going to get tedious, isn't it?"

"A lot of police work is tedious."

"I was talking about for me," she said. "Come on, Shadow. I'll try to keep you posted when I'm about to change directions."

"Believe me, from now on, you couldn't lose me if you tried."

For the next week and a half Hank was true to his word. The only time he let Callie out of his sight was when he handed her off to Jason like a football in midplay.

And it really was tedious. Callie didn't have a single minute to seek out Paul Locklear to try to determine where he'd been at the time of the accident. More and more, though, she couldn't imagine why he'd want to kill—or at least put the fear of God into—a man he supposedly had a thing for.

By the time the Thursday night before the softball game rolled around, she was feeling the effects of the almost nonstop surveillance and even more constant tension. When Jason offered to take her and her mother out to dinner, she declined.

"She's probably not even home yet. I don't know where she's been going lately, but she's been getting home later and later."

"Maybe she has a lover," Jason suggested. "Something you used to have, too."

"My mother?" Callie said incredulously, ignoring the comment about their own recent lack of privacy. "I don't think so."

"You never know. It's been my experience that the Gunderson women are quite provocative."

"Jason, you have never met a woman you didn't consider provocative."

"They all pale by comparison to you, though."

She regarded him curiously. "You sounded as if you meant that."

"I did."

"You also sounded surprised."

He sighed. "I am. One of these days I suppose we ought to talk about what it all means."

He looked so bemused, she almost felt sorry for him. After seeing him with his mother and gathering that his childhood had not exactly been filled with a textbook example of marital bliss, she could understand why the thought of commitment made him jumpy.

She'd had her own sorry example of marriage to overcome, but she'd leaped at the chance to marry Chad, anyway. She had vowed she wouldn't be so foolish a second time, but Jason had a way of making her doubts vanish like wisps of smoke. Love was amazingly sneaky that way.

"I'll walk you up," Jason said, following her out of the limo.

"You don't need—"

He cut off the protest with a kiss. "I'm hoping I can steal a few more of those before I go home to my cold, lonely bed."

"An intriguing notion," she agreed, her blood pumping a little faster at the prospect. Maybe she wasn't quite as tired as she'd thought.

The minute she turned the first key in the lock, though, the door flew open. Her mother practically tugged the two of them inside.

"Let me look at you," she demanded to Callie's confusion. She circled her as she might a Michelangelo statue, slowly and with great care.

"Mother, what on earth?"

"I have to see for myself that you're okay. Why didn't you tell me?" she demanded accusingly.

"About what?" Callie asked.

"The accident."

"Oh, hell," Callie murmured. She had made a deliberate decision not to tell her mother about that, and as far as she knew, everyone had kept the promise to keep Jason in the dark, as well. She winced when she caught his expression. He definitely did not look happy.

"What accident?" Jason demanded, his tone deadly.

Callie didn't want to deal with him, so she concentrated instead on her mother. "How did you find out?"

Her mother looked very put-upon. "The same way the rest of the world did, I suppose. From one of those sleazy tabloids. Eunice called asking all sorts of questions I couldn't answer. She finally told me what she'd read. I went down to the supermarket and picked one up for myself."

She gestured to the open newspaper, which had used a publicity shot of Terry and Callie to accompany a splashy headline: Hit-and-Run Stalker Endangers Daytime's Hottest Duo.

Jason had the phone in his hand and was jabbing in numbers before Callie could close her gaping mouth.

"We agreed there would be no publicity," she whispered as much to herself as to Jason.

"Get me Jenny Harding," he snapped, apparently to the network operator. "Now."

A moment later, he described the story and demanded, "How the hell did this happen?"

Apparently Jenny's stammered reply didn't satisfy him because with his next breath he fired her and slammed the phone down. He was cursing a blue streak, oblivious to the two women staring at him.

"Jenny might not have had anything to do with it," Callie suggested softly, feeling sorry for the poor girl who tried so hard to do a good job. It wasn't easy dealing with so many mega-egos, seeing that they each got their fair share of the limelight, but Jenny managed it. "She swore to us that she'd keep it under wraps."

"Us? Exactly how many people conspired to keep this from me?" Jason demanded.

Callie winced. "Just Terry and Hank. We knew it would just upset you. And we all ganged up on Jenny."

"Well, if she didn't leak it, who else would have?"

Callie studied the page again. When the byline finally registered, she gasped softly.

"What?" Jason demanded.

"Maybe it wasn't leaked. Look at the byline."

"My God," Jason whispered. "Bryan Davis, Terry's ex-brother-in-law."

An outrageous thought popped into Callie's head. "Who's to say he wasn't behind the wheel of that car himself?"

To her amazement, Jason didn't immediately label the idea as ludicrous.

"It's sure as hell one way to get an exclusive," he agreed. "And maybe some revenge for his sister at the same time."

His lethal expression suggested that it might very well be Bryan's last scoop, especially if Jason got his hands on him before the police did.

"That's it," he said. "I'm pulling you out of that softball game on Saturday. There's no way in hell I'll let you be in that kind of danger. Terry, either, for that matter. You'll be sitting ducks out there."

"We can't pull out," Callie protested. "The event organizers are counting on us."

"They'll understand," Jason said grimly. "In fact,

they'll probably be elated not to have the event spoiled by murder."

Callie wasn't especially overjoyed at the prospect of being an easy target in Central Park, but she refused to let the charity down. "Hank can handle security," she insisted. "He's already arranging for some help."

"Callie, he couldn't even keep the two of you safe crossing the street. How is he supposed to do it in a mob scene? I don't care how much help he pulls in. It's not possible."

"We will be in Central Park on Saturday," she countered just as fiercely.

Jason's expression hardened. "You know who you sound like? You sound exactly like my mother. She would never let mere security concerns stop her from campaigning."

Apparently he didn't consider it a flattering comparison.

"I'm sorry," Callie said. "I know you'll be worried, but this is a risk I have to take."

He looked at her long and hard, then shook his head. "You've turned into a publicity hound just like the rest of them, haven't you?" he said bitterly.

Callie couldn't believe he'd made such a ridiculous charge. "If I have, then you're the one responsible," she said. "Getting me on *Within Our Reach* in the first place was all about publicity, wasn't it? For all I know that's what our relationship has been about, too."

His eyes blazed with fury at that, but she ignored the reaction. She opened the door and gestured. "Leave, Jason. I really don't think you and I have anything more to discuss."

His gaze raked over her. Eventually, he reached some sort of conclusion because he shrugged. "No, I don't suppose we do."

After he'd gone, Callie let the tears that had been stinging her eyes flow. "Damn him," she murmured just as she felt her mother's arms enfold her. "Why does he have to be so stubborn and pigheaded?"

"Look who's talking," her mother said.

"Whose side are you on, anyway?"

"Yours," she insisted. "And his. This may be one of those times when you're both right. You need to compromise."

"There's no way to compromise. I made a commitment. I'm not backing out."

Through a haze of tears, she caught her mother's smile.

"I don't think you have the art of compromise nailed down quite yet, do you? Want me to explain it?"

"No," Callie said stubbornly. "Let Jason compromise for once in his arrogant life."

Even as the words were out of her mouth, she realized that her mother was right. She was being as pigheaded as Jason. At the moment, though, she couldn't see any possible middle ground. What really hurt was his refusal to see that her decision didn't have anything to do with the publicity. Sadly, it appeared that even after all these months, Jason didn't know her at all.

27

"Gina, you have been distracted all morning," Mikel complained, pacing the loft behind Regina like an angry bear. "There is not one new brushstroke on the canvas."

Regina sighed and set her palette and brush on a table beside the easel. "I have many things on my mind, Mikel," she said, massaging fingers that ached from clutching the brush so tightly.

He paused before her and took over the task of soothing her hands with his gentle touch. "Your decision about us, perhaps?" he asked, his dark eyes filling with hope.

She stroked his cheek with her fingertips. "I wish it were so simple."

"Simple?" he grumbled. "If that is so simple, then why have you not told me yes or no?"

She smiled at his impatience. "I thought I had."

"You have not said the words," he protested.

"You once told me words between us should not be necessary to explain the obvious," she teased.

His sensual lips curved into the beginnings of a

smile. "Then it is yes? You are telling me you will marry me?"

Her heart, which had been heavy ever since the worrisome discussion of Callie's accident the night before, brightened. "Yes, Mikel, I will marry you."

He swept her into his arms and spun her around. "When?"

Regina was giddy, either from the twirling or from contemplating the future. "Soon, I think. As soon as I can speak to my daughters about it."

"We will tell them together," he insisted. "It is my duty to let them know that you will be well loved and taken care of."

His body, pressed against hers, was not so solid or lithe as it once had been but it stirred her senses and made her anxious for the time when they would be together forever. In her mind she would always see him as the young, wildly exotic man he had been when they met. He filled her heart with such joy, there was little room left any longer for regrets.

"We can't tell them yet," she said. "Callie's life is in turmoil. I'm so terribly afraid for her."

She described the accident, the terrible headline in that tabloid, the fight with Jason and her own dread over what tragedy tomorrow's charity softball game might bring.

"I will be there with you," Mikel declared. "We will look out for her."

"You wouldn't mind?" she asked, surprised. "You have a full day of classes on Saturday."

"I will cancel them," he said without hesitation. "My students can work on their own, if they are dedicated enough. If they are not, then they will relish the unexpected day of freedom. My place is by your side."

Regina smiled at him in wonder. She had forgotten what it was like to be with a man who made her the center of his world. "Do you know how very much I love you?"

"And I you, my Gina."

"Will you come with me now?"

"Where?"

"There is someone I must see," she said, thinking of Jason's dark expression as he'd left the apartment the night before. Perhaps if Callie wouldn't initiate a compromise, Jason would. Mikel could help her to explain the high cost of stubbornness.

For the fourth time on Friday morning, Jason pulled the phone toward him and started to dial the organizers of Saturday's charity event to withdraw the *Within Our Reach* team. It was his prerogative as network president, to say nothing of his duty as someone who cared for one of the participants and feared for her safety. A man in his position should act, not waver, he thought fiercely, punching in the first numbers.

Once again, though, he stopped, muttering a harsh expletive under his breath as he considered how furious Callie would be if he did so.

If Callie wanted to risk her own neck and that of her best friend, why should it matter to him? A couple of murders or even a violent assault on one of the stars in Central Park would send the soap's ratings soaring, he thought cynically.

But even as the crude thought slipped into his head,

he shuddered. He couldn't bear the possibility of losing her. A huge emptiness opened up inside him just thinking about it.

When had she become so important to him? From the beginning he'd told himself that she was just another diversion, that he would tire of her as he had of all the others.

He hadn't. His body ached for her when she was out of his arms for too long. His mind seemed duller when she wasn't around to challenge it.

Of course, he had Freddie for the latter. Freddie had been poking his head into Jason's office all morning, looking increasingly worried about his boss's foul mood. He'd ventured inside only once, long enough for Jason to tell him to get the hell out.

This was one decision Freddie couldn't help him make. As Jason saw it, he could withdraw the team, earn Callie's wrath and risk losing her over his protectiveness and interference. Or he could let the game go on and risk losing her to a far more deadly fate. The decision should have been a snap for a man used to making difficult choices, but for once his innate decisiveness failed him. There was too damned much at stake.

When his secretary buzzed, Jason scowled at the phone. He'd ordered her not to interrupt him. She usually took his edicts seriously. Was everybody in his life rebelling these days?

"Dammit, I thought I told you I didn't want to see anyone," he bellowed without benefit of the phone. People three offices away probably heard him. He didn't care.

The door to his office inched open and Regina Gunderson regarded him with grim determination.

"I'm afraid I am the one at fault," she said, not looking all that apologetic. "I insisted. Is it all right to come in?"

"I'm sorry," Jason said at once. "Of course it's all right."

He still couldn't quite get over her transformation from mousy farmer to a self-confident, attractive, radiant woman. When a stocky, stoop-shouldered man with a full head of thick gray-streaked hair entered with her, Jason thought he understood what had happened. The adoration shining in the man's eyes would be plain to anyone, even a cynic such as Jason.

"This is Mikel Rolanski," Regina explained. "He is—"

"An artist," Jason said with amazement and genuine pleasure. He rose at once and grasped the man's hand. "I know your work. I have several of your paintings in my collection." They were, in fact, among the few he'd bought not as trophies but because he genuinely liked them.

"Then I am honored," the older man said. "You must come to my studio sometime and see Gina's work, as well as my own."

Startled, Jason stared at Callie's mother. "You paint?"

Regina blushed as Rolanski answered for her. "She was one of my best students once. I intend her to be again." He reached for her hand. "But first I must make her my wife."

Well, well, well, Jason thought, and wondered how

much of this Callie knew. He suspected she would be as stunned as he was.

"We did not come here to talk about us," Regina said determinedly. "It is this game."

Jason sighed. "I have thought of nothing else since last night."

She leaned toward him imploringly. "Could you not reach some compromise with Callie, one that would not put her in danger?"

"I wish I could think of one. Do you have any suggestions?"

"I've been thinking about it and Mikel agrees. Perhaps the team could play without her," Regina said. "That way the charity would still receive its money. That is really what she cares about, you know."

"That would work," Jason agreed, then smiled ruefully. "But your daughter would never agree to it. If Terry and the others are there, she will insist on being with them because she arranged it."

Regina studied him intently. "That is what you believe, isn't it? That she is honoring a commitment? You don't truly think she is doing it solely for the publicity, as you accused last night?"

"No," he admitted. "I was angry when I said that. That doesn't mean I think she's any less of a fool because she won't withdraw."

Mikel's penetrating gaze settled on him. "Would you feel as you do about her," he asked lightly, "if she were anything less than courageous?"

"What makes you think…" Jason began, then let the denial die on his lips when he saw the sympathetic, knowing look in the older man's eyes. "No, her bravery is to be admired."

"But you are scared for her," Mikel said. "As any man would be, if the woman he loves were walking into danger."

Jason sighed deeply. "Is it possible to survive loving these Gunderson women?" he inquired with a glance at Regina, whose hand was enfolded in Rolanski's much larger one.

"They test a man's patience," the artist agreed, grinning unrepentantly at the indignant woman beside him. "But they are worth it. I have waited more than thirty years for my Gina."

"If you two are finished blaming all your ills on me and Callie," Regina said irritably, "could we concentrate on protecting my daughter from harm?"

"How many suspects do you have?" Mikel asked. "Are there so many that we could not each be assigned to watch one, while this security man you have hired keeps an eye on Callie?"

"There are only two that we know of," Jason conceded. "A director from the show and a reporter."

"There, then, that is simple," Mikel said matter-of-factly. "You will watch one, and Regina and I, the other."

"My gut is telling me that we're missing someone," Jason said. "The motives for these two exist, but..." He shook his head. "I can't explain it."

"Still, if we neutralize these two," Mikel said, obviously relishing his new role as bodyguard, "and this Hank that Gina has told me about protects Callie, all should be well, don't you think?"

"I don't know what else we can do at this point," Jason conceded. "I'll have my assistant get a picture of the director for you before you leave so that you'll recognize him tomorrow. He's scheduled to play, I believe. Callie said something about right field."

He met Regina's anxious gaze. "And I think it would be best if Callie doesn't learn of this discussion."

"I agree," Regina said. "It would only upset her that we're interfering. In the meantime, I suggest we pray for a little help from above tomorrow."

Jason nodded. He'd prayed for so little in his life, perhaps there was some small amount of goodwill left for him in heaven. He promised to ask for nothing ever again, if only God would keep Callie safe.

28

Those familiar butterflies were once again dancing a rumba in Callie's stomach on Saturday morning.

The team was expected in Central Park by nine-thirty for a ten o'clock game, the day's first. Hank had decreed that he would personally pick her and Terry up just after nine. He'd brushed aside all arguments. He'd also mentioned that several of his off-duty cop buddies would hang out at the ball field to help him keep an eye on things.

To Terry's obvious astonishment, Neil had announced he was planning to ride with them. Normally Neil wouldn't be caught within miles of an event like this, but clearly he knew what the stakes were today. His fierce expression dared Terry to tell him to stay home.

Callie's mother slipped out at eight-thirty without mentioning her destination. If she was coming to Central Park, she hadn't said a word to Callie about it.

Rather than pacing around the empty apartment until her nerves frayed completely, Callie went downstairs, where she could pace with Terry. Neil regarded them both with a disgruntled expression.

"You could both stay home," he said. "That's what anyone with half a brain would do."

"But as we all know, no one in TV has half a brain," Terry shot back irritably. "Give it a rest, Neil. You've made your opinion known. We made a commitment and we're living up to it."

Neil retreated to the bedroom in a huff. But the minute Hank buzzed, Neil emerged and followed them downstairs. His grim expression made it clear he wasn't happy with any of them.

The ride to the meadow in Central Park passed in tense silence. When they parked illegally, Hank slapped a police vehicle ID on his windshield, then turned to Callie.

"You don't move from that playing field without telling me where you're going, okay? No quick solo trips to the restroom or a refreshment stand, nothing. Same for you, Terry."

"Got it," Callie promised. Terry nodded, his expression drawn. Callie could only guess the toll all of this was taking on him. Guilt and fear were lousy companions.

A crowd was already assembled on the grass. Callie spotted Jenny Harding walking among them, handing out photos and *Within Our Reach* buttons. Clearly Jason had thought better of firing her and had reinstated her. Photographers, a couple of TV newsmen and a handful of reporters were lined up behind the backstop, waiting for the soap stars to arrive. She recognized many of them from prior interviews and photo shoots.

Hank fell into step beside her. "Anyone in that gang you don't know?" he asked, gesturing toward the media.

"Several," she admitted. "Most of them are from the soap magazines, *People,* places like that, but I'm sure the others are here because it's a slow news day in New York."

"How does this work? Is it a free-for-all or does that Jenny person keep it under control? I see she's already out there working the crowd."

"I'm sure she'll do her best to set things up in an orderly manner," Callie said. "But these guys have a job to do. If she gets in their way, they'll run right over her, especially the TV guys who don't have to rely on her for future tips. The fanzine guys are a little more circumspect about offending her."

"Terrific," he said sourly as one reporter pushed Neil aside to get to Terry. With surprising force, Neil pushed right back even before Hank could intervene.

"Sorry," Hank said, muscling his way between the two men. He gestured toward Jenny. "See Miss Harding, if you want to talk to Mr. Walker."

The reporter looked as if he might argue until Hank flashed his badge at him.

"Jeez, man, I was just going to ask how he was feeling after his accident."

"And you are?" Hank demanded.

"Gil Haver, *Newsday.*"

Hank glanced at Terry. "Want to answer?"

"I'm certainly up to playing a little ball," Terry said.

The reporter moved off, apparently satisfied that that was as much of a comment as he was likely to get.

Callie moved closer to Terry. "What about your ex-brother-in-law? Any sign of him?"

Terry was tall enough to scan the crowd, despite the

number of people who were pressing closer, hoping for an autograph or a snapshot of the star. "I don't see him," he said, before turning his attention to the gathering of fans. "But I can't even swear I'd recognize him after all these years."

Then Callie lost sight of Terry as her own horde of fans surrounded her, waving photos under her nose for an autograph and pleading to have their pictures snapped with her. Hank did his best to maintain control, but it was a losing battle.

It was event organizers who finally managed to put a little order into the chaos by calling for the first game to begin.

They made it through six innings without incident. Once or twice during her times at bat, Callie was certain she spotted Jason in the crowd, but each time she lost him. Her heart thumped unsteadily as she thought about the fight they'd had. Until the very last instant, she'd been expecting him to follow through on his threat to cancel the game. As gut-deep scared as she was, she was still glad he hadn't. The charity would have lost thousands of dollars.

At the beginning of the seventh inning, just when her team was about to take the field, Lindsay Gentry slipped up beside her.

"Where's Terry?" she whispered. "Nobody's seen him for several minutes now, not since we came off the field before this at-bat. I figured he'd gone to the restroom, but one of the guys checked. He's not there."

Callie's heart leaped into her throat. She scanned the bench until she caught Hank's eye. He was beside her in an instant.

"Any problems?"

"Where's Terry?" she asked.

"He was here a minute ago," Hank said, glancing toward the field as if he might materialize in his position at third base.

"Blast it all," he murmured, then muttered something into his handheld radio, alerting his buddies that there was possible trouble.

Callie panicked. "Hank?"

He squeezed her shoulders. "Don't worry. I'll find him," he promised. "Put one of the substitutes at his position. Go on as if nothing is wrong. I've already radioed one of the other cops to keep an eye on you until I'm back. He's on his way over here now. I won't budge until he's in place."

When Callie stood frozen, filled with dread, Hank snapped, "Just make the substitution. We don't want this crowd to start wondering what's going on. Do it now, so I can start searching."

Acting by rote, her mind caught up in a swirl of panic over Terry's disappearance, she grabbed Jenny off the bench and ordered her to play third base.

"Me?" Jenny protested. "How come?"

"Please. There's nobody else."

Jenny looked confused, but apparently she sensed Callie's desperation because she finally nodded. "Okay, I'll try. What's going on? You look scared."

Callie mustered a weak smile. "Just afraid of having to forfeit this late in the game," she improvised. "We're down to our last substitute player and I might need him to pitch. Grab a glove, okay?"

Used to the eccentricities of the stars with whom she worked, Jenny shrugged and took the field.

Isolated in left field, the next three outs were the longest moments of Callie's life. Fortunately, the opposing soap team was not exactly packed with power hitters. Three ground balls dribbled into three quick outs. Jenny nailed the last batter with a solid throw to first base that had her teammates cheering.

Even over the exuberant shouts, Callie heard the distant wail of sirens as she was coming off the field. There wasn't a doubt in her mind about what they meant. Terry's disappearance had resulted in trouble, big trouble. Her stomach lurched as she tried to get a fix on where the sirens were headed.

Racing toward the bench, she spotted Jason running toward a secluded spot off to the left in the direction of the access road. She sprinted after him.

Whether Jason actually knew where he was going and what they would find or only anticipated the worst, he turned back and grabbed her just when she saw Hank kneeling down, bending over a body half hidden in a bright bed of tulips. The sneakers and jeans she could see weren't distinguishable from hundreds of others in the park, but Callie recognized Terry's vivid orange socks at once.

"No!" She thought she'd screamed, but the sound seemed to be little more than a whimper as Jason buried her face against his chest. She struggled to free herself. "Let me go! I have to see him."

"Callie," he protested.

"It's okay," Hank called out. "He's alive, but barely."

Callie tore herself free of Jason's grasp and ran to

her friend. Terry's face and clothes were covered with blood. It looked as if someone had taken a bat to his head. She might have gagged and faltered then, but Jason's grip on her arm steadied her.

She knelt down and gently shifted Terry's battered head and shoulders into her lap, cradling him. Her tears spilled over onto his face.

"Damn you, Terry Walker," she muttered. "Don't you dare die. I love you." Swallowing back a sob, she looked up at Jason. "Find Neil. Please."

He glanced at Hank. "You aren't budging?"

"Not on your life."

Jason still looked reluctant to leave her there, but he nodded finally and went in search of Neil. The two of them came back just as the ambulance screeched to a halt on the nearby road.

All of the color washed out of Neil's face when he saw Terry. "Oh, God, no." He tried to get closer, but the paramedics pushed him gently aside.

Callie went to him and held him. "It's going to be okay. It's going to be okay," she repeated over and over, clinging to Neil. He said nothing at all, but she could feel his tears dampening her hair where his head rested against hers.

When they lifted Terry into the ambulance, Neil approached and shot a defiant look at the paramedics. "I'm going with him."

"I'm sorry, sir. Not in the ambulance. You'll just be in the way."

"We'll follow," Jason said, grasping Neil's elbow and guiding him away. He glanced at Hank. "Where's your car?"

Hank looked torn. "I should stay here, help with the investigation."

Jason nodded. "Just give me your keys. You can meet us at the hospital."

"I'm coming, too," Callie said.

Jason took her hand and squeezed it reassuringly. "Of course you are. Terry will need both of you."

Hank tossed Jason the keys to his car. When they were inside, he reached in, grabbed the police light and placed it on the roof. "Try not to break any major laws," he warned Jason as he started it flashing and hit the siren. "They could have my badge for this."

Despite Hank's warning, Jason ran three red lights and took several corners on two wheels as he sped through the streets in the wake of the ambulance carrying Terry.

Callie worried about Neil. He was entirely too ashen. She reached into the backseat and clasped his hand. It was icy. "Are you okay?"

He glared at her. "Just swell," he said sarcastically.

"Hey," Jason protested softly. "Don't take it out on Callie."

"It's okay," she said.

Neil sighed. "No, it's not," he said, squeezing her hand. "It's just… I can't bear to think of what will happen if I lose him."

"We are not going to lose him!" Callie protested. "Don't even go there."

Their noisy arrival at the hospital drew startled looks from the paramedics. Jason silenced the siren as he let Neil and Callie out by the emergency room door. "I'll park and be back in a minute."

Inside was bedlam. Terry had already been whisked off to some inner sanctum for treatment. Children sobbed as frantic mothers tried to soothe them. One man, his expression desperate, clutched a plastic cup of coffee so tightly it looked as if it might bend in two, spilling the contents all over the already dingy floor. The nursing staff looked as though it were under siege as relatives demanded information and doctors barked out orders.

Neil was too used to being in charge to sit quietly and wait. He joined the others clamoring for information, finally threatening to break down every door in the place until he found somebody who could tell him something about Terry.

Oblivious to Callie's pleas, he was standing toe-to-toe with a burly security guard by the time Jason came inside. Jason sized up the situation and intervened before Neil ended up being banished to the parking lot.

"Come on, pal. Let's go track down some coffee," Jason said. "Callie can wait here for news, but I have a feeling it's going to be a while."

Neil resisted. "You go. I don't want any coffee."

"I do and I think the walk will do you good," Jason countered. "Come on. I know waiting is hell. At least we can kill a few minutes of it." He glanced at Callie. "You'll be okay here by yourself? You won't leave the area and go off on your own?"

She nodded. "I won't move an inch. I'll be fine. Just take care of Neil."

Jason put a comforting arm across Neil's sagging shoulders and steered him off toward the hospital cafeteria. Callie thought she had never loved anyone more than she did Jason right at that moment.

For all of his frequent protestations that he was cold-blooded and aloof, labels which had made their way into most of his media profiles, she knew that he was anything but. His sensitivity to Neil's anxiety was proof of that.

She sat back in the hard plastic chair and waited, her gaze fixed on the automatic doors through which Terry had disappeared. Her eyes, already gritty from too many tears, ached from the strain of nonstop surveillance.

When she could stand it no more, she approached a nurse who looked half-dead on her feet but who still managed a smile for everyone.

"Excuse me, could you see if there's any word at all on Terence Walker?"

The woman glanced at Callie and her expression softened. "You play on that soap with him, don't you?"

Although she was surprised anyone would equate the glamorous Cop Kelly with her own grubby appearance, Callie nodded. A tear leaked out before she could stop it. "I'm so scared for him," she confessed. "There was so much blood and his face—"

"Will be more ruggedly handsome than ever, once they get him patched up," the nurse promised her with a wink. "He was conscious and cursing a blue streak last time I passed by his cubicle. The X-ray tech was just going in there. Let me see what I can find out for you."

Callie turned away just in time to spot Lisa and Lindsay hurrying through the door. When they saw Callie, they raced over and enveloped her in a fierce hug.

"How did you know where we'd be?" Callie asked.

"Hank told us," Lisa explained.

"What's happening? Is he okay?" Lindsay demanded.

"He's conscious. I think that's a good sign. A nurse is trying to get some information for me now. What's happening back at the park? Did they arrest anybody?"

Lisa nodded, her eyes wide. "Some guy I'd never seen before," she said, then paused dramatically, "and you'll never guess who else."

"Jenny Harding," Lindsay said, refusing to draw out the suspense. "Can you believe it? That little twit was helping some sleazoid reporter get close to Terry."

Callie's heart leaped into her throat. "The sleazoid reporter wasn't by any chance Bryan Davis, was it?"

Lisa's head bobbed. "That's it. Hank told me, right before he took off for the precinct. How did you know? Had he interviewed you or something?"

Callie sighed. In deference to Terry's desire to keep his marriage a secret, she said simply, "No, I didn't know him, but Terry knew him from years ago." All of the rest would come out soon enough.

She was puzzled, though, by how the police had zeroed in on Bryan and Jenny so quickly, especially since Jenny had been in plain sight on the team's bench when Terry had disappeared. Was there a witness? Or was Hank merely hedging his bets by questioning a man who'd been under suspicion?

"Did they charge this guy and Jenny?" she asked.

Both women regarded her blankly. "They must have. They took both of them to the precinct for questioning," Lindsay said. "Jenny was crying like the little twit she is and swearing she didn't know anything about the attack on Terry, that she'd never leaked information to this reporter about that hit-and-run accident. I don't care what she said, though, the two of them looked awfully cozy to me."

Callie thought about Jenny's protests. This job on *Within Our Reach* was clearly her entry into big-time PR. Would she have put that at risk to help some tabloid reporter, especially with Terry's promise of dire consequences hanging over her head if she did?

But if Jenny hadn't been Bryan's inside source, then someone else had been and Callie suddenly thought she had a pretty good idea who it might be. In fact, realistically, there was only one person it could have been. She should have thought of it sooner, but she'd gotten sidetracked by the discovery that Terry had been married and by the likelihood that his sexual preference was behind the threats.

"When Jason and Neil get back, tell them I had to leave. I'll be back as soon as I can. A nurse should be coming out any second with news about Terry. She recognized me from the show, so she's bound to recognize both of you. Find out everything you can, okay?"

Outside, she cursed the fact that she didn't have a cell phone to call Hank and tell him what she suspected. It might be nice to have backup in case her suspicions proved to be correct, but she convinced herself that if the person really wanted her dead, she would have been killed long before now. This was about Terry. She'd merely gotten in the way.

She was halfway to the taxi stand when someone grabbed her elbow from behind and yanked her to a halt. She whirled around and found herself staring into

Jonathan Baines's eyes. They filled instantly with compassion, but there had been one brief instant when Callie had detected something every bit as hard and cold as the villainous Victor he played on the soap.

That tiny glimpse into Jonathan's soul told her everything she needed to know, confirming her guess at once. She wondered if she hadn't sensed it instinctively way back in that very first scene they had done together, the one in which she'd been so frightened of him that she'd impulsively placed her gun on the table between them.

Now, with his hand still clamped firmly around her arm, she simply had to come up with a way to keep him from figuring out that she'd guessed the truth, that he was the one behind the threats, that he'd been witness to a hit-and-run he very likely had arranged and that he had staged today's vicious attack on Terry.

She also realized belatedly that perhaps she had miscalculated. Judging by the cold gleam in his eyes and the painful tightness of his grip, Jonathan wasn't nearly as fond of her as he'd convinced everyone on the set he was.

The only thing she hadn't figured out was why he hated her so much. Admittedly, though, with her life very clearly on the line, Jonathan's motive probably didn't matter a whole heck of a lot.

29

Jason thought he'd go out of his mind when he discovered that Callie had taken off alone.

"How could you let her leave?" he demanded of the already shaken Lisa. "Dammit, don't you know she's in danger, too? Why the hell do you think Hank's been on the set every day?"

Apparently Lisa had never thought to question the good fortune that had plunked the cop into her path day after day. She didn't reply. She just turned those big brown eyes of hers on him and wept. Jason was immune to the tears. He wanted to shake her until her teeth rattled. Lindsay Gentry was not so reticent. Nor was she intimidated by Jason's fury.

"How were we supposed to stop her?" she demanded indignantly, putting a consoling arm around the younger woman's shoulders.

"Lay off, Jason," Neil warned. "I'm as worried about Callie as you are, but they didn't know. Yelling at them won't find her."

Jason didn't linger to debate the point. He scowled at the whole lot of them and took off for the parking lot, punching in Hank's beeper number on his cell phone as he ran. By the time Hank returned the page, mere seconds later, Jason had scanned the parking lot in every direction. There was no sign of Callie.

He headed for the taxi stand as he told Hank what had happened. "I'm going to talk to the drivers. Maybe one of them saw a cabbie give her a lift."

What he learned from the drivers moments later made his heart climb into his throat.

"The guy came up behind her just as she got over here," one man said.

"Didn't seem like there was anything wrong," another confirmed. "Looked like she knew the dude. She didn't struggle with him or nothing. We would have helped her, if she'd looked like she needed it."

Jason wasn't convinced of that, but this wasn't the time to question their likely heroics. "Describe him," Jason demanded.

"Medium tall," the second driver recalled. "Brown hair. Looked like he'd been playing ball or something. Had dirt from head to toe. Grass stains, too. His face was all red, like it had been too much for him."

There were half a dozen men in the cast who fit that description, Jason thought, fighting panic. He didn't have time to play this kind of guessing game. "Young or old?"

"Middle-aged, I'd say," the driver who looked to be about twenty said.

"Hell, no, older than that," the other countered. "Didn't you see the wrinkles when he smiled at her? The man's face crumpled up like tissue paper."

Paul Locklear? That couldn't be. Besides, he was

balding a bit. On top of that, Regina and her friend hadn't let the director out of their sight all day, any more than Jason had let that tabloid reporter out of his. Jason had checked with Regina and Mikel back in the park an instant before he'd gotten Hank's message about Terry's disappearance and taken off for the perimeter of the ball field.

The last thing he'd told them had been to keep an eye on Locklear until the director reached his own home. Mikel clearly understood the importance of doing just that. There was no way they would have failed to tail him to his front door. Surely Locklear couldn't have given them the slip and made it to the hospital so quickly.

And whoever had Callie was also behind Terry's beating. Locklear hadn't been out of sight long enough to have harmed the actor. Nor had young Davis been out of his sight all afternoon.

Damn, damn, damn! he thought, running through mental images of the rest of the cast, cursing the fact that more of the men weren't blond or old or bald.

It seemed to take forever before the right image clicked into focus: Jonathan Baines. The only other man in the right age range would have been Randall Trent, and he was much taller than the drivers had described, at least six-two and so lanky he appeared taller. He was also athletic enough that a romp on the ball field wouldn't have winded him. It had to be Baines, then.

But what the hell did Baines have to do with this? They'd never even considered him a suspect. Jason didn't wait to try to figure out the answer to that before punching in the number for the network switchboard and asking to be patched through to the producers. Marty Malloy answered.

"Marty, Jason Kane. I need to know an address for Jonathan Baines," he said, hopping into the backseat of the first taxi in line. There was no time to waste running back to where he'd left Hank's car, even though he regretted the lack of flashers and a siren to get him across town in a hurry. Of course, cabbies would drive like the proverbial bats out of hell for the promise of an exorbitant tip. He waved a large bill under the driver's nose and they squealed into traffic at a satisfyingly fast clip.

"Got it," he said when the producer read the address off their cast roster. He repeated it for the cabdriver, then told Marty, "No, I can't explain right now. I'll be back in touch. I can promise you that. If you hear from Baines, don't let on I was asking about him."

He paged Hank again and gave him the address. "I can't think where else he'd go. At least it's a starting point."

"I'll meet you there," the policeman said. "Whatever you do, don't go in without me."

"Yeah, right," Jason said with no intention of complying.

"Dammit, Jason! I mean that."

Jason hung up on him, then made another call, this one to Henry. "A lunatic has Callie," he told his driver succinctly. "Meet me at this address."

Henry didn't waste time asking a lot of questions. He just said, "I'll be there, sir. No harm will come to her. We'll see to that."

Somehow reassured by Henry's calm response, Jason told the driver to step on it. They careened around a corner so fast that Jason skidded from one side of the slippery backseat to the other.

"You okay, mister?" the driver asked, glancing into the rearview mirror.

"Don't worry about me. Just get there."

Apparently satisfied that Jason was indeed fearless, the driver tore through traffic with the skill of an Indy 500 driver trying to take the lead on the last lap. When he skidded to a stop in front of the Upper East Side apartment building where Baines lived, Jason tossed the hundred into the front seat and leaped from the taxi.

"You need any backup?" the driver shouted after him, apparently caught up in the thrill of the chase.

Jason shot him a rueful look. "That's okay. The cops are on the way."

More importantly, Henry, who would crawl through hot coals for Callie, was on his way. And Henry was not saddled by anything as mundane as police procedures to hamper the rescue effort.

Now that he was actually in front of Baines's building, Jason stood on the sidewalk debating what to do next. Hank had instructed him to do nothing, but there was no way he could stand by idly while Callie's life might be at risk just a few floors above him.

Think, he ordered himself when rage made cool logic all but impossible. Acting in haste could quite likely put Callie in more danger. The first thing he had to do was make sure this was where Baines had brought her.

Forcing a calm he was far from feeling, he approached the doorman. "I'm looking for Mr. Jonathan Baines," he said in the most imperious manner he could manage. It always got results. "Is he in?"

"I believe I saw him return a few minutes ago," the man said. "Shall I buzz him for you?"

"Was he alone?"

The doorman looked suspicious at the question. "I'm not sure I should say, sir."

"Was there a young lady with him?" Jason persisted. "Perhaps one of his costars from TV?"

When the doorman remained discreetly silent, Jason debated whether to wave money or his ID under the man's nose. He opted for both, along with a far more confiding, genial attitude. Throttling the man, as he very much wanted to do, wouldn't get results.

"I'm his boss," he explained, forcing a smile. "I have some big news for him and for Miss Smith. I was hoping to catch them together."

The man grabbed the two fifties and barely glanced at Jason's business card. "Fifteen-oh-six. They've been there about twenty minutes."

Long enough for Baines to do serious harm to Callie, Jason thought with a shudder. But why bring her back to his apartment? Why not do whatever he intended someplace else, then abandon her? It didn't make sense that Baines would want to draw Jason or the police right to his own front door.

With impeccable timing, Henry cruised to a stop in his own late-model economy car and parked it in a no-parking zone right in front of the building. The doorman looked as if he might protest, but Henry's scowl turned him away as if he'd noticed nothing at all.

"Is she here, sir?"

"Fifteenth floor."

"Then I suggest we go calling," Henry said.

They rode the elevator to the fifteenth floor in silence. In the corridor outside of Baines's apartment, Henry gestured for Jason to ring the bell, while he plastered his back against the wall next to the door and pulled a gun in readiness for his own unexpected entrance on Jason's heels. The gun looked perfectly natural in his hand. Henry was very resourceful, and Jason had seen to it that he was well trained to counter any attempts that might be made on Jason's life. Henry might appear to be nothing more than a courtly limo driver, but he was a skilled bodyguard, as well, should that talent ever be required. Jason had never been more grateful that he'd had the foresight to insist on the training.

Baines opened the door without hesitation and with absolutely no hint of surprise at finding the network president on his doorstep.

"Kane," he said with a nod. "I've been expecting you. Come in and join our little negotiating session."

Jason's gaze followed the direction in which Baines glanced. Outrage simmered at what he saw.

Callie was seated at a large dining room table, her hands painfully bound behind her back, a piece of duct tape over her mouth. He was relieved to see that her eyes, when they met his, were filled with fury, not fear.

What troubled him more was the gun that Jonathan Baines had trained right on her heart. Unfortunately, it more or less neutralized the one Henry was carrying.

30

Callie frantically tried to signal Jason with her eyes, pleading with him to stay cool. She could tell from his clenched jaw that he wanted to break Jonathan Baines in two. In the past half-hour, since Jonathan had abducted her at gunpoint from the hospital, she had seen just how close to the edge he was. He was clearly a man who was convinced he had nothing to lose by murder. If Jason alarmed him in any way, the actor would shoot them both without a qualm.

"Over here, Kane," Jonathan said, gesturing toward the dining room table with his gun. "Sit where you can keep an eye on your girlfriend. I want you to have a front row seat, in case I find it necessary to kill her."

Jason's complexion drained of all color, but there was no mistaking the fury in his eyes as he complied. He fixed his gaze on Callie. "Are you okay?"

She nodded.

He stared at Jonathan then. "What's this all about, Baines? Why are we here?"

Callie had been wondering that very thing herself. Although she'd guessed about Jonathan's involvement, she hadn't been able to pinpoint the motive. He'd said precious little to help her out.

"We're here to renegotiate my contract," he said now.

If her mouth hadn't been taped shut, it would have gaped at that. Jason looked equally startled.

"Your contract?" Jason repeated incredulously.

"It seems the producers have planned to write me out at the end of my current contract," Jonathan explained. "They've tried to convince me it will be a glorious ending, a hail of gunfire and all that. Unfortunately, I have bills to pay. I'm not prepared to die so soon."

Callie thought of the scads of alimony Jonathan was reportedly doling out to ex-wives and the probable cost of maintaining this elegant apartment with its spectacular view of the East River. She didn't doubt for a second that the prospect of being fired would terrify him.

But what did all of that have to do with Terry? Had he hoped to drive him off the show, assuming that the producers wouldn't want two popular stars to leave at the same time? Had the notes been nothing more than a clumsy attempt to frighten Terry away or had they been more? Had he also wanted to make Terry pay for replacing him as the show's lead?

Jason must have been wondering the same thing because he asked, "What do Terry and Callie have to do with this? Shouldn't you be talking to Marty and Katrina?"

Jonathan regarded him incredulously. "I thought you were supposed to be a smart man, Mr. Kane. Terry's the hottest thing on daytime. If he goes, the show won't be able to afford to lose me. Besides, he's a fraud, as we all know. Sooner or later, he would bring the show down when the public learns that he prefers men to women. I need *Within Our Reach* to continue to flourish. Getting rid of Terry serves several purposes. It protects the show from scandal and keeps me on the air."

The response confirmed Callie's earlier guess, but she didn't take much satisfaction in being right.

"And Callie?"

Jonathan smiled. "She is my bargaining chip, of course. You're the real power at *Within Our Reach.* I have a great respect for power. Wasting time with underlings serves little purpose. If you tell the writers I have to stay, they'll find a way to redeem my character and keep me alive. Whatever your personal ties to Ms. Smith might be, I'm sure your purposes are better served if she remains in one piece. Am I correct?"

Callie tried to gauge Jason's reaction to Jonathan's negotiating strategy, but he seemed to be looking past the actor toward the door of the apartment. She realized he had probably called for backup, something she foolishly hadn't done. The question was, had it arrived? And how would they be able to take Jonathan by surprise, when he was facing the door? He could fire at Callie and, most likely, Jason before anyone entering could get a clear shot at him. She realized that Jason's arrival hadn't guaranteed a safe outcome.

A muffled sound from the hallway answered one of her questions. Jason's quick, surreptitious glance in that direction confirmed it.

That meant it was up to her and Jason to distract Jonathan so that the cops or whoever was out there could make their move. She doubted conversation was the answer. They needed noise, noise enough to cover the sound of the door opening, chaos enough to distract Jonathan's attention from his target—namely, her.

She debated whether she could succeed in upending the dining room table. Trussed up as she was, she doubted she had the mobility.

But there was a pedestal table just to her left. It held a lovely vase. Possibly Ming or some other outrageously expensive Chinese dynasty from the look of it. Seeing that tumble to the floor was definitely likely to get Jonathan's attention. Given his financial difficulties, she doubted he'd want anything broken that might be auctioned or pawned.

Her feet were bound together at the ankles, but she tested and discovered if she moved cautiously, she could probably stand or at least launch herself sideways into that table.

Before she moved, she tried to catch Jason's attention with frantic glances sideways, indicating the direction in which she planned to go.

Timing was all-important. Jonathan was growing increasingly agitated by Jason's failure to commit to a new contract. Jason, apparently alerted to Callie's intentions, suddenly started throwing out salary terms and legalese that only a lawyer could appreciate.

Just when Jonathan's expression was about to turn smug, Callie dove for the table. The vase flew into the air.

With a shout of outrage, Jonathan scrambled to catch it, letting his gun drop in his haste to save the precious vase. Jason dove for the gun, just as the front door burst open.

Hank sized up the situation at a glance and trained

his gun on Jonathan, who was sitting amid the shards of broken glass, sobbing. He looked even more broken than the vase.

To Callie's astonishment, it was Henry who knelt beside her, set a very impressive gun down on the carpet and began loosening the ropes that bound her, *tsk-tsking* at the marks on her wrists and ankles. He shot a venomous look toward Jonathan Baines that made Callie glad that Hank had gotten to the actor first.

With the ropes off, Callie was able to sit up. She was just reaching for the duct tape across her face, when Jason nudged a reluctant Henry aside and hunkered down beside her. His gaze searching hers, he pushed her fumbling fingers away from the tape.

"I'll do it."

His own fingers trembled as he gently peeled away the tape. When it was off, he gathered her in his arms and sat there rocking her as if she were the most precious person on earth. To her amazement, she actually thought she felt his cheeks turning damp with tears. She reached up and touched his face to be sure. When she withdrew her hand, her fingertips were indeed damp.

"Oh, Jason," she murmured.

A ragged sigh tore through him. Even now, with Jonathan in custody, she could feel his heart pounding wildly.

"It's over," she whispered. "It's over and we're both okay."

He stood then and drew her to her feet. When she studied his face, a chill swept through her. He looked so distant…and so very, very sad.

He turned to Henry. "Would you see that Callie gets home, Henry?"

Callie stared at him in dismay. She could feel him slipping away from her, not just physically but emotionally. "Where are you going?"

"To the police station with Hank," he said, avoiding her gaze. He glanced at the policeman. "You can wait to get Callie's statement, can't you?"

Hank nodded. "I'll be by the apartment as soon as I get Baines booked."

Still shaken by everything that had happened and thoroughly confused by Jason's withdrawal, Callie shook her head. "I'll be at the hospital."

Alarm flared for an instant in Jason's eyes. "Are you hurt?"

"No, I have to go back and check on Terry."

Hank nodded. "I'll meet you there and give you a lift home."

Callie couldn't bring herself to ask Jason where he would be going after he'd given the police his statement. She knew in her heart he wouldn't be coming to find her.

What she didn't understand, would never understand, was why. Surely the stark terror she'd seen in his eyes earlier meant he loved her and cared desperately what happened to her. And yet he was going and she couldn't think of anything to do to stop him.

"You hurt her," Henry told Jason accusingly later that night. He'd picked Jason up at the police station and was driving him back to his apartment. "Why don't you let me take you to her? You know that's where you want to be."

"Stay out of it," Jason advised.

"I never thought I'd say this, but you're a fool," Henry said, clearly undaunted. "You know you're in love with her. Why can't you admit it?"

"You don't know anything about what I feel."

"The hell I don't," the driver countered. "You figure it's your fault she was ever in danger in the first place. You figure you got her on that show, and as a result, she nearly got herself killed. Somehow you should have known that a psycho actor was stalking Walker, right? So now you're going to do penance for the rest of your life to make up for it." He glanced over at Jason, who was riding in the front seat beside him. "How am I doing so far?"

"A veritable Freudian genius," Jason said bitterly. "You're so smart, why don't you buy a couch and go into the shrink business? It'd pay a hell of a lot better than driving me around town."

"Most people's hard heads don't interest me. Yours does."

Jason shot him a foul-tempered look. "Am I supposed to be grateful for that?"

"You should be," Henry said complacently. "Should I take you to her apartment?"

"No," Jason said stubbornly. "You can let me out right here, so I won't have to listen to any more of your blathering."

Henry's disapproving scowl spoke volumes. He braked his car so hard, it rocked on its frame. Jason climbed out, slammed the door, then stood there a minute, uncertain how to thank Henry for being willing to be there for him and Callie.

"I'll never forget what you did today," he said eventually.

Henry's expression didn't lighten a bit. "I did it for Miss Callie."

Jason smiled. "I know that. Like I said, I won't forget it."

Now it was Henry who looked hesitant. His expression filled with compassion. "You going to be okay?"

"Sure," Jason said. "By this time next century."

He stuck his hands into his pockets and started to walk. It was a surprisingly cool night for early June, with a hint of rain in the air. The air should have cleared his head, but it didn't. Images of Callie with that gun pointed directly at her ate at him. Images of Terry's shattered face and blood-soaked clothes taunted him. He kept telling himself there must have been a way to prevent everything that had happened.

It didn't seem to matter that the man responsible for both was clearly mentally unhinged. He blamed himself. It was his obsession with ratings, with proving his programming genius that had brought Callie into the middle of a nightmare. Henry was right. He would never forgive himself for that. He was no better than his ambition-driven mother.

He vowed then and there, standing on the corner as rain began to fall and soak him to the bone, that he would release Callie from the life he'd forced her into. He would call Whittington on Monday morning and tell the attorney there would be no problem if she wanted to get out of her contract early.

And he would make a few calls to brokerages that had made a fortune betting on his success at TGN. Callie would have the kind of job she loved by the end of the day on Monday. It was all he could think of to do to make amends.

He wondered if he would ever be satisfied that it was enough.

31

Callie sat quietly beside Terry's bed while he slept. In the past twenty-four hours she'd been home only long enough to reassure her mother that she was okay and to change clothes. The hospital had become her haven.

She could have stayed away. Terry was in no danger. The doctors said he was going to make a full recovery and that any scarring to his face could be repaired with plastic surgery.

The truth was, though, that she didn't want to be at home where she would be forced to think about Jason and his sudden abandonment. Of all of Saturday's tumultuous life-threatening events, that had been the most traumatic. He had walked away and not looked back.

Neil came into the room and walked up behind her. He rested his hands on her shoulders, gently massaging them.

"You're tense, Callie. And you're exhausted. Go home."

"I can't," she said simply.

"Because the big shot won't be waiting?"

She nodded as a tear escaped and slid down her

cheek. "Silly, isn't it? I fought letting him into my life. Now I can't bear to see him go."

"Love's a bitch, isn't it?" he said, his gaze on Terry when he said it. "I sure as hell never thought I'd be crazy for an actor. Yesterday, when I thought I might lose him…"

His voice trailed off and Callie could feel him shudder. She reached up and put her hand on his. "He's going to be fine."

"No thanks to Baines."

"Have you heard any more about Terry's ex-brother-in-law?"

"Actually, he stopped by while you were off being kidnapped. He apologized to Terry." He hesitated, then added, "And to me."

"You? Why you?"

"Because he tried to blackmail me into getting Terry to cooperate. He came to the apartment one afternoon. Your mother saw him there. She just didn't know who he was. She thought I was having a fling behind Terry's back."

"No way," Callie said with absolute confidence. Her own relationship with Jason should be as strong as the bond between these two men. "Tell me about Bryan."

"He's ambitious. He only wanted to catch a big break by using his connection to Terry's past. He promised me anonymity, if I'd talk Terry into going public. I refused. Then Baines practically handed him an even bigger story by clueing him in on the threats Terry'd been receiving and that hit-and-run he'd set up. Bryan swears he had no idea Baines himself was behind them. Also, he told the police Jenny had nothing to do with any of it.

They'd been out a couple of times so he could pump her for material, but he swore she'd refused to give him any inside information at all. That's why he was so thrilled when Baines started passing along these scoops of his."

Callie shook her head. "I can't believe he tried to blackmail you into feeding him even more inside stuff on Terry."

Neil looked thoughtful. "Bryan's not such a bad guy, actually. He's promised to try to get his sister to let Terry see his daughter, if he wants to."

"Will he?" Callie asked, trying to picture Terry as a father. She couldn't help feeling sad about how much he'd already missed of his daughter's life.

"We talked about it earlier today. He's thinking about it. He may decide to leave it up to her. She's old enough to choose whether she wants a gay father in her life."

Neil pulled another chair up beside Callie's. Instead of facing the bed, though, he turned it toward her. "Now what about you? You going to fight for the man you love?"

Callie thought of everything Jason had brought into her life—excitement, approval, challenges, *bowling* and love. How could she walk away from all that, except maybe for the bowling?

"I want to," she admitted eventually, then looked sadly at Terry. "I have a feeling, though, that it's too late. Maybe you've noticed, Jason is a very stubborn man."

"It's never too late," Neil told her forcefully. "If you don't believe me, ask your mother."

Callie stared at him in confusion. "My mother? Why?"

Neil smiled. "Just ask, okay."

Something in his voice and in his eyes told her she ought to be asking very soon. "You won't tell me?"

He shook his head. "Not a chance."

Intrigued, Callie stood up. "Then I guess it's time for me to go home."

Back at the apartment, she found her mother fussing around in the kitchen, humming happily off-key. Nothing so odd about that, she decided as she settled herself at the kitchen table and studied the woman who had transformed herself into someone Callie barely recognized.

"How about some hot chocolate?" her mother asked, regarding her closely. "Are you okay?"

"Just tired," Callie insisted. "It's too warm for hot chocolate. How about iced tea?"

Her mother reached for the teakettle. "Fine. It'll be ready in a minute. How's Terry?"

"Recovering nicely, according to the doctors." She studied her mother intently, fascinated by the lighthearted mood she detected. "Mother, what's going on with you?"

The question was apparently a little too direct. Her mother dropped the glass she was holding and blushed furiously.

"With me?" she asked, trying belatedly for an innocent tone. She borrowed time to compose herself by sweeping up the broken glass, then asked, "What makes you think anything is going on with me?"

"You've changed, for one thing."

"A new hairstyle and a little color for the gray," she insisted nonchalantly. "That's all."

Callie refused to accept the easy response. "It's more than that. Neil said something at the hospital."

Her mother stared at her, clearly alarmed. "What did he say?"

"Just that I should ask you about it never being too late for some things."

A smile softened her mother's features. "That's true enough. He was talking about you and Jason, I assume."

Callie was not about to be distracted by a discussion of her own problems. "Yes, but I'm asking about you. He made it sound as if you had some special insight into the subject."

Regina Gunderson sighed, then pulled out a chair. "I suppose now is as good a time as any to get into this, though I was hoping that Mikel…" Her voice trailed off.

"Mikel?" Callie repeated, seizing on the unfamiliar name. "Who is Mikel and what does he have to do with anything?"

"Mikel Rolanski is an artist, a very fine one," her mother said.

New pieces for the puzzle kept turning up. Callie couldn't seem to keep up with them. "Here in New York?" she asked.

"Yes."

"And you know him?"

Her mother's chin rose a notch and she fixed a steady gaze on Callie. "I'm going to marry him," she said in a rare burst of defiance. Her tone suggested that she expected Callie to argue with her.

Callie couldn't have argued if she'd wanted to. She was too dumbfounded. She simply stared. Marriage? Her mother was getting married? When had this happened? And how? All she could think was that Eunice was going to find some way to blame this on her, too.

"Maybe you'd better begin at the beginning," she suggested when she could finally form a coherent thought.

The beginning wasn't, as she'd expected, a few short months ago, but years in the past. "You were in New York before you married my father," she repeated in amazement.

"For two incredible years," her mother confessed. "I was an art student. Mikel was my mentor."

"But nothing more?" Callie asked.

There was that soft, knowing smile again. "Much, much more," her mother said quietly.

"Oh." Callie fell silent, letting that bombshell sink in.

Slowly, the whole incredible story began to unfold. She was spellbound as her mother described that long-ago love affair, her foolish decision to run home to Iowa when she became convinced that Mikel would never marry her and the even more impetuous decision to get involved with Jacob Gunderson and settle for the staid, uneventful life her family had envisioned for her.

"So, you see," her mother said. "When you left for New York, no one understood that need better than I. And no one knew the possibilities for heartache better than I."

Callie thought of the old art book that had come to mind so recently that night at Jason's. Those elusive memories of her mother's wistfulness when they'd looked at it made sense now. It reminded her of a life she'd left behind.

"You've never talked about living here before. I thought this was your first trip. Why didn't you tell me?"

Her mother's shoulders rose and fell with a heartfelt sigh. "Because it always hurt too much," she said simply.

Tears welled up in Callie's eyes then, tears of understanding and compassion. If she didn't fight for Jason now, would she spin out the rest of her days as her mother had, filled with regrets?

"But you've found each other again," she repeated, desperate for some sense of hope, for a promise that love survived.

Her mother nodded. "He's very anxious to meet you and Eunice. He's old-fashioned. He wants your blessing."

Callie reached for her mother's hands and held them tightly. "He makes you happy?"

She didn't need her mother's nod or the shy smile to tell her the answer. It was shining in her eyes and it was wonderful to see.

32

Freddie wasn't speaking to him because Jason had turned down his pet sitcom project for a second time, in roughly the same belligerent tone with which he'd rejected it before.

His secretary wasn't speaking to him because he'd bitten her head off once too often.

Henry wasn't speaking to him because of Callie.

In fact, the only person in the world who seemed anxious to talk to him was his mother, and she wanted to see where things stood between him and Callie.

It all came back to Callie. She was everywhere he turned. He hadn't had a peaceful moment since he'd walked out of Baines's apartment and out of her life.

By now, though, that attorney of hers must have told her that she could be released from her contract if that's what she wanted. And Dave Stoddard at Stoddard, Bentley and Gates would have called her with a job offer on Wall Street. He'd done his damnedest to set everything right. Her life was her own again.

And his was his.

The only trouble was, he suddenly hated his life. It

felt empty and lonely and a whole lot like a prison sentence. He'd given Callie her freedom and sealed his own pitiful fate. It was no worse than he deserved for dragging her into his world in the first place.

He was balling up unread memos and tossing them halfheartedly toward a trash can when he heard a commotion in his outer office. It sounded suspiciously like a faint cheer, uttered by his secretary and Freddie. He shrugged and dismissed it. Maybe they were watching a Mets game. Nobody seemed to be interested in getting a lick of work done around here, anyway, least of all him.

He crumpled up another memo—*Within Our Reach* ratings this time, he noted without bothering to read them—and aimed for the trash can just as his office door burst open.

In sailed Callie, followed by Walter Whittington.

Uh-oh, Jason thought, suddenly sitting up a little straighter. His blood pumped like a fire hose at a four-alarm blaze. His gaze locked on Callie. He couldn't seem to tear it away. She looked gorgeous. Every bit the femme fatale he'd envisioned.

She also looked just the slightest bit furious. Jason swallowed hard and forced his gaze to the attorney.

"What can I do for you?"

Whittington glanced nervously at Callie, then met Jason's gaze directly. "A bit of a problem has arisen," he said.

"Oh?"

"It's about Ms. Smith's contract."

Jason braced himself for the news that she wanted out. He'd offered her the chance to go. Why did the expected decision create this terrible sense of loss deep inside him? This was exactly the plan he'd set into motion.

"Whatever Ms. Smith wants is fine with me," he said.

Whittington cleared his throat. "I'm not sure," he began.

Callie glared at him.

The lawyer tried again. Jason was beginning to get the idea that Whittington was uncomfortable with whatever Callie's demands were. Jason decided to cut to the chase.

"As I told you the other day, if she wants out, I won't fight her. She's probably anxious to get back to Wall Street."

"Not exactly," Whittington said.

Jason caught on then that whatever Callie wanted, it was so outrageous that even the attorney couldn't bring himself to spell it out. He directed a look straight into Callie's eyes. They were blazing with anger and something else. Vulnerability, Jason realized with a sudden clenching of his stomach. What did that mean?

"Perhaps, Ms. Smith ought to spell this out for me herself," he suggested.

"Fine," she said, walking up beside his desk and removing what appeared to be her contract from her purse. She ripped it in two.

Jason winced. "I get the message."

"I doubt it," she said. She glanced toward Whittington, who pulled new papers out of his briefcase. She laid them on Jason's desk. "I think it's self-explanatory."

"You may find it a bit unconventional," Whittington began but fell immediately silent at a scowl from Callie.

Jason skimmed over the first paragraph. It was a personal-services contract, not unlike the one she'd just destroyed. He went through it paragraph by paragraph. It was identical to the contract they'd negotiated months earlier, which made no sense at all.

Then he reached the final paragraph. Jason read it, then read it again. "This sounds like a…" He couldn't even form the words.

"A prenuptial clause," Callie said sweetly. "It's my newest perk. It has been brought to my attention recently that I have a lot of clout around here. I figured it was about time I exercised a little of it."

Jason swallowed hard and tried to calm the sudden racing of his heart. "You're not serious about this?" he asked nervously.

"Oh, but I am." She glanced at the attorney. "Aren't I, Walter?"

The attorney grinned at last. "Oh, yes," he assured Jason. "She's very serious."

"But this is unprecedented," Jason protested. It was the most massive understatement he'd ever made.

Callie moved slowly until she was behind his desk. She swiveled his chair around until their knees were touching. Desire ripped through him with predictable speed and savagery. It was raw and primal and urgent.

"Perhaps," she said softly, "no one has ever wanted you as badly as I do."

The words were an echo of Jason's own taunting remark on the day they'd signed that first agreement. He was no more able to resist the deal now than he had been then, outrageous perks and all. But he couldn't help negotiating one final detail himself.

"I notice there's no lifetime guarantee," he said to Whittington, even as he pulled Callie into his lap. "Pencil it in and we have a deal."

Callie's eyes met his and held. "Walter, I think I can handle it from here," she said. Her voice was vaguely breathless, despite the confident statement.

The attorney slipped silently away just as Jason sealed their bargain with a sweet, lingering kiss.

"Are you absolutely sure this is what you want?" he asked when the kiss finally ended. "A few months ago all you cared about was getting back to Wall Street."

"I found something more challenging."

"Acting?"

"No, you," she told him. "I just hope you realize what you're taking on."

Jason grinned. "Oh, I think I've known what a handful you are from the beginning."

"What about my mother?"

"I don't think we'll have her to worry about much longer. Mikel seems to have that situation well in hand."

She regarded him with obvious surprise. "You knew?"

"The day before the ball game," he admitted. "The man is totally smitten, has been for years. He assures me the Gunderson women are worth waiting for."

"There is actually one other Gunderson woman we need to talk about," she confessed, looking uncertain.

"Your sister?"

Callie nodded. "It seems she's finally decided to leave that jerk she married."

"Good for her," Jason said approvingly.

"She's moving to New York."

"Uh-oh." He searched her face. "How do you feel about that? I know you two haven't always gotten along."

"We did once," Callie said, her expression wistful. Slowly a smile spread across her face. "Of course, New York does seem to be amazingly lucky for the Gunderson women, doesn't it? Maybe Eunice will find what she's looking for here, too."

"And you?" Jason said. "Have you found everything you were looking for?"

Her gaze met his. "And more," she said quietly. "Much, much more."

Amazing, Jason thought. His golden gut had done it again. Only a genuine femme fatale could steal his heart the way Miss Calliope Jane Gunderson Smith had.

* * * * *